TAKE
BACK
THE
SKIES

TAKE BACK THE SKIES

LUCY SAXON

BLOOMSBURY

NEW YORK LONDON NEW DELHI SYDNEY

First published in Great Britain in June 2014 by Bloomsbury Publishing Plc
Published in the United States of America in June 2014
by Bloomsbury Children's Books
www.bloomsbury.com

Bloomsbury is a registered trademark of Bloomsbury Publishing Plc

For information about permission to reproduce selections from this book, write to
Permissions, Bloomsbury Children's Books, 1385 Broadway, New York, New York 10018
Bloomsbury books may be purchased for business or promotional use. For information
on bulk purchases please contact Macmillan Corporate and Premium Sales Department
at specialmarkets@macmillan.com

Library of Congress Cataloging-in-Publication Data
Saxon, Lucy.
Take back the skies / Lucy Saxon.
pages   cm
Summary: To escape from a planned arranged marriage, teenaged Cat Hunter disguises
herself as a boy and stows away on a smuggler's airship where she discovers a world
of excitement and adventure.
ISBN 978-1-61963-367-4 (hardcover) • ISBN 978-1-61963-368-1 (e-book)
[1. Fantasy. 2. Adventure and adventurers—Fiction. 3. Love—Fiction. 4. Youths' writings.]
I. Title.
PZ7.S27432Tak 2014   [Fic]—dc23   2013050276

Typeset by Hewer Text UK Ltd, Edinburgh
Printed and bound in the U.S.A. by Thomson-Shore Inc., Dexter, Michigan
2 4 6 8 10 9 7 5 3 1

To Grandad Adams and Grandad Aldridge,
who never got to read this book
but were eternally proud nonetheless

1

Rain fell lazily from charcoal-coloured clouds as Catherine Hunter sprinted through darkening streets, her long hair tied in a tight braid and tucked beneath a black knitted cap. Her thick woollen coat and black work trousers disguised her gender quite nicely. She was practically unrecognisable; only the people who knew her well would have been able to tell who she was.

A faint smile tugged at her lips as she reached the familiar tree beside the high stone wall that surrounded the area in which she lived. It took barely any effort to swing herself up into its branches, the knots worn into footholds by constant use. With practised ease, she scrambled up as high as she could manage, edging on to an outstretched branch that just brushed the wall's peak. From there it was just a short jump over the wall, her thud upon landing muffled by the grass. Taking no longer than a second to regain her balance, she resumed running, diving into a gap at the base of a bush. The fence panel behind it was open, as she'd left it, and she crawled through without a care for the mud on her clothes. Her father would never see them.

Flitting across the garden to the back door, she pulled a

pin from her hair and slid it into the lock, opening it effortlessly. Leaving her boots at the very back of the hall closet, she shut the door soundlessly behind her, hurrying in socked feet towards the stairs. It was her habit to be silent, though she knew she was unlikely to draw her father from his office. Catherine would rather not risk it; the punishment for sneaking out was one she didn't like to think about.

After a brief detour to her bedroom to change into more appropriate clothing, Catherine wandered down to the living room, pulling her hair loose as she did so. She was unsurprised to see the newscast screen on in the corner; rarely did her father turn it off, even if he was nowhere near it. She sank on to the plush grey carpet, pulling her knees up to her chest and trying to regulate her breathing. Her father probably wouldn't want her to join him for dinner, but if he did decide to summon her and she gave herself away by looking out of breath, she could expect to be unable to sit down for at least a week.

She sighed to herself as upbeat music began to blare from the newscast screen and another recruitment broadcast played out. She wished that, just once, they might show something other than the war. Yes, she understood that the war with Mericus was important and people wanted to know what was going on – but didn't people also want to know what was going on in Siberene, or how the storms were in the East?

'*Your child will be one of many, expertly trained to protect their country,*' the cast told her in a proud, tinny voice. She sighed once more, tightly hugging her knees. Had she been a common child she would have been one of those sent to fight so the adults could stay behind and keep the country from crumbling. She wasn't sure whether to be thankful for her birth, or dismayed by it. Surely even war was better than the life of pseudo-freedom she had now. No amount of sneaking out to roam the streets could change the fact that she was trapped by her father's demands and expectations.

Gears whirred and she looked up to see the family servant – a mecha she had affectionately named Samuel – walking jerkily into the room, a tray of food in his claw-like hand.

'Is Father not eating dinner with me, Sam?' she asked, standing to accept the tray. The purple-white glow in Sam's eyes dimmed.

'No, Miss Catherine. Master Nathaniel is working,' he answered in his gravelly voice. Nathaniel was *always* working. Not that Catherine minded, as she liked being able to eat without being interrogated or insulted.

Sam reached out a thick bronze arm to straighten the silk throw over the back of the sofa, puffs of pale purple steam spilling from the thin chimney on his shoulder in time with the mechanical tick of his metal insides.

'And Mother?' she asked, setting her plate on the low table and sitting on the floor to eat.

'Mistress Elizabeth is sleeping.'

Her mother was always sleeping these days. Sleeping, crying or having a shaking fit. Her father kept telling her that the doctors were doing their best, but she couldn't remember the last time she'd seen a doctor at the house.

They had probably given up, just like her father, and were waiting for Elizabeth Hunter to die.

'Thank you, Samuel. You may leave.'

Catherine half-heartedly forked potatoes into her mouth. From the living room, there was a very good view of the shipyard, second only to the view from her bedroom. She spent a lot of time staring at the shipyard, watching skyships lifting gracefully into the air with canvas wings outstretched, the propellers beneath giving enough momentum for the ships to quickly latch on to the fierce updraughts that wound through the docks. How she wished to fly in a skyship: the freedom, the boundless space, with no expectations from anyone but herself and her crew. The ability to travel to countries she only dreamed of seeing, meeting new people and immersing herself in different cultures . . .

But that was all a fantasy.

She was destined – as her father had reminded her many times – to marry a high-born man, and produce many strong, healthy little boys and beautiful, gentle little girls to continue the family line. Though her father educated her like he would a son, that didn't extend to learning about the family business as a proper heir should. She was to serve her husband in every way, obey his orders, and swear fealty to the Anglyan government – just as her mother had. No one asked *her* whether she wanted to swear fealty, or raise lots of children, or even marry a respectable man, she thought resentfully. What if she wanted to marry a scoundrel? Gods, how she wished she could be a commoner! She would give up some luxuries for freedom of choice –

'Are you watching those silly ships again, Catherine?'

She jumped at the familiar sharp voice, almost spilling gravy down her blouse. Turning, Catherine tried not to grimace upon seeing her father's tall, imposing form in the doorway, his jaw set and his dark blue eyes stern.

'Yes, Father. And they're not silly! They're beautiful,' she insisted petulantly, for once, sounding much younger than her fourteen years.

Her father laughed coldly.

'Rusting piles of gears and timber, that's all they are. You'd best remove all that fanciful dreaming from your head now. It won't get you very far.'

Catherine didn't say anything; she knew better than to argue by now.

'I need to tell you something,' Nathaniel declared, and she refrained from rolling her eyes. Storms forbid her father talk to her just because he wanted to.

'You will be accompanying me to the dockside office tomorrow morning. I have a meeting with Thomas to discuss cutting rations, and he wishes you to be present.'

'Of course, Father,' she agreed, trying to hide her distaste. The only reason Thomas Gale wanted her there was to discuss her betrothal to his loathsome son Marcus. He was an arrogant, bull-headed boy whom she despised with every fibre of her being, but her opinion mattered little. It was a good match from a political perspective and her own feelings were irrelevant.

'Good. Wear your best dress, I want you presentable,' her father instructed, eyeing with distaste her plain white blouse and tatty leather breeches. 'I intend to formally offer the

7

betrothal contract, though I can't submit it as you're not yet a woman.'

Catherine nodded dutifully, thanking her lucky stars for her late development, and Nathaniel left the room, no doubt to go back to his office and continue working. Sometimes she wondered if he ever actually slept.

On the screen, a war report followed yet another recruitment cast, and she paused to listen.

'Massacre by Merican soldiers at an Erovan medical centre, no survivors. Five hundred dead.'

She felt suddenly nauseous. How could things like this be happening to Erovan civilians? There were only a few leagues of raging ocean and a single small storm barrier between Anglya and Erova, and the barrier had been there for as long as anyone could remember. Navigating the thicker clouds and tightly grouped whirlwinds was child's play to most pilots. Erova was closer than any other country, and took two days of flight at the most to reach, yet Catherine seemed so far removed from the troubles there. Not for the first time, she felt helpless. She wished that she were older, that she were stronger, that she could get out from under her father's thumb and do something to help. All too often she saw people gathering at the shipyard, dressed in combat uniform and boarding a military skyship. Boys and girls as young as thirteen stood shoulder to shoulder, led by stern guards who looked to be older than fifty. She yearned to be among them. Those brave soldiers were the only reason Anglya was safe from Merican attack.

She turned the newscast screen off and left the room, wandering to her mother's bedroom. Knocking, she nudged the heavy door open, her eyes adjusting to the darkened room. A lamp flickered at the bedside table.

'Mother?' she called softly.

'Catherine, dear,' a feeble, whispery voice breathed in reply, surprising Catherine. It wasn't often she found her mother awake and coherent. She smiled, crossing to the bed.

'How are you feeling?' she asked quietly, clambering up on to the soft bed and peering into the cocoon of quilts to see her mother's small face, clouded eyes staring dazedly up at her. Elizabeth's skin was pale and papery, and her once shining golden hair was dull and prematurely grey, but the barest hint of a smile tugged at her colourless lips as she looked up at her only child.

'No better or worse than usual,' said Elizabeth, and Catherine bit her lip. That was always her mother's answer. 'How are *you*, dearest?'

'Father wants to betroth me to Marcus Gale,' she announced, scowling.

Elizabeth's smile faded.

'When you were but a baby, and I was in better health, I used to talk of betrothing you to a beautiful little boy who would grow up to be a great man. But alas, he's gone, as is his mother . . .' Her voice trailed off and she stared wistfully at the familiar photo on the nightstand. It showed Elizabeth as a younger, healthier woman, with a beautiful blonde woman at her side. Both were dressed in exquisite gowns. The other woman was Queen Mary Latham, and the picture had been taken at the ball celebrating her son's seventh birthday. It was one of the last photographs taken of the woman before the entire royal family disappeared.

Before the war escalated and everything started to go downhill.

As Catherine was about to leave Elizabeth to rest, her mother spoke again with unexpected force. 'Don't let your father decide your future, Catherine! I let my father decide mine, and while I got a lovely daughter out of it . . .' She didn't need to finish her sentence. 'Your heart is yours and yours only to give away, and one day, you will find the man you wish to have it, and he will give you his. That man does not have to be Marcus Gale.'

Was her mother telling her to defy her father? How could she? She was the sole heir to the Hunter fortune – she might as well burn herself from the family tree.

'You are a brave girl, Catherine, and destined for greater things than becoming Marcus Gale's wife,' her mother said, her grey eyes clear for once. 'Your father is . . . a difficult man. He doesn't always understand how his actions affect others. And he certainly doesn't expect a woman to have a mind of her own, especially his daughter. Stand up for yourself, sweetheart, and make your own way in the world. Perhaps a shock like that would teach him an important lesson.'

Catherine's own eyes sparkled with understanding and excitement.

'But what about you?' she asked, drawing a faint smile to her mother's lips.

'It is a parent's job to look after their child, not the other way around. Don't worry about me, dear.'

'Mother, you do know how much I love you, don't you? More than anything,' Catherine told her firmly, leaning in to press a gentle kiss to her mother's brow and swallowing back the lump in her throat.

'And I love you, my dear one. But you're almost a young woman now, and you're beginning to need your mother less and less. Just ... teach that father of yours that he's not lord of the storms, would you?' Elizabeth replied with a look of fierce determination, which Catherine matched, rendering the family resemblance astonishing.

'Oh, trust me. He won't know what hit him.'

Catherine stayed with her mother until she fell asleep, then turned off the lamp and crept out. Knowing her father was in his office, she ran silently along the corridor and up the stairs to her room. She loved having the room at the very top of the house; if she imagined hard enough, she could pretend the rest of the house didn't exist.

'Hello, Samuel,' she said, finding the mecha in her room, making her bed.

'Good evening, Miss Catherine. Can I assist you in any way?' he asked tonelessly.

She wished she was good enough to program complex emotions into him, but despite all her tinkering down in the basement when her father was out, she wasn't yet anywhere near that level.

'No, thank you, Sam. You can, however, swear not to tell my father what I'm doing.' Technically, Samuel was meant to obey her father over her, as he was head of the family, but as far as the mecha comprehended the feelings of like and dislike, he disliked Nathaniel. Like the few aristocrats who could afford a mecha, Catherine's father treated Sam as nothing more than a lump of metal: useful, yet unimportant and unworthy of courtesy. Nathaniel owned a mecha merely as a mark of status, and would have preferred human servants if they weren't looked upon as the cheaper alternative. Catherine, though, had learned from her mother that even mechas deserved kindness and respect. Besides, having taken Sam apart and put him back together countless times, she knew there was a lot more to him than just gears and chains. Fuelled by tyrium, there was more technology involved in his design than in most full-sized skyships. That was half the reason mechas were so rare and expensive.

'What is it that I must not tell Master Nathaniel?' Samuel asked her.

Opening her wardrobe she pulled out the biggest bag she owned. Then she balled up a shirt and breeches, along with some undergarments, and stuffed them in the bag. She rummaged through her bedside drawers for a pair of scissors and the little money she had stashed away and hid those under the clothing.

'I'm running away,' she declared defiantly. 'I refuse to be married off to that awful Gale boy. Tomorrow I'm going to the shipyard to stow away.'

'Indeed, Miss Catherine. I shall endeavour to keep your secret.' Samuel sounded, though she knew it was impossible, somewhat forlorn.

'Oh, Sam, I wish you could come with me!' she said, reaching up to run a finger over the ornate Erovan festival mask covering Sam's 'brain'. She hated the mask, but her father thought that having so many gears visible was unsightly. 'But I can't take you. The common people don't have mecha servants so you'd be an obvious giveaway that I'm government-born. You do understand, don't you?'

'I do, Miss Catherine. I believe the correct response would be to wish you good fortune in your escape.' Smiling, she leaned up and pressed a kiss to the cold porcelain cheek.

'I'll come back for you, one day. When things are different. I shan't forget you, Samuel,' she declared, letting her gaze slide to the hand-drawn map pinned to her bedroom wall. The only reason she was allowed it was because her father wanted her to be aware of each and every bit of land Anglya ruled over; the land that seemed to be decreasing with every passing month. Once upon a time, Anglya had ruled the whole lot peacefully: each country had its own royal family and government, as they still did, but Anglya's royal family had been at the very head of things. That all changed when Mericus tried to claim Erova for itself. That had been the breaking point; since then, it seemed every country had decided to fight to break free of Anglyan rule. Catherine had been born in the midst of the war, and had no knowledge of what life was like before, but she at least remembered a time when the monarchy was in place. Before her father had been running things, when Collection hadn't even been an option.

Dashing over to the large glass half-dome that was the window of her bedroom, she hauled herself up on to the small window seat, pressing her nose to the glass and staring out over the city. She could see almost all of it from her room. The sun was setting, bathing everything in a purple-gold glow through the rain. Lamps twinkled from atop high posts in the city centre, lighting the way for those still going about their business. Excitement bubbled at the thought that tomorrow *she* would be part of the real world for good. Maybe she could catch a skyship to Siberene, or even Dalivia. Anywhere that wasn't Anglya.

Outside the government district the city was a sorry-looking place, dirty and rusting, and Catherine knew it was full of painfully thin children and parents scraping by to survive. She'd heard the countryside wasn't much better. All the food grown there was taken by the government and rationed, the excess sold at prices most people couldn't afford. Aside from the farmers, many country folk worked long hours in the mines, gathering tyrium for the government to sell.

It made Catherine sick to think of her privileged place in this world. Merely by being born a Hunter, she had secured a life of relative comfort, a high-born life for which most of the population must surely hate her. Ever since the monarchs disappeared and the government took over rule of the country, a deep loathing had grown in the hearts of the commoners for anyone born to aristocracy, regardless of how much influence they had in government. They understood that the government was doing its best to end the war quickly, but aristocrats were exempt from Collection, and for most people that alone was enough to breed hate. It must be heartbreaking, Catherine supposed, having every child bar your eldest taken from you soon after they turned thirteen. On Collection days with low numbers, even the eldest child was taken from some of the poorer families, and the government wasn't above ignoring birth records to take children who were younger. Some families tried to avoid the trauma of Collection by only having one child. But storms help you, if you were an orphan, or a street rat; you stood no chance of escape.

'No more,' she muttered to herself, her gaze steeling in determination as she looked at the shipyard. 'I won't sit back and let things happen any more.'

As she spoke a government skyship rose into the air, wings outstretched and tilted to catch the wind, pale violet smoke billowing from the engine pipes, the stern propeller unfolding to give it a boost away from the landing deck, into the nearest updraught. The Anglyan flag waved proudly from the secondary mast. No doubt it was heading to Erova, to fill the front lines with more unfortunate young souls destined to die.

The shipyard was huge. It had to be, given the size of some of the ships – and to allow enough space for each ship to unfurl its wings without tangling with its neighbours. With some larger trade ships standing twice the size of her house, which was one of the biggest houses in Breningarth, the shipyard was practically a city in itself.

'Miss Catherine, you should retire, it is past sunset,' Samuel said, interrupting her thoughts. She pulled away from the window, hopping back down to the floor. As Samuel went to get the lights, she changed into her night-gown and crawled under the thick blankets.

'Goodnight, Sam,' she murmured as he extinguished the last lamp, pitching the room into darkness but for the glow of light behind his eye lenses.

'Have a pleasant resting period, Miss Catherine.' As Sam left her room, she turned over and buried her head in the pillow, letting out a long breath. There was no way she was going to be able to sleep tonight.

2

Pale sunlight woke Catherine the next morning, for sleep had come, eventually. Remembering her plans, she grinned widely and stared up at the ceiling. If all went well, that had been the last time she would sleep in this bed. Finally, she pulled herself out of the warm sheets, opened her wardrobe and found her best dress. It was a gaudy purple monstrosity consisting mostly of petticoats upon petticoats, with silver lace at the cuffs and collar, as well as the trim of the corset, and masses of elaborate embroidery. The bodice was too tight and the fabric uncomfortably itchy. She hated it. She took the dress into the bathroom, where Sam had already drawn her bath. Her mind on her plans for the day, Catherine slid into the hot water. The hardest part would be giving her father the slip . . .

Later, she gathered the skirt of her dress so she could make her way downstairs to the kitchen. That was one reason she disliked dresses with huge skirts; they were completely impractical for just about everything fun. You couldn't run, or climb, and you had to be constantly aware of where your skirt was and whether you were accidentally showing more skin than was deemed appropriate.

Trousers were far better, but, of course, ladies didn't wear trousers.

'Good morning, Father.' She walked into the kitchen, every bit the perfect, dutiful daughter.

Dressed in an impeccable navy three-piece suit, his greying brown hair combed to the side and his sideburns neatly trimmed, her father was already eating porridge, and Catherine could see a generous bowl waiting on the table for her. If there was one thing the country had in abundance, despite the food rations, it was porridge.

'Good morning, Catherine. Can you not do something with your hair? It looks like a bird's nest,' he snapped.

'I had a bath and it's still drying. I'll sort it after breakfast.' He hummed in disapproval, but didn't say anything, looking back down at the newspaper spread over the table beside his bowl.

'Anything in the news?' she asked politely.

'Nothing unusual. Another battalion has fallen in Erova. There's going to be another Collection soon.'

Catherine felt a shiver go down her spine. She loathed Collection day. The screams and cries of parents could be heard for hours after the soldiers left.

'Are there even any children left to be Collected?' she asked, trying to mask her horror. Every time she went into the lower city, there seemed to be fewer and fewer children about. She feared there would soon be none left at all.

'Another twenty more have turned thirteen since the last Collection,' her father said dismissively. 'It's low, but it's better than nothing. Besides, we shan't need many more – if all goes well, the war should end before long. Now go and comb your hair. We're meeting Thomas at nine.'

Catherine hiked up her skirts and ran back up to her room, pondering her father's unexpected words. What had changed? Was the war truly coming to an end after all this time?

Swiftly she set about untangling the mess that was her long brown hair. The resulting plait was a little rough and uneven, and she knew her father would complain, but he would have to live with it.

'Hurry up, Catherine!' Nathaniel called impatiently.

Catherine fastened her favourite silver-buckled boots, choosing comfort over fashion – her father wouldn't be looking too hard at her feet – then hoisting her bag over her shoulder, she rushed back down to meet her father in the entryway.

She watched his eyes trail over her less than perfect hair.

'I suppose you'll have to do. Let's hope Thomas will forgive your appearance,' he muttered, lifting his satchel over his shoulder. Stomach churning anxiously, Catherine followed without a glance back at her home of nearly fifteen years, not wanting to question even for a second her decision to leave.

Catherine braced herself against a metal bar protruding from the floor of the carriage as the tram jerked to a noisy halt in the station at the heart of the city. Once sleek and near-soundless, years of neglect had made the trams rusty and unsteady. People tried to avoid using them if they could help it, but for some journeys there was no alternative.

Apparently, with the war going on, the government had better things to spend money on than maintaining public transport. Her father was mostly to blame; he was the one in charge of domestic issues.

Nathaniel herded her out on to the platform, where they were immediately assaulted with the sounds and smells of the city. The rain had stopped, but it was still cold enough for Catherine to feel a chill through the layers of her dress, and she found herself wishing she'd brought a coat.

The streets of Breningarth were alive with people, bustling past the rundown buildings and avoiding the large puddles that spanned the roads. This close to the outer city, half the shops had gone out of business years ago due to lack of both interest and stock. On street corners poorly dressed men sold government-produced newspapers or food from small carts, women aired laundry and sold clothes, and a few children darted like lightning from one stall to the next, slipping goods into their pockets on the way. Catherine, always on the alert, hid a grin as one boy stole the expensive pocket watch from her father's coat. His indigo-smudged face showed surprise when he realised she'd seen what he'd done. She winked at him rather than telling her father, and he sprinted away before she could change her mind.

Her boots clicked against the dirty cobbled street, and she couldn't help but notice how people backed away as she and Nathaniel approached, crossing to the other side of the street to avoid them. Catherine's dress immediately set her out as government, and most people would recognise Nathaniel Hunter from the public newscasts that were constantly shown on the screens in pubs and squares; he wasn't a popular man. Catherine followed her father past an entrance to the shipyard. The busiest place in the city, its noise was almost deafening, and the smell of burning tyrium was heavy in the air, a faint purple tinge tainting the clouds above. Catherine loved it.

The dockland government building was still several streets away, towering over the buildings around it, and Catherine hung back, heart pounding, as her father proceeded. It was now or never. If she could just get to the bustling shipyard, she would be free. She crouched as if refastening her bootlace, looking up through her fringe to make sure her father had carried on walking. In fact, he had quickened his pace; he hated being close to the shipyard as it was full of commoners. He often complained to Catherine that people of government status should not have to inter-act with the lower levels of society.

Seizing her moment, she straightened up and slipped down a narrow, empty side street between a pub and a bakery. Glancing both ways, Catherine opened her hand-bag, pulling out the breeches and tugging them on hastily under her dress. Struggling slightly to unlace the back of her bodice, her fingers shaking with exhilaration, she managed to wriggle her way out of the dress and pull her shirt over her head. She stuffed her money purse into the crotch of her breeches, knowing it would be safest there.

The only thing left in her bag was the pair of scissors she'd packed. She held them up, sliding her plait between the blades, and nearly cut her finger off as she heard foot-steps nearby. She spun round with her heart in her throat.

No one was there that she could see, but she had to get a move on.

Taking a steadying breath, she tried again, feeling little resistance as the sharp steel cut through the top of the thick brown braid. Her neck itched as short strands brushed the nape. She threw the plait down a nearby drain and left the dress and scissors in the bag, dumping it against the wall. She hoped that some lucky soul would find the contents and sell them. Running her hands through her unevenly cropped hair, she prayed it looked boyish enough that no one would comment. Her chest was easily hidden under the baggy grey blouse.

'I'm too clean,' she murmured, looking down at her pale hands and pristine shirt. All the children she'd seen near the shipyard were covered in dirt and tyrium smudges. The look of the ground below her feet made Catherine shudder, but she muddied her fingers regardless, smearing her shirt and breeches. Lifting her hands to her face, she wiped across her brow and cheeks, her eyes and mouth shut tight. A shiver went down her spine at the slick, wet feeling on her skin, and she determinedly ignored the smell. Finally, she spread the dirt through her hair so the dark strands stuck out haphazardly. Disguise now in place, she ran on along the alley, her heart thumping furiously against her ribs. She had done it! She had escaped her father. She was free.

It didn't take Catherine long to gain access to the shipyard – a quick sprint across the square and ten minutes of hiding behind crates, waiting for the guards to pass. Once she was in, she blended easily into the crowd of workers.

Her eyes were as round as coins as she wandered through the organised chaos of the shipyard. Burly men hauled enormous crates on deck with such ease that they might have been throwing pillows, while small boys scurried from ship to ship, fetching rope and gears and whatever else their captains asked of them, ducking the occasional wave of seawater that towered over the edge of the docks. Many of the docked skyships were vast government vessels, squeaky clean and resplendent in their military colours, banners flying proudly; others were authorised trade ships, gigantic and well-travelled, with huge canvas and metal wings furled at their sides. The number of other ships she could count on one hand; it was near impossible to get a permit for pleasure travel these days.

Steering well clear of the rows of government ships, Catherine made her way past the trade ships. Suddenly, she paused. A skyship at the end of the port had caught her eye. While it was still bigger than her house, it looked as if it were too small to be a trade ship. Its design was beautiful, if somewhat mismatched, with gleaming hazel boards and shiny bronze struts. Cream canvas wings were folded tightly to its sides and the mast was flagless, but the lowered sails were a matching cream colour, rippling slightly in the breeze. Gold calligraphy was scrawled neatly across the bow – *Stormdancer*, it read. The name seemed fitting. She imagined that such a small skyship would dance through even the harshest storms as easily as a master of ballet. Her breath caught, and she instantly knew which ship she was going to board. It was only a matter of how to go about it.

As she moved closer she saw a man sat straddling the boom, working at the rigging. *That* was going to make things difficult. She crept as close as she dared to where the ship's narrow gangplank met the dock, looking out from her hiding place between some large crates. The man had to head below deck sometime!

Her feet had begun to fall asleep before he hopped neatly down and dropped to his knees, opening the trap to slip below deck. Yes! This was her chance. Darting silently up the gangplank, she stepped as quietly as she could on to the ship's deck. Clothes were strung up over a line to dry, and she smiled at seeing a dress. There was at least one woman on the ship; surely she couldn't turn away a homeless child?

Catherine lifted the trap, sighing in relief when the narrow corridor below proved to be empty. She leaned up against the ladder to pull the trap closed and jumped down, landing with a quiet clatter on the metal floor. The inside of the ship was as mismatched as the outside: bronze and steel struts in the walls and floor were interspaced with the occasional section of gleaming wooden panels. The owners genuinely cared about their ship, and it showed.

Creeping as quietly as possible through the short corridors, peering into doors to find a hiding place, she was disheartened to discover only small, packed storage rooms and the main control room. As much as she longed to stay and marvel over the control room and its many dials and levers, she knew she had to hide before someone came back. There was another manhole at the end of the corridor and she dropped straight down it, ignoring the ladder.

There were more doors on this floor, which was U-shaped. Behind the first door was a washroom with a porcelain bath, and the door beside that was the loo. Further down was a wooden door stained with tyrium. Curious, Catherine tried the handle and the door swung open. A narrow bed was shoved against one wall, the patchwork sheets all in a mess, and beside it was a desk covered in blueprint papers and scrawled notes, weighted in place by twists of pipe and wire. A pair of chunky knee-high leather boots rested on the floor beside the bed, and a thick fleece-lined jacket with a high collar hung on the back of the chair at the desk. This was clearly a man's room.

It seemed as good a hiding place as any, so she shut the door behind her, eyes wandering over the messy blueprint stuck to the back of the door. For the life of her, she couldn't decipher its purpose.

She looked around the room for an even smaller place to hide and pulled open the doors of a large oak wardrobe that was bolted to the wall and floor. Heart racing, she pushed aside a heap of clothes at the base of the wardrobe, squeezing herself right into the corner. Covering herself with a long wool coat, she hoped she looked just like another pile of clothes. Catherine laughed shakily to herself. She wrapped her arms around her legs, and leaned her chin on her knees. All she could do now was wait.

3

A loud *thunk* snapped Catherine out of a doze, and she very nearly forgot how to breathe as she heard footsteps approaching. She heard voices before the door opened; three men, she thought. One with a common accent, the other two sounding government with a lingering undertone of inner city. Guards, maybe?

'If you insist, gents, but I assure you, you won't find anything,' the common man was saying, sounding somewhat amused.

Definitely guards.

'We'll be the judge of that, sprog,' one of the guards announced. Sprog? The commoner didn't sound like a child. She heard the thump of heavy boots kicking at wood, and assumed the guards were searching the room. Panic gripped her, her heart pounding as the door of the wardrobe rattled and opened. She froze – until everything went pitch-black around her, and another thump signalled the door being closed again.

'There's still plenty of other rooms for us to check, boy. Don't think you've got away with anything.' The other guard's voice was colder, sharp.

'Well, we have a take-off schedule to keep to, y'know. Places to be, stormwake to catch,' the commoner retorted, his voice growing fainter as the three walked out of the room.

When Catherine could no longer hear the bickering, a thrill went through her. She had successfully evaded the shipyard guards. She was practically free! She just needed the ship to take off while she was still aboard.

She leaned back against the side of the wardrobe and thought with satisfaction of how her father would explain to Thomas Gale that she couldn't marry Marcus because she had run away; no one had attempted to kidnap her since she was small, when the first attempt had ended with ten men being killed. Her father would know she'd left of her own volition. Oh, how it would embarrass him!

Catherine's backside was beginning to feel numb when she heard a faint rumbling that turned into a fearsome roar as the entire ship quivered. They must be preparing for take-off. She threw out her hands to brace herself against the walls of the wardrobe. Vaguely remembering something she'd been told once at worship, she murmured a quick request to the gods for safe travels through their domain. Not that she knew where she was going, but regardless, she would be travelling through the storms. Catherine didn't want to take any chances.

The vibrations increased, and she could hear the engine pumping steam through the pipes in the wall to power the propellers, a hissing sound joining the roar of burning tyrium and the loud creak of the wings being unfurled.

Faintly she heard shouts from the rest of the ship. She was filled with excitement until the wardrobe door opened suddenly. A pair of amused pale blue eyes stared at her.

'I thought my wardrobe floor looked a little lumpier than usual. Who might you be, then?' he asked. She placed him as the commoner who had been with the guards earlier. Unable to speak, she merely stared up at him, wide-eyed. She had never seen someone with such red hair before.

'We're already airborne,' he informed her, pulling his desk chair over and sitting on it backwards, propping his chin on the back and staring at her. They were up already? It had been amazingly quick! 'So who are you, and what might you be doing in my wardrobe? I assure you, it's not the finest place in the world,' he added with a wry grin, making Catherine giggle, despite herself.

'Cat —' she began, cutting herself off quickly with a cough. Telling him her name was Catherine would be a very obvious indicator that she was not, in fact, a boy. 'Just Cat,' she finished, making the effort to deepen her voice somewhat, letting her accent loosen. She couldn't go around speaking like a government brat. 'I . . . I just need to get away.'

The boy eyed her contemplatively. He looked about sixteen or seventeen, she guessed, and the awkwardness about his long-limbed frame suggested a recent growth spurt. A faint ginger shadow graced his purple-smudged jaw.

'Well, Just Cat, if that's what you want to call yourself,' he said with a smirk, clearly aware that this wasn't a real name. 'You've succeeded. This ship is heading straight to Siberene. Is that far away enough for you? The Collectors won't find you there, and you look the age, just about.' His piercing blue gaze travelled over her in a way that made her want to cross her arms over her chest.

'Are you going to leave me in Siberene?' she queried before she could stop herself, hating how scared she sounded.

'We might do. That's usually how it goes with the kids we smuggle out. Depends how entertaining you are,' he answered, his smirk not faltering for a moment.

'I'll have to be at my wittiest, then, shan't I?' she replied easily, and he smiled.

'I think we're going to get along just fine, brat. You can call me Fox. Are you going to be getting out of my wardrobe any time soon?'

She shrugged.

'I don't know, it's rather comfortable in here.'

He let out a short bark of laughter, swinging a long leg over the chair and reaching out to grab her by the wrist, pulling her out of the wardrobe and on to her feet. He was a good head taller than she was and this made her feel even more of a child than usual. Pausing, Fox eyed her appraisingly. 'You must be freezing in just a shirt – here.' Reaching into the wardrobe, he pulled out a thick knitted jumper, tossing it at her. The dark blue wool was soft and well worn, and Cat didn't argue at the gift, pulling it over her head. It swamped her, and she had to roll the sleeves up three times just to see her hands.

'Blimey, you're a short 'un,' he teased, making her blush.

'Leave off,' she muttered in annoyance, ducking out from under his hand as he attempted to ruffle her hair.

'Ooh, touchy. We'd better introduce you to the gaff, make sure he lets you stay. He might toss you overboard like the last one.'

Fox turned to leave the room, and Catherine stared after him in alarm.

'You're joking, aren't you? You wouldn't really throw me overboard? That would be murder!' she protested. She hadn't thought what might happen if the crew didn't let her stay. He chuckled as she chased after him, seeing that she had to take two quick steps for every one of his long strides.

'No, throwing you overboard would merely be displacing you from the ship – the water would do the murdering.'

'Don't be such a brute,' she told him with a scowl, which only made him chuckle harder.

'Lighten up, shortie. You'll never survive if you take yourself so seriously. Where you from, anyway? 'S not every day we get stows. Not even the bravest of little boys have the balls to dare escape Collection, so what's your story?'

Forcing herself not to blush at his words, she shrugged.

'I guess I'm just braver than most,' she replied evasively. She needed to think of a story before she could tell him anything. What would be believable? They scrambled up the ladder, and Catherine stumbled as the ship rocked violently for a moment. The sudden movement didn't faze Fox, who braced himself easily against the lurching, then walked on.

'You'll get used to that,' he assured her.

'So what's the captain like?' she asked curiously, quickening her pace to keep up.

'He's a decent sort. Bit loud at times, but he's a nice bloke. Been travelling since he was younger than me,' he explained, pulling open a door to their left that Catherine knew from her earlier exploration led to the control room. There were two other men in the room now who looked up when Catherine and Fox entered. One seemed a little older than her father, she thought, in his late thirties perhaps. His hair was steely grey, and he had a neatly cropped beard covering his cheeks and chin. His brown double-breasted coat was done up to his throat with shining buckles, and a neat white shirt collar peeked over the top of it. A black leather hat was perched jauntily on his head. The other man, sitting at the wheel, was much younger, early twenties, maybe, and somewhat baby-faced, with a smooth jaw marred only by a twisted scar on his left cheek, and honey blond curls falling into his hazel eyes.

'I didn't know we had another crew member,' he remarked quietly, one hand resting cautiously on the wheel. 'He looks a little young.'

The bearded man snorted, raising a bushy eyebrow at Fox. 'We don't, as far as I remember. Where'd you find this one, lad?' he asked.

'My wardrobe. Seems he managed to slip past those morons who were searching it. I thought I'd let you decide whether to throw him overboard or not,' Fox replied calmly.

The panic must have shown on Catherine's face because the older man laughed heartily.

'Don't scare the poor sprog! He's petrified enough as it

is. What's your name, kid?' The man directed a warm smile towards Catherine, who smiled back unsurely.

'He calls himself Cat,' Fox answered for her before she could speak, his scepticism clear. The blond man laughed, and the grey-haired man raised both eyebrows.

'First Fox, now Cat? What is this, a sodding menagerie?' he muttered to himself, but didn't question her chosen moniker. 'I'm Harry, lad. Captain of this fine skyship. Which, I might add, I don't remember giving you permission to board,' he added with a stern look. 'Better to ask forgiveness than permission – but you'd do best to tell me exactly why I shouldn't get Ben here to turn this ship around and drop you right back in Anglya where you presumably came from.'

Catherine's eyes widened in alarm, and she took a step forward.

'Please, sir, don't take me back. I won't survive if I go back there!' That was probably true. She was almost certain her father would kill her for running away if he ever set eyes on her again. 'I heard there's going to be another Collection next week!' Again, true. Just not necessarily relevant to her. 'I won't be a bother if you let me stay. I'm a fast learner. I can work wherever you need me, even if it's scrubbing floors or feeding the furnace! Just don't take me back to Anglya!' Catherine turned her shining grey eyes on the older man. His face softened and he sighed, rubbing at his beard.

'I suppose we can take on one more. We'll have to see how good you are around the ship. And the government won't miss one child this Collection, will they?' he mused, the weathered skin around his eyes crinkling. 'But if you're not up to scratch, we'll let you go in Siberene. There's no dead weight on this ship.'

Catherine beamed, fighting the temptation to hug the man in gratitude.

'Thank you, sir. I won't let you down, promise,' she declared. Harry clapped her on the shoulder.

'That's the spirit, lad.' He pulled a pocket watch from his coat. 'Not long until supper. Enough time for you to get cleaned up and shown around.' He glanced over at the man at the wheel. 'This is Benny, by the way, Benedict Talbot. He's our pilot.'

Benedict gave her a small wave and a reserved smile.

'Hi,' he said, and she replied with a grin.

'Fox, show our new boy around, would you? Let him have the room two down from yours. I'll talk to the missus and try to persuade her another sprog can't hurt us. And get her to change the bedding.' He looked thoughtful. 'I'll bet you don't have anything other than the clothes on your back, do you, Cat?' Harry asked.

She shook her head. She wouldn't tell him about the purse of money in her trousers; she didn't trust them enough for that yet.

'Well, we have plenty of Fox's clothes from when he was your age and I'm sure they'll fit fine. I'll see if I can persuade Alice to dig them out. Go on, then, brats, run. Don't let the new one get lost, Fox,' he added sternly.

'I would never do such a thing,' Fox replied, feigning outrage. 'Come on, then, Cat. Let's make this quick. I'm meant to be helping Matt with the engines.'

Catherine scurried after Fox as he hurried out of the control room.

'So, that was Ben and Harry,' he said. 'You've only two others to meet – Matt, the engineer, and Alice, Harry's wife. Alice is a proper sweetheart. Be nice to her, or you'll get storms from Harry. Matt's a cheeky sod, but all right. You'll see.'

'It's just the five of you?' Catherine asked, surprised. 'I thought you'd need more people for a ship this size.' From what she could remember, there were thirty crew members on each of the small government ships, and about a hundred on the larger ones. Her father had once told her that some trade ships had up to three hundred crew members and were practically a small town in themselves.

'We probably do. We get by just fine, though,' Fox told her with a shrug. She wondered how long he had been on the ship. She didn't dare ask, however; maybe she'd try when they were a little friendlier with each other. 'This level is controls and storage,' he continued. 'And the trap topside. Level below is crew quarters, washrooms, galley, and a bit more storage. Below that we've got more storage and the engines: that's where Matt and me spend most of our time. And bottom level is just storage.' Catherine nodded, surprised that a ship this size had four levels. She'd only anticipated three.

'So what is the ship for? I can't imagine a pleasure ship with that much storage, and I definitely can't see you getting a permit.' Pleasure permits were solely for the incredibly wealthy. Her father had one, but he rarely used it, as he deemed travelling unnecessary. As far as he was concerned, everything important would come to him rather than the other way around, and if it didn't come to him, then it clearly wasn't important enough.

Fox's lips twisted into a devious smirk, and his eyes sparkled mischievously. Catherine unconsciously leaned closer, curious to know what could cause such amusement.

'Well, that's where things get interesting.' Fox paused. 'Not that I should be telling you this until Alice gives you the OK. But you look like you can keep a secret.' He raised a questioning eyebrow.

'Course I can,' Catherine said. What could they be hiding?

'Well, I suppose you'll figure it out sooner or later,' he relented. 'As far as the government knows, we're fur traders shipping from Siberene. With the storms getting more active over the past year or two, not many ships are willing to make the journey there. Especially not the bigger trade ships. But we're small enough to nip round the bigger tornadoes with Ben at the wheel. The man can't half fly,' Fox said with no small amount of admiration in his voice. Catherine smiled; there were obviously strong bonds between the crew of the *Stormdancer*. The storms worsening was news to her, though; she never paid much attention to weather reports. She barely knew the difference between storm classifications, and the bigger ones hadn't come close to Anglya in years.

'And what do you do, really?' she asked shrewdly.

Fox's grin turned wolfish.

'We may or may not fill the lowest level – which doesn't exist in the ship's registered blueprints – with items monitored under rationing. And we may or may not happen to misplace those items among the needy of Anglya.'

Catherine stared at him, realisation dawning. 'You're smugglers!' she gasped. How did they get away with smuggling goods so blatantly? They docked in the city shipyard and everything!

'Any problems with mildly illegal business?' Fox asked, dropping down the narrow manhole, then stepping aside so Catherine could do the same. 'Because if so, we'll drop you off in Siberene and leave you to make your own way. You wouldn't be the first kid we've smuggled out – though it's usually because their parents ask us to. We don't usually keep them.' He smiled wryly, and Catherine smiled back.

'No problems.' Catherine resumed the thicker accent and low-pitched tone she practised on her excursions to the common areas of Breningarth. 'You're helping people and that's an admirable thing. Most people I know are just happy to look after themselves.' She thought of her father and his associates, who laughed at the poor and hungry from the comfort of their grand homes. She hadn't been able to sit for days the one time she'd dared give a copper to a common girl even younger than she was. 'How do you do it without getting caught, though? Aren't the guards meant to check every ship after it docks and before it leaves?'

Fox shrugged.

'Kid, nine out of ten guards at the Breningarth shipyard don't give a rat's arse about what we're smuggling – they're not even looking for goods. Their job is to stop anyone smuggling *people*. That's what they get their bonuses for.

The smuggling we do is a lot easier than you'd think – it's just that most are too scared of the punishment to bother trying.'

The punishment for smuggling was either death or forced conscription, which tended to result in death in any case.

'And you aren't?' she challenged, raising an eyebrow. He looked at her, a sort of sadness in his eyes, masked with amusement.

'Why would I be scared of a punishment I know isn't likely to happen?' he answered. 'It's like being scared of a storm that never comes.'

'It has happened, though. People have been executed for piracy plenty of times before,' she argued.

'Well, for a start we're not pirates. Pirates attack other ships. And those people were stupid. The key is to fade into the background, become part of the scenery. Don't give people a reason to question you being there, and they won't think you suspicious.'

Catherine conceded the point, then frowned.

'Are there more of you? Smugglers, I mean.' She imagined a whole network of people working beneath her father's nose, and couldn't help but grin. It was just like one of her fantasy books. 'Lots of people bringing in goods to help during rationing?'

'If there are, we haven't found any,' Fox replied with a shrug. 'And they don't work the same areas we do. But Breningarth is a big city. For all we know, there could be dozens more. Good luck to them, if there are. But either way, we work alone.'

He gave her a look that put an end to her questioning, though not to the thoughts racing through her mind, and they continued the tour.

'This is the washroom and there's another one at the other end of the hall. Next door is the loo, and opposite is the linen cupboard. Next to that is my room, as you know.'

Catherine blushed at the pointed look Fox gave her. 'Over here is the galley,' he told her, pushing against a thick oak door with his shoulder. The air immediately filled with the scent of food. 'We take all our meals in here, and you can usually find Alice in here. If not, she'll be next door in the laundry room.'

Stepping a little closer to Fox to peer through the open door, Catherine was surprised at the amount of space in the galley. With two long wooden tables, they could have easily seated about twenty people if they wanted to. There was a door at the back that she assumed led to the kitchen.

'Do I get to meet Alice now?' she asked.

Fox grabbed her by the back of the collar, hoisting her into the corridor.

'Alice is not to be interrupted while cooking except in the most dire of circumstances. Wait until supper,' he told her.

Fox shut the galley door behind him, leading her further down the hallway.

'That's a spare room, which is currently used for storage. And that's your new room,' Fox declared as he pointed to the two doors beside his own. 'Keep it clean and don't attempt to put a lock on the door. Harry will have your hide,' he added with a grimace. He pushed the door open, allowing her to stick her head in for a look. It was similar to Fox's room, just without all the clutter, and while it was drastically smaller than her room back home, she rather liked it.

'Brilliant. What about everyone else?' she asked curiously.

'They're around the corner,' Fox explained. She followed him down the U-shaped corridor, peering around at the four doors located there. 'Harry and Alice's room, other washroom, then Ben's room and Matt's room. Stay out of here – they take shifts and sleep odd hours.'

'So what will I be doing? You seem to have everything covered rather efficiently.'

'Matt will keep you busy. We'll just have to hope you're good at things, I suppose,' he teased, causing her to bristle in affront.

'I'm good at plenty!' she insisted, making him laugh.

'I never said you weren't,' he said. 'Why don't you wash up and then knock on my door? I'll take you down to Matt.'

She nodded, and the pair of them doubled back into their own hallway, Fox stopping outside the door to the linen cupboard and nudging it open.

'Towels and bed sheets and things are in here. I'm afraid you'll have to stick with the clothes you're wearing until Alice finds you something. Gods only know where she's put my old things.' He waited for her to grab a towel before shutting the door behind her.

'You've been here for a while, then?' she asked hesitantly.

'You could say that,' he replied shortly, jaw clenched, and moved to pull open the washroom door. 'I'll see you when you're finished.' Without waiting for her to say anything, he stalked off, his bedroom door slamming shut behind him. Catherine sighed; she hadn't meant to upset him. Shaking her head, she went through the open door of the washroom, slid the lock into place and turned to the large porcelain bath.

As much as she wanted to have a long, luxurious soak, she knew Fox was waiting for her, so she took as little time as she could. Eventually, she was dried and re-dressed. She rather enjoyed just being able to rub a towel over her now short hair and leave it. Tossing the towel into the hamper in the corner, she unlocked the door, and hurried across to Fox's room, knocking hesitantly.

'Now you're looking less of a street rat and more of a human boy,' he remarked as he opened the door, and she resisted the urge to laugh. If only he knew! 'Let's show you the rest of the ship, then.'

He set off down the corridor, and Catherine rushed to follow, half jogging at his side.

'You could slow down a bit, I've only got short legs!' she complained. He snorted, reaching out to cuff her shoulder.

'Maybe keeping pace with me might make you grow a bit. How old are you, anyway? Eleven, twelve?' he queried, eyeing her small frame.

'I'm fourteen, thank you very much. Almost fifteen, actually,' she retorted.

His eyebrows shot up. 'You're not serious?' he scoffed, and laughed when she nodded. 'Blimey, you're a midget! You'll want to put on a bit of muscle soon – you won't be much good if you can't lift anything. No wonder you've not been Collected yet.' The government tended to stay away from scrawnier kids, waiting until they bulked up a bit.

She wished she could reply that she was a perfectly acceptable height for her age and gender. But she stayed quiet, scowling in embarrassment. Fox seemed to realise that he'd gone too far, and ceased his teasing.

'Careful, here. The ladder is a bit shaky, but it holds all right,' he warned her as they reached the manhole. Nodding, she lowered herself slowly on to the steel ladder, gripping tightly as it swayed with her weight. Once they reached the ground, she immediately noticed the difference in temperature between the two floors. Humid air clung to her skin, drawing a thin layer of perspiration. She wiped a hand across her face, annoyed by the fact that Fox seemed unfazed by the heat, despite being dressed in both a tight long-sleeved shirt and leather waistcoat.

'The furnace must be around here, then,' she presumed, remembering the sweltering heat of the basement at home, where the burners were kept.

'Right you are. Everything to the left is storage, everything to the right is engines,' he told her, rolling up his shirtsleeves as he pushed open a door. 'Oi, Matt, where are you hiding? We've got a new one!' he called into the large, loud room. Steam hissed from pipes, the furnace roared quietly, and gears clanked and ground as they propelled the ship forward. Catherine had to duck as she walked, narrowly avoiding being hit on the head by a jutting piston. She heard the thunk of boots meeting metal, and recognised the stranger walking towards them. He was the man who had been sat on the boom earlier!

'New one? How in storms did we manage that?' the man asked in surprise, his dark brown hair plastered to his forehead with sweat, tyrium stains on his jaw and arms. He was dressed in a plain cotton undershirt, which was clinging to his muscular chest, and braces hung loose from his waist. Catherine blushed, despite herself. This man was built like a giant!

'Stowaway. Harry wants to keep him, soft-hearted pushover that he is. Figured you might be able to put him to use,' Fox replied, grinning at the large man. 'Cat, this is Matthew. Matt keeps the ship airborne and running smoothly. Matt, meet Cat. Storms know what his real name is, but that's all we're getting from him,' he added, ignoring Catherine's scowl.

'You're a wee'un, aren't you?' Matt commented. 'Well, welcome aboard, I suppose. What can you do?'

'Whatever you ask of me,' said Catherine earnestly. 'I have some experience with basic household mechanics, but I'm a very fast learner, sir.' Matt chuckled, amused at her enthusiasm.

'We'll see about that, sprog,' he told her. 'I suppose you're more useful here than anywhere else on this ship. I'll take him from here, Fox, no worries.'

Fox nodded. Catherine felt alarmed at the thought of being left alone in the engine room with such a hulk of a man. Her trepidation must have shown on her face for Fox laughed.

'He doesn't bite, shortie. He'll look after you and I'll see you at supper.' Lightly nudging Catherine's shoulder, he left the room by a door to their right.

Catherine stared up at Matt. Despite his massive build, he had a friendly face, with a chiselled jaw, a thin goatee and striking green eyes that contrasted with his pale skin. He held out a hand and she took it, his callused fingers dwarfing her slender hand.

'It's a pleasure, kid. Now come on, I'll show you the ropes before supper.' He tugged her forward – and Catherine only had time for one brief thought: 'What on Tellus have I got myself into?'

4

Catherine was startled out of her work when a loud bell rang through the room. She glanced up through her tinted safety goggles at Matt, who was just setting his wrench down.

'Food's waiting. Come on, Alice will have both our heads if we let the grub get cold,' Matt told her, tugging off his own goggles and reaching for the grey button-up shirt hanging on a pipe end.

Catherine wiped her oil-stained fingers on her trousers. They hadn't been doing anything too difficult; just basic maintenance on the engines, with Matt showing her what things looked like when they were working perfectly, and common signs of something malfunctioning. She picked it all up quickly, and was hooked already. She'd always been intrigued by machinery – her father had loathed her interest in it because he felt it was beneath her station. But learning how several innocent-looking pieces of metal could be shaped and put together to create something complex was fascinating to her. Working on Samuel had been her only experience of mechanics, and it thrilled her to learn more.

Letting Matt lead her back up to the galley, she hung back slightly when they reached the door. She had one crew member left to meet, and she had no doubt that if Harry's wife disagreed with her staying, she'd be out on her ear before she could say Anglya.

'Go on, lad. Alice is lovely,' Matt urged, nudging her through the door. Everyone but Ben was already inside, and they looked up at the noise. Alice was standing at the head of the table, spooning a thick stew from a large tureen into bowls. She was a short, curvy woman, her blonde hair threaded liberally with grey and tied in a bun. Her warm blue eyes fixed on Catherine. By no means overweight, she was differently shaped from the painfully thin, tightly corseted women of the government. She looked natural and homely, wearing a blue dress with ruffled skirts that swept the floor and a short brown jacket with large brass buttons. Catherine found herself instantly relaxing.

'You must be Cat, then,' Alice declared, her voice clear and friendly.

'Yes, ma'am. It's a pleasure to meet you,' she said shyly. Matt and Harry broke into loud guffaws.

'Oh, hush up, both of you! There's nothing wrong with having a bit of manners,' Alice scolded, hitting Harry sharply on the shoulder with her serving spoon. 'You just ignore them, Cat, lad. They wouldn't know politeness if it smacked them in the face.' She walked around one of the long tables, her laced boots clicking on the waxed floorboards.

'You're an orphan, I presume?' she asked.

'Something like that,' replied Catherine, remembering Fox's own phrase. Alice frowned.

'No parents waiting who might be pleased to hear their little one has escaped Collection?' She peered down at Catherine, one hand resting on her waist.

'No, ma'am, no one waiting for that,' Catherine replied quickly, pleased not to have to tell a lie. Alice pursed her lips.

'One more mouth to feed won't kill us, I suppose. I expect you'll work hard?' By now she was addressing the crew. Matt nodded his head readily.

'He's been a good lad, Alice. It's good to have a sprog to scrabble under the narrower pipework.'

'All right, then,' Alice agreed. 'Welcome aboard, Cat. We run a tight ship and don't you forget it! I'm Alice.' She smiled and reached out a soft hand. 'Unfortunately shackled by marriage to this scoundrel.' She jerked her thumb towards Harry, who faked an offended look. 'I can't say it'll be bad to have a sprog on the ship again, now Fox is almost grown.' She smoothed a hand over Fox's messy red hair. He ducked out from under her hand, but his expression was fond.

'Just sit right there, dear,' Alice prompted, setting a bowl at the empty space next to Fox. With a tentative glance towards him, Catherine slipped on to the bench. Alice poured from a bottle of mead for the rest of the crew and herself, and Catherine and Fox were given water.

Jumping as a brass spoon was shoved in front of her face, Catherine took it from Fox's hand, smiling in thanks.

'Aren't we waiting for Ben?' she enquired, looking around as everyone else dug in.

'He's still in the control room,' Fox explained. 'Harry will

45

relieve him after dinner, he'll grab his own food then. How did you and Matt get on?' he asked quietly, shooting a glance towards the bulky man, who was deep in conversation with Harry.

'He's great, I've learned so much already! I never knew there were so many small parts involved in keeping an engine running,' she gushed. Fox laughed.

'So you're enjoying yourself.'

'Definitely. What were you up to?' she asked curiously, spooning more stew into her mouth.

'Just stuff,' Fox replied evasively.

'What do you think, Mattie? Can the sprog stay?' Harry asked, his loud voice interrupting their conversation. Matt looked Catherine up and down, seeming to consider.

'Yeah, he's a sharp lad, fine by me.'

Catherine glowed with pride from the praise. Harry looked around the crew in turn. Alice shrugged, having already said her piece. Fox scowled.

'Well, I can't exactly say no, can I?' he pointed out.

'Come on, Fox, you know we're all run a bit thin on this ship. One more can't hurt, and it'll give you more time to work on your little projects.'

'Yeah, it's fine by me.' Fox smiled cheekily. 'Good to have someone younger to bully.' Alice rolled her eyes.

'Well, that settles it. Welcome to the crew, Cat. Alice, love, would you dig out some of Fox's old clothes for him?' Harry added. His wife smiled and nodded.

'Will do. They might still be a little big on him, though.'

'Thank you, I'm sure they'll be fine,' Catherine insisted.

'Where are you from, anyway, Cat?' Matt asked.

'Breningarth, born and bred,' she answered, hoping she could think quickly enough so as not to get caught in her own cover story.

'We assumed as much, but where specifically?' Matt continued, holding his bowl out towards Alice with a hopeful look on his face.

'Just outside Greystone,' Catherine told him. It was technically true; Greystone was the closest part of common city to the government district she lived in. A lot of kids in Greystone were educated alongside government children.

'Ouch, hard luck. No wonder you ran,' Matt said sympathetically. Being the closest to the government district, Greystone barely had any children over the age of thirteen due to the ease of Collecting from there. 'Are you sure your parents won't miss you?' he asked in a low voice, frowning. He clearly hadn't believed her earlier words.

Catherine's smile vanished, and her eyes fixed on her bowl.

'Like I told Alice, my parents ... aren't around,' she said awkwardly.

Fox patted her shoulder 'Yes, well, that's always the story,' he muttered quietly. Catherine wondered again what *his* story was.

She looked over to include the rest of the crew.

'What about you, where have you all come from?' she asked.

'Well,' Alice began, glancing at her husband. 'Harry and I met years ago in Mericus – I'm from there originally. I was sixteen, he was seventeen and flying with his father. My parents owned an inn by the shipyard, and I was working behind the bar when Harry and his dad's crew rented rooms with us. I fell in love with him and when he asked me to come with him, I couldn't say no.' Her eyes shone at the memory, and Catherine smiled as the two kissed, their love obvious.

'I asked her to marry me as soon as it was respectable – wasn't going to let her get away!' Harry said. 'When my dad died, I inherited this little beauty, and we made it our own. Had a few issues when the war began – we lost half our crew to the army, and the other half to their families. Wasn't so bad back under King Christopher's reign, gods bless his soul. No rations, no need for us to smuggle. We carried supplies out to the soldiers in Siberene, since it was easy for us to pass the storm barriers. When the monarchy went, well . . . Collections and rationing began, and we became a little less reputable. People were starving, and it felt wrong not to help. We picked up Fox about six years ago.'

Fox remained silent, unwilling to volunteer any further information. 'Benny a year later,' Harry continued, 'and Matt followed within six months, making enough of a crew to let the old boys go. Couldn't bear to be apart, these two,' he teased, elbowing Matt in the side.

'Benny and I grew up in Stratton,' Matt explained in response to Catherine's confused look. 'We lived next door to each other, went to the same school, did everything together. I was doing an apprenticeship at Tinker's when Ben got the offer to fly for Harry, and had to finish up my contract before I could leave and join him. Wasn't going to let him have all the adventures without me, was I?'

Catherine was impressed; Tinker's was a very prestigious

mechanics company – her father had shares in it. Its workers practically maintained the docklands single-handedly
now, though they were spread too thin to use their exper-
tise on other things, such as the tram system. Matt must
have been the best of the best to get an apprenticeship
there.

'And you, Fox?' she tried, turning to the freckled teen
beside her. Fox's shoulders tensed, and he stood abruptly,
not meeting Catherine's eyes.

'If you'll all excuse me, I've got work to do before bed,'
he announced quietly, not waiting for a reply before leaving
the galley, the door swinging shut behind him.

'What did I say?' Catherine asked, hurt.

Alice reached over and patted her on the shoulder, offering a smile.

'Nothing, dear. Fox just doesn't like talking about himself.
He's had a bit of a rough past,' she confessed, making
Catherine bite her lip.

'I'm sorry, I . . . I didn't know.'

'Of course you didn't, lad. That's why you were asking,'
Matt remarked. 'You wouldn't have asked if you had
known it would set him off like that. He's a mite sensitive,
is our Fox.'

Catherine shrugged, still feeling guilty, but the movement was cut off by a yawn. Her belly full, it was finally
beginning to hit her how tired she was. Suddenly, the
thought of her new bed down the hall was all too inviting.

'If I'm excused, I think I'll head to bed. It's . . . been a
long day,' she said ruefully, and Matt chuckled.

'Running away from Greystone and stowing on a skyship?

I'll bet. Goodnight, brat, I'll expect you down in the engines after breakfast.'

She nodded, standing.

'I'll be there. Thank you for the meal, Alice, it was lovely.'

Alice smiled at the compliment, piling Catherine's empty bowl on top of the others.

'You're very welcome, poppet. Breakfast is at seven – there should be a clock in your room. Either way, Fox will wake you up, if he's not still in that foul mood of his.'

Saying her goodnights, Catherine left the galley thankful to have been accepted by at least most of the crew. Fox's door was firmly closed and while Catherine was tempted to knock, she didn't dare.

Opening the door to her own new room, she sat down on the bed to unlace her boots. Placing them neatly aside, she stowed her purse away in one of the desk drawers and turned to the bed, not wanting to undress any further. She'd definitely give away her gender if one of the crew walked in on her in her undergarments. Sleeping in the clothes she'd been wearing all day might not be the most comfortable thing in the world, but she'd make do for one night.

There was a grubby mirror bolted to her wardrobe door, and she took the chance to get a proper look at herself, astonished by how much of a boy she looked with her hair cut short. It came down to just below her ears – a little longer than the current style, but nothing she hadn't seen on boys before. Fox was right, though; she definitely looked closer to twelve than fourteen. And she didn't look like Catherine any more. 'I look like Cat,' she murmured, staring at her unfamiliar appearance.

Slipping under the thick fur blanket, she curled up tight on the comfortable mattress, her brain racing. In just a few short hours she'd gone from Catherine Hunter, daughter of Nathaniel Hunter and future wife of Marcus Gale, to Just Cat, skyship dogsbody.

She had to admit, she preferred the latter.

Cat woke when a hand shook her shoulder. She blinked and squinted up at the face looming above her. She squawked as she realised Fox was standing over her bed, staring at her in amusement as she instinctively pulled the blanket up to her chin.

'Easy, there. It's half past six. I thought you might want to be up for breakfast. Also, Alice left these outside your room.' He held up a sack which Cat assumed was full of clothes. 'You'll get used to waking in the dark – if you had a proper porthole, you'd be getting sunrise at four in the morning,' he remarked, glancing up at the small porthole in the wall over her desk, which glowed dimly with the morning light.

Cat growled at the prospect of such an early hour, making Fox chuckle.

'I'll see you at breakfast. Don't take too long, or Matt will have eaten your serving.' With that he left, the room becoming silent save for the faint hiss of steam through the pipes in the walls, and the rhythmic chugging of the propellers, prompting her to realise her room was towards the stern of the ship.

She dug through the sack of clothes. Clearly Fox's style hadn't changed much since he was her age; smart collared shirts, waistcoats, trousers, knitted jumpers and buckled leather coats, and even a long winter overcoat and a pair of sturdy knee-high boots similar to the ones he wore now. She grinned to herself, imagining she'd look rather like his miniature once she was dressed, except for her brown hair, of course.

She picked out some black trousers, which were baggy on her, as well as a dark blue shirt and a black leather waist-coat. Buckling the heavy boots over sock-clad feet, Cat gave herself a once-over in the mirror to check she looked suitably boyish. It was odd, not getting ready for worship at the end of the week. Did the crew even observe Anglyan religion? Maybe she would ask some time, if she grew brave enough. She crossed the corridor to the galley, where the noise drifting from the open door told her she was the last one to arrive.

'Morning. Did you sleep well?' Alice asked as she entered. 'I know some people can't sleep when the ship rocks, but we had quite a smooth flight last night. We shouldn't hit the Siberene storm barriers for another few days or so yet.'

Cat stretched her arms out as she sat, hearing her shoulders pop. Harry was absent, and Cat presumed he was on shift.

'I slept like a log, thank you. Thanks,' she added grate-fully as a bowl of porridge was placed in front of her. Reaching past Ben for the pot of honey on the table, she poured in a small amount and mixed the golden liquid into the thick porridge. 'Does it usually take so long to get to the barriers?'

'Not usually, but we like to take our time. If we work too efficiently, the guards will start getting suspicious. Besides,

Harry thought you might like a few days to settle in before we bring you into the business,' Alice explained. Cat raised her eyebrows, pleased and surprised at their thoughtfulness.

'Ready for a hard day's work, sprog?' Matt asked.

'Always,' she replied.

'That's the spirit. We got a little battered last trip, and some of the plates are sticking. Nothing serious,' he added in response to Alice's worried look. 'We'll have it fixed no problem. Ben, just do your best to keep us out of the worst of it, if you can.'

Ben smiled, his brown eyes meeting Matt's gaze confidently.

'Sure. There's a relatively clear patch to the West that we should be able to squeeze through, if it's still around when we get there. Besides, when have you known me to fly us into a rough patch?'

Matt merely raised an eyebrow, bringing a faint flush to Ben's pale cheeks.

'Where are we going, anyway?' Cat blurted out without thinking. 'I mean, I know we're headed to Siberene, but . . . how do you manage to smuggle goods in without being noticed? I know Siberene isn't particularly involved in the war, but surely there are Anglyan guards at every shipyard,' she said. It was customary to have Anglyan soldiers present in every country under Anglyan rule, to monitor trading.

Her question earned a shared look from everyone in the crew, giving her the impression she was missing something.

'What?'

'He'll learn when we get there. It'll be easier to explain then,' Fox said from across the table.

'What will I learn? What's going on in Siberene?'

Matt smiled at her, somewhat apologetically.

'You'll see when we get there, sprog. Just . . . remember that things aren't always what they seem, and the newscasts don't always tell the whole truth.' His statement only served to confuse Cat, who looked around the table for clarification. When they all stayed stone-faced under her gaze, she gave up and went back to eating the last of her porridge.

'I'd better go and relieve Harry,' Ben declared, getting to his feet.

'You coming, then?' Matt asked with a glance at Cat. Standing, he leaned down to press a kiss to Alice's cheek. 'Delicious as always, sweetheart. I'll see you for lunch.'

Alice tutted.

'You and your stomach, Matthew Wylde,' she muttered fondly. 'Go on, the lot of you. You've got work to do. We'll need to have something to show for ourselves at Syvana.'

Cat followed Matt from the room and down the manhole to the floor below.

'I'll start you off with the basics,' Matt told her, leading her through to the engine room. 'Most of the steering system's parts are kept here.' He gestured to a large gear plate with a clear glass casing, right next to the furnace, and Cat almost groaned. She couldn't remove any more layers than she had already or she'd give herself away, but the heat was sweltering. 'They connect to belts that run through the walls, from the struts of the wings to Ben's control panel. The propeller motors are over there.' He pointed across the room, where Cat could see four large cog towers, one of which was rotating.

'What do you do if one of the belts in the walls breaks?' she asked curiously.

'Send a wee brat like you in the gaps to fix it,' he retorted.

'But surely I wouldn't fit!' Her eyes widened, making him chuckle.

'Calm down, brat, I'm only joking.' Matt rolled his eyes, amused. 'You Greystone lot are an odd bunch. Always taking things so seriously.' Cat tried to look offended at his words. With any luck, her so-called Greystone background would account for any other oddities they might notice. Most folk thought people from Greystone were strange, in an odd limbo between the commoners and the government.

She heard a creak, and Fox walked through the door. Unbuttoning his waistcoat, he draped it over a low-hanging pipe, rolling his flared sleeves up to his elbows.

Matt was grinning.

'Come to give us a hand, Fox? Better than sitting around doing sod all, I suppose.'

'Yeah,' Fox agreed, moving to stand beside Cat. 'But why don't we let the sprog give it a go. See how good he is.' Cat huffed at the raised eyebrow Fox directed at her, her eyes slipping to the small triangle of exposed skin at the base of his throat.

'He's good enough,' Matt assured Fox. 'But go on, then, Cat. See if you can find the problem.' He handed her the screwdriver.

Sweating uncomfortably, she turned to the encased gear plate. First, she unhooked the casing, eyes scanning the ordered entanglement of cogs, sprockets and chains. Before she could get too engrossed she was startled by a loud metallic clang, followed by a short bark of laughter. When she turned, Matt was rubbing his forehead and scowling at a steam pipe protruding a few inches from the ceiling.

'Every bloody time,' he grumbled, and Cat suppressed a laugh, meeting Fox's amused gaze.

'You'll get used to that,' he told her. 'Five years, and Matt still can't remember which parts are lower than others.'

Cat smiled at Matt's sheepish look and turned back to her work. At first, everything seemed to be working normally ... until she noticed a stretched link on one of the chains, which caused a bit of jarring when it passed between two gears.

'You need to change that chain. Is there a replacement in here or next door?' she asked, turning her head. She was surprised to see that Fox had stripped to his undershirt and was working on tightening an overhead piston. Her cheeks flushed as she tried to ignore the sight of his tensed biceps. She felt a strange sensation in her stomach, which was quickly replaced by a feeling of dread. She'd heard other girls talk about that type of feeling at the government school she'd attended, and in her current situation, it didn't bode well. No, she decided, this was just not the time. She had to act like a boy.

'Nice eye, lad,' Matt said, rummaging in a box and handing her the correct chain, clearly unaware of her current dilemma. 'You'll have to be quick about it, though. We can't have the steering offline for more than a few seconds.'

'No pressure or anything,' Fox piped up wryly, ruining her hopes of ignoring him. Cat turned back to the gear plate, staring at the chain. It was awfully long, and the top was hooked to a gear very high up.

'I'm not sure if I can reach,' she admitted, standing on tiptoe and stretching up to test.

'I'll give you a hand, shortie,' Fox assured her. She bit her lip as he stepped close, taking one end of the chain from her hands. The heat in the room seemed to increase tenfold as Fox leaned over her, reaching the gear easily.

'On three,' he murmured, fingers poised and ready.

'One, two, three.' On the last count, Cat quickly unhooked the chain from its cog, waiting two beats before looping the new one tightly in place, and clipping the two ends together before the chain could tangle. She stepped back in satisfaction, nearly colliding with Fox, the redhead squeezing her shoulder.

'Easy does it, brat. Not bad, though. Let's see how you do with some of our more complicated pieces.' As she turned, he wiped a hand across his forehead, pulled his undershirt off and dropped it to the floor to join his shirt and waistcoat. Cat's cheeks turned a fiery red upon seeing his bare chest, and she resisted the urge to groan. She'd never been attracted to anyone before; why did it have to start now?

5

For the first time since arriving on the *Stormdancer*, Cat managed to wake up at the right time on her own. It had only taken her four days to get used to the schedule. She shuffled into the galley, rubbing her eyes.

'Sleep well?' Fox asked as she slid on to the bench beside him, earning himself an annoyed look.

'Who decided that this unreasonable hour would be the perfect time to start the day?' she grumbled. But things improved as Alice placed a steaming plate of eggs and ham in front of her. Cat was surprised by the richness of the fare Alice fed them, but didn't comment, assuming their travelling allowed them to escape the rationing.

'I believe that would be the sun, when it decided to rise at dawn,' Ben remarked as he dropped into his own seat with a yawn. 'Are you all right? You sound a little ... off.'

Cat's eyes widened a fraction, and she coughed, making a mental note to remember to disguise her natural voice. She welcomed the distraction when Matt bounded into the room, smiling brightly and looking perfectly refreshed. His green eyes were alert, and he clapped Ben heartily on the back as he swung his long legs over the bench.

'Good morning!' he greeted chirpily.

Ben shot him a glare. 'It's far too early for you to be so bloody chipper. Especially since I was up all night in the control room.' Matt's bright grin immediately became a worried frown as he stared into his friend's tired eyes.

'You should go back to bed – you'll be in no fit state to fly like this. Can Harry not take over for a while?' he asked.

Ben shrugged, swallowing a mouthful of egg.

'He's up there now, but we'll hit the Secondary in about an hour, so he'll need me for that. It's been getting worse lately – even the natives are struggling to pass. They're mostly detouring through Mericus. It's not like they want to stop in Anglya, anyway.'

Cat frowned at that comment; sure, the relations between Anglya and Siberene weren't as good as they used to be. At the start of the war, with Anglya fighting in both Erova and Kasem, Siberene had bid unsuccessfully for independence, but she had thought they were on relatively agreeable terms now. And wasn't Mericus steadily becoming a war-torn wasteland as Anglyan soldiers pushed them out of Erova? Filing it away under 'things to ask about once they've told me what on Tellus is going on', she leaned forward.

'Are we nearly at Siberene?' she asked hopefully, eager to get off the ship and see somewhere new.

'Almost. Depending on how fast we can get through the Secondary storm barrier, we should be there by noon,' Fox informed her. His hair was messier than usual, and there was a small violet smudge on the bridge of his freckled nose that made her wonder if he'd been working before breakfast.

'Brilliant! Is there anything I can do to help?' she offered, but Matt shook his head.

'No, I've got it covered. Fox, why don't you babysit the sprog today?' he suggested.

Fox turned, his gaze meeting Cat's. 'I think I can handle him until lunch,' he agreed.

'What are you planning?' she asked suspiciously.

'Nothing you should worry about, shortie. Come on, let's get going, if you're finished?' he prompted, staring pointedly at her empty plate. She nodded, thanking Alice as she followed Fox with some trepidation. Instead of taking her towards the manhole, Fox turned towards his bedroom. Hovering unsurely in the doorway as he rifled through the haphazard piles in the bottom of his wardrobe, she most definitely did not stare at his backside as he bent over, though the faint pink on her cheeks betrayed her. She longed for days past when silly things like hormones and attraction didn't factor into her life, but hoped whatever she was feeling for Fox would dwindle in time. She would soon get used to his features – no matter how handsome she might find them – and think of him as nothing more than a friend.

She snapped out of her reverie when Fox straightened up, turning and facing her with an odd look before holding out a pair of leather-cushioned brass goggles similar to the ones hanging around his own neck. She stared at the item blankly for a moment before the meaning clicked into place.

'You're taking me up on deck?' she breathed. She'd been yearning to see what the world looked like from the sky.

Fox's grin widened, and he nodded, pushing the goggles into her hands.

'I need to tighten some of the rigging, and you're going to help me. Grab your coat, it'll be chilly outside,' he warned.

She didn't waste any time in rushing to her own room and grabbing the heavy wool and leather flight coat she'd been given by Alice, shrugging it on and doing up the silver buckles and buttons as she jogged back. Fox had on a long charcoal wool coat, buttoned tightly up to his chin. The grey made his eyes look even brighter than usual, and she tried to ignore the fluttering of her heart.

'I'm sure I don't need to warn you to be careful up there. As safe as the ship seems, we are, in fact, miles in the air. You won't bounce if you fall out,' Fox said, climbing the ladder.

'I'm not simple,' she retorted sharply, scrambling up after him. His patronising words had irked her – after all, she wasn't a baby! Fox merely smiled, a look in his eyes that she couldn't quite decipher. He stopped at the door to the control room, sticking his head in. Cat peered round, seeing Harry sitting in Ben's usual place at the wheel, eyes fixed on the curved glass viewing screen.

'Keep her steady – I'm taking Cat topside,' Fox called.

'Aye. Will do, lad, but keep an eye on him up there. And don't stay up too long. I don't want you up there when we hit the Secondary.'

'Don't worry, we won't be up long. I just need to tighten some of the rigging on the mainsail – I noticed it was start-ing to slip the other day.'

They hurried to the ladder under the trap, Fox hoisting himself up first and Cat securing her goggles before scurrying after him. It was odd, wearing flight goggles; they were tighter around her head than work goggles, and tinted the world a few shades darker. When she poked her head up through the trap, the wind buffeted her, and she was immediately glad of them. Fox took her hand, hoisting her up the rest of the way. She was embarrassed to have to grip his arm tightly as she tried to get her balance, her feet set apart as she stood her ground against the fierce wind. Fox waited patiently, not commenting on her death grip on his forearm, until she finally let go, only wobbling slightly.

'You all right?' he checked, and she nodded, looking up at him. His hair looked brown through her goggles, and his freckles stood out even more than usual.

'Fine. This is incredible!' she exclaimed breathlessly, staring up at the tall cream sails billowing from the main mast, the red and silver wind pennant at the top streaming straight out behind them. Clouds drifted lazily above them, the endless blue-grey sea churned far below them, and she could see for miles. Right on the horizon there was a growing dark area, the near-black clouds swirling ominously. Cat assumed it was the Secondary storm barrier, and could see why Harry didn't want them on deck when they reached it. It looked terrifying. She could hardly imagine how the earliest, primitive skyships had made their way through it, nearly five hundred years ago when Anglyans first began exploring outside their own land. Surely they would have been blown to pieces!

Fox stood behind her to keep her from getting buffeted too hard by the wind, and she leaned against the high wooden railing, standing on tiptoe to peer over the edge.

'Careful, don't lean too far,' Fox warned, his voice rough in her ear as he craned his head down to make himself heard. The hairs on the back of her neck stood up, and she arched away from him instinctively; it was that or lean towards him, and she couldn't risk giving anything away.

Fox raised an arm, pinning her even closer to the railing, and pointed to a dark shadow off to the left. 'If you look over there, you'll see Adena. There's a little town, right in the centre, full of people who don't ever leave the island. They grow their own food, have their own society rules, and marry their cousins to keep their numbers up. Some of them have up to eight or nine children,' he told her. 'Their island is slap bang in the eye of the Secondary so very few people ever visit, and no native has ever left there.'

Cat's eyes widened; how did a woman have nine children without her body giving out? She hadn't known anyone in Anglya to have any more than three.

'Have you ever been?' she asked, having to shout to be heard over the roar of the wind. It whipped at her hair and numbed her cheeks, and she wished she'd brought gloves like Fox.

'Oh no, we can never get close enough, even with Ben's excellent flying,' Fox said with a sigh, sounding wistful. 'I've been to Ropastal, though, round the other side of Siberene. The people there are beautiful,' he added.

'Wow. I'd love to travel to every country one day, and the islands! I've read stories and seen pictures in newscasts, but I'll bet it's even more amazing in reality,' she murmured, imagining flying in the *Stormdancer* all the way across the world as far as the exotic and colourful Kasem, meeting people and seeing animals she had only seen drawings of in her books. She said as much to Fox, who smiled.

'Now Kasem's somewhere I definitely haven't been. Harry's taken me to Mericus and Erova plenty, Siberene the most, and even Dalivia once. But maybe one day I'll bug Harry and Ben into flying us to Kasem. That would be an adventure.'

Cat turned, smiling at the infectious grin on Fox's face.

'It would that. Now, what was it you were saying about tightening the rigging?'

Tightening the rigging, in actual fact, turned out to be more of a lesson on the different knots used to secure different parts of the ship. It was interesting, and surprisingly fun, though Fox did jokingly threaten to tie her to the mast and leave her there more times than strictly necessary. Cat was just finishing a bowline knot to secure the rigging nets to the deck when Fox whistled sharply, causing her to look up. He didn't say anything, merely pointed towards the horizon. The dark grey storm clouds she'd spotted earlier were far closer now, and Cat gaped. No wonder most ships didn't attempt to fly through the Secondary; it was terrifying!

No one knew how or why the gods had formed the storm barriers where they did, but they were all over the world, and never seemed to move very far. Most seasoned pilots knew ways around the worst parts, and some – like Ben – dared travel through them.

'Time to go in?' she called, and Fox nodded, the tail of his coat whipping out behind him. Tugging on the running end of the knot to tighten it, she tucked it neatly out of the way and clambered ungracefully to her feet, having to hold out her arms to steady herself as she hurried over to where Fox stood by the open trap. He let her go first, dropping down behind her and stopping halfway up the ladder to fasten the catch on the heavy metal trap.

'So, what do you think?' he asked, a grin on his wind-flushed face, pulling his goggles down to hang around his neck. Cat didn't try to hide her delight in what she'd just experienced.

'It's amazing! I can't believe how far you can see from up there, and the sea is so fierce!' she gushed.

Fox nodded, his expression telling her he understood exactly how she felt.

'Humbling, isn't it? Knowing there's all that space out there, all those people in foreign lands, and you're just one of them. But . . . it's beautiful when the sky is clear. Especially when the sun rises and sets – the water glows purple, it's really quite something.'

'That sounds wonderful,' Cat breathed. Fox hummed in agreement, glancing over at her, and there was so much awe on his face that Cat's breath caught in her throat for just a moment. He was beautiful when he wasn't scowling. 'Possibly even worth getting up earlier than usual for.'

Fox laughed, and the moment was gone, leaving Cat feeling strangely bereft. 'I'd definitely say so,' he replied. 'But you won't see it for days yet – the storms are far too wild for a clear sky. No chance of anyone from Siberene being unlucky,' he joked. Cat smiled ruefully; in any of the six countries, being born under a clear sky was considered bad luck. Anglya was seeing more and more clear skies, and people were beginning to regard it as a sign that the country was cursed.

'Nice for them. I don't suppose Alice might make me some tea? I can't feel my hands all that well,' she confessed, her numb fingers stuffed deeply in the fur-lined pockets of the coat.

Fox sent her a somewhat sheepish look.

'I'm sorry. I should've told you to grab gloves as well. Remind me next time.'

She shook her head.

'No harm done. At least, not if I can beg a cuppa,' she added.

'You'll find Alice in the laundry room. Go and ask nicely and she'll no doubt oblige.'

Entering the galley, Cat timidly knocked on the laundry-room door. Waiting for Alice's call of 'Come in!' she pushed the door open. Alice looked up from a large pile of assorted fabrics that were damp and ready to be aired.

'Hello, poppet, what can I do for you?' she asked.

'Well, ma'am, Fox just took me up on deck, and I didn't take any gloves so now my hands are near numb with cold, and I was just wondering would you mind –'

'Putting the kettle on, dear?' Alice finished for her. 'Course I can, just let me fold this bolt,' she said, holding up a large square of thick black wool fabric, 'and you really needn't be so formal, dear. Don't call me ma'am, just Alice will do. I won't bite.'

'I'm sorry, I just ... I'm not used to ... women.' She wanted to say 'having a mother', but she wasn't sure that would go down well. Alice seemed to get her meaning, though, and smiled in sympathy. Setting the folded cloth down in a basket, she crossed to Cat, ruffling her hair.

'You might not have had much of a family in the past, poppet, but you'll find one here. Matt seems to like you, and Ben likes almost anyone Matt likes. Harry thinks you're a bright spark, and as for Fox ... he might seem a little distant, the poor lad, but compared to how he is usually, he's practically a new person since you turned up! You'll settle in soon enough, I'm sure of it.'

Cat felt a lump in her throat. She'd never had someone *want* to be her family before, not truly. Her mother loved her dearly, but Elizabeth had been ill for most of Cat's life, so not really there for her, and her father saw her as something to trade for greater power, not as a daughter to be loved.

'Thank you,' she said quietly, her voice slightly choked. 'That means a lot to me. And thank you for letting me stay in the first place.'

Alice squeezed Cat's shoulder.

'No reason not to trust you, is there? You're an orphan, and just by coming to us you've put your life in our hands – we could turn you in any day. But we won't, so long as you keep working as hard as you are. Now, what say you come with me to the kitchen? I'll stick the kettle on and start lunch and you can sit by the oven and warm up. I don't know what that boy was thinking, taking you topside so close to the Secondary. You could have been blown right off the deck! Honestly, I wonder where his brain is sometimes,' she huffed, shaking her head to herself as she led Cat through to the kitchen.

'But it was so pretty, Alice, the storms were incredible! I've never seen a storm that close up before,' Cat replied, a dreamy smile lighting her face. Alice took a long look at her as she filled the kettle, then laughed.

'That's another one hooked,' she remarked. 'You'll never stay on land for longer than a week from now on. That's what my Harry is like – the longest he stayed in one place was when he was courting me, and even then he whisked me away after three and a half weeks.'

'Sounds awfully romantic,' said Cat.

Alice grinned at her, a reminiscent look in her eyes.

'It was. Especially considering he hardly has a romantic bone in his body. That's something you should remember, poppet, for when you're older. The best way to a woman's heart is romance, plain and simple.'

Cat ducked her head to hide a grin.

'What are you making?' she asked as Alice began to pull supplies from cupboards.

'Beef and tomato sandwiches.'

'Sounds brilliant! I love tomatoes.' Cat's words earned her an odd look.

'You've had them before?'

Cat was perplexed by the question, then remembered that most common people would never have had tomatoes. Even her father had only ever got them off the black market.

'Uh, just once,' she said hastily. She'd have to be more careful. 'Friend of mine was in the black market. Is there anything I can do to help?' she queried, hoping to move on swiftly.

'You can slice the bread for me, if you like. I must say, I'm not used to boys knowing their way around the kitchen. I've tried to teach the others, but they're so hopeless it's best they stay well away.' Alice slid the loaf of bread over to Cat.

Just as she was getting started, the kettle began to whistle, and Alice turned to make three mugs of tea. She set two of them on a tray.

'There you are, dear, take that up to Harry and Ben in the control room. Be careful on the ladder,' she added with a pointed look.

Cat nodded, and taking the small tray she hurried from the kitchen.

It took longer than she would have liked to figure out how to climb the ladder without spilling the drinks, but she managed it, eventually.

'Tea,' she announced, drawing the attention of both men.

'Fantastic. Thanks, lad. Any idea when lunch will be ready?' Harry asked, downing half his cup in one go.

'Alice was just putting sandwiches together when I left. How far are we from Siberene now?' she queried.

'About sixty miles,' Ben answered. 'So we should be there in an hour or two. Tell Alice I'll pass on lunch today, will you? I can't leave the wheel. We're only a little way into the Secondary.'

They left the pilot to his work and as Harry shut the door behind him, he chuckled.

'I bet two coppers that Matt takes his lunch up as soon as he hears Ben's not coming down.'

'Even I know that's a fool's bet,' Cat retorted, earning a hearty laugh and a clap on the shoulder.

'You learn fast, lad. Then again, a blind man could see those two are joined at the hip,' Harry conceded, hoisting himself down the ladder after Cat. 'Actually, I wanted to talk to you. How do you feel about pickpockets?'

Cat stared at him, confused by the random question.

'They're not the worst people in the world,' she answered slowly, remembering how she'd let that boy steal her father's watch. 'Why?'

'It's always good to get a little extra, to distribute back in Anglya. Goods can only have come from one place, but money can come from anywhere so it's easier to spread around without suspicion. I used to send Fox out – he likes to keep his skills sharp – but he's getting too big now. You're small and nimble. Think you can swipe a few purses without getting caught?'

Cat frowned, thinking it over. She'd never tried to steal a purse before, but she'd stolen things from her father's office all the time – usually things he'd confiscated from her to begin with – and he'd never noticed. But would anyone in Siberene have a purse worth stealing? According to their news reports, even the upper classes were poor.

'I think I could do that. And I like a challenge,' she replied boldly, trusting Harry not to make her steal from those already in need.

Harry pushed the galley door open.

'That's the spirit! See how you go, but don't risk it too much. We won't be able to get you out of jail if you get caught. And, uh, don't tell the missus. She doesn't approve.'

'Why's Cat going to jail?' Matt asked casually from where he was loading sandwiches on to his plate.

'Pickpocketing in Siberene. And he's not going if he can help it,' Harry replied. 'Oh, Ben's staying up to get us through the rest of the Secondary. Be prepared for a few bumps, by the way, Cat. It will be a bit of a rough crossing.' As if to emphasise his point, the ship shunted sideways, and Matt made a frantic dive as one of his sandwiches attempted to make a getaway on to the floor, catching it just in time.

'I'll take Ben's up. I'm sure he'd appreciate the company,' he announced, putting more sandwiches on a separate plate and balancing it on top of his own meal. Harry shot Cat a look, and she grinned back at him as Matt left. She was learning.

6

'Hey, Cat, get your coat and gloves.'

Cat looked up at Fox, leaning in the door frame of her room.

'We're here?' she asked in excitement, and he nodded.

'Landing in ten – thought you might want to be on deck for descent. Get your gloves,' he repeated, a half-smile tugging at his lips. She hurried to obey, digging through the clothes she'd been given and eventually finding a thick leather pair in the pocket of one of the coats.

'Don't you have work to do during landing?' she questioned, bringing her goggles up over her eyes.

He shrugged.

'Matt won't mind if I skip out just this once to take you topside. He spent half his first months here on deck every time we took off or landed. He acts like he only ever stays with the engines, but he's as guilty as the rest of us,' he confided.

Seeing Cat was properly attired, he grabbed her by the crook of the elbow, tugging impatiently.

'Hurry up, or you'll miss all the good parts,' he urged, practically dragging her from the room.

The pair ran up to the top deck, Fox chivvying Cat every time she even looked like she was slowing. Emerging on to the deck, Cat raced to the raised section of the bow, scrambled up the ladder and practically threw herself over the railing. Below her she could see the sprawling icy tundra of Siberene. In the centre, enormous white mountains sliced through clouds with ease, and stretching from the coast almost to the base of the closest mountain was the city. Syvana, closest to Anglya, was the biggest of the four Siberene cities – and it looked to be bustling with energy. Cat let out a breathless laugh; the people looked like ants from this height. She could see the shipyard with its sparse rows of berthed skyships, plumes of steam rising where some were getting ready to sail. She wondered if her mother had ever made the journey – perhaps accompanying the queen on royal business – but thinking of her mother made her heart ache, and Cat forced her mind elsewhere.

'You might want to hold on to something.' She spun on her heel to find Fox standing a little way away, clutching a rigging rope. 'This part gets a little rough,' he warned.

She nodded, glancing around for something to grab, and decided to wrap her arms around a thick railing post. The sails sagged and she could see them getting lower and lower, the buildings getting bigger as they drew nearer. Most of them were quite squat, built plainly with thick slabs of steel and stone; a striking contrast to the towering spires and ornate buildings commonly found in Anglya. The people were all dressed in dark colours, thick leathers and furs. She didn't blame them, she decided, clasping gloved hands in an effort to keep her fingers from freezing.

'Where are the palaces? All the beautiful buildings from the newscasts?' she called to Fox, not wanting to turn away from the incredible sights for a second.

'Those are in the South – furthest from Anglya, so furthest from possible attack. Southern Siberene is probably the safest place you can be, mainly because you've got to navigate around the mountains to get there, and it holds the biggest military base in the country. Only an idiot would attempt to fly over the Kholar Mountains. The safest way is to ride. Although from what I heard during our last visit, the king was gathering men to create a four-way tunnel connecting the four cities.'

She let out a low whistle. That sounded like an awfully large job.

Cat clung on tight to the post, her eyes practically popping out of her head as their descent became steeper and the ship began rocking madly.

'This bit does get bumpy,' he told her, his grip on the rope tightening. Despite the nonchalant look on his face, there was the smallest curl at the corners of his lips and a sparkle in his eyes that he couldn't quite hide behind his goggles. He was enjoying this just as much as Cat was, she could tell.

They dropped past the lowest clouds, heading for an open landing deck in the shipyard, just on the end, out of the way of the trade ships. Cat immediately noticed that not only were there no Anglyan government ships, there were also no Siberene government ships, and very few trade ships. That could, of course, be because the storm barriers around the country were steadily getting worse, and few people dared to venture through them, yet it was strange that there was no Anglyan presence in the city. Siberene was still under Anglyan rule, wasn't it?

Even stranger, most of the ships in port seemed to be pleasure ships, or small-time merchant ships similar to the *Stormdancer*. There was a large jolt as they hit solid ground, sending Cat pitching forward to hit her head on a post with a thump. She yelped in pain, and Fox burst into laughter. Leaning back and rubbing her sore forehead, she gave him a dark look.

'You're awfully mean sometimes, you know that?' she told him.

'I have been told that, yes,' he replied evenly, still looking amused. 'We should head back inside, if you're ready. Harry will be waiting.'

Cat hummed happily at the warmth inside the ship, frowning when Fox led her to the door opposite the control room, finding the rest of the crew in there with a pile of large crates.

'Enjoy the view?' Harry asked, and Cat nodded rapidly.

'It was incredible! I can't believe how huge the mountains are!'

'Yeah, makes you wonder how people dare mine them, doesn't it? They have to travel for miles through all that snow,' Matt said with a shudder.

'Right, I want us to be in and out as quick as we can,' Harry said, his face serious. Everyone leaned in closer, and suddenly, all eyes were fixed on the captain. 'We need to be past the Secondary by sundown. That means leaving port by six at the very latest. I'd like it if everyone were back by half past five, though, just in case it gets a little tricky. Cat, Fox will take you into the city centre and show you the best way back.' He glanced at his wife, who seemed disapproving of his decision to send Cat pickpocketing. But she didn't interrupt. 'Just do your best, and don't get caught, because if you're not back by six, we'll have to leave without you.' Harry's face was apologetic, but Cat knew that regardless of how bad it would make him feel, he would carry out his threat. She nodded resolutely.

The greying man turned to Fox.

'Fox, once you've dropped off Cat, I want you to meet me at our usual supplier's. We're bringing in more than usual this trip, and I'll need all hands to carry things.'

'You're leaving him alone in the city on his first try?' Fox asked in shock, jerking a thumb in Cat's direction.

Harry shrugged.

'He'll have to learn sooner or later. Being part of this crew means being part of a family, and that means the lad has to help where he can, same as the rest of us. And we left you alone on your first try,' he pointed out.

'Yes, but I'd been pickpocketing for years before you found me. I knew what I was doing. He's completely green – you can't expect him to know what to do all on his own!'

Cat flushed at the implication that she needed someone to hold her hand.

'I can handle myself, Fox. I'll be fine on my own,' she insisted hotly.

'See? Lad says he'll be fine. Let him prove it,' Harry cut in before Fox could turn his anger on Cat. 'Like I said, we don't have deadweight on this ship. No arguments, the boy's flying solo. Now get on with it – we'll see you in a bit. Remember, Cat, half past five. The clock tower is the tallest building in the city, you can't miss it. Keep an eye on the time, and don't stray far from where Fox leaves you.'

Cat nodded, and Harry nudged Fox's shoulder.

'Go on, then, brat.'

Still scowling, Fox turned away from the group, walking out of the door without waiting for Cat to catch up. She sighed under her breath in frustration and raced after him, wondering again if all teenage boys were like him, or if he was just a special case.

Catching up with Fox halfway down the corridor, she elbowed him in the stomach, annoyed.

'What was that for?' he exclaimed.

'You're being an arse,' she told him frankly, feeling a small thrill as she said one of many words deemed 'impolite for ladies of her breeding' by her father. 'I'd appreciate it if you stopped. Besides, that can't have hurt, you've got about six layers on,' she added, rolling her eyes.

'I haven't "stopped" being an arse since I was younger than you. You'll just have to deal with it.'

Cat scoffed, climbing the trap ladder with ease.

'I highly doubt that. You were relatively personable before. So, to borrow a phrase from Matt, who peed in your porridge?' she asked, standing to the side while Fox lowered the gangplank.

'No one. And I don't believe my bad mood is any of your business,' he retorted sharply.

Cat let out a triumphant sound.

'So you admit you're in a bad mood?'

He growled quietly, ignoring the question, stalking past her down the slightly wobbly plank. Cat followed, picking up her pace while trying not to fall off the edge. Fox didn't turn to check she was following, but strode on, weaving through the growing crowd with ease, coat flaring out behind him. She was surprised to see a distinct lack of military purple among the clusters of people; she hadn't expected any men in work uniforms – everyone knew that Anglyan traders weren't allowed off their ships in foreign docks, so as to avoid causing riots – but she'd anticipated plenty of sharply dressed government men keeping an eye on goods distribution, and soldiers in their bright purple uniforms to keep the peace as people of all nations mingled. She couldn't even see a single low-ranked Anglyan officer.

Cat kept her eyes fixed on the shock of red hair that stood out among the crowds of people with either dark or incredibly fair features. In Anglya, most people had brown hair, blue or brown eyes, and very pale skin. There were some variations – such as red or blonde hair, and green or grey eyes – but they were few and far between. Here, there seemed to be just as many fair-haired people as there were dark-haired. Maybe if Fox ever got out of the sulk he was in, he would explain it to her.

She eventually managed to reach his side, jogging to keep up, a scowl on her face.

'Slow down, would you? I've never been to this city before – if your hair weren't so distinctive, I'd already be lost by now,' she snapped.

At the reminder that he was meant to be looking after

Cat, Fox slowed, glancing to the side with the faintest of apologetic looks.

'Sorry, I forgot,' he said grudgingly.

Cat didn't know whether that was 'I forgot you were following me' or 'I forgot you were new to this', or even 'I forgot I had to keep you safe'.

'Well, don't, in future,' she muttered, grabbing on to a loose buckle strap at the waist of his coat. He raised an eyebrow at her, and she grinned impishly. 'Just making sure you don't run off again. Now I can actually pay attention to street names and find my way back to the shipyard. It's not like I can ask for directions – I don't speak a word of Siberene.'

'*Casechz da stromseil jyetta,*' Fox said, the words harsh and guttural.

Cat stared at him blankly.

'Excuse you?' she replied. He half smiled, turning down a narrow street with squat slate houses on either side.

'*Casechz da stromseil jyetta.* That means "where is the skyship port" in Siberene. Of course, you probably won't be able to understand the response, but ... maybe if you let them know you're Anglyan, they'll draw you a map or something.' He shrugged, hands in his pockets. 'Better than nothing.'

'You speak Siberene?' Somehow Fox didn't seem like the type of person to learn foreign languages. She would have expected it from Ben maybe, or even Harry, but not Fox.

'A little. I speak enough of most languages to get by in their country of origin. Merican is easiest because their language is basically Anglyan. I have a fair grasp on Erovan and Siberene, and I can say "where are the pretty women?" and "could I have an ale?" in Dalivian. The man who taught me insisted that should I ever visit again, those would be the only phrases I'd need to know,' he explained, making her giggle.

'Impressive,' she conceded. 'Maybe you could teach me a little?'

Fox's eyes were unreadable behind his tinted goggles.

'Maybe. If you don't get left behind today. Which you will do if you don't remember the name of this street. It's the main connector between the central courtyard and the district where the shipyard is.' He removed a gloved hand from his pocket to point to an engraved sign hanging from a tall metal post at the end of the road. It read *Stratzephyn*, and she wondered aloud what it meant.

'Literally, it means "marriage street",' Fox explained, 'because it marries the business district with the housing district. The river separates them, and this street is part of the bridge.' Fox gestured up ahead as the street seemed to rise. As they drew closer, Cat realised there was indeed a bridge, and she looked over the steel railings to see a fast-flowing river full of large chunks of ice.

'It's half-frozen! Surely they can't fish in it?' she asked.

The river Brenin, which flowed through Breningarth, contained fish, and was fast-flowing and big enough to fit water turbines – even if it was full of the filth of the city – but the flow was nothing compared to this. She imagined that trying to place a waterwheel in this river would only result in the wheel snapping.

'The ice is brought down from the mountains, not from

the river itself. But actually there are plenty of ice water fish further outland, and the water is crystal clear and can be drunk straight from the river. It's also a free source of ice, so a fair few butcheries have underground rooms built out into the riverbed where they can keep their meat cold,' Fox told her.

Cat's eyes widened, impressed.

'Oh, so is this the main courtyard, then?' she queried as they reached the end of the bridge. For the centre of the city, it didn't look like much.

'Not quite,' Fox replied, leading her between a bakery and a tailor's. When she could see past the crowds, she stopped in her tracks, gaping. The main courtyard was just that: one gigantic courtyard, surrounded by shops and small businesses. In the centre was a large ornate fountain, a jewelled eagle taking flight in the centre, spraying water up into the air and glistening in the sun as it fell back down to the pool below. Diamonds tipped the eagle's golden wings, while dark rubies crested its shoulders and large vibrant sapphires glittered from its eyes.

It must have cost a fortune, Cat thought, amazed.

A dark grey stone path stuck out from the fountain at each compass point, with squares of an odd white grass in the centre. Children were kicking balls to one another, running and laughing, while adults strolled leisurely around the courtyard, some with bags of shopping on their arms. It looked wonderful and peaceful; nothing like the frostbitten wasteland she'd seen on the newscasts, with people struggling to survive under the harsh punishments enforced by Anglyan law.

Maybe that was one of the other cities?

'What's the fountain for? It's beautiful,' she observed, and Fox nodded.

'One of a kind, isn't it? It's the Rudavin fountain, commissioned by King Andrei Rudavin nine years ago when Siberene gained complete independence. The Siberene eagle is on the royal family's crest.' She frowned at his words, sure he was mistaken; Siberene wasn't independent. Their monarchs and government still answered to Anglyan rule.

'People believe that if you throw a copper in the fountain when the wind blows North, your deepest desire will be granted,' Fox continued, not noticing her confusion.

Cat licked her finger and held it up to the wind, her face falling when she realised the wind was blowing East. Fox laughed, patting her on the head.

'Not today, shortie. Anyway, stay within the central courtyard, keep an eye on the clock tower, and if you want something hot to eat there's a little shop in the Southwest corner that does fresh pasties for a couple of coppers. They're usually pretty good, but I wouldn't ask what's in them. You're probably best off not knowing.'

Cat made a face at that, but nodded, her eyes seeking out the Southwest corner. The clock tower was as noticeable as she'd been told it would be – a tall, sturdy building with a huge black and white clock face, and a steel bell encased in glass on the top.

'OK, stay in the courtyard, don't lose track of time, don't ask what's in the pasties. Got it. Anything else I need to know?' she asked, and Fox shook his head.

'Not that I can think of. Good luck, and be careful. Don't do anything foolish,' he told her seriously. Then, reaching out to clap her on the shoulder, Fox turned on his heel and sprinted off the way they had come.

Cat felt suddenly bereft without him. She set off towards the fountain where most people seemed to be gathered. Keeping her head down, she walked at an easy pace, trying to blend in. Seeing a girl about her own age chatting in exuberant Siberene with a woman that could only be her mother, Cat felt a pang of longing. Her mother would know she was long gone by now. Would she be pleased? Unhappy? Cat couldn't quite be sure, but she at least hoped her mother was proud.

Looking around, she had to admit she was very confused. The Anglyan newscasts had led her to believe that Siberene was recovering after their failed fight for independence. The pictures showed the people dressed in rags far too thin for the intense cold weather, with barely anything to eat.

But Siberene seemed to be prospering, and Fox had said the fountain was commissioned after their independence *nine years ago*. That certainly didn't match up to anything she'd been taught or seen on film. She wished she understood the language, so she could figure out what was going on.

Deciding she needed to find out as much as she could while she was here, Cat walked along the path, keeping her eyes peeled for anyone who looked an easy target for pickpocketing. She might not have done it before, but she knew the idea behind it; be sneaky and silent enough to pinch a purse while the person is distracted, then slip away as quickly and quietly as possibly so that you don't get caught. Watching the crowd carefully, she noticed she wasn't the only pickpocketing child about; she counted at least three, and smirked to herself. Some things were the same wherever you went. Fox knew what he was doing, dropping her off here; even if she got caught, she probably wouldn't stand out that much from the others. She knew back in Anglya, very few people bothered to take pickpockets to the authorities, just taking their money back and sending them on their way. Still, she couldn't risk missing the ship's departure. Getting caught wasn't an option.

She spotted a man sitting on a bench reading a newspaper. He was wearing expensive clothes and had a large emerald ring on his middle finger. She understood that jewels were a lot less expensive here than in Anglya, as Siberene was where most jewels and metals were mined, but even so, the man was obviously rich. His money purse was by his side, attached by a buckle to a strap on his heavy coat. It had evidently slipped out of his pocket.

Cat glanced around to see if anyone was watching her, and seeing the coast was clear, sidled up to the bench, dropping down behind it as if playing hide-and-seek. As she pretended to hide, she curved her body to conceal the fact that she was unbuckling the purse and sliding it into the inside pocket of her coat. Straightening up, she tried not to laugh triumphantly as she ran away.

Success!

Grinning to herself, she stopped by the edge of the fountain. It was even more beautiful up close. The jewels were of the highest quality, and the silver – for she was sure that was what the statue was made of – was sculpted perfectly. She wasn't surprised to see no less than four uniformed men around the fountain, each with a pistol at his belt. She wouldn't leave such an extravagant item unguarded either.

Kneeling on the wide concrete rim, she saw the bottom of the pool was littered with shiny pieces of copper. There was a big blue, white and black pennant with the Rudavin family crest flying high from a pole near the Eagle, showing the wind direction. It was slowly edging round from East to Northeast, and Cat crossed her fingers that it would reach North before she had to leave. Even if it was only a silly superstition, there had to be a reason so many people believed the fountain worked. Sighing to herself, Cat stood up and wandered in the direction of a group of women who were in heated discussion. One of them had left her handbag on the floor to her side.

She had work to do.

7

Two hours and four bulging purses later, Cat was well and truly into the swing of things. Syvana was so different, and yet so very similar to Breningarth: the overcast sky, almost as dark as the stone buildings themselves, threatening snow at any moment; the upper-class people going about their daily business, walking past the lower class with their noses upturned. Their inattention was something Cat found useful as she walked through a crowd of well-dressed men with her eyes on a blue velvet purse hanging from one man's belt. She reached out with nimble fingers, slipping the purse off his belt and into the folds of her coat, and turned away, darting from the crowd before she could be caught. Her stomach rumbled, and she let her eyes drift to the clock tower. Plenty of time for a short lunch break.

Sneaking a couple of coppers from one of the pouches, she looked for the pasty shop Fox had recommended, her body freezing cold despite her many layers. Finding the shop by smell rather than attempting to translate the signs, she slipped inside, welcoming the warmth of the small room. The display case on the counter was full of cakes and pastries, and the oven at the other end had a sign above it reading, *Pasty, 3c.* Pleased that the word for pasty was evidently the same in both Siberene and Anglyan, she walked up to the counter where a cheerful-looking elderly woman stood in a thick long-sleeved dress and dark blue knitted shawl. Setting three coppers on the counter, Cat bit her lip nervously and pointed to the oven.

'Pasty?' she asked, praying she came across simply as a nervous young boy rather than a foreigner.

Luckily, the woman smiled, tottering out from behind the counter and pulling on a pair of thick oven mitts. Opening the oven door, she removed one of many pasties sitting on the rack over the glowing embers, wrapping one end in newspaper and handing it to Cat with a quiet '*Spa'asza.*'

Cat nodded with a shy smile, having no idea what the word meant.

Hurrying from the shop, she winced at the blast of cold, lifting the pasty to her lips. It was buttery and delicious, and she was smiling as she set off for a wander, staying close to the edges of the courtyard and looking at what the shops had to offer. As expected, there were a fair few jewellers', as well as shops selling clothes, rugs and blankets made or lined with furs. She had the brief thought that had she been with her father, she could have probably bought whatever she wanted from any of the shops, before reminding herself that had she been with her father, she wouldn't have been in Siberene in the first place.

She remembered what Matt had said about not believing everything in the newscasts, and resolved to demand answers from the others when she got back to the ship.

Passing a newspaper stand, she desperately wished she could read Siberene; so much information on those pages that she couldn't have, it was infuriating.

Cutting across the Eastern path back to the centre of the courtyard, she paused by a vendor selling sweets and eyed a small paper bag of toffee squares wistfully. They were her favourite. Finding the price tag on the shelf below the bag, she saw it was a silver. Maybe ... surely Harry wouldn't know that there had been an extra silver in one of the purses when she'd stolen it? She could always replace it with money from her own purse once she got back to the ship.

Unable to resist, she dug a silver out of the purse. Approaching the vendor and pointing at the paper bag, she placed the shiny coin on the counter. With a smile, the man took a bag off the shelf, pressing it into her fingers. She beamed at him, taking her prize and running off towards the fountain, thickly gloved fingers fumbling with the string tying the neck of the bag. She managed to get it open, and popped a toffee square in her mouth with a quiet moan of pleasure as the sweetness hit her tongue. Sucking on the treat, she stuffed the bag in her coat and looked up at the pennant by the fountain, her eyes widening as she saw the wind was blowing North. Obviously other people had noticed too; they were tossing copper coins into the water and murmuring under their breath.

Hastily finding a copper in one of the purses, she squeezed through the crowd to the edge of the pool, pressing a kiss to the coin before throwing it into the water. It hit the surface with a small splash, sinking to join its fellows.

She closed her eyes tightly. *I want for Anglya to prosper again. I want to stay on the* Stormdancer *forever.* Concentrating hard on her deepest desire, she opened her eyes, wondering if anything magical was supposed to happen.

Only time would tell, she supposed.

Cat started to look for her next victim. She noticed a finely-dressed man standing outside a jewellery shop, and her eyes landed on the purse at his belt. That was far, far too easy. Feet light on the crisp white grass, she made her way over. Just as Cat approached, one hand outstretched to slip the purse from its strap, she froze. Two men were walking past, dressed in heavy black coats and thick boots, talking in low voices – in Anglyan.

'We should just cut our losses and run,' the taller man said to his companion, accent marking him as government. 'Empty the family accounts, leave Anglya and start over here, before someone catches the government in their own web of lies.' Cat was surprised she didn't recognise either of the men – she was usually good with faces – but continued to listen intently.

'How, though? There's no way we'd be able to get our families out. We make one move to leave, and they'll take the girls for Collection before we can blink. I'm not leaving without my daughters,' the shorter man replied vehemently. 'We're safe as long as we keep working, and junior enough that even if the truth does come out, we can claim innocence. It'll happen soon enough – they can't keep up this whole war charade much longer. When it does, we act like we've never seen any of the kids in the lower levels, never even *been* down there, and we get off scot-free.'

'Oi!' Cat jolted as a meaty hand grabbed her outstretched wrist, hoisting her up to stare directly into the eyes of the man she'd been about to steal from. His face went red, and he let out an angry stream of Siberene.

'No! Let me go!' she exclaimed, struggling in his grasp. 'I didn't do anything, I didn't touch it, let me go!' Panic rose in her chest as the man lifted her clean off her feet, carrying her effortlessly towards the fountain, and the guards that surrounded it.

Cat struggled harder as she realised his intent, kicking him in the shins with little effect. She couldn't let him turn her into the guards! If she got arrested, Harry and the crew would leave without her, and she'd be stranded! But the man's grip was too tight, his hands as big as dinner plates, as he dragged her in front of a guard, barking out something in harsh tones. The guard's brow furrowed, and Cat wished more than anything that she could understand Siberene.

'No!' she shouted again as the guard pulled some handcuffs from his belt, clipping them around her wrists as her captor held her still. 'No! Stop! I'm innocent, I didn't do anything! Search me, I'm innocent!' The coat was full of hidden pockets, as Fox had shown her the night before, and the purses she'd already stolen were safely tucked away where the guard could never find them. Maybe if she got him to search her, he'd think she hadn't actually stolen anything and let her go. A glance at the clock tower showed it was already quarter to five; she had forty-five minutes to get back to the ship. It wasn't looking good.

Her captor muttered something to the guard, sounding disgruntled, and the guard replied in an assuring tone, gripping the handcuffs tightly and yanking Cat forward. Her feet finally touched the ground as the man released her, but it was no use; she was cuffed, and there was no escaping from them on her own.

The guard left his post at the fountain, tugging Cat along with him as they headed for a narrow street – in the opposite direction to the shipyard. She could see people laughing and jeering at her, but had irritatingly lost sight of the two Anglyan men that had got her into this mess. What had they been talking about, anyway? What kids in the lower levels?

'Where are you taking me?' she demanded. In all her years of sneaking around and getting into trouble, she'd never been arrested before.

'Cells,' the guard spat out in thickly-accented Anglyan, sending a wave of cold fear through Cat. Struggling frantic-ally, her shoulders ached as she tried to wrench her hands free of the metal cuffs, heels dragging on the paving stones as the guard continued to tow her along regardless. He was about as broad as she was tall; Cat didn't stand a chance. Still, she resolved not to give up; she had tasted freedom now, onboard the *Stormdancer*, and would do anything not to be parted from it.

The guard stopped in his tracks as there came a loud crashing noise, followed by a series of screams and exclama-tions. Cat could just about make out a crowd of jostling people further down the street. Turning to her, the guard pulled another pair of cuffs from his belt, looping one of them through both of her wrist cuffs and hooking the other end tightly around a railing.

'Stay,' he instructed in his low, gruff voice, turning on his heel and jogging over towards the commotion. Cat immediately turned to her cuffed hands, wincing as she contorted her wrists painfully in an attempt to break free. It proved fruitless; the cuffs were strong and thick, and she had nothing with which to pick the lock.

'Shut up and keep still.' The voice startled her so much she almost slipped on some ice, and her eyes widened at the familiar head of red hair that seemed to appear from nowhere.

'Fox!' she hissed in astonishment, throwing a frantic glance in the direction of the commotion. The guard was nowhere in sight. 'What are you doing here?' Fox crouched, pulling a thin wire from his pocket and immediately setting to picking the lock on her handcuffs.

'Rescuing you – what does it look like? Idiot brat, I can't believe you let yourself get caught! You were just standing there like a statue, I'm not surprised he noticed!'

'You were watching, in the courtyard?' she asked. Had he heard the two Anglyan men talking?

'I was passing through,' he replied evasively, a look of concentration on his face. 'Saw you causing a bit of a scene there. Foolish boy, what were you thinking?' There was a soft click, and Cat couldn't help but beam as the cuffs fell from her wrists and were left dangling from the railing.

'We haven't got time – I'll explain when we're safe,' she assured him under her breath, rotating her wrists and grimacing at the pain. Fox grabbed her by the shoulder and urged her forward, faltering at a loud shout.

'Hey!' Glancing behind her, Cat cursed as she saw her guard racing towards them, fury on his face.

'Run,' Fox muttered, practically throwing her ahead of him as they both started to sprint.

'What if he's got a gun?' Cat exclaimed.

'He's not going to shoot a sprog. You only stole some purses.'

Cat panted with relief as they drew further and further away from her guard, getting closer to the courtyard with every frantic step. Suddenly, all she could see was stars as she ran head-first into something solid and fell backwards, the back of her head slamming into the stone ground so hard she thought she might vomit. She heard Fox cry out in alarm, but couldn't focus on anything but the blinding pain in her skull, the world spinning as she tried to sit up.

'Cat, get up!' A hand grabbed her under the arm and hoisted her to her feet, sending her vision lurching again. She let out a moan of protest at the motion, which morphed into a shout as a larger hand gripped the collar of her coat, trying to wrestle her from Fox's grip.

The solid thing she had run into turned out to be another guard, and Cat's heart raced as the first guard caught up with them.

'Fox!' she screamed, not caring that it was definitely not a masculine noise. Through her blurred vision she could make out Fox trying to tug her forward by her arm; the pain in her shoulder was excruciating. Fox's grip slipped, and she felt herself reeling backwards. Cat fumbled with the buckles on her coat and let it fall from her shoulders. Unfortunately, one of the guards dropped her coat as soon as he realised it was no longer on her, and grasped her jumper and shirt collar in one hand, pulling her away from Fox.

The teenager's hands wrapped around her wrists as he tugged, Cat's fingers feeling small and weak as she tried to grip him back. Her head pounded, willing her to just close her eyes and let the guards take her.

It all happened within a few seconds. The sound of ripping fabric was the only warning she had before her jumper and shirt split down the sides, leaving a handful of fabric with the guard as she fell into Fox's arms for a second time. Prepared, the older teen urged her aside and swung a fist into the closest guard's face before he could regain his balance, breaking the man's nose with a satisfying crunch.

'Cat, go! Back to the ship, I'll catch up!' It took several seconds for her pain-fogged brain to process his words, and Cat stood there watching as he fought off the two guards single-handedly. Her coat, heavy with stolen purses, lay abandoned on the street in a pile of snow, and she bundled it in her arms.

'I'm not leaving you!' she argued, merely for Fox to growl in frustration, dodging a well-aimed kick.

'Run, you moron!'

Cat looked around for anything she could use to help, wondering why no one seemed to be coming towards them. They were certainly making enough noise. Fox cursed loudly as he got caught across the jaw with a huge fist, sending him stumbling back several steps. Cat took the chance, reaching out to get Fox's attention, jerking him towards her and the exit to the courtyard. He looked up wild-eyed, seeing the coat in her arms, and seemed to agree with her decision, grabbing her wrist and running away from the guards as fast as he could manage.

Fox took the lead and dragged her down a side alley, and through several more until he evidently deemed them far enough away from the guards to stop. Cat panted, trying to regain her breath while her head resonated with white-hot pain. She dropped the coat to the floor, the remnants of her jumper and shirt falling off her too, and she saw Fox freeze, his eyes widening. Opening her mouth to ask what was wrong, the words died in her throat, goosebumps rising on her arms as she realised that she was standing in the alley in just her undershirt, and Fox's eyes were fixed firmly on her chest.

8

Fox gaped, staring at her incredulously.

'I can explain,' she stuttered, head pounding.

'I think I can manage without an explanation,' Fox retorted stiffly, not taking his eyes off the area where her thin undershirt clung to her skin. 'How long did you think you could hide that one, hmm?'

'I was going to tell you,' Cat insisted feebly. She was still trying not to be sick, and Fox's accusing stare wasn't helping. Bending to grab the coat from the ground, Cat shrugged it on and wrapped it tightly around her. 'I didn't think you'd let me stay if you knew.'

'Maybe you were right,' the redhead muttered, glaring at her. 'Storms, I should have let the guards have you.' Before she could respond, Fox turned on his heel, coat flaring out behind him as he left Cat alone in the alley, ruined clothing at her feet. A faint sob bubbled in her throat, but she swallowed it down, clenching her jaw in determination. Just because Fox had reacted badly didn't mean the rest of the crew would do the same; she had to at least try and convince them to let her stay. And that meant getting back to the ship before half past five.

Tentatively reaching up to check the wound on the back of her head, Cat grimaced as her fingers came away wet with blood. She could do nothing about that now, though. She noticed the peak of the clock tower just above the building to her left, and headed towards it, hoping to eventually reach the courtyard.

She was in luck, ending up at the edge of the Eastern side within a few minutes of walking. There were still three guards around the fountain, and she nervously edged out into the main courtyard, staying hidden behind a crowd of women who were walking in the direction she needed to go. There was a chance the guards wouldn't recognise her, but her arrest had caused a fair amount of noise. It wasn't a risk she was willing to take.

It took her a lot longer to make it back to the shipyard than she'd anticipated, but at last she stumbled over to the *Stormdancer*, wanting to cry with relief that the ship was still docked. Dragging herself up the gangplank, she spotted Ben and Matt playing cards on deck. They looked up when she approached, and Cat's heart sank; their expressions said it all. Fox had obviously made it back before her.

'All right, girlie,' Matt greeted, getting to his feet. 'Storms, you look awful. Fox said you'd had a bit of a bump, but if I'd known you were hurt this bad I'd have gone looking for you myself!'

Ben frowned, moving over to examine her head wound.

'He told you, then?' she said, resignation in her tone.

'He did,' Matt confirmed, an unreadable expression on his face. 'Why didn't you tell us sooner?'

'Boys are more useful. Girls are weak, helpless and only good for cooking, cleaning and pleasing men,' Cat replied without missing a beat, repeating what had been drilled into her from a young age by her father.

'Well, that's a load of rubbish' Matt muttered, rolling his eyes. 'Come on, lass, let's get you below deck. I want Alice to have a look at that head of yours.'

'You're not going to make me stay in Siberene?' Cat asked. Ben smiled at her, squeezing her shoulder gently. There was blood on his fingers from her head, and it smeared on her coat.

'Of course not, Cat. We're not that cruel. Now, come on, it's cold out, and you need to sit.'

'Wait,' Cat said abruptly. 'I want some answers first. If I'd known the truth to begin with I wouldn't have got caught.' She told the two men how she'd overheard the Anglyan men, squinting as her vision doubled. Matt and Ben shared an uneasy glance, Ben biting his lip.

'You'll get your answers,' the blond man promised. 'But inside, after Alice has seen to you. You've no doubt got concussion and you're in no state to stand out here chatting.' He glanced pointedly at her legs, which were shaking with the effort of keeping her upright.

'I'll carry you down,' Matt offered, making Cat scowl.

'Don't need to be carried,' she insisted. 'Not a helpless little girl.' The large man ignored her, hoisting her into his arms with ease.

'Humour me.'

Groaning as the world spun on its axis, Cat buried her head against Matt's chest. She was hardly aware of him carrying her below deck and through to the galley, opening her eyes as she was deposited gently on the bench.

'Oh, Cat,' Alice sighed, coming into her line of vision with a frown on her face. 'What have you got yourself into?'

'I didn't want to lie,' she insisted quietly, eyes half-shut. 'Tell Harry. I never wanted to lie to you. It was safer, but I didn't want to.'

'I know, lass.' That was Harry's voice, though she couldn't see him in the room. 'Just let Alice sort you out.'

'Answers,' Cat reminded pointedly, opening her eyes wider to give Matt a prompting look. He sighed, running a hand through his hair as he sat opposite her.

'I don't know what to tell you, lass,' he admitted, shuffling over as Ben came to sit beside him.

'The beginning is usually a good place to start.' Fox's voice made her jump, and she turned to watch as he entered the room. Wincing as Alice poked at a particularly tender spot, Cat didn't let her gaze drop from him, the expression on his face making her heart clench with guilt.

'There you are! I've half a mind to take you over my knee. you're not too old, you know!' Alice exclaimed, fixing the redhead with a stern look. 'What were you thinking, leaving the poor lass on her own with a wound like this in the middle of the city?'

'She lied to us!' Fox protested, only for Matt to interrupt him with a scoff.

'Like we've not been lying to her in return!' he argued, turning to Harry. 'We need to tell her, Harry. She knows too much.'

'How can we trust her?' Fox shouted. 'She's lied to us about this – what else don't we know about her?'

'My name is Catherine Elizabeth Hunter,' Cat declared loudly, staring Fox dead in the eye. 'And I ran away from home because my father is an arrogant git with delusions of grandeur and plans to betroth me to some brutish boy I can't stand.' She took a deep breath, trying to calm her nausea. 'Now, can you please stop shouting? I have one *hell* of a headache.'

'Hunter?' Ben repeated, brows furrowing. 'Nathaniel Hunter's daughter? You're a government brat?'

'Oh, brilliant,' Fox remarked sarcastically, pacing up and down the galley. 'Now we know we can't trust her!'

'I hate the government just as much as you do!' Cat argued, making him snort.

'I sincerely doubt that,' he replied, voice cold.

'I didn't ask to be born government,' Cat murmured, turning imploring eyes on Harry. He was the captain; it was his word that would decide her fate. 'I hate my father, I hate his associates, I hate the whole bloody aristocracy. Make of me what you will, but if you're going to get rid of me I ask you to do it here rather than in Anglya. If my father finds me, he'll kill me.'

'Hold on a minute,' Matt soothed, holding up a hand. 'No one said you're going anywhere, lass. Let's just take a minute to talk this over *rationally*.' There was a long silence, and the dark-haired man let out a slow breath. 'So Cat's a girl. I don't see how that could be a problem – we're not the type of crew who believe all women belong in the home. And so what if she's government? She's not done anything but help us since she arrived. Storms, Fox, she doesn't even *know* about the war! Don't blame her for the faults of her elders, she's just a sprog.'

'So she's staying, then?' Fox spat, looking at the rest of the crew. 'You're keeping her, even though she could be a government spy?'

'William Michael Foxe!' Alice exclaimed, to Cat's surprise. William was Fox's real name? Somehow it suited him. 'How dare you! I thought we'd raised you better than to judge someone by their birth. I thought your *parents* had raised you better.'

Fox flinched at her words, and Cat could hear Ben and Matt wince in unison.

'Well, it seems I'm outvoted,' Fox muttered angrily. Not looking at Cat, he turned on his heel and made for the door, slamming it shut behind him. Alice sighed, smoothing a hand over Cat's blood-matted hair.

'Don't listen to him, poppet,' she urged. 'He's just sore on certain subjects. Now, I'm just going to get you some ice.' She got to her feet, slipping into the kitchen, and Cat looked up at Harry.

'I still want answers,' she insisted. 'Trying to make sense of it all . . . it's making my head hurt.'

'I don't think that's the reason your head hurts, lass,' Matt remarked, making her laugh softly.

'Making my head hurt *worse*,' she corrected. 'Siberene looking like this, everything those Anglyan men were saying . . . it doesn't add up.'

'You'll get your answers, sprog, I promise,' Harry assured her. 'But not tonight. You need to rest. I'm not having you get even more worked up with that head of yours. Tomorrow morning, we'll explain everything.'

Cat made a face, and Matt chuckled.

'It's for your own good,' he insisted, reaching over the table to squeeze her shoulder. 'Harry and I need to get this old girl up in the air, anyway. It's getting late. Ben will keep you company until Alice sends you off to bed. Goodnight, girlie.'

'Night,' Cat murmured, managing a brief sleepy smile. 'And thank you, Harry. For letting me stay.'

Harry chuckled.

'Did you really think I could just leave you behind, after seeing how you've wrapped my crew round your finger? Storms, girl, if you've forgotten, Fox actually went back to stop you getting arrested! He might be sour now, but he doesn't do that for just anyone.' He winked at her, squeezing her hand where it lay on the table. 'Get some sleep, Cat. I'll see you at breakfast.'

The two men left, and Cat turned to the only other person in the room. Ben was staring at her with a nonplussed look on his face, and Cat couldn't help but ask.

'You knew, didn't you?' she said.

'I had my suspicions,' he admitted with a nod. 'I figured if you were hiding something, you'd tell us in your own time. But ...' He paused, biting his lip. 'I had a little sister once. Sophie.'

Cat gasped, eyes widening in horror. She didn't need to ask what had happened to her; she was the second child in a common family.

'Oh, Ben, I'm sorry,' she breathed, reaching over to slide her hand over his. 'How long ago?'

'Six years,' he replied, swallowing thickly. 'She was one of the earlier ones.' He looked up, meeting her gaze, and managed a half-smile. 'I've been wondering why you seemed so familiar ... now I know. You remind me of her,' he confessed.

Cat looked at him in surprise.

'I do?' she queried, and he nodded.

'She was always trying to prove she could be just as good as us boys, if not better. Always beating me at games, despite being five years younger,' he told her with a fond grin. 'Even beat Matt a few times.' He didn't say any more when Alice walked back in, a watertight bag full of ice in one hand and a bowl of warm water in the other, a dish towel over her shoulder.

'Have the boys gone to get us airborne?' she queried, earning a nod from Ben as she sat down beside Cat once more. 'Good, we need to get moving. Cat, dear, this is going to sting.'

The warning came mere moments before the damp dish towel was pressed to Cat's head wound, and the girl yelped, jolting. Alice tutted, and Ben stifled a grin, hand still in Cat's.

'Well, you won't need stitches,' Alice declared once she was done, allowing Cat to press the ice to her head. 'But I'll want to keep an eye on that over the next few days.'

'I just want to go to bed,' Cat admitted. The lantern hanging from the ceiling was sent swinging as the ship jolted upwards, and Cat fought against the surge of nausea.

'Of course, dear. Keep the ice with you, it'll help you sleep easier. Ben, walk her back to her room before you go to relieve Harry, would you? This bloody ship is bad enough to walk in on its own, let alone with a head wound.'

Helping Cat up, Ben slid an arm around her shoulders, keeping her steady.

'Goodnight, Alice. Thanks for cleaning me up.'

'You're very welcome, lass. Sleep well,' Alice replied fondly, giving her one last smile before Ben walked with Cat out of the galley into the corridor.

'I'd offer to carry you, but despite being older than Matt, I don't quite have his build. At least it's not far,' the curly-haired man mused, a wry smile on his face.

'You're older than Matt?' Cat asked, surprised.

'By two years,' Ben confirmed. 'I'm twenty-four, he's twenty-two. How old are you, by the way? I've been assuming thirteen for obvious reasons, but if you're high-born that's not really an issue.'

'Fourteen,' Cat told him. 'Fifteen in four days, actually. And trust me, if I weren't my father's only heir, he would have shipped me off to wherever Collected children go years ago.'

Ben frowned at her words, and she gave him a pointed look. 'I'm not stupid, Ben. You might not be telling me anything, but I can work some things out for myself. Those men in Siberene talked about kids in the lower levels, what-ever that means – clearly not all of the Collected are going to war.'

Ben sighed, and they stopped outside her bedroom door.

'Still, fifteen is quite an age to reach in this country. I'll have to get Alice to bake you a cake, or something. We'll explain everything in the morning,' he added as she went to

104

open her mouth. 'Sleep well, brat. I'll try and keep her steady through the Secondary so as not to wake you.'

Cat hugged him goodnight and slipped into her bedroom, shrugging out of her heavy purse-laden coat as soon as the door was shut. She was exhausted, and it felt like every muscle in her body had turned to lead. Barely having the energy to unbuckle her boots, she crawled beneath her blankets in her trousers and undershirt, the ice still pressed to the back of her head. For now all she cared about was getting some sleep.

9

Cat's head was still aching the next morning when she woke up, the ice pack little more than a bag of lukewarm water on her pillow. However, the pain was bearable – and nothing a good cup of tea wouldn't help. Dressing quickly she walked out of her door – and froze. Fox's door had opened at the same time, and he emerged, stopping in his tracks when he saw her.

'Catherine,' he greeted neutrally, making her wince at her full name.

'William,' she retorted in the same tone.

He blinked, then scowled.

'Don't call me that,' he muttered, heading for the galley door.

'Then don't call me Catherine. I told you when we met, it's just Cat.'

'That's because you don't get many boys called Catherine,' he mocked in reply. 'Not that Cat is much better. I should have known.'

She glared, resisting the childish urge to kick him in the shin. That was a bit rich coming from someone who went by the name Fox.

'Please, Fox, can't you give me another chance and just trust me?' she pleaded, latching on to his arm. He shook her off.

'I did, and then you turned out to be a girl. I don't trust easily a first time, let alone a second,' he told her, pushing past her to get to the galley.

The rest of the crew apart from Harry were already eating breakfast, and smiled when the two youngest members entered. The smiles faltered when they saw the mood Fox was in, and the look on Cat's face.

'Morning, brats,' said Matt through a mouthful of porridge.

'Matthew, don't speak with your mouth full,' Alice scolded, spooning out two more bowls of porridge.

'Morning, Cat. How's your head?' Ben asked.

'Still throbbing a little, but I'll be fine,' she assured him, rolling her eyes when Alice rounded the table to check for herself.

'Yes, that's healing up nicely,' she declared in satisfaction. 'But I still want you taking it easy for a day or two. No working downstairs – all that heat and tyrium dust can't be good for you in this state.'

Cat wanted to protest that she wasn't in any sort of 'state', but kept quiet, not wanting to argue with the older woman.

'Is Harry upstairs?' she asked Ben, who nodded.

'Yes, but we won't need him for the explanations,' he assured her, his shoulder bumping Matt's as he shifted to rest his elbows on the table. He met Cat's gaze evenly. 'You deserve answers.'

Both men shared a look, and Matt sighed softly.

'You were right when you told Ben last night that not all the children were being sent to war,' he began. 'The truth is we don't know where the children are. The war ended over eight years ago, Cat. About three months after the monarchs disappeared. Mericus gained control of Erova, Dalivia have control of Kasem, and Siberene is a fully independent country. It has been since before the war was over.'

Cat gasped. Sure, she'd had doubts, but to hear the truth spelled out so plainly . . .

'Then why the lies? Why the false newscasts, the war reports? Storms, why the *Collections*? If the Anglyan government doesn't need the kids for war, why are they still taking them from their families?' Why was the entire country still on rations if there was no war going on? It didn't make sense.

'We've always assumed that they've been using them as free labour in the tyrium mines,' Ben admitted. 'But after what you overheard, now we're not so sure. All we know is, the Collection ships go straight out to the Anglyan countryside, and the kids are never seen again.'

'The rest of Tellus have an agreement to leave Anglya alone,' Matt explained. 'They have a vague idea what's going on – they must do, the amount of kids that get smuggled out – but after all the damage the Anglyans did in the war, no one wants anything to do with us. They're happy to leave us to rot.'

'That's awful,' Cat breathed, and Fox snorted, the first sound he'd made since they'd sat down.

'That's politics,' he retorted. 'They get along much better without us, and don't want to risk the Anglyan government trying to regain control. If we happen to kill ourselves off by putting all the children to work, it's no skin off their noses.' His voice was grim, and Cat shivered.

'You think that's what they're doing, then?' she questioned intently. 'Killing off the commoners by taking the children?' It would make sense; gods knew her father and his associates would love to be able to toss all the commoners into a storm and be done with it. 'Hang on,' she murmured, pausing. 'You said the war ended about three months after the monarchs disappeared, right? And then the Collections began?'

Ben nodded, and Cat felt unease grow in her stomach.

'That's around the same time the aristocracy took over government. I remember there were about two or three months after their disappearance when everything was up in arms, and no one was in charge. Then my father and his colleagues took over.' Her mother had been absolutely inconsolable when the monarchs had disappeared. Queen Mary had been her closest friend. Cat could barely even remember them, having been only six when they disappeared, but she remembered asking her mother why she wasn't having lessons with Prince James any more. She'd hardly seen her father over those few months.

'What a coincidence,' Fox muttered under his breath, earning a scolding look from Alice. 'What? I'm just saying. The country went to the storms once her father and his ilk took over running it. All the deception is down to them.'

It wouldn't surprise Cat to find out that her father was aware – and in favour – of a plan to wipe out the commoners. The overseas effort wasn't his department, but he no doubt knew the man who had come up with the idea. He liked to involve himself in all aspects of government.

'You've known this since the beginning, then?' she asked Alice. 'You and Harry. And you haven't done anything?'

'What could we do, lass?' Matt cut in. 'We'd be arrested as soon as we dared say anything. They're already blackmailing half the people who know into keeping quiet. Anyone not in government who has to leave their ship in another country is told they can keep all their kids in exchange for silence. Like you saw, it's impossible not to find out the truth as soon as you step on foreign soil – the government knows it can't hide it. They threatened for years to take Fox from us. He's too old now, but we know what's at stake.'

'And what about what's at stake for all those people who aren't being blackmailed?' Cat retorted angrily. 'Those people whose children are being taken from them for no good reason? Those people starving on rations, living in fear of foreign invasion?' She turned to Ben, eyes wide and imploring. 'How can you stand back and let it happen when you know how it feels to lose someone to Collections?'

'What do you propose we do, then?' Fox cut in, voice flat. 'Go on, government girl. Tell us in your infinite wisdom how we should be fixing this whole mess all by ourselves.'

Cat swallowed, steeling herself and meeting his eyes defiantly.

'We infiltrate the government building,' she declared, her voice shaking. 'I've been sneaking in and out of there since I was barely old enough to walk. It'll be harder now I don't have my . . . family influence.' She coughed, looking away as Fox's eyes flashed with something hateful and ugly. 'But it can be done. We get in, find out why they're really Collecting the children, and we get enough evidence of their corruption to trap them in their own lies. Even if – even if the rest of Tellus doesn't care, maybe we have some people left in Anglya who *do* care enough to fight back.'

There was silence after her words, in which Cat tried to look as confident as she sounded, before Matt let out a bark of laughter.

'You've certainly got guts, I'll give you that,' he remarked.

'Something needs to be done, before it's too late,' Cat reasoned. She couldn't help but wonder, however, how often she'd come close to uncovering things. If she'd just made it through those locked doors, just *once*, things could be so very different. If she'd overheard the right conversation, or read the right letter. Then again, her father probably would have beaten her for sticking her nose in his business. She couldn't believe it had been eight years and no one had tried to stop them, though. Did people not care?

'Don't be ridiculous,' Alice scolded. 'We didn't spend years risking our necks smuggling just to throw it all away on a suicide mission. It's an awful situation, Cat, but there's very little we can do about it.'

Cat's lips pursed, her brow furrowing in frustration. Surely they could do something?

'There's one thing I don't understand,' she began, frown deepening. 'Before I left home, my father told me they wouldn't be needing Collections much longer. He said the war was coming to an end. If there was no war in the first place, what on Tellus was he talking about?'

There was another long silence, and Ben and Matt shared a glance.

'It's true, then,' Matt said, looking grim. 'There were rumours something big was happening. Something was changing. We dismissed them as just talk, but if Hunter was talking about stopping Collections ... they must have all the kids they need for whatever they're planning.'

'Surely if they stop taking the sprogs, that's all that matters?' Fox groused.

'Don't be thick,' Matt retorted, 'if they stop taking them, it means they've finished what they needed them for. Gods only know what that may be.'

Fox scowled, but a slow smirk tugged at Ben's lips, his eyes calculating. 'We'd need information first,' he murmured thoughtfully. 'Guard shift schedules and locations. Then blueprints, schematics ...' He looked up at Fox, raising an eyebrow. 'You've been wanting to find out what's actually going on for years.' The sulky teenager shrugged to acknowledge the point, but he didn't seem any closer to agreeing to Cat's suggestion. Ben broadened his appeal to the whole crew.

'Cat's right; we've been letting it lie for far too long now. The government seems to be escalating their plans, and who knows what their next step is. We need to stop them before they can implement it. And I think it's time I found out what happened to my sister.' He met Cat's eyes with a tentatively determined expression, and she grinned back.

'Hardly much point in arguing the matter,' Fox remarked. He looked at Ben. 'You're right about one thing. If we're going to change something, it'll have to be soon, before it's too late. Any Collection from now on could be the last.'

Fox's sudden acquiescence came as a surprise to all of them, and Cat smiled hesitantly at him. He met her eyes, his expression blank for a long moment, before he smiled back. It was barely there, but it made her beam.

'I still think it's a death wish,' Alice said. 'But you have a point – something needs to change. If anyone can manage it, we can. Especially with Cat's inside knowledge. Anyway, we do nothing until Harry's had a say.' Her brow was ridged with worry lines, but there was something in her eyes that made Cat sure the woman would do everything to convince her husband to go along with things.

'We can talk to Harry about it at lunch,' Matt suggested, pulling his pocket watch from his waistcoat. 'But for now, we'd all better get to work. Except you, Cat. It's rest and recuperation for you,' he ordered. He and Ben got to their feet, slipping into quiet conversation as they left the galley.

Cat was aware of Fox following her as she made for her bedroom, intent on taking a bath to clear her head, but didn't acknowledge him until they were outside his room, when it became clear he wasn't going to leave her alone.

'Did you want something?' He didn't rise to the bait.

'I hope you know what you're doing,' he said instead. 'This isn't one of your little fantasy stories where everything has a happy ending. People could die. *We* could die.'

'People are already dying,' Cat retorted. Whether the children were in the tyrium mines or elsewhere, they certainly weren't likely to be alive and well. 'Something needs to be done. I'm just surprised you're agreeing with me.'

'Like you said, something needs to be done.'

Cat paused, taking several moments to get the words out. 'Are we all right, then? Last night you all but hated me!'

Fox's gaze fell to the ground, and he scuffed the toe of his boot against the floorboards.

'Last night I found out that not only are you a girl, but you're a government girl. Excuse me for reacting badly to that information,' he said quietly, walking past her to enter his bedroom.

She followed. She wasn't going to let him escape *that* easily.

'The others managed to react just fine,' she said, sticking her booted foot in the doorway as Fox tried to shut the door on her.

'I'm not the others. I've not met a single government brat who wasn't an arrogant, egotistical scumbag.' His posture was tense, his shoulders hunched. He looked like he was preparing to either run or fight.

'You've met *me*!' she argued, bringing a snarl of rage from his lips.

'I don't *know* you!' he exclaimed, taking a step forward. 'I *can't* know you, because everything I thought I knew about you was a lie. I . . . I don't know what to believe about you, Cat.' His voice was a tight whisper.

'Believe what you've learned since you met me,' she pleaded, resting a hand on his arm. 'I'm Cat. Not Catherine Hunter, government brat, and if I have my way I never will be again. Just trust me, Fox. Would any of the other government brats you've met ever plan to infiltrate the compound?' she pointed out.

'I'll give you that one,' he conceded with a snort. 'That definitely makes you one of a kind. Still ... I trusted you, and you were lying to me the whole time. I don't appreciate that.'

Cat bit her lip guiltily.

'I know. I'm sorry. I thought it was best ... boys are more useful than girls. No one wants a silly little girl around, unless there's some cleaning to be done,' she said with a wry smile.

Fox's brow furrowed in a frown.

'You've proved rather useful so far,' he told her. 'And regardless of whether I trust you or not, you've got guts ... for a girl.'

Cat scowled, glaring at him.

'I never pegged you for a chauvinist.'

He blinked. 'A what?' he asked blankly.

'Sexist,' she explained, making him laugh.

'That wasn't being sexist, that was being truthful. Now, if you don't mind, you're in my bedroom ...' He raised his eyebrows.

'Right,' she muttered, feeling her cheeks burn. 'If and when you decide you can trust me ...'

Shutting the door on her way out, she sighed, shaking her head.

'Boys.'

Cat spent most of the morning in her room, thinking. She did, at one point, venture down to the engine room, but Matt wasn't there, and she wasn't confident enough in her own abilities to start working on anything without supervision. Still, by early afternoon, she itched to do something productive. Wandering restlessly through the ship's corridors with no real destination, she bumped into Alice at the corner that led to the galley.

'Hello, dear. Bored?' the older woman asked knowingly.

Cat nodded.

'Matt's with Ben and Harry up in the control room, Fox is being ... Fox. Is there anything I can help you with?' she queried.

'So long as you don't do anything strenuous, with that head of yours. You could help me sort lunch out,' Alice suggested. 'The boys have sped things up a little, so we'll be landing the day after tomorrow. It's safer to stay away for a while, after the little incident in Siberene.' Cat blushed, making the woman roll her eyes. 'It's not your fault, lass.'

Having followed Alice into the kitchen, Cat hopped up on the table – both chairs were currently housing crates of food – her legs swinging slowly.

'At least I managed to keep the purses I stole,' she mused. 'What do I do with those, by the way?'

'Give them to one of the boys, they'll put them downstairs with the rest. I'd recommend Harry – Matt and Ben won't be in the best of moods, now Ben's started thinking about poor Sophie again. And Fox, well ...' She trailed off, and Cat stifled a smile.

'Won't want to talk to me right now,' she finished. 'Why's Matt like that? With Ben, I mean? I get that they're best friends, and have been for years, but ... It always seems like Matt's protecting Ben, never the other way around.'

Alice smiled, knife swiftly peeling potatoes. 'They've always been that way. From what they've told me, Ben was rather scrawny as a sprog, and got picked on quite a bit at school. As you can imagine, our Mattie has never been a small lad and has always protected Ben. It used to annoy poor Benny, but I think he's rather used to it now.'

'I think it's sweet,' Cat admitted.

Alice met her eyes and winked.

'Isn't it? Poor Ben, bless him. Matt's just showing he cares. Here, slice this for me, would you, dear?' She gestured to a knife and a loaf of bread and Cat nodded, hopping off the counter to take up the knife.

'And what's Fox's story? You said he's been with you for years. What happened before that?' she questioned tentatively.

Alice frowned deeply.

'I think you'd best wait for him to tell you that, sweetheart. He isn't one to bandy his business about. Keeps himself to himself, does Fox. He shouldn't have been so rude to you, though.'

'It's fine. I don't think he meant most of it.'

Alice frowned, stirring the stew somewhat more forcefully than usual.

'Regardless of that, he shouldn't have said the things he said.'

Cat held her tongue; she didn't want Fox thinking she had complained about him.

Alice began to plate up, and Cat moved to help, carrying some of the food through to the galley. Just as she was setting the plates down, the door opened and Fox slunk in, face like a thundercloud. When he saw her, he got that unreadable look in his eyes that infuriated her.

'I thought you said women weren't only good for being in the kitchen,' he muttered as he sat, dragging a plate towards him.

'I did. But that doesn't mean I won't help Alice. It would be mean of me to leave her to carry all those plates herself when I have two perfectly good arms of my own.'

Fox held his hands up in surrender, rolling his eyes.

'All right, fine. Have you spoken to Harry yet?'

Before Alice could answer, the man himself walked in, accompanied by Matt.

'What's this I hear about you sparking a rebellion on my ship, young lady?' the grey-haired man asked Cat with raised eyebrows, his words light but his face serious. 'You've got some nerve, I'll give you that. But if you say you can get us in, I'm all for it.'

'It'll take a bit of planning, but I can do it,' Cat replied confidently, glad Harry was on board. She had memories of sneaking about the government compound with Prince James, she'd been doing it from such a young age.

'Then we'll get started as soon as we've landed. If we're going to be doing this, we need to go big. It's not enough to get evidence to shut the government down – we'll need to do it manually too,' Harry told them, and Cat watched as a large smirk crossed Matt's face.

'Benny's going to love what you're implying there, Captain,' he remarked, making Harry chuckle.

'Too right he will, the little pyromaniac. We need to reduce the building to rubble when we're done with it. A fresh start is exactly what this country needs. We can't go back to the old ways, but maybe we'll get close to how things were with some new ones.' Cat gaped, about to protest, but shut her mouth abruptly. Yes, it was perfect. The government couldn't smooth things over if their whole building was dust and debris.

'We'll need blueprints, then,' Matt told the older man, easily balancing two bowls of stew on top of each other. 'I'll have a chat with Ben, and see what he can make on such short notice.' With that he disappeared, and Alice rolled her eyes, spooning out stew for the rest of them.

'Honestly, those boys and their explosives,' she muttered fondly. 'We never should have taken that job clearing rubble in Mericus, it's spawned an addiction.'

Harry winked at his wife. 'They had the addiction before that, we just perpetuated it.'

Alice shook her head, exasperated. 'Come on, Cat, eat up, you need your strength. And let me check over that head of yours.'

'Isn't blowing the whole place to kingdom come a bit . . . drastic?' Fox said, lips curled in a frown. 'Don't get me wrong, I'm all for the destruction of government property, but not everyone in that building is government scum. There's cleaning staff and whatnot.'

Cat bit her lip; he had a point. Moreover, her father would likely be in the building. Yes, she hated him, but she wasn't sure if that extended to wanting him dead. 'But if we don't, they'll worm their way out of punishment. If we time it right, we can do it at maintenance shift change. I'll write the times down later and we'll work something out.' Knowing when the maintenance staff were off-duty had been one of the first things she'd learned as a girl. It was much easier to sneak around when they weren't there. And as for her father . . . even if he wasn't involved in Collections, he was guilty of plenty of other heinous crimes. If he happened to be in the building when it blew, then that was the will of the gods, and Cat would rather not dwell on it.

Fox still didn't look happy, but he kept silent through the rest of lunch, obviously aware of how little choice they had in the matter. Excusing herself quietly when she finished, Cat left the room. She didn't quite feel like she fitted in yet, and the rift between her and Fox was only exaggerating that feeling.

Remembering how horrid he had been to her recently, she scowled, asking herself how she could find him attractive.

'Physical attractiveness has nothing to do with actual personality,' she muttered, sitting on the workbench in the engine room.

'That's true, yes, but I have known people to find Fox's personality attractive in the past. Storms know why, the boy's as prickly as a hedgehog.'

Cat squeaked, falling off the workbench, her face as red as a tomato as she looked towards the door to see Matt leaning in the doorway. Picking herself up, she glared at him.

'Don't you make any noise when you walk?' she asked, and Matt snickered, scratching at his goatee where it was beginning to grow scruffy.

'I was hardly quiet – you were just thinking too hard.'

Her scowl deepened, and then she registered his earlier words.

'You knew?' she asked simply, not needing to elaborate. The large man shrugged apologetically.

'You weren't particularly discreet. I don't think anyone else has noticed, not since we only just found out you're a lass,' he assured her.

She sighed in relief, then looked up at him suspiciously.

'You thought I fancied him before you knew I was a girl?' she asked.

'It's not unheard of, you know,' he replied. 'But no, I just thought you were shy and suffering a bit of hero worship. Then the other night happened, and it clicked.'

Cat bit her lip, and sighed, running a hand through her short brown hair.

'You don't have to tell me it's fruitless. I already know. It'll pass in time, though,' she insisted, wondering which of them she was trying to convince. 'So, what needs doing?'

'Are you cleared to work, then?' he asked, eyeing her in concern.

'Fit as a fiddle, promise,' Cat vowed. 'Alice said I could help so long as I didn't do anything dangerous.'

'Excellent. You can crawl under there and see if the bolts are as rusty as I think they are,' Matt instructed, pointing to a large cog tower raised about two feet off the ground.

Cat obligingly dropped to her back and slid into the small gap the best she could, yelping when Matt playfully tugged her ankle. A small smile played at her lips as she set about examining the machinery. At least some attitudes hadn't changed.

10

Cat fell out of bed as the ship rocked violently, waking abruptly. Scrambling from the floor and out into the hallway, she stared at a calm-looking Fox just outside her door.

'What in the name of storms was that?' she asked, alarmed.

'It's called landing. It happens every now and then,' Fox replied drily, leaning against the wall.

Cat's eyebrows rose.

'We're here?' she queried, and Fox nodded.

'We are indeed. Harry sent me to wake you up, but I see that's not necessary ... though you may want to get dressed properly first.'

Cat looked down at herself, blushing when she realised she'd run from her room in the undershirt and long cotton shorts – which, admittedly, were almost trousers on her – that she slept in due to lack of real nightwear.

'Uh, yes. Right. I'll ... get dressed,' she agreed, attempting to stay casual. The widening of Fox's grin told her that she'd failed. Retreating back into her room, she let out a long wail of despair, cursing under her breath.

'I can hear you, you know!' Fox called from the other side of the closed door, obvious amusement in his tone. Cat cursed even louder, causing the older teen to laugh as he walked away. Willing her cheeks to return to their normal colour, she dressed for Anglyan weather, wrapping a scarf around her neck. It was nearing winter and the weather was unpredictable around this time of year, though a glance out of her small porthole confirmed it wasn't currently raining.

Arriving in the galley, she sat beside Matt.

'Good morning, girlie. Ready for some sneaking and subterfuge?' he said perkily.

She laughed, nodding.

'Not so fast, young lady,' Alice cut in with a frown. 'You're not going anywhere with that head of yours. Besides, Harry wanted you and Fox to do a bit of maintenance. We had a rough journey over, pushing her as fast as we did.'

Cat glanced over at Fox, who was ignoring her and eating his breakfast as if he couldn't even hear the conversation. She had to spend the whole day with *him*?

'I rested all of yesterday, and I feel fine,' she insisted, though Alice didn't budge.

'Captain's orders, brat,' Matt pointed out. 'Shame I can't join you, the old girl really does need some work. But Ben and me are heading to the shipyard pub. A fair few men who are now working on government ships also work guard shifts at the compound, and some of the traders used to be in masonry and might know where we could go about getting the blueprints. After a bit of liquid persuasion, of course,' he told her with a wink.

She looked at him in disbelief.

'You're going to a pub at this hour?' she exclaimed.

Ben snorted.

123

'It might be early but that won't stop the men; they'll want a pint or two before setting off,' he told her.

When Matt and Ben had finished eating, they bid the rest of the crew goodbye and went off into the city in good spirits. Despite Harry's orders for them to both work in the engine room, Fox disappeared soon after Matt and Ben left, so Cat wandered down on her own to begin work.

It was strange being down there without Matt, and she was reluctant to touch anything for fear of breaking it. She wandered over to the large furnace in the centre, checking the tyrium levels inside. It always amazed her that just one of those small cubes of bright purple rock could power an entire skyship for several hours. That was why Anglya had controlled an empire at one point, she supposed; if there was one thing everyone needed to trade successfully, it was tyrium, and Anglya had it in abundance.

Sighing to herself, she left the furnace how it was and got to work cleaning some of the propeller belts where they were sticky with grease deposits. Maybe Fox would give her a hand, once he returned.

Cat was glad to get back on track the next day, her head healed over and Harry having no excuse to postpone things. Matt and Ben had been successful in finding blueprints – she'd hardly seen them since they'd returned from the pub, tucking themselves away with the papers in Matt's room – so now they just had to figure out which of the four government entrances was the best to use. That was where she came in.

Dressed in fairly respectable, clean clothing, Cat met the rest of the crew at breakfast in the galley.

'Alice is going with you, brats,' Harry told her and Fox over breakfast. 'Just in case the Collection crews come a-calling. I know you could probably escape, but we don't want to risk anything. Especially not with you, Cat.'

Cat bit her lip nervously, but nodded, glancing at Fox, who was staring back.

'I'll keep an eye on you, shortie, don't worry,' he assured her quietly.

She smiled in relief, glad that even in his foul mood, he understood how bad it would be for her to get Collected. He was probably too old to be taken; though Cat didn't actually know his age he looked possibly seventeen, maybe eighteen if he hadn't shaved. Almost a grown man.

'Sure you'll be able to restrain yourself wandering around Greystone?' she teased. 'We won't go unnoticed if you're punching government workers in the face.'

Fox snorted, giving her an amused look.

'I'm sure I'll manage.' The plan was to eavesdrop on as many people as possible, in the hope of learning more about the guard shifts around the entrances. As Nathaniel Hunter's daughter, Cat had always entered and exited through North Gate, but it was far too well guarded for street rats to sneak through.

'We'll be docking for a while, so I need to file for a long-term permit with the warden,' Harry added.

'We'd better get going, Mattie,' Ben urged quietly, nudging his friend's shoulder. Matt nodded, standing, and after a short whispered conversation with Harry, the two left. Cat wasn't sure what they were up to; they hadn't seen fit to tell anyone but Harry. Presumably, Alice wouldn't approve.

'Come on, Alice, let's get going,' Fox said. 'Coming, Cat?'

Waving goodbye to Harry, the three of them headed up on deck. Cat stood for a long moment, just peering out over the railing into the city. It was bizarre to think that she'd left – had gone all the way to Siberene – and it was only having seen the prosperity of the foreign country that she was able to see how truly desolate Anglya was. The crumbling brick and lopsided stone of the housing districts was more obvious to her, and the broken streetlights hard to ignore. Even the richest of common men wore threadbare clothes that had seen many better days. Everyone looked thin and haggard, and the city itself was dilapidated and filthy.

'Shocking, isn't it? You don't realise until you've seen what everywhere else is like. What we *could* be like, if your lot weren't ruining it,' Fox muttered, nudging her in the back to get her moving. Cat elbowed him in the stomach.

'They're not *my lot*! I hate them just as much as you do.'

He scowled darkly.

'Whatever you say, girlie. Now, hurry up.'

Cat hurried down the gangplank. As she reached the bottom, she narrowly avoided being run over by two men carrying a large crate. They cursed at her as she darted out of the way and went after Alice.

'Which end of Greystone are we looking at?' Cat asked, keeping her voice low.

Fox shot her a funny look.

'What on Tellus are you talking about, ends of Greystone? Either end is full of pretentious middle-class bastards.'

Cat rolled her eyes. Now was not the time for prejudice, even if it was well founded.

'Well, if you go up the Highdene end, it's right by the South entrance of the compound, which is where people like the Cantfields and the Mayfairs live. That end, you'll probably only get petty gossip about who's been seen stepping out with who, which families are currently in good standing and which have members who've done something rather naughty. Useless, boring drivel that delights the ladies and makes them think they've got access to some secret scandal. We might get something useful about the compound, but I doubt it. The Kentridge end is near . . . near where people like my father and the Gales live, and is also close to the gentlemen's club. That's where we'll get the more solid information – what's going on in the compound, who has business meetings they're being terribly tight-lipped about. But it's very difficult to get close enough to hear anything.'

'We'll go there, then,' Fox snapped irritably and scowled.

Cat looked sideways at him.

'Or . . .' she continued, elongating the word, 'we could head to Kentridge through Appleby, which is furthest from the compound walls. We're less likely to get business information, but more likely to eavesdrop on workmen – guards, government mechanics, the ones who actually do what people like my father order them to. And trust me, the workmen like to complain. If we're going to learn anything, it'll probably be there.'

'How in blazes do you know all this?' Alice asked, impressed.

Cat shrugged.

'I went to a lot of meetings with my father. As his heir I was allowed to meet his associates, but as a girl I had to sit and wait outside while they discussed their business.' Her voice showed exactly how she felt about that. 'A lot of the time, there was no one checking I was actually sitting outside, and those meetings would go on for hours. So I'd slip off into Greystone and no one would touch me, knowing who I was. No one dared bring the wrath of Nathaniel Hunter down on their heads,' she explained matter-of-factly.

Alice tutted, disapproving of a young girl wandering the streets alone. Fox just looked grim – at the inattention paid to a small girl, or the reminder of just how important she was, she didn't know.

'So you recommend we go through Appleby, then?' he asked her, and she nodded.

'It's been a little while since I've been there, but Mr Perkins should still live at number seven, and he's the commander in charge of coordinating the guards' shifts,' she replied, turning down a corner towards the familiar dark grey paved streets. 'We're bound to learn a thing or two. He tells his wife everything, and she's an awful gossip.'

For once, she was leading the way, Fox and Alice trailing behind her. She could tell it was infuriating Fox that she was more knowledgeable than him in this area, and that made her smile. He deserved a taste of his own medicine.

'You can't just walk into Greystone,' Fox hissed, grabbing her by the shoulder as she made to cross the street. 'Not as a commoner, anyway.'

Impatiently she eyed her two companions.

'Your clothes are fairly decent. Fox, stuff your goggles in your pocket and just walk in like you own the place. You manage to do that everywhere else, so it shouldn't be too hard for you.'

He blinked, taking a few moments to register that she'd insulted him. Far from being offended, he grinned.

'Little girl has some fire in her belly.'

Cat stomped on his foot.

'*Don't* call me little girl,' she warned.

'If you had pigtails, lass, I'm sure he'd be pulling them,' Alice murmured wryly, and Cat saw the faintest hint of red colour in Fox's freckled cheeks.

Greystone was in markedly better condition than the inner-city areas, but most of the buildings still looked shabby and in need of repair, and she could count more broken windows than she had fingers. Glancing over her shoulder, she waved a hand impatiently, and Fox sighed before starting forward, confident swagger out in full. Alice kept her usual warm smile on her face, hiding her nervousness well.

'Just keep an eye out and walk slowly,' Cat muttered under her breath, peering around the streets. It was relatively quiet, as most people were currently at work. However, that meant the wives were left to their own devices, and if she remembered correctly . . .

'There.' Sure enough, they turned a corner and reached the small park in the centre of Appleby, where a group of women were sitting on benches chatting quietly, a few of them with babies on their laps. There were four young children, three boys and a girl, playing with a ball on the grass. The trio stayed back, wary of getting too close.

'Perfect,' announced Cat.

'Why perfect?' Alice queried.

'See that blonde woman in the dark blue skirt with the grey corset and shawl? That's Mr Perkins' wife. I thought she'd be here at this time. The baby the woman next to her is holding is hers, and she'd never resist an opportunity to show him off. She practically threw a party when he was born.'

'You know a worrying amount about the social habits of government scum,' Fox murmured, ignoring the sharp look Alice shot him.

Cat just shrugged.

'One thing my father taught me that I actually bothered to listen to – always know what those who work for you do with their free time, just in case they're using it to betray you.'

Fox's eyebrows rose slowly.

'That's ... really quite paranoid,' he told her, and she nodded.

'Completely, but it works. Now, how are we going to get close enough to listen in without being noticed?' She eyed the surrounding area, looking for somewhere that would shield them from curious eyes.

'And just what do you think you're doing, you little brat?' Cat froze at the familiar voice, turning on her heel. Standing in front of them, proudly wearing his guard's uniform with a shiny new stud at his collar signifying a recent promotion, was Finnegan Rowley, son of Jeremy Rowley, head of ration allocation. Finnegan was a pompous idiot with delusions of grandeur – he had once told an eleven-year-old Cat that he was going to marry her and become the head of the Hunter family. Fortunately, her father had overheard and laughed himself breathless, taking great pleasure in telling the boy that he would never give his daughter away to someone with so little standing.

'Walking, what does it look like?' she retorted coolly, crossing her fingers behind her back, hoping desperately he wouldn't recognise her.

'I don't know you,' he declared.

Cat rolled her eyes, staring up at the boy – man now, she supposed – through her ragged fringe.

'Well, that tiny brain of yours can't be expected to remember every name you try and shove in it, Finnegan. I live down in Lethbridge at Miss Kasey's. This is my friend from school, Will, and his mother Alice.' She hoped Miss Kasey was continuing to take in higher-class orphans, or her plan was down the drain. Luckily, Finnegan nodded slowly, still eyeing her with distrust.

'Tell Miss Kasey that if she doesn't stop letting in strays my father will have to cut her rations. I don't care for little orphan brats like you, and neither does the rest of the country. We'll start shipping you off if you keep asking for food.' Cat felt Fox stiffen behind her, a low growl escaping his throat. She reached back discreetly, placing a hand on his arm.

'We're of the same blood, Rowley, so don't act like you're better than me,' she said curtly.

'Yes, but I actually have parents who care about me,' he replied nastily. Cat wished she could tell him who she really was, just to see the look on his face, but giving the game away wasn't worth a petty grudge match. Fox's growl grew louder, and he started forward, but Cat held him back. Finnegan's eyes darted between the two of them, completely ignoring Alice and lingering on Fox for a long moment, before he evidently decided that Fox looked too big a threat to try brawling with. Finnegan may have been solidly built, but it was obvious that most of it was not muscle. His double-breasted uniform jacket strained around the middle, and one row of buttons was uneven, betraying the need to adjust them in order to fit his girth.

'Hurry along to Miss Kasey's, then, brat, and watch your attitude around your betters,' he spat.

Cat gave him a look of wide-eyed innocence.

'Oh, I will, when I see them,' she replied, nimbly stepping aside when he aimed a punch at her face. 'Oh, was I meant to stay still for that? Terribly sorry. Maybe next time I'll let you hit me, and then you can explain to your commander how you punched an orphan boy. I'm sure he'll agree it was a valid use of the power you've gained with that pretty new scrap of silver. Commander Grange, right?'

He winced almost violently, face going pale, and Cat knew she'd guessed correctly. Only Grange could inspire that reaction in his men.

'You'll get yours one day, boy,' Finnegan muttered, turning on his heel and stomping off down the street, away from the park.

When he was gone, Cat let out a chuckle at the looks on her companions' faces.

'That was fun,' she remarked.

'You, young lady, are far too devious for your own good.

That poor boy looked about ready to mess his trousers after your last comment,' Alice muttered with a shake of her head, making Cat snigger. 'Though with his attitude, I don't blame you!'

'That poor boy is a brute and a bully, and deserves everything I gave him and more. That was merely a bit of retribution. I couldn't resist, not when he doesn't recognise me.'

Alice sighed.

'I suppose it did the trick. We're just lucky it was a guard you knew, rather than one you didn't.'

Cat grinned at her, then looked at Fox, who was still staring at her.

'Anything to say?' she queried neutrally.

Fox shook his head, a bemused grin stretching across his lips.

'That was impressive. And it makes me wonder what he did to you before you were Cat to get you to react that way,' he admitted.

Cat wasn't sure how she felt about Fox making that distinction – Catherine and Cat, two separate people. It was like Fox was splitting her personality, and only wanting to know half of it. She may have given up her Hunter heritage, but she wasn't completely disregarding the person she'd been.

'He bullied a lot of younger sprogs when we were in school, thought he was sent from the storms himself because his father's head of rationing, and tried to betroth himself to me when I was eleven. That was when my father drew the line – he's had plans for my marriage since I was born,' she replied.

'You government types and your arranged marriages,' Fox muttered. 'Do any of them actually work?'

Cat thought about that for a long moment. She knew some people who were content with their spouse, and lived perfectly happily. But she couldn't state with any certainty that any of them would have *picked* that person.

'I don't think so. But marriage to us – them,' she corrected hastily, seeing the look on Fox's face, 'isn't so much about love, it's political strategy. Joining two families of status together to increase the status of both. No one cares if the people involved love each other. We're usually betrothed before we're old enough to know what love really is.'

'Everywhere else in the world did away with them decades ago,' Alice mused. 'One day Anglya will catch up.'

'I don't know how you can think they're normal,' Fox remarked to Cat, wrinkling his nose.

'I never said it was normal. It's just what happens,' she told him with a shrug. 'Now, back on topic, how are we going to get close enough to listen in on Mrs Perkins and her friends? Even if I keep my cover as one of Miss Kasey's lodgers, they won't want a little orphan brat playing with their precious children.'

'We could just sit on the grass nearby and talk. It's not like they own the place,' Fox pointed out, one eyebrow raised. 'Unless they do.'

'No, no, it's free land,' Cat replied. 'And I suppose we could. We'll have to look busy, though, or they'll tell us to go to work.'

'Well, we look more suspicious just standing here, so we'd better get a move on,' Alice urged, glancing at the group of women in the park.

Cat led the way over, sitting on the closest piece of grass; far enough away from the gathering of women that they wouldn't be caught eavesdropping, but close enough to hear most of what was being said. Urging Alice and Fox to start a light, superficial conversation, she leaned back on her hands, straining to hear what the ladies were saying. Most of it was frivolous chit-chat, but she perked up at a mention of guard duty.

'Oh, my John has been working ever so hard these past months. But if he carries on the way he's going, he says, his commander will grant him another stud. And, of course, you know what that means,' one of the women told the group, and all of them burst into girlish giggles. Cat was given two near identical perplexed looks.

'If John Catton gets a fourth stud his commander will give him leave to have a second child. Also, a pay rise,' she explained quickly.

'Was John involved in that dreadful scuffle I heard about from Mr Graham the other day? I know it was in his area,' asked a woman with a squealing baby in her arms.

'You have to get *permission* to have children in government?' Fox asked in an incredulous whisper.

Cat shushed him, but she'd missed Mrs Catton's response.

'Only the second one onwards. Now, shut up and keep talking, they said something about a scuffle in John's area. That's South district.'

'Shut up and keep talking?' Fox muttered with raised eyebrows, but resumed his fake conversation with Alice.

'They're tightening security in the area, Harvey told me. Pulling in ninth and tenth for extra shifts.'

Cat winced; there went the easiest prospect of entering. South Gate was known to be the least guarded, being the one closest to Greystone.

'How long for, do you know? Daniel is in tenth, and he's barely home as it is,' a woman with pale blonde hair asked, frowning, and Cat hid a smirk. The reason Mrs Ashdowne's husband was barely home was because he was having an affair with Mrs Bates's sixteen-year-old daughter. Something the older woman was obviously aware of, if the shifty look she had on her face was anything to go by.

'It's all worth it, though, if it brings in the money,' Mrs Bates said kindly.

'Are you getting anything from all this drivel, or can we carry on to Kentridge?' Fox asked impatiently, his foot bouncing. For a moment he reminded Cat of one of the young boys tugging on his mother's skirts a few feet away.

'I've already ruled out South Gate entrance, so unless you count that important progress as drivel, cease your whining and let me listen,' she scolded sharply.

He looked both surprised at her tone and abashed at his childishness, and went quiet once more, turning as if he were listening to Alice talk.

'Did you hear about Linda Bowen? She's been seen meeting Nathaniel Hunter for lunch.'

Cat froze.

'Oh yes, apparently they're looking rather cosy. The man isn't even waiting until his wife passes, and he's making no secret of his dalliance. How very shameful! Especially after what happened with his daughter.'

'Does anyone know what happened to her? There was

an article in the newspaper, but I'll admit, I was much more interested in the news that Marcus Gale has been betrothed to the Carter girl.'

Cat snorted quietly – Amelia Carter could have him.

'According to the news, Lord Hunter says she ran away. It seems awfully suspicious, though. Harriet Cantfield says Lord Hunter sent her away with the Collection because she was being so dreadfully disobedient. She's his only heir, so maybe that's why he's stepping out with Linda. Elizabeth Hunter isn't likely to give him another from what I've heard. They say she's barely hanging on as it is.'

'We're going. I've heard all I need to know,' Cat announced abruptly, tugging Fox to his feet with her as she stood. His eyes were knowing as they met hers, and she couldn't return his gaze. Alice got to her feet gracefully with Fox's aid, a look of concern on her face. She opened her mouth to speak, but Cat shook her head pointedly. She didn't want to hear it. She didn't waste any time in crossing the grass, and turned down the street that would lead to Kentridge.

'We'd have to be mad to go in through North Gate, so East or West would be the better option,' Cat declared, determined to ignore what she had just heard about her father's new relationship.

'What kind of man is your father that they believe he'd do such things to you?' Alice asked softly.

Cat shrugged, smiling humourlessly.

'Not one you'd want to meet, I assure you. Personally, I'm surprised there's not a rumour saying he murdered me himself. It's what I always thought would happen to me.'

Alice paled, and she gave Cat a mildly horrified look.

'Don't say that, that's awful!' she protested.

Cat didn't bother pointing out that it was simply the truth.

'Keep an eye out here. Especially for anyone who looks like they're staring at me too long – I'm more likely to be recognised in these parts. I used to walk through here all the time. My house isn't too far past the walls.'

Fox nodded shortly, immediately wary, and Alice shuffled in a bit closer to both of them. Cat almost forgot to breathe when they turned a corner, only to walk straight past Thomas Gale himself. The man didn't even pause, his shoulder bumping into Fox's as he pushed past them, his stride quick. Fox was about to turn and shout after him, but Cat grabbed him and forced him forward.

He glared at her.

'Why didn't you let me have a go at him? The arrogant sod needs to learn some manners!' he exclaimed angrily.

Cat elbowed him in the gut.

'That "arrogant sod", as you so aptly put it, is Thomas Gale. He's practically royalty – you must have heard of him. Calling him out on his lack of manners is like putting a *Shoot me* sign above your head.'

Fox's eyes widened, and he glanced back over his shoulder.

'I expected him to be ... taller,' he mused. He paused suddenly, looking over at Cat. 'Didn't you say your father was going to betroth you to a Marcus Gale?'

Cat nodded, shuddering at the mention.

'Thomas's second son. He's fifteen, and one of the most

awful boys I've ever met. And I've met you,' she added, a slight smile letting him know she was teasing. Still, he feigned hurt, holding a hand to his chest as if wounded. 'But yes, that was Father's plan. As you can see, it didn't work out so well. Alice,' she called, surprising Fox at the abrupt turn in conversation. 'How willing would you be to go alone around here?'

Alice stopped, looking at her curiously.

'Alone? Why?' she asked. Cat pointed over at a small café full of women sipping tea and eating tiny sandwiches.

'Mrs Gale's housekeeper is sitting just over there, the brunette in the grey skirt and green corset over her blouse. If you could get a cup of tea and listen to some of the women, you might learn a lot. But obviously it's not the type of place to let in ruffian teenage boys,' she added with a small grin.

Alice straightened her blouse nervously. She was visibly steeling herself, and nodded, holding her head high.

'I'll meet you back at the ship,' she told them before walking off. Cat and Fox watched as she went calmly into the café, sitting at a table as if she'd done it every day for years.

Fox grinned proudly.

'The woman has guts.'

'That she does,' Cat agreed with a smile, 'but she'll be fine in there. Let's go, we don't have much time.'

She reached out, grabbing him by the arm to urge him towards a narrow alleyway.

'Time for what? Where are we going?' he asked.

'I'm taking you to the smithy. His apprentice is a blabbermouth, and he's in charge of gate maintenance. After that I have a quick errand to run.' She wasn't sure when she'd next get the chance.

'What sort of errand?' Fox's voice was suspicious, and he stopped in his tracks. 'Planning on dropping home to see your father? I'm sure if you asked nicely and married that Gale boy, he'd take you back.'

Cat smacked him across the face before he could say anything more.

'How *dare* you! When will you get it through your thick skull that I wouldn't go back for all the money in the king-dom!' she hissed, taking a step closer to him. 'I'm not going to sneak off, and I'm definitely not marrying Marcus Gale! Now, come on.'

She practically dragged him the rest of the way to the smithy.

'I'll meet you back here when I'm done,' she told him, and he raised a copper eyebrow.

'If you say so.' Huffing, Cat ignored him, turning back to sprint towards the high wall separating Greystone and Government Housing. She had to be quick, if she didn't want to be caught out.

11

It took barely any time at all for Cat to get to the tree she usually used to sneak back into her house. Fox's words were ringing in her ears as she ran; how could he possibly believe she wanted to go back to her father? Did he not know her at all? Seething with anger, she scrambled up the tree and over the wall, easily crawling through the loose fencing panel behind the bushes. Her father was supposed to be at work; she could only hope he was sticking to his schedule.

The spare key was exactly where it usually was, and as Cat didn't have a lockpick with her she dug it out from beneath the flowerpot, unlocking the door with a quiet click. The house looked strange after her time away from it, and the extravagance she had grown up with suddenly made her nauseous. Leaving her muddy boots beside the door so as not to leave footprints all over the house, she raced up the stairs, heading straight for her mother's room.

'Mother, I —' She trailed off as she pushed through the door, eyes widening. All her mother's things were there, her photographs on the shelves and her clothes in the wardrobe, but the bed was empty, the sheets turned down. Cat stepped forward, running a hand over the blanket at the foot of the bed. Where was her mother?

'Mistress Catherine.' Cat startled at the voice, whirling around to see Samuel standing in the doorway. He looked a little worse for wear, but was still functioning well. 'You have returned.'

'Not for long, Sam, and you *mustn't* tell Father I was here. I just came to pick up a few things, and have a look around. I . . . Where's Mother?'

'Mistress Elizabeth is gone,' Samuel's voice was blank, and a lump rose in Cat's throat.

'Gone? You mean . . . she's in the hospital, right? With the doctors?'

'Mistress Elizabeth is gone,' the mecha repeated. Cat didn't ask again, not sure she wanted clarification. Surely it couldn't have happened so soon. The women had said Elizabeth was on her way out, but not . . . not dead. She had to be in the hospital.

Pushing the thought away forcefully, knowing she didn't have much time, Cat set about rifling through the drawers, looking for anything helpful. Had her mother known anything about the truth of the war? She *had* been best friends with the queen; surely if Mary had confided in anyone, it would have been Elizabeth. Still, if Elizabeth Hunter had known what the government was up to, it wasn't visible in any of her possessions. She didn't keep a journal, or any sort of written account. No old letters to her best friend, just a small stack of photographs. Cat pocketed one of them, a faint smile on her face as she looked upon her five-year-old self in the arms of King Christopher,

Prince James on the floor with an arm wrapped around his father's leg. The king had been a kind man, and a fair ruler from all accounts. It was truly a shame, his disappearance.

Coming up with a frustrating lack of useful information, Cat gave up, pocketing two framed photographs and one of her mother's necklaces. With any luck, Nathaniel wouldn't notice them gone, or would assume Samuel had tidied them away somewhere.

Her next stop was her father's office, her heart pounding as she crept into the room. She wanted to ransack the entire place, look in every nook and cranny for information. But she was short on time, and Nathaniel would notice even a hair out of place in his domain. She had to leave the office exactly as she found it. Leafing carefully through piles of paper, Cat searched for some sort of record or flight plan for the Collection ships. Collection wasn't her father's area, she knew, but surely he had some sort of information on it? He had information on everything.

Surprised and dismayed to find only dull meeting reports, and expenses records for the government offices, Cat glanced up at the ornate silver clock on the wall. She wasn't willing to risk it; if her father even thought for a second that someone had been in his personal office, he'd triple security in all the government areas. They'd never get into the compound. She had stayed too long, anyway. The crew would be wondering where she was.

Still, she figured she had a few more minutes to spare, and went upstairs to her room, nudging the door open. It was exactly as she had left it, though Samuel had clearly been in to tidy. A grin on her face at being back in her bedroom, Cat crossed to dig out a leather satchel from beneath her wardrobe, throwing the wooden doors open to look at her clothes. It would be wonderful to have some clothing that hadn't previously belonged to Fox, even if she could only wear it on the ship.

All of her dresses and skirts were far too government-looking for her to even consider bringing, but she packed the few outfits she used when going out disguised as a boy, and some of her more ragged breeches and shirts. They fitted her better than Fox's clothes did. Adding some under-garments to the bag, she set about grabbing some of the more personal items which she hadn't been able to take when she'd first run away.

She packed a photograph of herself and her mother, on one of her good days, back when Cat was nine. Her mother's hair was still blonde rather than grey, and her pale cheeks were dimpled with a smile. Cat also seized some of the jewellery her mother had given to her just a few months before, knowing she would never wear it again. It was Ingate family jewellery – her mother's family – and Elizabeth had been determined that if her husband married again after her death, his new wife would never have it. A stuffed toy dog Cat had been given as a baby went into the bag, after she'd run her fingers over his floppy velveteen ears. He'd been a gift from the king and queen upon her birth, and her favourite toy throughout childhood. She just couldn't let Fox see him; the teasing would be *endless*.

With one last look around her room, eyes lingering wistfully on the tall bookcase stuffed to bursting – she would take far too long if she decided to choose only a handful of books to take with her – Cat shouldered the satchel and left, wondering if she would ever return again. She doubted it.

'Are you leaving again, Mistress Catherine?' Samuel queried, waiting for her in the hallway as she reached the bottom of the stairs.

'I'm afraid so, Sam. I am sorry I can't take you with me, but . . . I'm safe, and happy, where I am.' Safe was a relative term, but the specifics were too complicated to explain to the mecha.

'Then all is well,' Samuel replied, bowing his head with a faint creak. He needed maintenance. Cat wished she had the time to do it; storms knew Nathaniel never would.

'Goodbye, Samuel. Look . . . Look after my mother when she returns, won't you?' Cat didn't give the mecha a chance to respond, but shoved her boots back on and slipped out of the house, locking the door behind her and replacing the spare key. Within minutes she was climbing the trellis and over the wall, back on the Greystone side. Dusting off the knees of her trousers, she hitched her satchel further up her shoulder, running to see if Fox was where she'd left him. She only hoped he hadn't gone back to the ship and told the crew she'd abandoned them.

Luckily for Cat, Fox wasn't far from where she'd left him, leaning against a lamppost with his hands in his pockets.

'It's about time you showed up,' he said by way of greeting. 'I was beginning to think you'd wandered off for good. What's in that bag?'

'Just some things,' she replied evasively, tugging on his

sleeve to get him walking back in the direction of the shipyard.

'Things from where?' Fox eyed her shrewdly, realisation dawning. 'You went home, didn't you?'

'It's not home,' Cat murmured. 'Not any more.'

'I bet you told your lord father everything about us.' Cat paused, glaring at Fox as he spoke, wishing she could shout at him once more without causing a scene.

'He wasn't even *there*, if you must know! Besides, if I told him everything, I'd be in just as much trouble as you, wouldn't I?' Fox didn't seem to have an answer to that, and his silence made her grin smugly. 'I went back to get some things from my room, and snoop around my father's office. There was nothing – no mention of Collections, nothing but useless paperwork.'

'Sometimes a lack of evidence is as damning as evidence itself,' Fox said, frowning. 'He probably keeps it all hidden somewhere. If you've been sneaking about since you were a wee'un, he must've known to keep anything truly incriminating where you'd never find it.'

'You're probably on to something there,' Cat mused. 'Anyway, did you hear anything at the smithy?'

Fox grinned wolfishly, a slight spring in his step as they crossed out of government territory. 'Eventually, yes. East Gate is faulty,' he relayed. 'Apparently there was a bit of a riot out there after the last Collection, and one of the gear plates got broken. The apprentice was complaining that the replacement won't be here for two days yet.'

Cat beamed at his words, feeling hope rise in her. That made their entry *so* much easier.

As they turned a corner, a flash of silver and black caught Cat's eye, and she froze, throwing out an arm to halt Fox. A little way ahead of them, two guards walked side by side, sporting distinctive long black coats with silver adornments, a silver armband around the left bicep. Collection officers.

She felt Fox's hand grip her shoulder, and the pair of them watched silently as the two officers stepped up to the door of a crumbling brick house, knocking sharply. A woman answered, her face draining of colour immediately upon spotting the uniforms.

'She's not thirteen yet!' the woman cried, but the guards remained impassive.

'Our records state otherwise,' one of the guards replied as his partner pushed his way past the woman and into the house. Cat's heart was in her throat as the woman began to sob, shouting her protests at the two men, who ignored her, the guard at the door restraining her. It wasn't long before a second set of cries joined the woman's, and the guard reappeared with a squirming dark-haired girl in his arms. There was no way that girl was over thirteen.

'No! Please, don't take my daughter!' the woman begged, falling to her knees as the guard released her to help the other man with the girl, who was kicking and screaming. By this point, several people were watching from their own doorways, blank-faced. Collections were routine enough to not draw much attention, though there were still plenty who couldn't look away.

'We should leave,' Fox murmured quietly, hand squeezing Cat's shoulder as they watched the two guards march the girl away, leaving the mother on the floor in her doorway, sobbing into her hands. 'If the officers are about, we don't want to risk being on the streets alone.'

Tearing her eyes away from the distraught woman, Cat nodded, swallowing back the lump in her throat and following Fox as he crept towards a narrow side alley. Soon they were far enough away to no longer hear the woman's cries, but they echoed in Cat's mind the entire way back to the ship.

Back on the *Stormdancer*, they slipped straight below deck, Cat darting away to deposit her bag in her room and compose herself before meeting with Fox to head over to the galley. The three men were sitting around the table, a large blue paper spread out in front of them. Ben had a notepad on his knee, and a pen in his left hand.

'Morning! How did your little snooping trip go?' Matt asked cheerily, looking up. There was an ink smudge on his cheek.

'Rather well, actually. Although Cat's knowledge of the upper-middle class is disturbingly intimate,' Fox declared, swinging his leg over the end of the bench beside Matt, peering over the blueprint. 'And yours?'

'Equally well. We got more blueprints of the three upper levels of the main building from a friend who owes me a favour, as well as schematics for all four entrance gates. We were just wondering which one would be the easiest to go for,' he replied.

Cat sat beside Harry, and leaned forward to get a better view of the blueprint.

'East Gate,' she told them. 'Fox found out that the gears are jammed, and it's going to take at least two days for a replacement gear plate to arrive. It's practically an open door. And these blueprints will be useful, though I've been in the upper two levels and there's nothing of interest there. It's mostly offices, conference rooms and apartments for anyone working through the night. I was never allowed into the ground-floor level, so it'd be a good place to start. I know more than enough about the habits and backgrounds of the higher class government workers, though. Father always said that the best weapon is information,' she said.

'I might not agree with your father's politics, but he seems like a smart bloke. Where's Alice, anyway?' Harry asked.

'She went into the café where Mr Gale's housekeeper was having tea. Thomas Gale is a very important man – if anyone's likely to know anything about the government's plan, he will. She should be back soon,' Cat assured Harry, who didn't look too pleased at the prospect of his wife alone in Greystone.

'So when are we going to do this, then? Tonight or tomorrow? I mean, once we're in, we should be fine. It's just getting past the initial guard that's the problem,' Matt said, looking excited.

'Not tonight, they'll expect a break-in in the dark,' Fox said instantly.

'Sunday morning, between seven and nine.' The group looked up as Alice entered, smiling cheerfully. 'That's when the bulk of the guards get time off to go to worship. They'll have a skeleton guard, so it shouldn't be too hard for you boys to keep out of their way.' She sat down beside her husband, kissing him on the cheek. 'I am so very glad we weren't born upper class. No offence, dear,' she added to Cat, who laughed.

'I wish I wasn't, don't worry,' she assured Alice vehemently. 'Did you hear anything else?'

'Only that Thomas Gale is going away for a spell, apparently. His housekeeper didn't say how long for, but it's all very sudden,' Alice explained.

Cat frowned; that was unusual. Where could Gale possibly be going? Did it have anything to do with her father, and his comments about the war coming to an end?

'So we'll spend tonight preparing, and move after daybreak tomorrow?' Harry checked. The other five nodded, and Alice stood.

'I'll get started downstairs, then.'

'Cat, lass, if you've nothing else to do, Alice and I could do with a hand delivering the goods.' Harry said. It took a few moments for Cat to figure out what he meant, before remembering that the *Stormdancer* crew were smugglers at heart. The plan to overthrow the government wouldn't deter them from carrying out their essential work.

'Of course. Just let me go get changed into something more suitable.'

Heading out of the galley, she found that Fox was following her. She glared over her shoulder at the redhead, and carried on to her room. When he didn't look like he was going to continue to his own, Cat turned around, folding her arms over her chest defensively.

'Am I not allowed to change on my own, or are you afraid I'll run off in my undergarments all the way back to Greystone?' she snapped.

Fox snorted, leaning with catlike grace against the wall opposite.

'Did you miss it? Being back in your old neighbourhood?' he asked.

Cat bristled, glaring.

'No, I did *not* miss it. We've been through this! I don't appreciate you making out that I enjoyed being a government brat, because I hated every second of it, and I've never been happier than I am now I've left,' she retorted.

He didn't get angry back at her as he usually did, which surprised her. He just crossed one ankle over the other, cocking his head to one side as he looked at her.

'I didn't mean it like that. I was just curious. You seemed like you had an attachment to it, even if you didn't really enjoy living there. You are allowed to get nostalgic, you know.'

Cat's glare faltered, and she looked at him in confusion.

'What? One minute you're twisting every word I say to get me to admit liking growing up as government, now you're telling me to get nostalgic about my time there?' she asked sceptically. 'I don't understand you.'

He shrugged, scratching at his jaw – Cat could see a faint dusting of copper-coloured stubble on his chin.

'The feeling is entirely mutual,' he retorted drily. 'I'm . . . just trying to figure you out. You're not like any other highborn girl I've met.'

Cat smiled at that, trying to keep the blush off her face. She didn't succeed.

'I'll take that as a compliment, I hope.'

There was a long, awkward silence between them, until Cat suddenly blinked, snapping out of her daze.

'I need to get changed.'

Not waiting for Fox to reply, she retreated to her room, staring at herself in the mirror. Her face was red, and she looked distinctly flustered.

'Bloody boys,' she muttered to herself, pulling more appropriate clothes from her wardrobe.

The coat from her pickpocketing excursion was still slung over the chair, and she quickly rifled through the hidden pockets, pulling out the purses one by one. She frowned when her fingers touched rough paper, and let out a laugh upon pulling out the small bag of toffee squares. Storms, it felt like such a long time ago, she'd completely forgotten she'd bought them. Stowing them away in her desk drawer, she gathered up the purses and made for the lowest levels of the ship, wondering how long Harry and Alice needed her for. They had a lot of planning yet to do, if they were going to be ready to slip into the government compound during worship hours. Still, she supposed, they could hardly let down the people who were relying on the smuggled goods. The world didn't stop for them; not yet, at least.

12

Seeing the trapdoor open at the very bottom of the ship startled Cat; it was the first time she'd seen evidence of the lowest floor since she'd joined the crew. Presuming she would find Harry and Alice down there, she cradled the purses to her chest with one arm, using the other to climb down the ladder.

'I brought these with me,' she declared upon seeing her captain's hat-covered grey hair. 'Completely forgot about them until now.'

'Excellent, excellent. Blimey, lass, you did do well!' Harry cried upon seeing the fat purses, a proud look on his face that made Cat feel warm inside. 'Set them up there.' Cat nodded, reaching up to put the purses in a small crate resting on a stack of larger ones. There were a lot more crates than she'd expected, and Cat was impressed that they'd managed to smuggle so much without getting caught.

'Where do we deliver to exactly?' she queried, wondering how they were going to get everything out without arousing suspicion.

'Danley. We've got friends there who'll share it around,' Alice told her.

'Danley's a good walk away. How are we going to get everything past the checks?'

Alice smiled mischievously.

'Most of the guards are lazy, you see, and so bored with their jobs that they won't check the crate thoroughly. It's easy enough to hide things, especially since we're legally permitted to transport furs. They'll see two or three layers of furs and let us past,' she explained.

'Fair enough. Still, I don't fancy carrying these crates all the way to Danley,' Cat mused, eyeing the stacks. Most of them were big enough for her to fit inside; how was she supposed to carry them?

Harry chuckled, shaking his head at her.

'No, no, we're not carrying them. I'll rent a cart and mule from the man by the gate, like most traders,' he told her. 'Right, we're ready to start unloading.'

Cat leaned against a crate, a frown on her face as she studied the tiny trapdoor hole. Harry dealt with her confusion by fiddling with a small gear plate on the far wall. Her jaw dropped as a panel of the wall folded and slid to the side, opening up a hatch that was big enough to offload the crates.

'That's genius,' she breathed.

'That was Fox's idea,' said Harry with a grin.

'Yes, well, I suppose he has to have some half-decent ones every now and then,' she replied casually. Alice snickered, clearly picking up on how the secret hatch had gone from 'genius' to 'half-decent' in a matter of seconds.

Shifting the crates down the ramp that Harry pulled out from the floor was tiring work, but eventually they got all eight crates on to the concrete outside. Alice and Cat sat on a crate while Harry went to rent a cart. Cat watched as huge, hulking men – some even bigger than Matt – carried barrels and crates on to other, larger trade ships, tossing them about as if they weighed no more than matchboxes.

'Are we ready to get moving, then?' Harry called, jogging up with his hand gripping the reins of a dark grey, somewhat scrawny mule that didn't seem to appreciate being made to move.

'He looks a little on the skinny side – are you sure he's up for the job?' Alice asked, surveying the animal critically. Harry shrugged, manoeuvring the mule so the cart was close to the pile of crates.

'Richie says he's stronger than he looks,' he insisted, patting the mule on the withers. 'Just a little reluctant to set off at first,' he added with a frown.

Cat eyed the mule; his ribs stuck out a bit, but his shoulders looked sturdy enough and his hips were full.

'I can ride him there, if you like. I've ridden before. Horses, admittedly, but a mule can't be much different,' she said, jumping down from the crate to help Harry load it up the cart's ramp.

'Without a saddle?' Harry asked, eyebrows raised.

Cat nodded, gently running a hand down the mule's flank as he started at the sudden noise behind him.

Having hauled the crates out from the ship itself, it didn't take too much effort to then get them on to the cart. Alice and Cat waited patiently as Harry retreated back through the hatch, closing it up behind him and emerging several

155

minutes later from the trap on deck, jogging down the gangplank to join them.

'Need a hand up, lad?' Harry asked, and Cat blinked – before realising that, of course, they would have to treat her as a boy in public.

'Please,' she said, shifting to the side. With Harry's help, she swung on to the mule's back with ease. It wasn't the most comfortable thing she'd ever sat on, but it was bearable.

Harry looped the reins back over the mule's head, passing them to Cat. She dug her heels firmly into the animal's skinny sides, tugging gently with the reins to turn him in the right direction. He didn't seem too bothered by her riding him; his ears twitched lazily every now and then, his pace slow and steady. Harry and Alice walked along beside her, arm in arm.

They got to the gate and were stopped by a narrow-faced guard. His mud-brown eyes landed on her, a sneer tugging at his thin lips.

'Is your brat too lazy to walk, or just too stupid?' he remarked, looking amused at his own wit.

'The brat isn't, but the mule is,' Harry retorted. 'Sprog's just keeping him going.'

The guard glared, reaching out to the nearest crate. Cat held her breath.

'Permit?' he requested sharply, and Harry handed over a ragged-looking piece of paper, which the guard ran his eyes over, handing it back within seconds. Leaning over the side of the cart, he peered into the crate, lifting several layers of thick fur. Cat crossed her fingers, silently praying to anyone who might be listening.

She sighed almost audibly in relief when the guard let the lid drop shut again, waving them forward.

'Next!' he called, looking to a much larger cart waiting behind them.

Cat kicked the mule's sides, urging him forward, and relied on Alice for direction as they entered the city. In a few minutes they turned into an area that was unfamiliar to her, and it was only when the streets got dirtier and the buildings smaller and more rundown that she realised they were heading to Danley through the slums.

As they moved deeper and deeper into the slums, Cat gripped the mule's ragged mane. This was unknown territory to her, and as reluctant as she was to admit it, it frightened her. Several buildings were half collapsed, missing doors and windows. She nearly jumped out of her skin when she saw a shadow down a side alley, and a small boy – probably no older than six or seven – emerged. He was dirty and in ragged clothes, his arms stick thin. Harry didn't look surprised to see him, and merely patted him on his greasy head, drawing a hesitant smile from the boy before he ran off again. Before she knew it, they were being followed by a small crowd of people. Still, Harry and Alice carried on confidently, and Cat forced herself to be calm.

'We were wondering when you would turn up. You're late, old friend.' The quiet, easy voice spoke from the shadows, and Harry broke into a grin.

'We've had a few unexpected changes in circumstance, Gareth.'

As Harry spoke, a tall, thin man in a threadbare green

jumper walked towards them, embracing Harry. He nodded respectfully to Alice, leaning in to kiss her on the cheek.

'You help us more than you can imagine – a short wait is no problem.' Gareth's eyes landed on Cat atop the mule, and his white-blond eyebrows rose.

'Who's this, then?'

'One of our unexpected changes in circumstance,' Harry explained. 'Gareth, meet the newest addition to my crew, Cat. Cat, lass, this is Gareth, a good friend of ours. He's the one who's so kindly distributing our goods to those who need them.'

Cat smiled hesitantly at the man, whose eyebrows rose even higher.

'Lass? Pardon my saying so, but you don't look much like a girl,' he told her politely, and she laughed.

'That's the plan. It's easier for me to pretend to be a boy than admit to being a girl and have everyone tell me I'm incapable,' she explained.

He nodded sagely, extending a hand to her. She leaned forward to shake it.

'Sound reasoning. How did you end up flying with our Harry?'

Cat shrugged.

'I ran away from home, and stowed away on the best-looking ship in the yard,' she said. Harry let out a bark of laughter.

'You flatter me, brat,' he said. They had a lot more people following them now; evidently word spread fast. 'She's bright as a spark and pretty sneaky with her fingers – got a good haul from the courtyard.'

Gareth gave Cat an approving look.

'That's what I like to hear. Oi, Josh, hands off!' he snapped suddenly, directing a sharp look at a young boy who had climbed on the cart, a hand reaching for the lid of the smallest crate. He looked up with wide blue eyes, then hopped off, backing away hurriedly.

'Sorry about him, he's new. Orphan,' Gareth said, startling Cat with his rapid changes in demeanour. Alice frowned.

'Poor lad. Is he staying with Jess?'

Gareth nodded.

'Joined us about a week ago and he's a bit of a wild one. Rory's taken him under his wing, though, and it seems to be serving well enough.'

As Gareth spoke, they turned a corner into a small open area. The floor was dirty, cracked concrete, with a single ragged tree in the centre, and it was almost full of people. As they drew closer they were practically flooded with children; climbing the cart, jumping on Harry and Alice, some even attempting to join her on the mule, hands grasping at her trousers and boots. There was a sharp, loud whistle from Gareth, which spooked the mule into tossing his head and skittering sideways.

'Give them some space, or you'll not get a crumb,' he ordered, and every single child stepped back. Cat slipped down from the mule and stood by Harry's side.

Several strong-looking men came forward to help Harry get the larger crates unloaded, while both men and women started pulling the lids off, setting the furs back on the cart to get to the goods beneath. Gareth took the smallest crate; lifting the lid a fraction, his eyes widened.

'Bless you,' he murmured, his eyes meeting Harry's. 'All of you.'

Harry smiled, clapping the man on the shoulder.

'Cat assures me that none of the men and women in Siberene will miss the contents of their purses terribly.' He paused, frowning. 'There seem to be far more of you since last time.'

Gareth smiled sadly, looking at the assembled group. 'There's fewer jobs than there were last time you were round. More and more people these days with nowhere else to go.'

'Who's this, then?' one woman asked, patting Cat on the head.

'That's Cat, Maggie. We actually have a favour regarding her; she ran away with nothing but the clothes on her back, and all we've got to give her is Fox's old things. Don't suppose you've got any dresses some of the girls have outgrown?'

Cat jumped as a hand grasped her upper arm, pulling her to the side. She sent a wide-eyed look of alarm at Alice as she was led over to a group of women, then stood quietly while Maggie explained the situation.

'She's about as tall as my Annie was, but smaller around the chest,' one woman remarked in a way that made Cat want to cross her arms over her front.

'It's a shame she chopped her hair off, she would look lovely in pigtails,' another said, stroking a hand over her short hair. Cat shuddered inwardly at the thought of having pigtails; she hadn't had them since she was five.

Her clothes were tugged at, her arms moved up and down,

and hands roamed all over her body as they decided whether they had anything to fit her. She threw pleading glances to Alice until the older woman finally took pity on her, thanking the women for their help and taking Cat back to the cart, where people were carefully distributing the goods.

'Was that really necessary?' Cat hissed under her breath, causing Alice to shake her head in amusement. 'I picked up some clothes from home.'

'They're only trying to help. They don't think it's proper for a young woman to be wandering around in boys' clothes.'

Cat rolled her eyes; there was nothing wrong with wearing boys' clothes.

'Whereabouts in Danley are we? I don't recognise the area,' she admitted.

'Harringford. And you wouldn't recognise it, lass. I don't doubt your lord father would tan your hide were he to find out you'd been here. The people of Harringford are those who can't afford to support themselves. The sick, the poor, the elderly, the unwed mothers. They band together here, and we help them the best we can,' Alice explained quietly, her eyes darting to a young woman – barely older than Cat – with a tiny baby cradled in her arms. The child was wrapped in threadbare swaddling blankets. The mother was even scrawnier than Cat, with large purple circles under her eyes, and no shoes. Cat had heard, of course, some of the older government boys bragging; how they'd seduced a poor common girl and had their way with her, or paid for one at a brothel. She should have realised such behaviour might end in situations like this.

'It's not much, but it should do her well enough,' one of the women said, approaching them with a bundle of clothing in her arms.

Alice kissed the woman on the cheek as she took the garments.

'Thank you, ma'am,' Cat said, and the woman smiled at her.

'Just returning the favour you've done us, dear,' she replied.

Cat really didn't think she'd helped that much, and she was touched that these women owned so little, yet they were perfectly happy to give her some of what they did have.

In the distance, Cat heard four loud gongs, and her eyebrows rose; was it really four in the afternoon already? Harry looked back in the direction of the clock tower, his brows furrowed.

'We should get going, I think,' he declared, looking at the men gathered around him. 'We need to get these furs to our buyer.'

They waved him off, smiling good-naturedly. With a boost from Harry, Cat climbed back on the mule, startling the dozing animal. Several of the children raced forward from the shadows to hug the older couple goodbye; a few braver ones even waved to Cat, who smiled hesitantly and waved back.

Clicking her tongue and digging her heels in, she turned the mule and cart around and the three of them set off.

'They were nice,' Cat said quietly to Harry, who was holding the mule's reins as they walked.

Harry nodded.

'Yeah, they're a decent sort. Had a hard lot dealt to them and they're just trying to make the best of it. They'll probably benefit the most if we succeed in our ventures.' He was being purposefully vague, which she could understand; you never knew who was listening in Breningarth.

'Why's that?'

'Well, if we're correct, most of the upper classes will be in a sticky situation. The perfect time for those less fortunate to take back some control and get what they need,' he pointed out.

Cat pursed her lips, thinking about it. Of course, if they did go ahead with blowing up the main compound building, it would leave the country with no government. Everything would change.

'What were you and the men talking about, while the women were practically undressing me?' she asked.

'Be nice, Cat,' Alice chastised.

'Leave her be, love. Even I could see the lovely ladies were being a little ... overenthusiastic,' Harry said with a chuckle. 'I was letting them know to spread the word that something's going to be changing soon, and that they should be prepared.'

When they returned to the shipyard, Cat easily slipped down from the mule, and Harry clapped her on the shoulder. 'Go on in and find the boys, lass. Alice and I can finish up here.'

Cat looked at him, surprised.

'Are you sure?' she asked. 'I don't mind ...' She trailed off, but Harry smiled.

'We'll be fine, go. We'll see you at dinner,' he insisted. She sighed but relented, and hurried up the narrow gangplank and towards her bedroom. She was surprised to see Fox outside her door, looking uncomfortable.

'Oh, good, you're back,' he started, taking a step towards her. 'I, uh, thought I'd best apologise,' he said somewhat awkwardly. 'For earlier.'

Cat raised an eyebrow, edging past him to get to her room.

'Go on, then.'

To her surprise, he stepped into the room, nudging the door shut behind him.

'I'm sorry,' he said earnestly. 'I was rude. That ... wasn't my intention.'

She couldn't help but snort, looking at him incredulously.

'You seem to do a lot of things that aren't your intention, don't you?' He shifted, obviously uncomfortable, and Cat decided to take pity on him. 'You're forgiven, and I admit I overreacted a little back in Greystone. But in future, *don't* accuse me of being like them. I'm not.'

'I didn't mean it that way!' he insisted. 'I'm just trying to figure you out. And another thing ... I'm sorry about your mother too.'

She froze at his words, tensing visibly.

'What's wrong with her? If you don't mind me asking,' he added hastily.

Cat sighed, clambering on to the bed.

'I'm not sure,' she admitted. 'I don't think the doctors know either. She's been ill for as long as I can remember, getting worse the older I got. I always knew she wouldn't live long, but . . . that's the only time I regret leaving. When I think of her. She wasn't home when I went back. I think she's in the hospital.' She willed herself to believe her own words.

'I'm sorry,' Fox said again. 'I wish I could say I know how you feel. I lost my parents quickly, so it's not really the same.'

Cat was silent, expecting him to elaborate, but when he didn't, she shrugged.

'I just wish I could have had more time with her.' She swallowed the lump in her throat, and was surprised when Fox reached out, squeezing her knee for the briefest of moments.

'Maybe you will,' he replied supportively. 'You have no idea what'll happen in the future. You could get home and, well, see her off peacefully.'

Cat frowned.

'I don't know if I can go home again,' she confessed quietly. She didn't even know where home was for her any more.

'We'll see,' Fox mused, shrugging. Silence stretched between them, before he cleared his throat. 'I should, um, leave you to your evening.'

'When did it happen?' she blurted out. He looked at her, confused. 'Your parents. How . . . how old were you?'

'Nine years ago,' he replied, voice somewhat hollow. 'I had just turned eight.'

Cat's heart clenched in sympathy; she couldn't imagine being alone at such a young age.

'I . . . I'm sorry,' she murmured.

His lips quirked wryly, and he pulled the door open.

'Yeah. Me too.' He left before she could say anything, and she sat for a while, stunned. She didn't know how long it would take her, but she was determined to get to the bottom of the puzzle that was William Foxe.

13

Cat didn't spend long in her room, not wanting to dwell too much on Fox's apology. It only made her wonder what his life might had been like before the *Stormdancer*. Instead she went to the engine room, finding Matt and Ben down there working on several devices she didn't recognise.

'What are those?' she queried, startling them.

'Nothing you need to worry about just yet, lass,' Matt assured her. 'Something for when we've got plenty of proof about what the government is up to.' Cat's mind cast back to Harry saying they would need to destroy the building once they were done gathering evidence, and it clicked; they were explosives. She hadn't expected them to have so many.

'We won't need one for East Gate, will we?' she queried, dreading the kind of commotion blowing up the gate would cause.

'No, no, not at all. We went to check it while you were out in Danley, and it's well and truly done in,' Ben assured, scratching at the scar on his cheek.

'Looks like some brave sod took a sledgehammer to it,' Matt mused. 'Makes it much easier for us, I have to say.'

They were interrupted by Harry's voice crackling over the loudspeaker.

'Meeting in the galley, lads and lass. We need to figure out a plan of action for tomorrow. Also, dinner is up,' he added.

'Fantastic, I'm starved!' Matt exclaimed, and Ben snorted, helping his taller friend to his feet.

'You're always starved.'

As they walked towards the engine-room door, the side door opened and Fox emerged, purple staining his fingers and jaw, the telltale shimmering of violet tyrium dust in his hair. He nodded to them in greeting, wiping at a streak of tyrium residue on his chin.

'What do you get up to in there?' Cat queried.

'Lots of things,' he replied evasively. 'Tinkering, mostly. Keeping an eye on the secondary propeller rotors, experimenting with a few bits and bobs.'

'Fox and I should go and wash up,' Matt said, cutting in before Cat could demand a better answer. Ben and Cat carried on to the galley. When they entered, a tureen of stew sat on one end of the table, next to a plate of crusty bread and six bowls – the rest of the table was taken up by Harry's blueprints. His head was bent low, and he was alternating between marking things on the blueprints and scribbling things down in his notebook.

'Matt and Fox are just cleaning themselves up,' Ben told Alice, dropping down on to the bench. 'How's it looking?'

Cat settled beside Harry, kneeling on the bench to look at the blueprints. They'd changed a lot since she'd looked at them the day before; there were several rooms with pencil crosses through them, or little notes in messy handwriting she couldn't read. East Gate was circled, and a thick black ink line led from there to a door on the side of the main compound building.

'Pretty good. We've ruled out a fair number of the rooms on the top two floors as the more public offices, so they're off the list – it's far too dangerous. They won't likely be hiding anything there anyway.' Harry gestured with a wave towards several pages of folded blue paper that Cat assumed were the two higher floors. She knew those floors well, and Harry was right; they were busy, and not likely to be of use. 'Any lower, however, is a bit more difficult. I've heard a little bit about these, but Cat was never allowed in. If the government is hiding anything, it'll be there.'

She frowned, leaning over to take the pencil from Harry, trying to visualise things.

'These two are out,' she murmured, crossing through two rooms. 'They're the stairwells down from the upper level, if I remember correctly. And all these over here are far too close to North Gate to risk investigating – they'll be full of people.'

Fox and Matt entered, and Alice started ladling thick stew into the bowls.

'Put those away would you, love? At least while you're eating,' she said to her husband, who nodded, folding the blueprints away.

Alice slid the plate of bread into the centre of the table, and Fox, sitting down next to Cat, reached past her unceremoniously, grabbing the nearest hunk of bread. Cat shot him a look, which was ignored, and she sighed, reaching for her own bread.

'So how are we doing this, then?' she asked, swallowing a mouthful of delicious hot stew.

'Explosive canisters are sorted,' Ben piped up, his grin barely restrained at the thought of being allowed to cause large explosions. 'We'll take a look at the blueprints in a bit, figure out where to put the canisters to cause maximum damage.'

'Could you save the talk of explosives until after we've eaten, please?' Alice sighed, causing Cat, Fox and Matt to snigger in unison.

'What happens if we get caught?' Cat asked. This was all suddenly becoming very real. Matt paused, looking at her as if he hadn't even contemplated the prospect.

'We die,' Fox said simply.

Alice gasped, looking at him aghast.

'William!' she exclaimed. 'There's no need for that!'

'What? I'm only being honest. If we get caught, do you really think they'll let us trot home after a slap on the wrist? They've killed people for less,' Fox pointed out bluntly.

Cat winced; he had a point.

'He's right, love,' Harry piped up reluctantly, patting her hand. 'It's a risky business. But we have a chance to try and we'll keep our wits about us. Would you really want to leave things as they are? There'll be no sprogs left within a decade if we do.'

Alice's expression was unreadable, and she tugged at a stray curl that had come loose from her bun, before eventually nodding.

'I . . . I suppose you're right,' she admitted with a sigh. 'I just don't like the thought of everything going so wrong.'

Harry wrapped an arm around her, pulling her close to his side. Cat bit her lip, wishing she hadn't brought up the subject, and nearly fell off the bench in shock when fingers brushed the back of her hand. Looking down at her lap, she followed the arm up to Fox's face. He was determinedly staring into his stew, even as his hand closed around hers, squeezing it gently in reassurance. The hand left almost as suddenly as it had arrived, and her eyes stayed fixed on Fox's face for a long moment, waiting for him to turn and look at her. Eventually, he did, and their eyes met; his surprised and guilty, hers simply confused.

They were all silent and contemplative as they ate. When the bowls and plates were cleared away, Harry spread out the blueprints once more.

Matt and Ben had their heads together as their eyes scoured the paper, Ben marking points with little crosses. They passed the pencil between them without any words, working as one person rather than two.

'There,' they murmured in unison, not seeming to realise they had done so.

'That should wipe out the majority of the building with only nine canisters. I can't say for sure. I don't know how deep it goes down. If we're sending someone in, it might be best to have them plant a few more on the inside, just to be safe,' Ben said.

Matt slipped the pencil from his friend's fingers, circling a small outbuilding on the map, which had a cross drawn against one wall.

'That is the newscast centre. That's where we can contact the foreign authorities, so we'll need to get in there before we send it up in flames. Fox, we'll need your hacking skills for that.'

'Doable,' Fox assured them. 'If it's anything like East Gate, it shouldn't take more than five minutes. Ten if I'm having a particularly difficult day.'

Cat half smiled, knowing that Fox could quite possibly hack whatever locks they had in a matter of seconds, let alone minutes.

'Not just the foreign authorities,' she cut in quickly. Her brain was racing. 'If there were a way to film whatever was going on inside the compound ... we could broadcast it to the entire country, if we kept the government out of the loop. Maybe the whole world. Anglya, Siberene, Erova, Mericus, Dalivia, Kasem, they all need to know. The last two might not be able to help, but ... Father told me once that when Anglya ruled the six kingdoms, the newscasts shown here were broadcast across the entire world, with constant stationary skyships acting as relay towers. I don't think those skyships were ever moved, even after the war began. Fox, how hard would it be to hijack the signal and take advantage of those?'

Despite Matt being the engineer, she knew Fox was the real mechanical genius on this ship. She'd seen him fashion a working miniature skyship out of a few scraps of metal and a half-melted gear plate.

His blue eyes narrowed in thought, and Cat could practically hear his brain whirring.

'Presuming they're arrogant prats who assume that no one could ever hack their locks, once we get in it should be wide open. Then it's just a matter of dismantling whatever protections they've set up against broadcasting world-wide ... I can handle it. Matt, you'll need to help me, though,' he admitted.

Matt nodded.

'Not a problem. And, Cat, don't you worry about filming evidence. Fox here has it all covered, don't you, Foxy?' he said with a grin, clapping him on the shoulder.

'Completely. And *don't* call me Foxy,' he snapped.

'There's just one question, then,' Harry said, a grave look on his face as he eyed his crew carefully. 'Which one of us is going in with Fox?'

Cat bit her lip, steeling herself.

'I am,' she announced.

'Absolutely not,' Fox retorted, turning to look at her. 'I – we're not risking you in there. You're too young.'

Cat huffed.

'Who else will likely recognise every man in that compound? You said it yourself – my knowledge of the government is disturbingly good. I can identify every person involved in whatever we find, and tell you who you'll be wasting your time following. I might not have accessed all the levels, but I've been sneaking around that building since I was old enough to walk! I know what I'm doing. Face it, Fox, you need me. Besides, this was my idea, and I'm not going to sit on the sidelines like a good little girl and let you have all the fun.'

'Fun?' Fox scoffed, rolling his eyes. 'You think risking our lives like this will be fun? Admittedly, you have inside knowledge, but Matt and I can manage just fine,' he retorted.

173

'Matt? Can you really see *Matt* managing to sneak around a top secret government compound? No offence, Matt, but you're hardly built for stealth,' Cat added with an apologetic glance.

Matt shrugged, smiling ruefully.

'She has a point,' he said to Fox, whose scowl deepened. 'Admit it, Fox, if she was a boy, you'd let her go. She knows what she's doing, and she's a darn sight better at going unnoticed than I would be. Stop being so bloody overprotective and give the girl a chance.'

'I won't be responsible for her,' Fox argued.

'I'll be responsible for myself, thanks,' she snapped. 'So that's it, – me and Fox.'

'I'd better go and prepare, then,' Fox declared, getting up.

Cat looked at him inquisitively.

'Prepare what?' she queried, and he stared at her for a long moment before sighing.

'Come on,' he muttered, gesturing for her to follow.

She grinned, bouncing up from her seat and following Fox out into the corridor. Her eyebrows rose when they walked past his bedroom door.

'Do I finally get to see what's in this mysterious room of yours?' she asked, as they reached the manhole. He shrugged, dropping down without using the ladder. Huffing in frustration, she jumped down behind him.

Fox pulled open the engine-room door and turned left. Cat couldn't help but grin as he pulled a key from his pocket and unlocked the mystery door.

He slipped inside and she followed tentatively. It was dark, with two low gas lamps in the furthest corners, a long workbench between them. Almost every inch of wall space was either covered by shelves, or had papers pinned up, all with drawings and blueprints on them. The shelves were full of boxes, and on the workbench sat a half-finished piece of machinery, while next to it a soldering iron leaned on its stand.

'Impressive,' Cat murmured, eyes wide. She yearned to study the schematics on the walls in more detail, but Fox was reaching up for a box on the highest shelf, his shirt riding up to expose a slim strip of pale flesh above the waistband of his trousers.

Cat felt a flutter in her stomach, and her cheeks grew warm.

The box slid off its shelf and into Fox's arms. He quickly lowered it to the floor with a thud.

'So what have you got in here, then?' she asked.

'Bits and pieces. I like to tinker,' he said quietly.

Cat peered at the object on the workbench, running a gentle finger over a delicate gear plate, one of the chains still hanging loose, as thin as a thread of silk.

'This is from a mecha,' she realised in surprise. She remembered having to repair the tiny gear plate several times after her father had lost his temper and lashed out at Samuel. It was part of a brain – the part that helped register images. But she couldn't see the thin, dark green film that usually accompanied the part. 'Where did you get it from?'

'Found a couple of broken ones in a rubbish cart just outside of government. How did you know?'

Cat shrugged.

'My family had a mecha, back home. Have – he's still there. Father was rather ... careless with him at times. I often repaired him,' she explained.

Fox had an amused look in his eyes.

'Ever the little gearhead, hmm?' he teased lightly.

'It was interesting. They're very complex machines, to have some semblance of intelligence and understanding,' she said.

Fox nodded, moving closer. He stood over her shoulder, leaning forward to point out a few things on the half-finished machine on the desk.

'Look and see what you can recognise. Figure out what it is,' he challenged.

Determined to pass his test, she turned back to the workbench to study the mechanisms closer. She recognised many basic components; they could have come from a mecha, but also from a delicate clock or something with equally small gear plates. Brow furrowing in concentration, she grinned triumphantly as she spotted the one piece that gave the game away. Then she gasped, realising exactly what Fox had built.

'That shouldn't be possible,' she breathed. 'You've built a video recorder. But ... it's so tiny!'

She'd seen a video recorder when a newscast team had come to their house, and her father had filmed newscasts in his office from behind his desk. The recorders they'd brought were huge, clunky things. Two people had been needed to carry one of those, whereas Fox's device could be worn quite easily on a jacket collar, the small lens peeping through a buttonhole. It would never even be noticed.

'This is amazing. How on Tellus . . . ?' She trailed off.

Fox's hand reached out to cover hers on the machine, his index finger pointing to the lens and its backing mechanism.

'That right there, that's the lens in a mecha's eye which allows them to "see" their surroundings and temporarily imprint the images on a dalivinite film, lasting long enough for the mecha to do its job, but without saving the images. If you adjust it to use the tyrium dalivinite film developed for newscasts, stored in here,' he gestured to a small metal box set aside, about the size of Cat's palm, with a hole in one end, 'it'll save the images permanently, so the film canister can then be inserted in the broadcasting machines over in the newscast building.'

Cat was gawping and she knew it, but she couldn't help herself.

'That's genius! You're a genius, Fox,' she insisted, bringing the faintest of red flushes to his freckled cheeks. He looked away, shrugging. 'But . . . there's no sound?' she asked.

He knelt by the box he'd just pulled down. Cat swivelled round in her chair to face him, curious. He neatly set aside the multitude of spare parts in the box and pulled out a device even smaller than the video recorder.

'You didn't think I'd dismantle a mecha and leave the ears in, did you?' he asked wryly.

She looked at him in confusion; mechas didn't have ears.

'Not literal ears,' he added. 'But the mechanism that allows them to process sound. I ripped that out, modified it a little, set it to store on a permanent yelenium core, and there you go. Audio recording device.'

He passed it to her carefully, and she cupped it in her hands, bringing it up to eye level. The thin strands of orange yelenium that made up the core were encased in metal-framed glass, buzzing with little violet sparks, stretched out between two strips of metal like a harp.

'I've been working on them for a while – weeks before you showed up. It's rather clever, really. The yelenium is so sensitive, the vibrations from sound create little ridges in it, so it remembers the pattern. If you make it a little thicker than usual, the ridges don't stretch, and you can replay the sound back by letting a little wire brush over the ridges,' he explained. He reached over, twisting the device so the small microphone pointed upwards, then ran a finger down one side of the casing until he came across a switch.

'Say something,' he murmured, flicking the tiny switch.

Cat bit her lip, glancing up to meet Fox's vibrant blue eyes, which seemed almost to glow in the dim lighting.

'This is brilliant,' she said, somewhat awkwardly.

Fox smirked, flicking the switch in the other direction. There was a speedy whirring of the few exposed gears, before Cat heard her own voice, somewhat tinny, but recognisable.

'OK, I'm impressed now. I can't believe you made all these yourself. You'd make a fortune selling them!' she breathed.

Fox raised an eyebrow.

'Then I wouldn't have the advantage in spying on government scum, would I?' he retorted. 'Besides, they're already being made outside of Anglya. I got my idea from something similar I saw in a shop in Siberene. The problem with isolating yourself so completely from the rest of the world is that you don't get to share in their advances. Did you know that in Mericus even the common people have newscast screens in their homes? Not just the aristocracy. Apparently they're thinking about using them for things other than news.'

'What else could they use them for?' Cat asked in confusion, and Fox grinned.

'Education, entertainment, all sorts of things. Think about it. If they can record news, why can't they record a professor giving a lecture, or a performer doing a show?' he pointed out.

Cat imagined being able to watch a performer on her newscast screen; it would be wonderful!

'It's a shame it isn't like that here,' she sighed.

Fox shrugged.

'Not yet it's not, but if we succeed it could well be. We'll open up communications with the rest of the world, and they'll probably be happy to bring us up to date. They really don't hate us as much as the government likes to make out. They hate our government, and they're bitter, but they don't hate Anglya itself. They did originate here, after all.'

'Yeah, several hundred years ago.'

'Still, they respect the First Men, and the country they came from. If we succeed, we'll be welcomed back with open arms, I'm sure of it.' His eyes were intense and serious, and his expression sent a shiver down Cat's spine. 'I want you to be careful,' he murmured, drawing closer. 'Worry about yourself. If at any point it looks like you're about to get caught, run and don't look back. I can handle myself, and I don't want you putting yourself in danger for me,' he chuckled humourlessly. 'I'm not worth you getting caught.'

'I'd rather us both get caught and go down together than for you to get caught and me run,' she argued.

He scowled, shaking his head firmly.

'I don't want you getting caught, Cat,' he insisted. 'Please, just promise me you'll be careful.'

Cat folded her arms across her chest indignantly.

'You don't need to protect me, you know. Anyway, you've made it very clear recently that you'd be happier on this ship without me here to disrupt things,' she replied.

He winced.

'I never said that,' he began, and she rolled her eyes.

'You never had to.'

Fox sighed, turning away from her, and Cat got the feeling that they had just taken two steps forward and about thirty in reverse; a feeling that was becoming increasingly common with the enigma that was William Foxe.

'I'll be careful. But I'm not going to leave you behind.'

The answer didn't seem to satisfy him, but quite frankly Cat didn't care. Turning on her heel, she left. She was tired of arguing.

14

The thick soles of her boots were almost soundless on the floor as she walked through the narrow halls of the skyship. Pacing the corridors was better than sitting in her room, waiting for breakfast. She'd been tossing and turning all night, and by half past four she'd given up on getting any real sleep.

She paused in the pale blue-grey light filtering in through the small portholes and sat on the edge of the manhole, her legs dangling down to the floor below.

'Happy birthday to me,' she sighed, somewhat wistful.

It had been a week and a half since she'd stowed away and she was, as of three o'clock that morning, fifteen years old. She didn't feel it; at times she felt ancient, and at others – usually when Fox was around – she felt like an awkward, stuttering twelve-year-old, trying to make sense of those around her, jumping head first into waters far deeper than she could handle.

'That you, Cat?'

She blinked, peering down the manhole, smiling when she saw Ben at the foot of the ladder.

'Morning,' she greeted him.

'Good morning, lass. Many happy returns,' Ben replied. 'Come here, I've got something for you.'

Intrigued, Cat dropped down, following Ben around to the corridor where the rest of the crew slept. Ben pushed open a door, beckoning her closer. She hesitantly peered inside. Ben's room was neat, with a few drawings pinned to the walls, all of different places in the world; some she recognised, some she didn't.

'These are beautiful,' she murmured.

'Why, thank you. I drew them.'

Her eyebrows rose in surprise.

He smiled sheepishly, tugging at a stray curl.

'I didn't have many friends as a sprog – except Matt, of course. I spent a lot of my time alone, drawing. Come here.' He gestured for her to enter, and she did so, watching him pull a brown paper bag from his desk drawer. He pressed it into her hands, smiling.

'I know I said I'd get Alice to bake you a cake, but in all the chaos it completely slipped my mind. So Matt and I got you this instead.'

Reaching into the bag, Cat's face split into a wide grin as she pulled out a large cupcake, bigger than her fist, with raisins dotting the golden sponge. It had purple icing, and a slightly lopsided *15* iced in silver.

'It's not much, but I hope you like it.'

Cat beamed, hugging him tightly around the waist, careful not to drop her cake.

'It's the best,' she declared. Her father had always bought her dresses and jewellery and perfumes on her birthday but she'd not had a present she actually enjoyed since she was young, when her mother had been well enough to buy them. 'Thank you, and Matt.'

'You're very welcome. Happy birthday, lass. Almost a grown woman now,' he teased, making her blush.

'D'you think I could have this now, or should I save it for after breakfast?'

Ben chuckled, ruffling her hair.

'Eat it now. I'll see you at breakfast.'

Leaving the pilot's room, she cradled the cupcake carefully in her hands, taking a bite as she rounded the corner and humming in contentment. It was delicious. Her next bite was far bigger, and she was so engrossed in the treat she didn't notice Fox standing in her bedroom doorway.

'There you are!' he exclaimed, startling her. 'Hurry up, we need to get moving. Where did you get that cupcake?'

'Ben gave it to me,' she replied, somewhat defensive. 'It's my birthday.'

He blinked, startled.

'Oh. Happy birthday. Get changed – you'll need darker clothes than that.'

She sighed, barging past him to get to her room, not expecting him to follow. She set her half-eaten cupcake on her desk and pulled her long-sleeved shirt over her head, standing in just her undershirt, whipping around when she heard a yelp.

'Storms, girl, at least wait until I'm gone before you start prancing about in your undergarments!' Fox exclaimed, squeezing his eyes shut.

'Well, wait outside, then,' she snapped, throwing open her wardrobe. She dressed quickly, taking her cake with her, and left her room only to find the corridor empty, and the galley silent. She stood there frowning – until the smell of the city caught her nose. Taking a large bite of cake, she went down the other end of the corridor, peering up through the manhole. It was lighter than it should have been up there; the trap topside was open. Hurrying up the ladder and continuing up on deck, cupcake cradled carefully, she wasn't too surprised to see Fox climbing up the rigging to sit on the boom. She climbed up behind him, and he didn't seem shocked when she shuffled out beside him.

The two sat in silence for several long minutes, Cat finishing off her cake and watching the sun rise over the city. When it became clear that Fox wouldn't be starting the conversation, she spoke.

'What's your problem with the government, anyway? I mean, besides the obvious.' Everyone hated the government, but Fox seemed to have a particular loathing. He remained silent, and Cat was about to give up and leave him to it when he spoke.

'I used to live in Marleytown when my parents were alive,' he told her, head turned in the direction of Marleytown itself.

Cat looked at him in shock; Marleytown was a fairly well-off middle-class area near Greystone, and Fox definitely didn't seem like the type. 'We had to scrimp a little, but we earned enough to get by and keep our house. When I was eight, Dad's workshop in the basement caught fire, and our whole house went up in flames. Everyone assumed I'd been in there with them, and I let them – it was better than being taken into government care. They weren't Collecting,

184

then, but there were a fair number of orphan kids disappearing. I don't think the monarchs knew about it. They were too caught up in the war, and it was only a year or so before they too disappeared. If they'd known, I'm sure they would have stopped it. Shame, really. If they hadn't gone, none of this would have happened. The king wouldn't have stood for it.'

Cat stared at him, listening intently. Was Fox actually opening up to her?

'I lived in the slums for three years – nearly got Collected a few times – but the people in Danley helped out a lot. I saw a lot of things happen in those three years, things that taught me how cruel and heartless the government really is. Once I saw three government boys beat a fifteen-year-old girl to death because one of them had got her pregnant, and she wanted some money to help take care of the baby. They left her there, in the street, just . . . bleeding to death. I was nine and . . . and I couldn't do anything, though storms know I tried.' Cat was silent, horrified, but Fox wasn't looking at her; he was staring out over the city with a look of disgust. 'I expected to be there forever, but then one day I was wandering around the shipyard and Harry found me.' He smiled bitterly, fiddling with a brass button on his coat. 'Things have been great ever since. Then . . . then you turned up. I thought you were like me at first. An orphan. No home, no parents, no one to miss you when you left.' He let out a hollow chuckle. 'Look how wrong I was. You were a spoiled little princess, protected from the cold, harsh world and given everything you could ask for, and plenty you didn't. It was hard not to hate you at least a little after that.'

Cat glared at him, half tempted to push him off the boom.

'Don't assume things about me just because of my name, and my birth status; we *spoiled little princesses* are allowed to have terrible childhoods too. You have no right to judge me by how you think I grew up, because I assure you, it definitely wasn't as glamorous as you're imagining.' Her voice was quiet, but hard. He *knew* her life hadn't been sunshine and roses before, so why did he continue to act like it had?

Annoyed, she swung her leg over the boom and jumped straight to the deck. Wrapping her coat around her against the early morning chill, she descended the trap, deciding to leave Fox to himself.

'There you are, sprog!' Matt's cheerful voice called as she walked past the open galley door, and she stopped, doubling back.

Matt, Harry and Ben were all in the galley with Alice, all three men dressed in black and looking serious. Trying to wipe the scowl off her face, she joined them, eyeing the mass of devices piled on the table, next to satchels for her and Fox. She recognised Fox's audio and video recorders, and the rest seemed to be Ben's explosive devices. He had one in his hand, and was patting it fondly.

'Where's our dear little thundercloud, then?'

Cat's scowl returned.

'On deck, being a pillock,' she muttered darkly.

Harry let out a low whistle.

'That is definitely not a happy face,' he murmured, frowning, and Cat snorted, despite herself.

'Blame Mr Thundercloud,' she retorted.

186

'He'll be down soon – with less of an attitude problem, I hope,' Matt assured her. 'Happy birthday, by the way.'

Cat smiled, hugging him briefly.

'Thanks. I just want to get everything over with. The sooner we get this done, the sooner things will change.'

Ben smiled at her from across the table.

'We'll be coming with you past the gate, but you're on your own after that. Mattie wants to have a look in the newscast building, see what kind of set-up they've got in there. We won't plant the canisters yet, as we don't know how long you'll be in there,' he explained.

The door opened, and a sour-faced Fox walked in; Cat thought the thundercloud nickname was rather apt. He didn't look at her; just sat on the end of the bench furthest away from her.

'We ready to go, then?' he asked, his gaze firmly on Harry.

'In a minute, lad, be patient,' Harry told him, looking around the table at his assembled crew.

'East Gate will barely be guarded from seven until nine today for worship, and then every day at one in the afternoon until half past two when they break for lunch. And, of course, they'll be on a skeleton guard during the night shift. One of us will be round the gate area every day at lunch break, just in case you need us,' he said to Fox and Cat, who nodded. 'Try and get as much recorded evidence as you can – but don't do anything stupid. Like Cat said, the sooner this is over the better. Mattie, give us a hand wiring these two up, would you?' he requested, getting to his feet and picking up one of the audio recorders, prompting Cat to stand up.

'Hold still, lass,' Harry murmured, reaching to fix the recorder to the inside of her leather waistcoat, the microphone hidden but unobstructed at the base of her starched shirt collar. She reached up, gingerly feeling for the switch, checking where it was so she didn't fumble for it when she actually needed to turn it on.

'I've packed some non-perishable food for you both in the satchels,' Alice informed them, passing the two leather bags over to them. 'Try and make it last.' She hugged them tightly, patting Fox's cheek. 'Stay safe. I'll see you both soon.' There was only a slight waver in her voice, betraying the very real possibility that she might never see them again.

Harry reached for a video recorder, while Matt secured Fox's audio recorder and Ben slipped one in his satchel just in case. When the pair of them were wired up, with the video recorder's film canister safely in the inside pocket of Cat's waistcoat, they pulled their coats back on and left the galley, all five of them heading up to the deck.

Ben reached out from behind Cat, squeezing her shoulders comfortingly, thumbs hooking through the epaulettes on her coat.

'Just trust yourself, and as hard as it sounds, trust Fox,' he said, his voice quiet in her ear.

She gave him a sceptical look, and he returned it with a lopsided smile.

'I know, I know. But I don't think you realise just how much you get under his skin.'

She snorted quietly to herself; *that* probably wasn't a good thing.

Climbing up on deck for the second time that morning, Cat squinted in the early morning light, and followed her companions down the lowered gangplank. The shipyard was, for once, almost empty. Even the guards were dozing in their glass-fronted office, allowing people to come and go as they pleased. There were a few people taking advantage of the early hour, loading up their ships ready to leave or slipping into the city. Their little group went, for the most part, unnoticed.

They stuck to the grimy back alleys as often as they could; the city was beginning to wake, people readying themselves for worship, and the main temple was right in the centre, nearest South Gate, the intricate steel spire visible from just about everywhere in the city. They would have to be careful, time things perfectly; if they arrived too soon, the guards would still be in place and their efforts would be wasted. Pulling her coat sleeves down over her hands to keep her fingers warm, Cat hurried along after Fox and Harry, with Ben close behind her.

When they reached the street that passed close to East Gate, Cat crept forward to check it was deserted, cursing under her breath when she saw a single guard leaning up against the solid steel wall of the obviously faulty gate, which had a steel rope looped around the handles to hold it together. A shallow ditch at its base, the wall was a good ten feet tall and circled the entire government district. Despite that, the government compound was easily visible behind it, the largest building in Breningarth. The entire building was unnecessarily ornate, the dark brickwork carved into patterns and water-dragons by expert hands and only slightly weathered by storms. She couldn't help but eye the rows of windows suspiciously, wondering if there was anyone looking out of them. She prayed to the gods that the place was deserted. She couldn't think of anyone in government who would be caught dead missing Sunday worship. Luckily, East Gate was like the other three entrances to the government district, in that there was hardly any housing nearby; no one wanted to live close enough to be caught up in government affairs, so there were no residents around to see them creeping about.

Sneaking back to the crew, she told them about the guard.

'Leave it to me,' said Matt, reaching into Ben's satchel without hesitation, and pulling out an unlabelled glass bottle and a rag. This earned him confused looks from the rest of the crew – even Ben – who were too perplexed to stop him when he rounded the corner, not even bothering to hide himself.

'Sir, I'm going to have to ask you to turn around and leave,' the guard called out, making Fox jump.

'Don't be so hasty there, friend,' Matt replied cheerily.

The rest of the conversation was too quiet for Cat to hear, until a muffled thump startled her into peering round the corner. Matt was standing with the bottle and rag in his hand, staring down at the unconscious guard at his feet.

'You can come out now,' he told them.

They all rounded the corner as Matt slipped the bottle and rag into his coat pocket then hoisted the guard over his shoulder as effortlessly as if the man weighed the same as Cat.

'Where in the gods did you get that from?' Fox asked, sounding both impressed and disturbed.

'That would be telling,' Matt replied, tapping the side of his nose. He sneezed, frowning. 'Still on my fingers. That tickles.'

'Can we hurry this up, please?' Harry prompted.

Matt saluted mockingly, dumping the unconscious guard unceremoniously in the ditch surrounding the walls of the compound. In wetter weather, the ditch would be filled with water, but right now it was just frozen mud. Fox strode forward and headed straight for the gate to deal with the steel rope. Cat peered into the ditch at the uniformed man slumped in the mud.

'Are we just going to . . . leave him there?' she asked.

Matt shrugged.

'Why not? If he raises the alarm when he wakes up, who's going to believe his story? They'll just think he's still drunk from last night.'

'Done,' Fox called a few moments later, pushing the gate ajar.

'You took your time,' Ben remarked.

'I've wired a loop into the secondary lock, opening both of them just by opening the secondary. It'll be easier than trying to wrestle with that primary lock after it's fixed,' Fox explained.

One by one, they followed Fox into the government compound. Cat had never been in via the east side before; she had only ever entered through North Gate near her house and where all the higher members of government had offices. Going by the blueprints, they were close to the newscast building, and there would be an entry door to the government building in an alcove round the corner to their left.

191

'This is where we leave you, then,' Harry declared reluctantly, glancing up at the imposing structure.

Cat swallowed the lump in her throat, knowing that if things went badly, it could be the last time she saw the three men who had become such close friends. She rushed forward, wrapping her arms around Matt's waist and burying her face in the soft fabric of his coat.

'Be careful,' she told him, turning to direct her statement at Ben and Harry too.

Matt hugged her back tightly.

'You too, girlie. Trust each other, and don't take risks. We'd rather have you out alive than have all the information in the world.'

She nodded, releasing him to hug Ben.

'Fox will look after you. Even if he makes you want to throttle him at times,' he whispered into her ear.

'And Matt will look after you. As always,' she replied.

Ben nodded back at her.

'That he will.'

She moved to hug Harry, who kissed the top of her head in a fatherly manner that almost had tears welling in her eyes.

'If this doesn't work out, thank you for everything,' she told him sincerely.

He smiled back, clapping her shoulder.

'It will, but you're welcome, anyway. Now, get going before someone comes.'

15

As soon as they found the alcove, Fox knelt by the security-locked door, flipping the panel and pulling a pair of pliers from his coat pocket.

Cat kept watch as Fox worked; she was expecting guards to pass by on their rounds at any moment. Finally, she heard a loud click, and the door swung inwards, revealing a long, empty corridor. Slipping inside, Fox closed the door behind them. There were three branches to the corridor where they stood: left, right and forward.

'Which way?' Cat whispered.

Fox shrugged, pointing left.

'Why?'

'No reason, just feels like left is a good way to go,' he replied with a wry smile.

'Left it is, then.'

Cat had never been so pleased to see the pretentious architecture and decoration; the deep, shaded alcoves set every few feet down the hallway were invaluable for hiding from the occasional person going from room to room. Obviously not everyone had been allowed to leave for worship. The walls were painted a deep purple above the wooden panels which covered the bottom half, and wrought silver lamps lit the way, the thin flames causing flickering shadows to dance across the walls and floor. As they walked further and further, sticking to the shadows and staying near silent, Fox was both impressed and disgusted at Cat's continued ability to identify the majority of people who passed them while they were safely concealed in alcoves.

'How on Tellus do you know these people? Surely your father didn't meet *all* of them?' he queried in a hushed tone. Cat shrugged.

'He was a very busy man,' she replied. 'And some of them live in our square,' she added.

Fox shuddered at the thought of living in the same area as such pompous bastards, and asked her how she stood it.

'I didn't exactly have much of a choice,' she pointed out drily, before pressing a finger to her lips as they passed a door. He looked at her quizzically as she crept closer, crouching low to press her ear to the gap beneath the door. They heard strains of conversation, mostly complaints about long working hours.

'Boss said we need more for one last push, but I don't see where we'll get them from. I know we're running out of test subjects, but the Collections have taken just about every thirteen-year-old to be found,' one man muttered in irritation. She quickly reached inside her coat, flicking the switch on the audio recorder in her waistcoat. 'We can't start taking first-borns, or there'll be hell to pay.'

'What boss says, boss gets, though,' another man replied grumpily. 'Maybe we'll have to start taking them younger. If they carry on with all that war effort tripe people will practically give their kids away to fight for their country.'

Cat's eyes widened, meeting Fox's. *Test subjects?*

'Not like he has anything to worry about now, is it? Nor me, for that matter, I never had any brats of my own.'

The man's companion guffawed loudly.

'That's 'cause you can't get a woman!' he jeered, earning a growl from the first man.

'Like you're any better,' he retorted. 'Still, I'll have to have a chat with Caden about it, tell him what boss said about needing more. He's bound to have a few ready to be brought in. If not, we can always clear out Miss Kasey's. Susie was saying how Miss Kasey was complaining about being short for cash with all those kids – she probably wouldn't mind us taking the runts off her hands.'

Cat gasped silently in horror. The truth was that Miss Kasey never said anything but kind words about her children. The poor woman had probably been fighting tooth and nail to stop the government taking them all.

'That might work. At least Johnno cleared up a little space, sending the successful experiments for further modification. We should be able to spread the current batch out a bit more, get a new lot in from the country. And it's freed up some of the equipment,' the second man said, sounding pleased.

'Yeah, Alex wanted to move the ones in Lab Seven over to Lab Sixteen this afternoon. We should probably finish up here before shift switches, or Trent will be complaining again.'

'Bloody Trent,' the second man muttered darkly. 'Him and his smarmy face and fancy suits, thinking he's better than us just because he's cosy with the Jacksons.'

Cat bit her lip, leaning down to whisper both into the microphone and to Fox, who was eyeing her curiously.

'Jackson family, of Haybury, secondary heirs to the Portland fortune through Mrs Jackson. Riley Trent, Connor Jackson's friend and business partner,' she muttered quickly, flicking the recorder off when she noticed the men had gone silent. She and Fox retreated to the nearest alcove, Cat letting out a breath she hadn't been aware she was holding.

'They're testing something on the kids,' Fox murmured.

Cat nodded, shuddering at the thought.

'Doesn't surprise me that Trent is involved, and probably Jackson too. Connor Jackson hates kids – his wife is barren, so he's lost any chance of inheriting her family's fortune if her older brother dies childless. It'll go straight to her younger brother, George,' she explained.

'Serves the bastard right,' he said angrily. 'Shall we get moving, then?'

Cat nodded, letting Fox lead the way to the end of the corridor. He stopped, causing her to run into his back. She swerved round him to see what had caused the sudden halt. Her jaw dropped; right in front of them was a seemingly endless spiral staircase, flattening out every few feet down to lead off to another corridor. Cat couldn't see how many floors it led to; she lost count after it went pitch-black at six.

'Bloody hell,' she breathed, stunned. This definitely hadn't been on any blueprints she'd ever seen, nor had she come across it during visits with her father.

Fox slipped his watch from his pocket, flipping the cover open.

'It's about to get busy in here,' he declared. 'How about we head a little lower?'

'We'll have to do it quickly,' Cat reasoned, biting her lip. 'All the way to the bottom?'

Fox nodded, and with a deep breath the pair of them started to run. He began practically flying down the staircase. Cat followed him, trying not to trip over her own feet. Fox's footsteps were almost noiseless, which surprised Cat; it was a metal staircase, and she was finding it difficult not to make a racket. They raced to the bottom, adrenalin pumping furiously, and Fox nearly hit the wall when he finally reached the end, stopping abruptly and turning to catch Cat before she could run into him. She landed in his arms with a soft thud, finding herself squashed against his chest.

'Sorry,' she mumbled, embarrassed.

'No harm done,' he said lightly, releasing her and turning to look around. The bottom floor turned out to be a small, round room, with just one door. Cat stared upwards, gulping at the expanse of blackness.

'We must be almost a hundred feet under the city,' she breathed. 'What could possibly be so important that they'd dig this far down?'

'Only one way to find out,' Fox replied. He knelt down to examine the lock of the door, sucking his bottom lip between his teeth. 'Bloody hell, this is some pretty intense lock work.' He swore softly, twisting to reach into his bag.

Cat moved closer, eyeing the lock over his shoulder. She couldn't make head nor tail of it, and it impressed her that Fox could. He pulled a small metal box from the bag, which

197

he opened to reveal several fine-tipped tools. He picked out a tiny screwdriver and set to work on the lock. Cat leaned back against the wall beside the door, letting him work in peace, trying not to panic. Someone could come down and find them at any moment, and they'd have nowhere to hide.

'There!'

'You've done it?' she asked.

'Did you doubt me?' he replied cockily, turning the handle. Heart beating frantically, Cat unconsciously reached out to grab the back of Fox's close-fitting jacket, standing behind him as he opened the door.

Far from what she expected, Cat was shocked to see what appeared to be a quaint, well-decorated living area that wouldn't have been out of place in her previous home. There was even a newscast screen in one corner perched on a dark wood table, and a pair of comfortable-looking brown leather sofas arranged at a right angle to face it, a matching coffee table between them. The room was decorated in purples and greys, the royal colours of Anglya. There were three doors off the room, and a small kitchenette area with a sink, a cold box, some cupboards and a kettle.

'Someone is living down here,' she murmured incredulously, moving out from behind Fox when it seemed there was no danger.

Suddenly, one of the doors opened, and both Cat and Fox froze, eyes darting for somewhere to hide. A skinny blond boy about Cat's age walked confidently through the door, stopping when he saw them. His crystal blue eyes widened in alarm.

'You're not the guards!' he exclaimed.

Cat eyed him curiously, wondering why he seemed so familiar. He certainly didn't look dangerous.

At his shout, a woman ran in behind him, causing Cat to gasp. She had *definitely* seen this elegant woman before, both in person and in photographs, though the former hadn't happened for over eight years. She was much thinner and paler, and her blonde hair was greying, but she was definitely the same woman. That explained who the boy was too. Storms, he'd grown.

'Who are you? And what are you doing in our rooms?' the ivory-faced woman asked imperiously.

'It can't be!' Cat breathed, stunned. 'Queen Mary?'

'Who are they, Cat?' Fox asked, his shoulders tense, watching the two strangers warily.

Before Cat could answer, the blonde woman's confusion turned to a gasp.

'Storms! You look so much like her. Are you ... do you know Elizabeth Hunter?'

Cat nodded dumbly, unsurprised the woman recognised her. She'd seen pictures of her mother at her age, and other than hair colour they were practically a mirror image.

'Cat, who is she? How does she know your mother?' Fox insisted urgently. Cat turned to him, still looking shell-shocked.

The woman's hand flew to her mouth. 'Catherine?'

'Fox ... if I'm not mistaken, this is Queen Mary Latham, and her son Prince James. The lost monarchs of Anglya.'

16

'Good one,' Fox said, forcing a laugh. 'You nearly had me there. Really, Cat, who are they?'

'She's telling the truth,' Mary told him gently, before gesturing to the two sofas. 'Quick, shut the door before anyone sees you. We haven't got long before the guards bring lunch.'

Still stunned, Cat led Fox over to the nearest sofa, sitting on the edge nervously. Mary folded her purple skirts under her and sat delicately on her sofa, James at her side looking perplexed, thin hands folded neatly in his lap. James was eyeing Cat as if he didn't know what to make of her. She now knew where the little boy her mother had wanted her betrothed to had gone. Did he remember her like she did him?

'If you're the monarchs, how long have you been here? You went missing before the war ended,' Fox said, and James looked over at him in alarm.

'How do you know the war is over?' he asked suspiciously. 'The newscasts tell everyone, especially the commoners, that it's still going on.'

Fox leaned back into the sofa cushions, though Cat could tell he was far from relaxed.

'Oh, the majority of the people are under that impression. But you didn't answer my question,' he added, eyes fixed on the queen.

'They kidnapped us when James was barely seven years old, and brought us here. They said the country didn't need a monarchy any more, that it had *outgrown* us.' Mary began, her voice bitter.

'My husband resisted,' she bowed her head, 'and … and they killed him.' Mary's face saddened as she spoke, and her son laid a comforting hand on her arm. Cat swallowed harshly; Christopher hadn't deserved that. He was a good man. 'We've been here ever since, never allowed out. Guards come three times a day to give us meals. They keep us updated on the rubbish they're feeding the rest of the country through that,' she gestured to the newscast screen, 'but they're quite happy to tell us how the war has ended, and that they have all our people fooled.' She scowled, hatred in her voice, and Cat thought that Mary was not a woman she'd like to cross any time soon.

'Who's "they"?' Cat asked. 'The government, I know, but who's in charge of this whole operation?'

A pained look crossed Mary's face, and she shook her head.

'I don't know, Catherine. I'm sorry.'

'Cat. Call me Cat. I … I don't use the name Catherine now,' she explained. 'You must have some idea of who it might be?'

'I can't say anything with certainty,' Mary said. 'I don't really know what to believe any more.'

Cat sighed, glancing sideways at Fox, who shrugged as if to say 'it's up to you'.

'Fine,' she relented. 'So you've been down here for the whole eight years?' she clarified, still remembering the day her mother had told her they were gone. Mary nodded, wrapping an arm around her son's shoulders.

'Why haven't they killed you?' Fox asked abruptly. Cat shot him a scandalised look, but Mary didn't look offended. 'It's an awful lot of effort, keeping you both alive down here.'

'We might be useful in future,' Mary explained wryly. 'So they're keeping us here just in case. If the country begin to lose faith, nothing will restore it more than "finding" their lost monarchs. I think the plan, should they ever need to enact it, is to tell everyone the Mericans have been holding us hostage, to spur them into taking revenge.' Cat was aghast. It had to be awful, knowing you were only alive to be pawns in the government's power play.

'But they won't let you reclaim the throne even then,' Fox mused knowingly, and a small half-smile flitted across the monarch's lips.

'Oh, of course not. They *allow* me to educate my son, but I'm forbidden on pain of punishment to teach him his heritage, and the role he would have taken had we not been kidnapped. Not that it stopped me,' she added flatly. 'I always knew one day someone would find us. I never expected it to be you, though, Cat. What on Tellus are you even doing down here?'

'It's a long story, but we're here to help,' Fox interrupted. 'How do you know Cat? Or should I just take this as another one of your creepy "knowing everyone in government" things?' he asked Cat.

'I . . . James and I grew up together, before they were taken. Ma'am was my mother's best friend,' she said. James looked so very different to the childhood friend she remembered; but she supposed she must look very different to him too.

Fox nodded, and James suddenly sat bolt upright.

'Mother, it's nearly two,' he pointed out.

'Quickly, you need to hide,' she urged, standing up. 'The guards will be by with lunch soon. Is the door lock reset?'

Fox stood, eyeing her with a raised brow.

'I don't leave any trace of my work, ma'am,' he said frankly, and she smiled.

'I think I like you, young man,' she told him, her brown eyes sparkling. 'Now, quickly, go and hide in James's room – we'll get you when it's safe again. And then I'll want an explanation.'

With no other choice, Cat and Fox allowed themselves to be ushered through a door off to the side, finding a bedroom that matched the decor of the living room. There weren't any personal possessions, though, making the room look cold and almost unused, if not for the unmade bed and clothes strewn over the chair and floor.

'You'd better hide in the wardrobe, just to be safe. Sometimes they check the bedrooms,' James explained quietly, pulling open the wardrobe door.

Fox shrugged, climbing into the wardrobe without hesitation. After a brief pause Cat scrambled in beside him.

'Stay in there and don't make a sound. I'll come for you when they've gone,' James promised, before shutting the door on them, sending them into darkness.

There was a brief moment of shuffling while they both attempted to get comfortable in the cramped space, before Fox sighed in annoyance and Cat found herself being pulled against his chest, his arm settled around her shoulders. She squeaked indignantly, and felt him shrug.

'It's more comfortable than having your elbow in my ribs,' he muttered under his breath.

Cat could hear his heartbeat through the thick wool of his jacket.

'Do you trust them?' he asked softly.

'Yes,' she breathed in reply. 'Like I said, Mary was my mother's best friend. James and I had lessons together and played together all the time as wee'uns. She always hated my father, and if the government killed Christopher ... she won't let the matter lie. We can trust them.'

Cat felt Fox relax somewhat, though he gave her an odd look when she referred to the queen by her first name. Cat knew no different; it was what she'd always called her. Mary had practically been family.

There was a long silence before Fox spoke again.

'You know, you seem to have an incredible penchant for hiding in people's wardrobes,' he told her, and she could hear the smile in his voice.

The next sound out of his mouth was a soft *oof* as her elbow impacted with his stomach. Hard.

Cat blinked in shock at the sudden influx of light, and it took her eyes a moment to adjust and recognise James staring at them, an odd look on his face.

'You look awfully cosy in there,' he remarked, making Cat

realise Fox's arm was still around her, and she was practically snuggling into his chest. She stood quickly, and almost fell out of the wardrobe in her haste to get out of the embrace. Fox exited far more gracefully, eyeing James warily.

'The guards are gone, then?' he asked.

'They are,' the blond boy confirmed. 'They left lunch, which Mother says you're welcome to share with us.'

He led them back into the living room. Mary was on the sofa and a tray of food rested on the coffee table. It wasn't much − bread, vegetables and chicken − but they shared what they had, anyway. 'Thank you,' Fox said sincerely, surprising Cat. 'For hiding us. You could have easily given us away.'

'I'm not stupid, lad,' Mary retorted, raising an eyebrow at him. 'If we've any hope of escaping, we'll need to stay on your good side. Besides,' her expression softened, and she glanced at Cat, 'if you're anything like your mother, I know you will do the right thing. I trust you.' Cat nodded, feeling oddly humbled by the woman's words, and hoped she could live up to the expectation. 'So how did you find us?' Mary asked curiously. 'I can't imagine you just happened to stumble across us. What were you doing here in the first place?'

'Well, that's a bit of a long story, actually,' Cat told her. 'It started when I ran away after Father told me of his plans to betroth me to Thomas Gale's son, Marcus.' Mary's eyes widened.

'Thomas Gale? Cat, dear, I don't blame you for running. I can only imagine what any offspring of his might be like. But how did that lead to you meeting . . . Fox, was it?' she checked, and Fox nodded, not offering his full name.

'I stowed away on a skyship, where he lives. In his wardrobe, in fact,' Cat said with a faint blush. 'I was pretending to be a boy – hence the haircut – and the crew allowed me to stay.'

Cat and Fox explained the events that had led them to find the room at the bottom of the compound, sharing their suspicions and uncertainties about what was going on in the city and with the children, and how they were there to find evidence enough to expose the government for what it really was. Mary and James were horrified when they heard that the children were being taken, though didn't know what was being done to them. They hadn't left their rooms since they'd arrived, and the guards didn't talk much.

'You're welcome to sleep here as long as you're around,' Mary offered. 'I'm afraid it'll have to be the floor, but the guards only come in at mealtimes, so you'll be perfectly safe overnight. I just ask that when you do leave, you take us with you.'

'Certainly,' Fox agreed, earning wide smiles from James and Mary. Cat smiled too; having Fox on the same page was always helpful. Besides, they could hardly leave them down there, with what they had planned for the building. 'Now,' said Fox, 'I'm assuming they've allowed you a washroom down here? Would you mind if I used it? There's no point in us heading back out there – not until they go on a skeleton guard for the night shift.'

'Of course,' said James, jumping to his feet.

Cat settled back down beside Mary as James led Fox through to the bathroom, and Mary smiled at her.

'I am so very glad to see you, Cat,' she said softly. 'I always wondered what had become of you – I worried that Nathaniel would corrupt you. However, I can see there's more of your mother in you.' She smiled briefly, covering Cat's hand with her own. 'Yet the fact that you're here shows you are, in only the best ways, your father's daughter.'

Cat scowled. There was nothing she hated more than being compared to her father. People had been telling her since she was young that she had her father's spirit. As far as she was concerned, it wasn't a compliment.

'And now I must know, though after hearing you speak about your father's plans I think I can assume the answer. How is Elizabeth?' she asked as James returned. Cat's smile faltered.

'She . . . she's not well, she never has been. She told me the illness started before she got pregnant, so you must have known . . .' She trailed off, and Mary nodded with a frown. 'She tries her best, but . . . she's been very ill for a long time, bedridden most days. The doctors say there's nothing they can do for her.'

Mary looked saddened by the news, and Cat wished she hadn't been the one to break it to her.

'Would you . . . tell me about her? She didn't tell me much about what her life was like . . . before me. She would always get too tired to finish her stories. She told me about you, but she never said much about how you met.'

'Of course. What would you like to know?' Mary queried.

'Anything,' Cat pleaded.

Mary laughed lightly, curling her legs up beneath her.

'Well, Elizabeth and I grew up together. Her father was my father's chief adviser, and we were companions. We shared the same governess, attended the same parties, we did everything together. Your mother was my very best friend, and I have never known a kinder person in my entire life.

'As we grew older, I was allowed my choice of the young men of aristocracy, and started being courted by my Christopher. But Elizabeth's father insisted she married Nathaniel. The only reason Nathaniel agreed was because it would give him even more money and status. He loathed her, and the feeling was mutual, as I'm sure you're aware. Then Elizabeth and I got pregnant rather close together, and we used to sit for hours and plan our children's futures.'

Cat knew where this was going, and eyed James warily; he was listening almost as intently as she was.

'Mother told me that part,' she interrupted, not sure she wanted Mary mentioning the planned betrothal. At that moment, Fox entered.

'What have I missed?' he asked, padding silently across the dark grey carpet as he took the space beside Cat.

'I was just telling Cat about her mother when we were young,' Mary explained, smiling. 'Anyway, as I was saying, we used to sit and plan our futures, and, of course, the futures of our children.' She laughed, shaking her head ruefully, not noticing Cat's desperate expression. 'As soon as you were both born, we couldn't help but imagine you growing older and falling in love, and being betrothed. The contract had been drawn up and everything.'

The young prince stared at Cat. Obviously he hadn't been told about it.

'We would have been betrothed?' he asked his mother. 'Cat and I? Had we not been kidnapped?'

Mary's giggle was almost girlish.

'Well, we were young, but that's what we had hoped. I doubt even Nathaniel would have objected to his daughter marrying a prince. After all, you were such good friends as young children, it only seemed natural for you to stay close.'

Cat wanted to bang her head repeatedly against the coffee table, and she didn't need to look sideways to know Fox was scowling. Now James was looking at her like she was his one true love. It astonished her how different he was to the rosy-cheeked, cheerful little boy she'd been friends with. With a pale, angular face and his blond hair cropped close to his head, he was clearly becoming a man, and yet compared to Fox he still seemed a child.

When the guards arrived with dinner, Cat didn't dare speak to Fox in the wardrobe, and Fox didn't wrap his arm around her like last time. Cat felt the loss more than she would have liked to admit.

Once they'd rejoined the others, Fox's gaze flicked to the clock on the shelf every five minutes or so. When it chimed eleven, he got to his feet abruptly.

'It's probably safe for us to have a wander, Cat,' he announced, going to put his boots on. Cat nodded without argument, grabbing her own boots.

'You're going outside?' James asked, and Fox nodded shortly.

It was very clear that Fox was going off James; whether it was because of the boy's personality or the way he looked at Cat, she wasn't sure.

'Can I come with you?' he asked.

'Absolutely not,' Cat and Fox responded in unison. James looked surprised at Cat's refusal and pouted.

'Why not?' he pressed.

'We don't know how many workers there will be out there and somehow I don't think they'll overlook a wayward prince wandering free,' Fox said sharply.

James's face fell. 'I suppose you're right,' he admitted reluctantly.

Cat could understand where he was coming from – she knew she would want to leave as soon as possible had she spent her whole life in the same set of rooms – but she was grateful to Fox for backing her up.

'Glad you see it our way. Cat, shall we?'

She nodded, stepping back to allow Fox to unlock the door. He pushed it open tentatively.

'Be careful,' Mary told them, and Fox flashed her a mischievous grin, before shutting the door.

'Where to first, then?' Cat asked.

Fox was staring upwards.

'Start at the top, work our way down? According to Harry's sources, there'll be hardly anyone about at this time of night.'

Cat nodded, and they set off up the long spiral staircase, Fox going first to check every floor was clear as they ascended.

'I wouldn't marry James, you know,' she blurted out, then blushed. She didn't want to admit, even to herself, exactly why she felt the need to clarify that to Fox. His step faltered for a brief second, but he didn't say anything. 'I mean, when this is all over, if he takes the country back and tries to put a betrothal contract in place ... I won't do it. I'm not Catherine,' she declared fiercely.

'I know,' he replied simply, his tone not giving anything away.

Cat bit her lip, wondering if he was just placating her, but could have sworn she saw some of the tension bleed from his shoulders as they hurried up the remaining stairs.

They made it to the top of the staircase, and Fox peered through the window of the closest door.

'Empty,' he told her, turning the handle and entering the room.

Cat followed quickly. 'Why so many mechanics' work-shops?' she wondered aloud, walking over to the nearest desk and looking at the project assembled on it. 'These look like parts of a mecha.' They looked very similar to what she knew Samuel contained, only ... not.

'This is a gun,' Fox added, pointing over her head to a metal box-like object mounted on the bronze-plated shoulder of a mechanical arm, the opening narrowing out into a gun barrel. He ran a finger down the back of the box, before flipping the arm upside down. 'Look, there.'

Cat stared where he was pointing, seeing only a complicated webbing of gears and chains, before the pattern began to click into place.

'The trigger is in the finger of the hand. There are bullets stored in the hollow of the casing.'

Cat's eyes widened; what were they doing with guns mounted on mechanical arms?

The other rooms on that floor were similar; all mechanics' workshops, all empty, none of them giving away their exact purpose. Cat and Fox went down to the floor below, where they saw three mechanics walking down the corridor. Ducking into an alcove, they waited for the men to pass. One of the men paused, a frown on his face and his gaze directed at their alcove. Cat flattened herself against the wall as much as she could, glad for the low lighting during the night shift. Her heart was so loud she half expected the man to hear her, and she didn't dare turn her head to look at Fox.

'What you dawdling for?' one of the man's companions called. The man shrugged to himself, shaking his head and continuing on. When they were alone once more, Cat let out a long breath.

'That was too close,' she murmured, and Fox nodded, looking spooked. Staying on their guard, they began to explore.

The rooms on this floor were a mix of yet more workshops and small office spaces. Cat tugged frantically on Fox's arm when she saw that the walls inside one room were pasted with blueprints, looking eerily similar to Fox's own workroom back on the ship. Checking there was no one around, they slipped inside, Fox immediately directing his video recorder to scan over the blueprints.

'These are all mechanical body parts,' he murmured quietly. 'Arms, legs, torsos. It's like ... they're building mechas, but more advanced models. Mechanical soldiers, armed to the teeth. But ... there's something wrong. There's no fuel source, and some of these connections don't seem to lead anywhere. They're ... unfinished,' he explained, frustrated.

Cat drew closer. She could see what he meant; most of the parts seemed to just stop halfway, like there was something they connected to that wasn't part of the schematics.

'They're preparing for war!' she exclaimed. 'Building a mechanical army that doesn't age, or bleed, or feel pain. An army with no limits – it can be rebuilt and replaced as needed. Soldiers with no morals or emotions. If it works, they'd be unstoppable.'

Fox looked grim, and stopped filming the blueprints.

'We'd better stop them before they get that far, then, hadn't we?' he retorted. 'There's one thing I don't understand, though. If they've got these grand ideas about mechanical soldiers, what are they kidnapping children for?'

Cat shrugged, staring at the blueprints as if they would give her answers.

'Commanders, maybe? Raising them away from their families, training them to be the perfect leaders for their metal army? They'll need someone to give orders, and I can't see many of the aristocrats wanting to get their hands dirty like that,' she suggested.

Fox tilted his head thoughtfully.

'Only way to find out for sure is to keep looking.'

Passing several workshops, at the end of the corridor they reached a locked door with no window, which instantly made them curious.

'Can you get the lock?' Cat queried, and Fox shot her an affronted look.

'Of course I can get the lock. But what if there are people on the other side?'

'Look, Fox, this is the only locked door we've found, other than the one to Mary and James's rooms. I think we should take the risk on the assumption that whatever's in there will be equally important. It's worth it.'

Fox nodded, dropping to his knees and pulling out his tool kit. Cat glanced around nervously as he worked, hating the feeling of exposure she got from standing there. She crossed her fingers, muttering under her breath and almost letting out a yelp of relief when the lock clicked.

'Here goes nothing,' he murmured, pushing the door open.

It was pitch-black inside and completely silent, and Cat relaxed somewhat, assuming it was empty. A strange smell, like meat that had gone off, reached her nostrils and she gagged.

'Hang on,' Fox muttered.

There was a click, and the lamps on the walls sparked, the small flames flaring to life.

Cat gasped.

Lining the walls of the room were large, steel-barred cages, locked with simple padlocks. Every single cage held at least a dozen children. They were all younger than Cat, and each one had some sort of mechanical attachment; a crudely fused mechanical arm or leg, similar to the ones Cat and Fox had seen in the workshops. Some of the children had entire sections of their heads missing, springs and gears jammed into the flesh of their brain. Others had metal plating in place of skin over their chests, and there were large, gaping wounds where the mechanics had failed to bond the metal to human skin. Bile rose in Cat's throat, and she gripped Fox's arm tightly. Not one of the children moved, and Cat realised in horror that every single one was dead.

'Oh, gods,' Fox breathed, face pale. 'Those twisted, perverted monsters. Cat, the mechanical attachments ... that's why they didn't connect to anything. They're not building mechanical soldiers – they're fusing metal and flesh, they're connecting wires to nerves and making *human mechas. Gods.*' His voice trailed off hoarsely, and a tear leaked from the corner of his eye.

'These must be the "failed experiments",' he continued after a pause.

Cat shook her head, her mouth opening and closing silently – she couldn't speak. The smell of blood and decay was making her nauseous, and she looked up at Fox desperately.

'Go and wait outside, Cat,' he told her softly. 'I need ... I need to film this.'

Cat kept shaking her head, clinging tighter to Fox's coat sleeve. She wasn't leaving him; she wasn't going out into the building alone. He looked at her, then sighed in understanding, squeezing her quickly around the shoulders and pulling out his video recorder with his free hand.

'Cat, I need to get closer. I need you to let go of me,' he urged softly, his fingers prying gently at the hand clutching his shirt cuff.

Reluctantly, Cat released him, watching with glassy eyes as he walked closer to the cages. He was two feet away from the front of the nearest cage before he stopped, unable to force himself any closer. Cat waited as he filmed the cages, his quiet voice letting her know that he'd also turned on his audio recorder. It wasn't long before he'd had more than he could take and switched both recorders off, returning quickly to Cat. She had slid down the door and was sitting with her knees tucked up to her chest, face buried in her arms. She jumped as she felt a hand rest on her hair, and looked up to see Fox eyeing her worriedly.

'Let's go,' he prompted, nudging her to her feet.

Outside, Cat dashed down the corridor to the nearest alcove, practically collapsing to the floor as she reached it, silent tears streaming down her cheeks. When Fox joined her, he sank to the floor beside her and hugged her. She latched on to him, burying her face against his chest, crying into his waistcoat. His cheek pressed against the top of her head, his arm around her.

'I feel sick. I don't want to be sick,' she murmured frantically, her breath coming short and fast. He rubbed her back soothingly, squeezing her hand.

'Just breathe, Cat. Nice and deep, copy my breathing, focus on me,' he whispered, exaggerating his own breaths. Eventually, she calmed down a little, though all she could see when she closed her eyes was the room full of children. It could have been her, had she not been high-born. It could have been Fox, had he not run away. Her brain conjured an image of a girl with Ben's features, and she went cold; how could they tell Ben about his sister's fate?

She didn't know how long they sat in that alcove until she managed to get herself under control. She realised that she was practically sitting on Fox's lap, and scrambled away. There was a wet patch on his shirt, and she bit her lip.

'I'm sorry, I . . .' she trailed off.

'Don't worry about it,' Fox said simply, squeezing her hand. She looked away, wiping her face on her sleeve. She was sure she looked a mess, with red-rimmed puffy eyes and tear-stains on her cheeks, but she didn't care.

'We should . . . keep looking,' she murmured, her voice croaky. 'Now that we know what we're looking for.'

But gods, how she wished she'd stayed oblivious.

17

The atmosphere in the compound had completely changed for Cat. No longer was there the buzz of excitement, the thrill of doing something against the law; now, all she could feel was a persistent gnawing in the pit of her stomach and the overwhelming urge to curl up and cry. Fox too was even quieter than usual.

Still, they doggedly kept on with their task, quickly sneaking to the floor below. There they found more workshops, which were bigger and more extensive than those they'd seen before, but Cat wasn't interested in figuring out how the devices worked any more. She was hoping they would find some children alive and untouched, but considering how the mechanics had complained about running out of test subjects, she wasn't confident that hope would be realised. The men had talked about bringing in a new batch from the country, though; maybe children were brought to the compound in groups at a time. Maybe there were hundreds of healthy kids still out in the country.

'Wait,' Fox breathed suddenly, pushing her into a dark corner.

Cat blinked, snapping out of her thoughts, and held her

breath as four men in overalls and lab coats walked past. She grimaced when she saw a rust-red stain on one of the men's white coat, knowing there was only one thing it could possibly be. The purple heart embroidered on his coat identified him as a doctor, sending a chill down her spine. How could a man trained to save people be doing something so awful?

'We're getting closer to something important,' Fox told her quietly, once the men were gone. 'There are more and more workers around here.'

Cat and Fox continued in the direction the men had come from. Near the end of the corridor they found another door and Cat stood on tiptoe to look through its window. A stifled gasp escaped from her mouth and she beckoned Fox closer.

The workshop inside was at least twice the size of all the others they'd seen and, unlike the others, it was a hive of activity. Cat counted twelve mechanics and two government men, both of whom she recognised. There were three large metal tables in the centre of the room with several carts full of medical and mechanical equipment surrounding them. In one corner was a cage similar to those they'd seen before. The only difference was the children inside these were alive. Unconscious by the look of it, but definitely breathing.

She hastily removed her video recorder from her buttonhole and lifted it up to point it through the window, watching in silent horror as three of the mechanics opened the cage and removed a sleeping boy, his light brown hair matted over his small face. The boy was naked and thin and she was sure he couldn't have been much older than thirteen. He was sleeping too deeply for his slumber to be natural, and Cat realised he had been drugged. The men laid the boy on one of the metal tables, and a doctor in a heavily blood-stained lab coat stepped forward, a scalpel in his hand. Cat looked away and saw Fox crouching down.

'What are you doing?' she hissed.

'Trying to get this door open,' he told her quietly. 'We need audio, and we can't do that with the door closed.'

Cat looked back through the window, her stomach lurching as she saw one of the mechanics raising a lethal-looking mechanical saw to the young boy's left arm. She ducked away as the blade whirred to life, not wanting to see any more. The lock clicked – Fox had the door open – but the hideous noise of the saw drowned out any conversation that might have been taking place in the room.

Unable to keep watching, Cat switched off the video recorder and crouched down to join Fox on the floor.

'Th– they're cutting off his arm,' she stammered.

'Just wait. We'll get our chance soon,' he assured her, one finger curled around the door's handle to keep it ajar, then they sat and waited for silence, trying to ignore the sickening grinding noise. Abruptly, it stopped.

Listening to the murmur of quiet conversation, both of them jumped at a sudden explosion, looking at each other in alarm. Cat stood and peered through the window. The mechanical arm the men had been attempting to attach to the boy's shoulder was twitching violently, and thick purple-black smoke poured from the wrist joint. Every man in the room had gathered around the table, and Cat knew this was their chance. Seeing a desk piled high with metal boxes, she kicked Fox in the side, silently gesturing for him to go through the door. He looked at her like she was crazy, and she rolled her eyes in impatience.

'Trust me,' she hissed.

He nodded, slipping through the open door in silence, and she followed. Together they crouched down behind some of the metal crates that spanned almost the entire wall. Fox tapped her on the arm, gesturing to his audio recorder and switching it on. Turning hers on, Cat pointed towards the other end of the room. Fox shook his head, sitting down to make it clear he was staying where he was. Cat steeled her nerve, then ducked low, rushing down the line of crates to the other end.

Standing in a small group on the other side of the crates, a few feet away from where Cat was crouched, were four doctors and one of the government men, Albert Jennings. He had worked for her father in the past, and it didn't surprise her in the slightest that the slimy man was part of this operation.

'We need to change our approach,' one of the doctors said. 'This isn't working well. We need to step back and try something different. Maybe keep them out in the country for longer, bulk them up a little more. They're coming in too scrawny.'

'We don't have *time* to step back and change our approach, Meyers!' Jennings hissed angrily. 'It's working in some cases, and we're running out of kids! The commoners will start asking questions if we take them any younger – they're sceptical enough as to what use a little brat could be in a war zone.'

'It's only working in one out of five children! That's still four dead kids we could do without!' a different doctor exclaimed.

'Getting a guilty conscience, Barton?' Jennings sneered.

'No,' Barton insisted defensively. 'I'd just rather we developed something more likely to work on *all* the children and reduce the rate that we're going through test subjects. You said it yourself – kids are in short supply these days.'

'The commoners aren't having kids any more.' A third doctor now jumped in. 'Not if they can help it. They can't see an end to the war, and they don't want to bring up kids in a country like this.'

Jennings snorted with disgust.

'Well, the sooner they wipe themselves out for good the better. Do what you have to do,' he snapped. 'Just do it quickly. If we run out of kids, we'll take adults.'

'That won't work and we both know it! The subjects need to be experiencing puberty for the enhancements to take. Their body needs to be in the process of changing already. Adults have finished growing, so it would be useless to try.'

Cat almost screamed as a loud bell rang sharply three times, positive it was someone raising the alarm about her and Fox. She met his eye at the opposite end of the room, and he looked just as scared as she did. The workers, however, didn't seem fazed, and one let out a contented sigh.

'About bloody time! I'm knackered!' Meyers remarked, rolling his shoulders and putting down the sharp metal tool in his hand. He glanced back at the boy on the table, who now had a new mechanical arm fused to his shoulder, the skin around the joint red and blistered, but not bleeding. The arm was held out at an angle, supported by a smaller metal table that had been pulled up beside the large one. Two of the workers were taping plastic sheeting around the boy's shoulder, keeping it sterile, and another covered the boy with a thin blanket up to his chest.

With that, all the men headed for the door, and, seconds later, Cat rushed back to Fox. This might be a shift change, and would be their only chance to get out before a bunch of new workers entered. They waited for a long moment before daring to sneak out of the room and slipping down a corridor in the opposite direction.

'Jennings – the government bloke – kept saying they didn't have much time, and were running out of children,' Cat said hurriedly. 'He told the doctors to do what they needed to do, so I think they'll be redesigning some things. I just hope that while they're doing that, they'll leave the kids alone.'

'We can but hope,' Fox agreed. 'But we'll need to start keeping an eye out for rooms with live sprogs in. If this whole building is going up, we can't leave them in here.'

Cat shuddered at the prospect, and nodded. If they were going to be evacuating the monarchs, they could take the time to save as many children as they could too.

'We should get back to Mary and James – it'll be light soon, and we both need sleep,' Fox prompted.

Peering around the corner, Cat followed Fox in a sprint down the corridor towards the staircase, while it was empty. The two of them practically fell down the stairs, jumping them two or three at a time until they reached the bottom floor. Fox fiddled with the lock on the door, pushing it open and Cat followed him inside, eyebrows rising when she saw a lamp was still on and that Mary was sitting on one of the sofas.

'You didn't have to wait for us,' Cat said by way of greeting.

Mary rolled her eyes.

'Did you really think I'd be able to sleep with you out there?' she retorted.

Cat shrugged, looking around the room.

'James gone to bed?' she asked, and Mary nodded.

'Now, tell me what you've discovered,' the queen requested, eyes serious.

'Nothing that need concern you until we're out of here. The less you know the better,' Fox said firmly.

Mary drew in a breath, but all she said was, 'There are blankets and pillows for you both, if you want to get some sleep. Fox, there's space on James's floor, and Cat, you can take my floor.'

Cat froze.

'No, I stay with Fox,' she said firmly, stepping closer to him. Mary frowned in disapproval.

'Cat, dear, really, it's not proper for a young man and a young woman to sleep in the same room,' she began.

'I don't care,' Cat cut her off fiercely. 'It's safer for us to stick together. I stay with Fox, no arguments.'

'I have to agree with Cat,' Fox added. 'We would have slept in the same place had we not found you. We can sleep on the sofas – it's not like we'll be sharing a bed.'

Cat blushed lightly at the mention of sharing a bed with Fox, but stood her ground. Fox's hand rested on her shoulder in a show of solidarity, and Mary sighed.

'If you're on the separate sofas, then I suppose that's acceptable,' she said sternly.

Fox raised a copper-coloured eyebrow, but Cat placed a hand on his arm before he could say anything. The last thing they needed was him picking a fight.

'The guards come at eight with breakfast. We'll wake you if you're not up already. Goodnight,' Mary muttered in resignation, turning down the lamp and turning to go to her own bedroom.

'She didn't seem too happy about being told no,' Fox mused when she was gone.

'I'm not letting you out of my sight,' Cat declared stubbornly.

Fox smiled at her, squeezing her shoulder.

'Me neither,' he agreed.

Cat sat down to unbuckle her boots while Fox gathered the blankets folded on the coffee table, tossing one to Cat and keeping one himself. Carefully removing both her audio and video recorders and leaving them on the coffee table, Cat removed layers until she was just in her under-shirt, shirt and trousers. Normally she would sleep with the shirt off, but she didn't dare with Fox there. He, however, had no problems, stripping down to his trousers and under-shirt. Cat couldn't resist stealing glances at his muscular arms as she crawled under her blanket. Fox collapsed wearily on to the other sofa. He tilted his chin back, meeting her eyes in the near-darkness.

'I'm scared,' Cat whispered. 'What if . . . what if this isn't good enough? What if we get caught, or we can't convince people?'

There was a pause, before Fox smiled.

'Cat, we've got video and audio proof of what those bastards are doing. Once we go public, they're going down. And as for getting caught, well . . . don't you trust me?' He flashed her a cheeky grin, and she smiled back timidly. Fox's arm slipped out from under his blanket, reaching across to grab her hand. He squeezed strongly, and Cat held on, closing her eyes. It was far, far easier to get to sleep.

When Cat woke, it was to a pair of bright blue eyes staring her in the face – and definitely not the pair she'd been expecting. She nearly screamed, seeing James standing beside the coffee table, eyeing her silently.

'What in storms are you doing?' she muttered sleepily.

He didn't answer, and she noticed that he was no longer staring at her. She looked at where his eyes were fixed, and coughed awkwardly. Her hand was still twined with Fox's.

'Is he your boyfriend?' James asked, his voice slightly higher than it had been the night before.

'No,' she answered quickly, trying to disentangle her hand. Unfortunately, she underestimated both Fox's grip and how light a sleeper he was. His eyes flickered open, and he looked at her with a small half-smile, squeezing her hand.

'G'morning,' he greeted, voice husky with sleep. Looking around, he spotted James, the smile immediately dropping from his face. 'Don't you have better things to do than watch us sleep? How long have you been there, anyway?'

James flushed, shaking his head.

'N-not long!' he insisted, stuttering slightly, the guilt on his face giving him away. 'I just thought I'd wake you both up before the guards bring breakfast in. Also, before Mother comes in and catches you holding hands.'

Fox glanced away at that, letting go of Cat's hand, and she felt somewhat bereft. Sitting up with a stretch, she yawned, running a hand through her sleep-mussed hair.

'What's the plan for today, then?' she asked Fox, once they were back in James's wardrobe.

'More evidence. We need names and faces so they can't worm their way out of punishment, and we need to try and find out who the boss is, even get him on film if we're lucky,' Fox replied softly.

They both went quiet when they heard voices from the next room – voices that didn't belong to either James or Mary. Cat didn't know how long they sat there, but eventually the wardrobe opened, and a sullen-faced James beckoned them back into the living room. Breakfast was tasteless porridge, but Cat and Fox ate their share without complaint.

'What time are you leaving?' Mary asked.

'As soon as we can,' Fox answered. 'We need to find out who's in charge of this whole thing. Unless you can tell us . . . ?' Fox trailed off expectantly.

'I don't know enough to tell you about anything,' Mary insisted.

'Fine.' The redhead stood, grabbing his bag from the corner. 'Cat, if you want to get washed and changed, go and do it now.'

She nodded, jumping to her feet and taking her bag with her into the washroom. When she returned to the living room, Fox was waiting for her, also fully dressed.

'Let's get moving, then,' Cat urged, clapping her hands together impatiently. They replaced their devices, Fox making Cat's skin tingle when he leaned in close to adjust her audio recorder, his fingers brushing her throat.

Ignoring James's glare and Mary's worried frown, the two left, letting the door shut and lock behind them.

'Where to?' she asked in a whisper, mentally cataloguing which floors they hadn't yet explored.

'Three floors from the top, where we left off?' Fox suggested. 'We'll get some more footage, then take what we've got to the rest of the crew and see what they say about it. We need to check in with them, anyway, and see how things are going from their end. If we get there in time we can be over to the ship at lunch, and back in here at evening shift change.'

Cat nodded and followed him up the stairs. They reached the level and stepped out into the corridor – and immediately backtracked around the corner, flattening themselves against the wall. The corridor was buzzing with activity, and Cat and Fox shared a dismayed look. No way were they going to be able to slip undetected through all of that. Not wanting to waste an opportunity, Fox removed his video recorder from his waistcoat, turning it to face the corridor in the hope of catching some faces for Cat to later identify. At this point the more proof they could get the better. They moved to an alcove containing a long oak desk and hid underneath it, preparing to wait out the flood of people.

Within about ten minutes the corridor began to clear, and Fox suggested they attempt to have a look around some more of the workshops. Several of them contained experiments in mid-process, and while it made them both queasy to watch, they knew they needed to get footage of it. Fox dug a scrap of paper and a pencil from his satchel to write down door numbers of labs that still had children in them, so they knew where to find them when they began to evacuate. There was an encouraging amount of unharmed children; around fifty, by Cat's count. She just hoped that the mechanics wouldn't move them in the meantime.

As the morning dragged on into afternoon, Fox began obsessively checking his pocket watch, waiting for the clock to tick over to one o'clock when lunch break began and the guard would be minimal. Finally, he deemed it safe for them to leave, and led the way back to the outer door they'd entered through the day before, then paused.

'There could be security guards on the other side,' he said, shaking his head. 'Not a risk I'm willing to take. Come on.'

He grabbed her hand, practically dragging her down the right-hand corridor, pulling her into an alcove with a small window just above Fox's head height.

'Keep an eye out and hit me if someone comes our way.'

Without waiting for a response, Fox reached up to grab the window sill, spreading his legs far apart, jamming the toes of his boots in the grooves between the wood panels on either side of the alcove. Cat alternated between observing the corridor and watching Fox as he awkwardly walked his way up the wall, holding on to the window sill until he was high enough to sit on it. He flicked the latch on the window, pushing it open. There barely looked enough room for her to fit through, let alone Fox.

'Are you sure that's going to work?' she hissed, and he flashed her a roguish grin, stretching right down to hold out his hand.

'Trust me, girlie. Now, let me pull you up.'

Eyeing him apprehensively, she gripped his hand tightly in hers, jumping as he pulled. There was a brief moment of panic as Fox nearly overbalanced, but he leaned back into the open window, bracing himself against the frame as Cat gripped the sill, hoisting herself up ungracefully to sit beside him. It was a tight fit, and Cat found herself pressed against him, their faces about half a foot apart.

He winked at her.

'Told you it would work. You go first.'

He let a hand rest securely on her shoulder as she twisted to lower herself out of the window. Forcing her thoughts away from the warmth she could feel through her coat – now *really* wasn't the time – she gripped the window sill tightly, not wanting to drop suddenly and make a lot of noise. She felt her toes brush the ground, and let go, landing on the damp concrete with a muffled thump. Looking up at Fox, she beckoned him, moving aside so he could lower himself down. When his feet touched the ground, he quickly darted round the corner to hide by the protrusion of building stretching towards the back of East Gate, followed by Cat.

'You all right?' he checked, and she nodded, taking a few moments to slow her breathing.

There was a gallery running along the wall, thick stone columns supporting decorated arches in the self-important government fashion. But the heavily shadowed walkway would be just as useful to them as the alcoves inside the building had been – it made perfect cover. Fox seemed to fade into the shadows as he slunk across to the other side, ready to dart out and pick the lock of the exposed East Gate.

Cat stepped out of her hiding place to join him, only to scurry back at the sound of footsteps. Her eyes widened as she caught Fox's alarmed expression, and suddenly she felt a hand grabbing the back of her collar, lifting her clean off her feet. 'What in storms do you think you're doing here, brat?' a voice hissed in her ear, the guard's breath hot on her neck. All she could do was let out a whimper, feeling herself tremble as she was forcibly turned around. She didn't recognise the man holding her, but his rumpled uniform had just one stud on the collar, and the putrid scent of alcohol was dizzying. 'Where did you come from, then?'

'Let – let go of me,' Cat mumbled, struggling feebly. She could see Fox hiding in the walkway, watching her, aghast.

'What would I do that for?' the guard said, chuckling darkly. He was swaying on his feet as he held her, and Cat stretched down to stand on solid ground once more. 'Bet you've escaped from one of them holding cells inside, hmm? Boss'll be awfully mad if a brat gets away. Don't know what they need them for, anyway.' The man's tone turned scathing as he muttered to himself, but his grip stayed tight. Cat struck a solid blow between his legs, making him howl in pain. His grip loosened just enough for Cat to squirm free and run off, but as she turned to see if he was following, a tall form blocked her vision and a sharp crack filled the air, followed by the heavy thump of a body falling to the floor. She swallowed her scream, frantic eyes landing on Fox, who had emerged from the shadows and held one of his heavy steel-toed boots in his hand. There was a smudge of dark blood staining the leather, and her gaze flicked to the crumpled form of the guard, who was unconscious and bleeding from a cut on his forehead.

'Is he . . . dead?' she asked, still trembling.

'No, just unconscious. But we need to get going before he wakes up,' Fox replied quietly.

She looked up at him warily. 'We can't just leave him here! He'll tell someone he saw me!'

Fox snorted, rolling his eyes. 'Cat, he smells like he took a bath in a distillery. No one will believe anything he says,' he said, tugging her away.

He didn't speak again until they were a good distance away from the unconscious man, hiding deep in the shadows of the empty walkway. Cat clasped her hands together, willing her fingers to stop shaking. 'You're OK,' Fox murmured, leaning his head against hers for the briefest moment. 'You're safe, you're fine. That was a good shot, actually. Good luck to him if he ever wants kids.' There was a grin on his face, and Cat giggled.

'I'm sorry,' she said softly, earning a raised eyebrow. 'That could've blown everything.'

'It wasn't your fault, it could've just as easily been me,' he said quietly. 'And you dealt with it well.' Cat bit her lip, but didn't argue. Her fault or not, it had been far too close for comfort.

Fox got the gate open with ease, and Cat was surprised to see it unguarded on the other side.

'Psst! Cat! Fox!' Her head snapped up, and she couldn't stop grinning when she saw Ben lurking in the shadows nearby. Racing towards him, she let him envelop her in a tight hug as he pulled her back into his hiding place, Fox following close behind. 'Oh, thank the gods you're both OK. We were so worried,' he breathed, dropping a kiss to her head before releasing her, bringing Fox into a brief hug as well.

'Where's the guard?' the redhead asked, and Ben smirked.

'Mattie's taking care of it. We're getting rather good at drawing guards away for twenty minutes or so, just in case you turn up. Oh, Alice is going to be ecstatic, she's hardly slept.' They all froze at the sound of footsteps, but relaxed when it turned out to be Matt, a faint purple bruise on his cheek and his hair mussed.

'Storms, you're back!' he exclaimed in a whisper. 'Are you OK?'

'We're fine,' Fox assured quickly. 'We've got so much to tell you, but we need to get back to the ship.'

'Of course,' Matt agreed, already setting off towards the shipyard. Cat followed, feeling safe for the first time since she'd stepped into the government compound. Storms, she just wanted it all to be over.

18

'So what did you find out, then?' Matt asked Fox and Cat once they were all settled around the table in the galley, Alice brewing tea for each of them. Cat grimaced, sharing a look with Fox, who looked equally sombre.

'It's bad,' he started, taking out their video and audio recorders and setting them on the table. 'What they're doing to those children ... it's despicable.'

'You – you actually saw some of them?' Ben asked tentatively, his face pale. Cat's heart went out to him, and she braced herself for what she was about to tell him, aware his mind was on his sister; she would've been nineteen now, but there was no way she was still alive. Cat wished he could've stayed oblivious.

'They're creating an army,' she said quietly. 'That much is true, at least. But it's not any kind of army you've seen before. They're *mutilating* the children, giving them mechanical limbs with guns on them, trying to create a half-human, half-mecha soldier. It ... it doesn't seem to be going very well. There are more failures than successes from what we can see.'

The entire crew had gone chalk-white at her words, and

Ben looked like he was about to pass out. Matt's arm was around him, squeezing his shoulders tightly.

'We gather Collected kids are being stored out in the country,' Fox continued, and Cat jumped as his hand slid over hers on the bench, entwining her fingers and holding her with a vice-like grip. 'Fed to put some weight on, then groups are brought back by train to undergo experiments. We don't know what happens to the successful cases.' He paused. 'There is some good news in all of this, though. Queen Mary Latham and her son are alive.'

You could have heard a pin drop in the galley.

'They're being held captive in a room right at the bottom of the government compound. Have been there since they disappeared. The king was killed, but his wife and son live,' Cat explained.

'Bless my soul,' Harry murmured, running a hand over his beard. 'I suppose that solves the problem of who will run the country once the government is gone. If they're up to the task.'

'Do you really think they'll be given a choice?' Alice pointed out. 'After all the government has done, people will want the monarchy back in place, whether the monarchs themselves like it or not.'

'We need to act quickly,' Fox said, sipping at his tea. 'The longer we're in there, the more likely we are to get caught. We need to find out who's in charge, film some conclusive evidence, then evacuate the children and the royals before we bring the place to the ground.'

'We're ready for that when you are,' Matt assured him, his arm still around Ben. The blond man seemed to be shell-shocked by the news of what had probably happened to his sister. Cat didn't blame him; she would have been sobbing if it had been her.

'I'll go back in tonight, and evacuate everyone who needs to get out. We're quite sure we know where all the kids are, but I'll look around for more when I'm planting canisters,' Fox declared. Cat froze, abruptly tearing her hand from his.

'What do you mean, *you're* going back in tonight? You talk as if you're going in alone.'

He nodded.

'That's because I am,' he replied slowly.

She glared.

'You most definitely are not! You're mad if you think I'm letting you go in without me! You need someone to watch your back!'

She couldn't believe they were having the same argument twice. Had she not managed to get it into his thick head the first time?

'It's too dangerous for you,' Fox insisted vehemently. 'We won't be able to keep sticking to the shadows.' Cat rolled her eyes.

'Like it's any less dangerous for you?' she snapped.

'Now, kids, calm down,' Alice attempted quietly, and both teens whipped around to face her.

'You agree with me, though, don't you, Alice?' Fox demanded. 'It's far too dangerous for Cat to go in. I can handle it on my own.'

'Don't get like that, lad,' Harry said with a scowl. 'I don't want you going in on your own. I might not like the idea of

Cat going in either, but it's better than you flying solo in a place like that. Even if you won't be there for long. It'll be easier to get the kids out with two of you, anyway.' His eyes were stern, and it was clear he didn't expect to be argued with.

Fox growled under his breath, tugging at his hair in a way that looked painful.

'Fine. But don't expect me to do all the work. I expect you to pull your weight,' he muttered reluctantly.

Cat raised an eyebrow sharply at him.

'Did I not pull my weight enough today, then?' she asked acidly.

Fox winced.

'That's not what I meant,' he backtracked hastily, and Cat snorted.

'Of course it's not.' She stood up. 'If you'll excuse me, I think I'm going to go before the urge to punch this idiot in the face becomes too overwhelming.'

Even Ben sniggered as Cat stormed towards the door. She knew Fox was following her – his steel-toed boots were loud on the floorboards – but she ignored him all the way back to her bedroom.

'I didn't mean what I said the way it sounded like I meant it,' he blurted out.

She paused for a moment to decipher his words.

'Your meaning was quite clear to me, I assure you,' she replied curtly, turning round to face him. 'Earlier you told me what happened with the guard wasn't my fault.'

'It wasn't!' he insisted. 'I wanted you out of things before that happened.' She folded her arms over her chest, wishing she were taller.

'Make your mind up, Fox. Either it was my fault, or it wasn't. But regardless, I'm not letting you go in alone tomorrow.'

He sighed in frustration, pulling at his fringe.

'It wasn't your fault. Storms, I say all the wrong things around you, Cat,' he told her earnestly.

She didn't budge, just carried on glaring.

'You say enough to prove that you're never going to trust me. I don't know why I bother any more. I'm just as capable as you, girl or not,' she said, looking him in the eye.

He held her gaze for several heartbeats, before looking away.

'I . . . I told you about my parents. I told you that I spent three years with no one. I learned to rely on myself . . . relying on others gets you killed. You might have hated your father, but at least you had him. You never went cold, or hungry, or wondered if you'd still be alive by morning. You don't understand. Trusting people is . . . difficult for me,' he said awkwardly. 'And you might like to think you're capable, but until you reach a situation where you truly need to *be* capable, you won't realise just how much you need help.'

None of this stopped Cat from wanting to clobber him.

'I've spent most of my life sneaking around places I shouldn't be and listening to conversations I shouldn't overhear, so I think I have more experience in this area than you. I know enough information to ruin the careers of half the men in the upper echelons of government, and I don't care how often you want to have this argument with me, my answer won't change. You need me in this, but we won't get anywhere if you don't bloody well stop trying to protect me!'

'You're a girl, it's my job to protect you!'

Furious, Cat slapped Fox across the face, leaving a bright red handprint on his cheek.

'It's times like this I wish I'd managed to stay a boy!' she hissed, storming off towards the manhole. She didn't care where she went, so long as it was away from Fox.

Still raging, Cat glared at the floor as she walked, glad that Fox wasn't following her. Almost without thinking, she found herself in the engine room, heading straight for Fox's private workshop. She expected to meet resistance when she pushed the handle down, but the door swung open. Feeling very much as if she was doing something forbidden, she crept forward into the low-lit room, noticing it was just as neat as it had been the last – and only – time she'd entered. Very few of Fox's little projects were out of their boxes; some sat on shelves of their own or on the floor.

She shuddered as a loud crackling noise filled the room, and one of the mechanisms on a shelf to her left began emitting violent purple sparks. She reached for it, wincing as the sparks burned her fingers. Quickly transferring it to the workbench, she sat in the chair and grabbed a magnifying glass. It was a complicated little piece of machinery, with many intertwined pieces.

Eventually, she began to recognise some of the components. She gasped. It was a mecha, but almost spider-like in its construction. Being so tiny, it held just the very basics, but the spindles she assumed were legs had feet of rough wire cloth, and there was a single eye lens in the centre of its 'head'.

The sparks resumed, this time accompanied by the tell-tale violet-grey smoke of an overheated tyrium core. She reached for a pair of needle-nose pliers and the soldering iron. It took a while to part the gear plate casing far enough to see into the very centre of the spider-mecha, and she hummed in dismay. Sure enough, the two gossamer-thin gear chains connected to the small cube of brightly coloured fuel were too close together, and kept rubbing against each other. That was going to be difficult to alter.

She worked in near silence, the only sound being the occasional splutter from the mechanism or thoughtful hum escaping her own lips. She was so engrossed in her work that she didn't notice the door opening, and leather-clad feet crossing the room.

'What are you doing?'

She squeaked loudly, jumping at the unexpected voice.

'Bloody hell, Fox, don't *do* that! Not when I'm holding hot things!' she exclaimed, shaking the soldering iron at him for emphasis.

He gave her an apologetic half-smile.

'I asked you a question,' he reminded, and she bristled.

'I came down here to get away from *you*,' she said sharply. 'I really wasn't going to touch anything, but then this started sparking and I figured I should at least attempt to fix it, rather than just leaving it to melt itself in a corner somewhere.'

'Oh,' he replied simply, leaning back against a shelf. 'And can you?' He nodded towards the upturned spider-mecha on the workbench.

She turned back to the machine with a nod, using the

pliers to feed a thin strip of solder wire into the crevice, pressing the tip of the wire to the tiny pinion and lifting the soldering iron against it. The gear slowed, fixing itself in place, and the two gear chains revolved – but didn't touch. She smiled to herself, carefully closing up the seam she'd created, flipping the spider-mecha back the right way up and balancing it on its thin legs. It shuddered for several seconds as the spark caught on the tyrium, before walking forward in a clumsy, uncoordinated manner. Small puffs of vibrant purple smoke escaped from the chimney on its back, showing that the tyrium was at the right temperature to burn as it fuelled the mechanism.

'Does that answer your question?' she replied, slightly smug.

Fox raised an eyebrow.

'What was wrong with it?'

'Gear chains on the inside were in contact, so the poor little thing was shorting out,' she explained. 'Did you not know?'

Fox shrugged, not meeting her eyes.

'I've been trying to figure out why he was being so disagreeable. I suppose it just takes a fresh eye at times,' he relented.

'Fresh eye, sure,' she said, trying to suppress a smile. She watched the spider-mecha wander across the workbench while the two of them stood in silence, occasionally redirecting it before it could wander off the edge and on to the floor.

Fox sighed. 'I feel like I'm spending most of my time either arguing with you or apologising for arguing with you,' he told her resignedly.

'There's an easy solution, then, isn't there?' she replied simply. 'Stop arguing with me.'

He laughed, the sound loud in the small room.

'Easier said than done, I assure you,' he murmured wryly. 'I am sorry, though. I'm just ... not used to girls like you.'

'What's that supposed to mean?' Cat asked.

'I'll try and stop being so overprotective,' Fox continued without answering. 'But I can't make any promises. Just ... tell me if I'm being an arse, and I'll try and stop.'

She chuckled, and he smiled back tentatively.

'All right, then,' she agreed, supposing it was the best she would get. 'We need to get back to the compound, don't we? It's getting late.'

'It's about time now,' Fox agreed.

Taking a few moments to figure out how to turn the spider-mecha off, Cat stood and followed Fox, the pair of them heading up to the floor above.

'What does he do, anyway? The little spider thing,' she asked Fox.

'He's meant to clean the inside of pipes that neither Matt nor I can fit our hands into – that's why there's wire cloth on his feet. He's a work in progress, but ... I'm sure I'll get him up and functioning soon. The biggest problem is trying to fit in enough components to get him to do his job, without making him so big that he'd get stuck.'

'That's ... actually quite clever,' she remarked, and he grinned crookedly.

'Don't sound so surprised,' he retorted.

She laughed, nudging his shoulder playfully.

'Kissed and made up, have we?' Matt teased, stepping out

of his bedroom just as they emerged from the manhole. Both of them blushed furiously, making Matt snicker. 'I'll take that as a yes. Ready to get moving, then?'

'If everyone else is,' Cat confirmed, thinking of all those children in cages, of Mary and James in their prison below the city. The sooner they got them out the better.

'We're all set. Harry's got a friend who's a whizz with film and audio, and he's going to cut together your footage into something we can broadcast to the rest of the world. We'll get you two in, Benny and I will start setting up the canisters and make sure the newscast room is clear for you, then when Alice and Harry meet us with the footage we'll wait for you to get out with the kids.'

'How is Ben?' Fox asked, voice low, and Matt's smile faltered.

'Not taking it well. But . . . he's got a focus for now. It'll be later when it hits him hard. Storms, poor Sophie. We knew Collection was bad, but something like this never crossed our minds.' Cat reached out, squeezing one of his large hands in hers. If Matt and Ben had been friends since they were kids, he must have known Sophie too.

'We'll make things right,' she said determinedly. 'For Sophie, and all the others.'

When they got up to the galley, it was to find the three remaining members of their crew geared up and ready to go. Ben's satchel was bulging, and Cat could see the telltale outline of several guns on his person. Many more were lying on the table, and Matt broke away to start equipping them with frightening efficiency.

'Matt tell you the plan?' Harry asked, his expression

serious. All of them were dressed in black, and his usual leather top hat had been replaced with a black flat cap.

'Yes,' nodded Fox. 'You'll sort out the newscast footage, Matt and Ben will plant the canisters. We get in, find out who's in charge, get the sprogs, get the monarchs, and get out as quickly as we can. Anything else?' Fox said evenly. Harry clapped him on the shoulder.

'The rest of it can wait until you have the kids out. You ready, Cat?' His brown eyes landed on her, and she swallowed, nodding. The clock was ticking.

'As I'll ever be.'

Getting back into the compound was much easier than Cat anticipated; the four of them were in within minutes. Harry and Alice had gone to take the video and audio footage to their friend, Fox replacing the film cases with fresh ones before wiring himself and Cat up. Splitting up with Matt and Ben as soon as they were past East Gate, Cat followed Fox round to the window they had left through, helping him up to the sill. 'It's clear,' he assured her, shifting on the ledge to hoist her up beside him. Cat was glad for the cloudy weather masking the lower rays of the sunset, making it near pitch-black as they slipped in through the window.

'Where to first?' she whispered, and Fox frowned.

'We'll head to where we haven't looked yet. We're on a time limit now, and we need to find something good. The closer we get to the stairs to the upper levels, the more likely we are to find out who's in charge.' That decided, he led the way further down the corridor, both of them as silent as ghosts.

A little way past the stairs down to the Lathams' prison, they came across a small crowd of people all leaving what looked like a conference room, a flood of chatter accompanying them. Cat flicked her audio recorder on. She saw Fox do the same, his body tensed. Latching on to the word 'children', Cat attempted to follow a conversation between two men lagging at the back of the group, wishing she could step forward a little further.

'They're bringing in another trainload of sprogs from the Greaves at the weekend,' the man on the left – a short, balding, rather chubby man by the name of Harold Woods – told his companion. Cat's brow furrowed. Since when had there been a train out to the Greaves Mountains?

'Another lot already? Bloody hell, we're going through them fast. How many are even being sent skywards these days? Seems like we're taking as many out to bury as we bring in.'

Cat couldn't get a good look at the second man, but by his significant girth and the unique red and purple velvet coat he wore, she assumed he was Robert McCrae, the only man she knew with such interesting choices in clothing. She frowned at his wording; what did he mean by "sent skywards"? Making a gesture to Fox, Cat crept behind the migrating group.

'Doesn't it just? Apparently they're confident about this lot, though. All Greystone kids, healthier than the street rats we got last time. Listen, I've got to split, I've got a meeting with the boss before I call it a night. He needs to talk expenses,' Woods told the older man with an annoyed frown.

McCrae snorted, patting Woods on the shoulder.

'Good luck,' he remarked.

McCrae turned into a room off to the side. And glancing at Fox, Cat knew they didn't need to discuss which of the men to follow.

Woods walked through a door at the end of the corridor and, after waiting for several heartbeats, Cat and Fox followed. To their surprise, there was a narrow staircase ahead, and Woods was on his way up. Careful not to make any sound on the steps, they crept along behind the squat man, who was muttering to himself under his breath.

When they reached the top of the staircase there was another door, and Woods had to remove a key from his pocket to open it. Luckily, he didn't feel the need to lock it behind him, and after a long pause Cat turned the handle slowly, waiting for it to creak. She let out a sigh of relief when it didn't, pushing the door open and stepping through. Immediately, her heart sank, and her stomach turned to lead. She knew this corridor. This was the corridor in the north wing of the second floor of the government building; the corridor she had been left in many times while her father conducted important business meetings in his office. She felt a deep sense of dread in her gut, and stopped in her tracks, causing Fox to bump into her. His bright eyes were fixed on the ostentatious decor of the corridor; the lush purple carpets, the varnished dark wood walls lit with far more ornate silver lanterns than the ones downstairs. Portraits of famous past government leaders hung on the walls, and Cat vividly remembered the time she'd drawn moustaches on several of them.

'What?' Fox hissed in her ear. Woods was still walking,

heading towards the worryingly familiar door at the end of the hallway.

'No,' Cat was murmuring, shaking her head, as Woods knocked on the door, waited for a beat and then entered, shutting it behind him.

Glancing around the empty corridor, Fox grabbed Cat forcefully by the arm, pulling her forward.

'Please!' she gasped frantically. 'Turn around and go back!'

Fox ignored her, and she closed her eyes tightly as he hovered near the door. She didn't need to open her eyes; she'd spent a good deal of her life staring at that door, bored out of her mind. She could tell Fox that there were twenty-four squares of glass in the window. She could tell him that the door handle was brass, and jammed if you lifted it upwards first, locking the door from the outside; she'd had a lot of fun fiddling with the handle, and a lot of fun locking people inside for hours. And she could definitely tell him that there was a spelling mistake on the plaque just below the window – the plaque that, spelled correctly, would have read *Lord N Hunter II*.

19

Fox froze, staring in shock at the nameplate.

'Hunter,' he breathed, eyes wide. 'Your ...'

'Father,' Cat finished, her voice small and scared. 'Gods ...
I had no idea he ...' She shook her head; she should have
known. Deep down, part of her had suspected as soon as
she'd learned the truth, but there had been plenty to suggest
he wasn't involved. Collection and war strategy weren't
anything to do with him, and while she hated her father she
hadn't believed him capable of such cruelty. In retrospect, it
all added up; the frequency of men in the compound she'd
recognised as working for him, his comment about the war
coming to an end. Still, she wouldn't believe it just yet.
There had to be more solid proof.

'You won't be able to get the door open,' she told Fox.
'He got an inside lock after I tried to eavesdrop one too
many times.'

She couldn't help wincing as she remembered the
punishment she'd been given on that particular occasion.
Things like breathing and swallowing had been hard for a
few days.

'Two minutes,' Fox said quietly, lifting his video recorder

up to the window, recording the discussion going on inside the office. Cat didn't move, not until Fox lowered the recorder and walked back to her. He didn't speak until they had returned to the stairwell they'd used to enter the public offices, sat under the stairs at the bottom.

'Did you know?'

Cat's eyes widened.

'*What?*' she gasped incredulously, staring at him in shock.

He stared back intently. '*Did you know?*' he repeated slowly.

'Of course I didn't know! How could I have known? But there has to be some other explanation! He couldn't be behind something like this . . . he couldn't!' she told him desperately, trying to believe her own words.

Fox snorted in disbelief.

'You're defending him? All that talk about him hating you and you wishing you'd never been born to him, and you're defending him?'

'He's my father!' she hissed. 'I hate him, but he's still my father! You wouldn't understand that, would you?'

Fox recoiled as if he'd been punched, and guilt welled in her chest.

'I'm sorry. I didn't mean that,' she said immediately.

'Yeah, you did,' Fox replied, his voice oddly low. Cat wished she'd kept her big mouth shut. 'We need to get moving. We're running out of time.' Fox didn't look at her when he said this, getting to his feet and leaving Cat with no choice but to do the same.

'He wouldn't do something like this. He works the home front, not Collections. And he's cruel, but not *this* cruel,' Cat continued. How could she have known her father for fifteen years, and not had an inkling that he was behind the mass mutilation and murder of *children*?

'From what you've told me, he's *exactly* this cruel,' Fox said sharply. 'Why do you care, anyway? I thought you'd disowned him, renounced your government connections. I thought you were one of us.'

'I *am*!' she said desperately. 'But excuse me for wanting to believe that the man who sired and raised me has at least a *shred* of kindness in his stone cold heart!' Not wanting to hear Fox's retort, she pushed past him and fled from the room.

Later, she would be amazed at how reckless she'd been, and how she'd managed not to run into a single worker as she sprinted down random corridors and staircases. She didn't know how long she kept running, just that when she stopped she had no idea where she was. Dropping to the floor in an alcove, she buried her face in her hands, choking back a sob. Why didn't Fox believe her when she said her father wouldn't do something like this? Yes, he was a bastard, she admitted that freely. And yes, he was probably supportive of what was going on – she wasn't naive enough to think that he had no idea; he knew everything that went on in government – but he wasn't unfeeling enough to be in charge of the whole thing, was he? There *had* to be some other explanation.

Wiping her wet cheeks angrily, she stood up, determined to get some work done and prove to Fox that not only was he wrong, but that she could do plenty without his help or protection. Emerging from her alcove, she walked up to the nearest door and peered through the window, feeling the now familiar tightening in her gut. A boy lay on a table, his midriff covered by a sheet that stopped high enough for her to see that both his legs were mechanical. She didn't dare think about how long he'd been lying there.

The door swung open easily, and carefully she tiptoed up to the table, breathing through her mouth in an attempt to ignore the smell of blood and burned flesh. At first, she thought it was another dead child, and she felt a pang of sorrow. Then she looked closer and almost jumped out of her skin when she noticed the gentle, barely there rise and fall of his chest.

Cat started as a low, rasping groan echoed around the room. The boy was attempting to open his eyes. She stared at him, flicking on her audio and video recorders as she did so.

'Hello? Can you hear me?' she murmured, stroking his sweat-matted brown hair. It was close-cropped, like a military cut. 'I'm not one of them, I'm safe, I promise,' she breathed, willing him to wake up. Slowly, unfocused blue-green eyes blinked open, eyeing her in dazed confusion.

'I . . . who?' he croaked, chest heaving with the effort.

Cat hushed him, still stroking his hair.

'My name is Cat,' she told him. 'I'm here to help. My friends and I are working to save you. We'll call in the foreign authorities, and we'll shut the government down, and we'll stop them taking children.'

She sounded far more confident than she felt inside, but didn't let her fear show. 'M'name's . . . Andrew,' he breathed. 'Andrew . . . Hale.'

251

'Hello, Andrew Hale,' she replied with a smile. 'How . . . how long have you been here?'

He gave the barest twitch of his shoulders. 'Two . . . years.'

Cat gasped, eyes wide. He'd been there for two years? She couldn't imagine spending two *days* in that kind of torture!

'Gods . . . I'm so sorry,' she murmured.

'Not . . . your fault, lass,' he told her with a huffing breath that she thought was meant to be a laugh. Her eyebrows rose in surprise that he'd recognised her as a girl, despite her hair and clothing.

'I wish there was more I could do for you,' she said. 'Even if I knew how to get those awful contraptions off you, I couldn't give you back your legs.'

He met her eyes, his breathing becoming a little more ragged.

'You're . . . stopping them?' he asked. 'You're . . . telling the . . . world what they've . . . done?' Cat nodded frantically, and his half-smile grew. 'Then you're . . . doing plenty. It's too . . . late for me . . . but not for . . . others.'

Cat felt a tear trickle down the side of her nose.

'You're incredible,' she told him. 'Most people would hate me for not being able to save them.'

Andrew smiled wryly, giving another twitch-shrug.

'Knew I . . . would die . . . here,' he breathed. 'Least now I . . . know there's . . . hope for . . . the rest.'

'I won't let this happen to any other kids,' she vowed. 'We'll stop them before the next Collection, I promise. They won't get away with what they've done to you.'

He smiled at her, sweat beading on his forehead with the

effort of talking and staying conscious. Cat imagined he must be in excruciating pain, and her respect for him rose even higher.

'You're ... sweet,' he told her with a choked chuckle. 'When it's ... over, tell ... my mum I'm ... sorry. Nancy Hale ... Friar's Way.'

Cat nodded, glad her audio recorder was on.

'I will, I'll find her. I'll tell her how brave her son is,' she assured him tearfully.

'Thank you,' he rasped. His eyes moved to look at something over her shoulder, and he frowned. 'You need to ... go. They'll ... be back ... soon. Apparently I need ... a new arm.' He smiled weakly, but Cat could see the fear in his gaze. He wasn't sure he'd survive a third 'enhancement'.

'I won't forget you,' she promised. 'I'll find your mother, and I'll tell her. Just ... stay strong, OK?'

He gritted his teeth and gave her a fraction of a nod. She leaned in, pressing her lips to his cheek. His skin was cold and clammy, and when she pulled back, he was grinning.

'Kiss goodbye from ... a pretty girl. What ... else do I ... need to ... stay strong?' he said, making Cat laugh.

'You charmer,' she retorted. 'Good luck, Andrew Hale.'

'You too ... Cat. See you ... around.'

'See you around,' she replied softly, fleeing the room before more hot tears escaped from her eyes. She ran, this time with a destination, retracing her way to the queen's prison.

Taking a small screwdriver from her bag, she started working the gears, thanking the gods that she'd paid attention when Fox was unlocking the door. It took three times as long as it would have taken him, but eventually she heard a satisfying click and pushed the door open.

'Cat,' Mary said in surprise. 'Where's Fox?'

'You mean he's not back yet?' Cat asked, shocked.

'No, we were getting worried. The guards have brought dinner already,' Mary told her, gesturing to the tray on the coffee table. 'We saved some, but it's probably cold by now.'

'Thanks,' Cat murmured, not feeling at all hungry.

'So where's Fox? Is he OK? I thought you two refused to split up?' Mary queried insistently.

Remembering what Fox had said about her father, Cat scowled, crossing her arms over her chest.

'I don't care if he's OK,' she replied stubbornly. Both Mary and James looked at her with raised eyebrows.

'That doesn't sound good. What happened?' James questioned.

Cat bit her lip, not sure if she wanted to tell them. But she needed answers, once and for all. 'We followed a man – Harold Woods – after he said he had a meeting with the boss, and . . . he went into my father's office. Fox immediately took that to mean that my father is in charge of this whole disgusting operation! I hate my father, but I can't see him doing something like this!'

Mary's expression faltered, and dread settled in Cat's stomach.

'I always feared my suspicions would be true. Cat, I . . . I'm sorry,' she began, and Cat shook her head.

'No, no, it can't be true,' she protested.

Mary took a step closer, resting a hand on her arm.

'I'm so, so sorry, darling. Nathaniel . . . he's a very troubled

254

man. When we were first kidnapped, he came down here and gloated about how we'd never be free, and he'd have control of government, and that his daughter would never marry my brat of a son. You won't tell me what is going on but whatever it is Nathaniel is involved, and it wouldn't surprise me to learn it was his idea. After all, our kidnapping was.' She scowled at those words, and James let out an indignant noise.

'You're . . . you're telling the truth, aren't you?' Cat asked in resignation, not wanting to face the evidence she could see building up all around her. Mary nodded, squeezing her forearm.

'You have to understand, Cat, your father was never in his right mind. He only cares about what he can get out of things. He married your mother to get to the Ingate fortune, he had you to have an heir and loathed it because you were a girl, and he gained control of the country for what *he* would gain from it. He doesn't care how his actions affect others because he simply doesn't understand that he's hurting people.'

Cat felt her knees buckle, but an arm slid around her waist before she could hit the floor. She vaguely realised James was helping her over to the nearest sofa, but couldn't have cared less, collapsing into the brown leather.

'How . . . how could he do *this*, though?' she asked mournfully. 'I don't understand. I knew he was a bastard, but I thought even *he* had some sort of moral code.'

Tears welling in her eyes, Cat ducked her head, not struggling when James's arm came around her, pulling her into his chest somewhat awkwardly. It wasn't as reassuring or safe as being in Fox's arms, but she was glad for the comfort all the same.

'I don't know why some people do the things they do,' he murmured into her hair as she leaned into him. 'But whatever your father has done, you can't blame yourself. He makes his own decisions. You're doing something good – you're trying to stop him.'

Cat managed a weak smile, which vanished when the door swung open and an all too familiar flash of red hair showed that Fox had returned. She wiped her eyes, and swallowed uneasily as she saw him looking angrily at her and James.

'You're back, then,' he noted. 'Do you have any idea how long I've been looking for you? You irresponsible moron, I thought you'd got yourself caught! I nearly got *myself* caught! I've been looking everywhere for you, and you've been here the whole bloody time! I'd have thought you'd know not to wander off in such a dangerous place, or don't you care any more now that you know getting caught will just take you to Daddy dearest?'

Cat wrenched herself from James's embrace, jumping to her feet and glaring at Fox.

'Wandering off? I can look after myself, thank you very much! And I wouldn't have had to "*wander off*" if you weren't being such a pillock! For the last time, I don't want to go back to my father! I had just enough faith in him still to not instantly assume things about him! I now know I was wrong, but ... I didn't want to believe it. Even *you* should be able to understand that.'

Fox rolled his eyes in exasperation.

'Cat, I really don't give a crap about your father. To me, he's just another government bastard trying to kill us all. I *thought* you were of the same opinion,' he snapped.

'Stop arguing, both of you!' James cut in desperately, standing beside Cat. He reached out to grab her hand, but she yanked her arm away, sending him stumbling into his surprised mother.

'This is none of your business!' Fox roared. 'So stay out of it! Gods, I don't need to deal with this right now.' He turned on his heel, storming off into James's bedroom, slamming the door behind him.

Cat felt as if she was a puppet with her strings cut, falling back on to the sofa limply.

'Well, that's just made everything ten times worse,' she muttered into her hands. 'You two need to pack. We're evacuating as soon as we've got something to show Nathaniel is in charge,' she told them. 'Pack only what you need – we can't be weighed down. I . . . I'm going to go talk to Fox.'

She stood, and Mary briefly laid a hand on her arm, urging James to follow her into her bedroom. Cat took a deep breath, steeling her nerves, and strode across to James's bedroom.

20

Not bothering to knock, Cat slipped inside and shut the door softly behind her. Fox was sitting on the floor, leaning against the foot of the bed.

'I'm sorry,' she began somewhat awkwardly. 'I shouldn't have run off, I know that. I was just . . . upset. I know I'd be just as angry if it had been you, so I'm sorry.'

'Is that it?' he asked flatly, making her flinch.

'No.' She took a deep breath, trying to calm her emotions. She'd done enough crying today. 'I'm sorry I argued so much about my father. But . . . you have to understand where I was coming from. I hate him, but he's my father, and no one wants to think their father capable of something so . . . so inhumane.' She shuddered, Andrew's pain-filled blue-green eyes drifting through her mind. Her father had been responsible for that. 'I was just so angry, but I . . . I don't want to fight with you any more, Fox,' she told him earnestly, eyes wide in apology. 'I can't stand having you angry with me.'

Fox was silent for a long moment, and Cat was about to leave when he held out an arm expectantly. She stared at him, uncertain of what to do. He rolled his eyes, curling his fingers in a beckoning gesture. Hesitantly, she moved closer, dropping to the floor beside him. When he didn't lash out at her, she scooted under his arm, allowing him to pull her into a half-hug by his side.

'I forgive you,' he said softly. 'It can't have been easy for you to find out something like that. And I'm sorry for all the horrible things I said earlier,' he added. 'I think we've both said things today that we regret.'

Cat nodded.

'Yeah, we have,' she agreed quietly. Suddenly, a small grin flickered across her face, and she rested her hand on his knee just above where his trouser leg tucked into his boot, her middle and index finger outstretched. 'Start over?'

He smiled slightly, crossing his index and middle finger over hers, curling them around each other. She hadn't done that since she was a young child; the instant forgiveness technique often used in the school playground. As soon as fingers were linked, the argument was forgotten.

'Start over,' he promised, before releasing her fingers. Her hand stayed on his outstretched knee, though, and his hand rested over it.

'I feel a bit of an idiot,' he mused, and she raised a questioning eyebrow. 'I can't believe I didn't connect the dots sooner, when I first met you. I'd seen him on newscasts ... you have that same sort of look about your face. I suppose your false gender threw me off – I knew Hunter didn't have a son.'

'He did raise me,' she pointed out. 'He hated that he didn't have a son, and brought me up as both son and daughter. It backfired on him though – by learning to be

259

the perfect son I became far more opinionated than any well-behaved lady of society.'

Fox laughed quietly.

'Isn't that the truth?' he agreed. 'So where did you go when you ran off?'

Cat shrugged, letting her head drop to lean against his shoulder.

'I don't really know – I wasn't paying attention to where I was going,' she admitted. 'I . . . I met a boy, though.' She didn't need to look to know Fox was gazing inquisitively at her. 'His name was Andrew. He . . . he's been here for two years already, and they've taken both his legs. He said he was getting an arm today.'

Fox let out a long breath. Cat squeezed his knee gently.

'He was so brave. He could barely talk, but he still told me about himself. I told him that we were going to stop it, and he just asked me to tell his mother he's sorry. He said he always knew he would die here, and . . . he didn't seem to mind that he was dying. He called me pretty,' she added with a smile.

'They hadn't taken his eyes, then,' remarked Fox, making her blush. She didn't know what to make of Fox when he made comments like that. 'He sounds like an amazing lad. I'm sure his mother, when we find her, will be very proud of her son.'

Cat looked up at him hopefully.

'You'll help me find her? He gave me her name, and said she lived in Friar's Way, but . . . it's an awfully big place.'

Fox squeezed her shoulders.

'Of course I will.'

She couldn't help smiling to herself. Despite where they were, and what was going on around them, she couldn't regret her part in it all. She had met Fox, after all.

'I think James has his eye on you, you know,' he told her.

'What makes you think that?' she asked, amused.

'The way he looks at you. He was awfully happy, having you in his arms and comforting you, when I walked in. And the way he looks at me whenever I touch you – he's jealous! Don't tell me you haven't noticed?'

Cat flushed at the implication that there was something between her and Fox to be jealous of.

'Maybe you should give him a chance,' continued Fox. 'Of course he's a prat, but then he's spent his whole life in solitude. He'll improve – I hope – in time. And he's your age, and he'll be king one day if we sort all this out. You could be Queen of Anglya.'

Cat grimaced, shaking her head rapidly.

'I don't want to be a queen. I just want to stay on the *Stormdancer*,' she insisted.

'Yes, but the country will need a queen after all this is over. And I can't think of anyone better than the girl who started the revolution in the first place.'

Cat's heart twisted painfully. It was clear Fox didn't have any feelings for her; he sounded far too at ease with the idea of her marrying James.

'I won't marry for duty,' she told him fiercely. 'If I wanted that, I'd have stayed with my father and married Marcus Gale. I'll marry for love, and I don't think I could ever love James.'

She didn't think – she *knew* she would never love James. Not now she'd met Fox.

261

'Hmm, well,' Fox murmured doubtfully. 'There's marrying for love, and then there's realising who would be best for you.'

'The man I love would be best for me,' she pointed out. 'Who could be better?'

Fox shrugged, sighing.

'We need to go back out there,' she declared softly. 'I told Mary and James to pack and be ready to leave, but we need to get more proof of who's involved and start getting the kids out. Ben will be getting impatient with those canisters of his.' Fox snorted, getting to his feet and helping her up.

'Ben can wait – we'll only have one chance at this. Come on, let's get back out there.'

Wiping the few stray tears from her cheeks, Cat followed Fox, suddenly very aware of how much time she had wasted by running away.

Mary and James looked up when the two entered the room, two satchels on the sofa between them.

'All better now?' Mary asked with a smile, and Cat nodded.

'Yes, thank you. We're ready to get going again. Stay prepared – we don't know how long before we'll be back. We still have some work to do here, but as soon as we're done we'll come and get you, and we'll need to be quick about it.'

Fox started for the door while Cat slung her bag over her shoulder and let Fox get the lock. When they were outside, he turned to her abruptly.

'I've just realised – you must have unlocked this door on your own!'

Cat rolled her eyes at him.

'Yes, because believe it or not, I'm actually *not* completely incompetent.'

He shrugged apologetically, giving her a lopsided smile.

'I know that, but I didn't think you paid all that much attention when I hacked it.'

Cat didn't respond, not wanting to sound like a soppy fool by telling him she paid attention to *everything* he did.

They retraced their steps back to the corridor that led to Nathaniel's office, and Cat was just about to walk towards the door when she saw the handle turn. Grabbing Fox's sleeve she yanked him around a corner as the door opened and an all too familiar man walked out.

Cat wasn't sure what she was meant to feel upon seeing her father again. He hadn't changed much since she'd last seen him; there were no bags under his eyes or extra grey hairs at his temples from worrying about his missing daughter. He strolled purposefully down the corridor, and Cat saw Fox reach into his waistcoat to turn on his recorders. She did the same, feeling some measure of guilt at spying on her father. But she shoved it away; he wasn't her father any more, he was a power-hungry bastard who was slaughtering and maiming innocent children.

They didn't have to follow him far; he went down one flight of stairs, turned a corner and entered a lab that neither Cat nor Fox had yet been in. Cat peered through the window, gasping at what she saw inside. A pair of mechanics were working on an unconscious young girl who lay on a table; a girl who looked disturbingly like Cat. Fox opened the door a crack, enough to hear what was going on inside.

Like many of the other labs, there were crates full of mechanical attachments in various stages of completion lining the walls, with enough of a gap between them and the walls for Cat and Fox to hide. When both mechanics and Nathaniel were absorbed in studying the girl on the table, Cat and Fox slipped through the door and scrambled behind a pile of crates. Finding a narrow space between two crates that she could peer through, Cat unhooked both her recorders to set them in the gap, resting on the crate below. Her father was looking closely at the girl.

'We just wanted to check, m'lord, that it wasn't her. Before we did anything irreversible, y'see,' one of the mechanics stuttered nervously. 'Only she looks awfully similar, and we didn't want to harm your lordship's daughter.'

Cat could feel Fox's eyes on her, but ignored them, watching her father.

'Very well,' he murmured, his hand reaching out to roll the girl over, examining her lower back. Cat's hand went almost instinctively to her own lower back, lifting up the tail of her shirt and feeling across the three twisted lines of scar tissue running down the line of her spine. She had been six years old, and her father had been *very* angry.

'This is not my daughter,' Nathaniel confirmed, letting the girl fall limply to the table. 'Do what you will with her.'

The mechanics nodded, relieved, and one of them scurried across the room to pick up a thick bronze chest plate with several thin chains and wires dangling from the underside. The other picked a scalpel up from a tray, lowering it on to the girl's ribs. Cat looked away, nauseous. It disgusted her that, despite the similarities, her father didn't flinch. She wondered what he would have done if it *had* been her on that table; would he let them continue with the experiment? She shuddered, unable to answer her own question.

'The Hale boy accepted the third enhancement, m'lord,' the mechanic with the chest plate told Nathaniel, and Cat perked up. Andrew was still alive? 'He'll be ready to send skywards by tomorrow morning, if he survives the night. One of the strong ones, he is.'

A smile tugged at Nathaniel's lips, and he nodded curtly.

'Good. Was that all you needed from me? To check the girl wasn't Catherine?'

Cat couldn't believe he was completely ignoring the girl on the table.

'Yes, m'lord. If you'll excuse us, we've got to get over to Lab Seven to help with a rather difficult arm addition. The subject's a little small, you see . . .' the mechanic trailed off, and Nathaniel chuckled.

'Small test subjects don't survive – you know that. But all practice is good, so if you must, then leave,' he dismissed them.

Cat watched as the mechanics drew a blanket over the girl on the table, not bothering to clear away their dirty surgical tools as they left. Nathaniel didn't follow, staying by the girl's side. She was surprised to see him put a hand on the girl's forehead, brushing her dark brown fringe from her closed eyes. Cat glanced sideways at Fox, who looked both disturbed and frustrated, his blue eyes darting between Nathaniel and the door.

'You don't think I didn't notice you sneak in, do you?' Nathaniel called out.

Cat's heart stopped. Fox turned to her, an expression of wide-eyed horror on his face.

'Yes, I know you're there,' Nathaniel called, his voice smooth and dark, amusement clear in his tone. 'You might as well show yourselves.'

Cat exchanged another frightened look with Fox, then stood on shaking legs, keeping her head held high as she met her father's gaze.

'Well, well, the prodigal daughter returns,' Nathaniel murmured, failing to hide his shock, turning his head as Fox stood as well. 'And you've brought a friend. How sweet! I must say, when you ran off, I wasn't expecting to see you again, especially not here. Marcus was terribly disappointed when I told him his little bride was no more.'

Heart pounding, Cat walked out into the centre of the room. Her audio and video recorders were sitting in the gap between two crates, but the glint of metal on Fox's waistcoat told her that his were still attached.

'Marcus can go jump in a hurricane,' she spat, making her father laugh.

'Oh, I have missed that razor-sharp tongue of yours, daughter dear,' he said fondly.

'I'm not your *daughter* any more,' she told him.

He smirked.

'Of course you're not. I would never stand for having a street rat as a daughter. I should have known you'd end up associating with commoners. Maybe I should have offered you up for Collection when I had the chance. You would have turned out far more useful than you are now.'

'You'll see how useful I can be! We'll bring down this

horrific experiment of yours, Nathaniel! We're going to let the authorities in Erova and Mericus know what's happening.'

Cat felt somewhat odd calling her father by his first name, but she wouldn't ever call him 'Father' again.

'We don't *need* those countries, Catherine. We *created* them. None of those countries would even exist in the way they do if not for the original Anglyan explorers who found them. They'll learn, though, they all will.'

'Learn what? That you have been lying to the entire world for years?'

Nathaniel threw his head back and laughed. 'When I set my army on them, they'll realise how wrong they were to demand independence from our glorious empire! You might stop the experiments in this compound, Catherine dear, but you'll never find my army! High up in a skyship, out of reach of your grubby little fingers. That's where the *real* experiments are – the successful ones, the ones that survive enhancement. And they're almost ready for war.' He smirked savagely and Cat suddenly realised that he was mad; completely and certifiably insane.

'You're a fool! Those countries are far better off independent than they ever were under Anglyan reign. You won't get away with this.'

He cut her off with a laugh, eyes glinting dangerously.

'And why is that, little Catherine? I've been kidnapping children for years, and no one has noticed. Not when I call it *recruiting*. And no one objects to rations if I tell them we're at war. Such mindless little sheep, doing what their lord tells them, not questioning a single word I say. They made it so very *easy* to get what I want, and I don't see how that's going to change just because you managed to run off, humiliate me and now "discover" what's going on here.'

Cat smirked triumphantly, not realising how frighteningly similar she looked to the man in front of her at that moment.

'That's because I know something you don't, Nathaniel,' she taunted. 'And what I know is that this entire conversation has just been recorded for the world to hear.'

Nathaniel's eyes widened, and he looked around, as if expecting a large newscast camera to suddenly pop into existence.

'You're bluffing,' he hissed.

'I most certainly am not. Fox and I have recorded everything in this room, and more. We've found the Lathams, and we'll make sure everyone learns the truth about what you've been doing to their children. Somehow I don't think they'll be too happy about that, do you?'

Nathaniel let out a loud roar of rage, clenching his fists.

'You little brat!' he growled. She stood her ground, chin jutting out defiantly. 'You won't get away with this, Catherine. You or your little friend.' He reached inside his long leather trench coat, and Cat froze in shock as he pulled a gun from a holster at his hip. He aimed it steadily at her, pulling back the hammer with a mechanical click. 'You can't expose me if you don't leave this room alive.'

21

Cat's heart pounded against her ribs and her brain whirled in panic. Nathaniel was armed; they weren't. And there was no scrap of sentimentality in Nathaniel that would stop him from shooting his own daughter. They should have taken one of the guns from Matt and Ben.

Suddenly, a blur of black wool and copper-coloured hair blocked her vision, and a muscular arm pulled her close against an equally muscular back. Fox had stepped in front of her. She growled in frustration. He was an idiot if he thought she was going to let him face a man with a gun.

'Oh, how disgustingly saccharine – you've taken up with a common boy!' Nathaniel jeered, the gun still pointed at them. 'That's all you'd be good for, little girl. Pity I didn't notice sooner – I could have made good money.'

Disgusted, Cat squared her shoulders, knowing anything that might have remained between them was gone. She would have no remorse, no regrets, whatever happened.

'I should have done the same with your worthless mother,' Nathaniel continued. 'She's dead, you know? Died crying her eyes out just days after you left. And as far as everyone else is concerned you're dead too. It's time I made that rumour true.'

Cat felt breathless. She'd had her suspicions about her mother, but to have it confirmed like that was a shock. 'You won't lay a finger on Cat,' Fox snarled.

'Oh, so it talks,' Nathaniel exclaimed in mock surprise. 'You're very sweet, little boy, but this is a family affair. It doesn't involve you.'

'Fox is more of a man than you'll ever be,' Cat said.

'Little Catherine, trying to stand up for her brat boyfriend. How quaint. It won't get you very far, though. I'll just shoot you both.'

Nathaniel moved to pull the trigger, but before Cat could blink Fox had jumped forward, diving for the gun. Cat screamed loudly, sure the gun would go off as Fox and Nathaniel crashed to the ground, both gripping the gun. Fox kicked out roughly, trying to get his opponent to release the weapon. Cat could do nothing but stand and stare as the two wrestled violently on the floor, the gun's hammer still cocked, ready to fire at any moment.

'Get off me, you little brat!' Nathaniel snarled. Fox tugged at the gun, feeling Nathaniel's fingers loosen, but the older man abruptly rolled to the left, causing Fox to fall back, Nathaniel on top of him. The dark-haired man struggled to his knees, then jumped to his feet, using the momentum to shove Fox hard against the wall, his head slamming back. Cat gasped, watching her friend lie immobile, the gun in his unresponsive hands.

There was no time to move as Nathaniel came rushing towards her, an ugly sneer on his face as he wrapped his large hands around her neck, shoving her down and pinning her forcefully to the ground. She choked and spluttered for breath, feeling his fingers crushing her windpipe, Nathaniel's family ring cutting into the flesh of her neck. She couldn't breathe, she couldn't think, her vision was full of black spots and her limbs didn't respond when she told them to move. She struggled desperately to hold on to consciousness. Just as she could feel herself slipping, there was a loud bang, and the fingers around her neck loosened. She inhaled a frantic lungful of air, which was squashed out of her almost immediately as Nathaniel's heavy body fell on top of her.

As she tried to push him off, she came into contact with something slick and hot. She stared at her hand, which was covered in thick, red liquid. Blood.

'Cat!' She flinched instinctively at the voice, her breath coming in short, harsh pants as the heavy weight on her was lifted.

'Cat, it's OK,' a voice murmured, and she scrambled away in panic, backing up against a crate.

'You killed him,' she murmured feverishly, shaking her head slowly as some dim part of her brain recognised the voice as belonging to Fox. 'You killed him!'

'He was strangling you, Cat,' Fox replied calmly. 'It was him or you, and I wasn't about to lose you.'

Yes, of course. Fox had saved her. Her breathing still uneven, she didn't back away as Fox approached a second time, allowing him to drop to his knees by her side, helping her sit up. His hand was on her back, rubbing gentle circles, and he pressed his forehead against hers.

'Breathe, Cat. Just breathe, it's OK, he's gone. He can't

271

hurt you or anyone else ever again. I've got you, it's all right, everything is going to be fine.' Fox's low voice was all Cat could concentrate on, and she buried her face in his shirt for what felt like the hundredth time that day. She was safe; her father was dead, and he'd never hurt her again.

'I'm OK,' she murmured, her voice coming out as more of a whimper than actual words. 'I'm OK.' She felt a finger on her cheek, and lifted her head, meeting Fox's eyes. He brushed away the tears clinging to her cheek, smiling softly at her.

'I've got you,' he repeated quietly. 'You're safe.'

Before she could say or do anything, his head moved forward and his lips pressed against hers. Her eyes widened, and she froze, her hands gripping his waistcoat. He held the kiss for only a few seconds, before moving back, a faint blush rising on his freckled cheeks.

'You kissed me,' she breathed, surprised. 'Why . . . why did you kiss me?'

He snorted, rolling his eyes.

'Honestly, how have you not noticed how utterly besotted I am with you?' he asked, stroking her cheek gently.

She blinked, stunned.

He what?

'But . . . you were telling me to give James a chance. I thought . . . I thought you didn't like me,' she confessed.

'James would be better for you,' he agreed in a whisper. 'If we change the way things work around here, he'll have better standing than I have, and he'll give you a better life. I'm not nearly good enough for a girl like you, but . . . I'm awfully selfish. So much so that it's going to be impossible for me to do the noble thing and let that prat of a prince have you.' His lips twitched, and Cat smiled, tentatively pressing her lips to Fox's for the briefest moment.

'Even if that prat of a prince does want me, I don't want anyone except you,' she assured him solemnly.

This made Fox grin broadly, and he tucked a lock of hair behind her ear. Her eyes widened as she saw the bloody handprint she'd left on Fox's waistcoat, and felt the liquid soaking into her trousers.

'This . . . really isn't the place,' she remarked with a shell-shocked laugh, trying not to stare at the dead body of her father lying a few feet away.

Fox had no such qualms and glanced over his shoulder, grimacing.

'No, it's not,' he agreed. 'We need to get out of here before someone comes back for the girl.'

Grabbing her audio and video recorders, her eyes landed on Nathaniel's prone body, and she saw something silver glinting on his hand. 'Wait.' Hesitantly, she approached the dead man, kneeling down on a patch of floor that wasn't covered in blood, taking his hand and slipping the ornate Hunter family ring from the man's finger. It was much too big for her, but it was hers now. She was the head of the Hunter family, whether she liked it or not. Stowing the ring away safely in the inside pocket of her waistcoat, she turned back to Fox, both recorders in her hand.

They had all the incriminating evidence they needed.

'Here, let me,' Fox urged, helping her attach her recorders. She smiled at him, and he grinned back, squeezing her hand when he was finished.

'Let's get moving, then. It looks like we've got even more work to do than before, if there's a skyship out there with more of these kids aboard.'

Cat nodded. She didn't let go of his hand, needing something to concentrate on other than the mental image of her dead and bloodied father, and the two of them rushed back to the staircase. Cat was amazed no one had responded to the gunshot, but reasoned that the workers were probably all too used to strange explosion noises from the workshops.

Once downstairs, Cat had to let go of Fox's hand to let him get the lock, and within two minutes the door was flung wide open, startling Mary and James.

'Grab your things, we need to go,' Fox said, urgency in his tone. The pair didn't even hesitate, seizing their satchels from where they'd hidden them behind the sofa. They'd changed into dark clothing, and Mary wore a scarf over her hair to cast her face into shadow.

'Nathaniel is dead,' Cat told them hurriedly, voice hollow. 'They'll know they have intruders as soon as someone finds his body, so the alarm could be raised any minute. We need to get out of here and meet our crew at the gate so we can get the sprogs, blow up the building and commandeer the newscast centre.'

James gaped like a fish for several moments, then shook his head.

'You don't do things by halves, do you?' he muttered. Fox smirked, reaching into his satchel to pull out one of the canisters Ben had given him to scatter inside the building. Ben had told them to put some on the lower levels, or only the building above ground would be damaged.

Leaving the canister in the middle of the room, right beside the lamp on the coffee table, Fox turned to eye the monarchs seriously, though he was clearly speaking to the younger of the two. 'Be careful and do everything I tell you. I won't risk us getting caught because you're being an idiot.'

Cat couldn't help but laugh quietly at the offended look on James's face.

'Cat,' Fox said to her, 'bring up the rear.'

Cat nodded, letting the other three leave ahead of her. She shut the door and waited for Fox to give the all clear before following the small procession silently up the stairs. At the top, Fox stuck his head out into the corridor, ushering Mary and James into the nearest alcove. They were about ten feet from the window they knew would lead them to the area outside the gate.

'Where to now?' Mary asked, and Fox jerked a thumb to the left.

'Window up that way,' he replied under his breath, checking the coast was clear. They followed him up the corridor, Cat at the back of the group, and reached the window without any trouble.

'How on Tellus are we going to fit through there?' James asked in an incredulous whisper.

Fox raised an amused eyebrow at him.

'You're scrawny – you'll fit. Hang on.' Climbing once again with spread legs up the walls of the alcove, Fox reached for the window latch and shoved the glass pane open. Peering over the edge, he held out a hand.

'Mary, you first,' he urged.

With a hesitant look, Mary gripped Fox's hand tightly, gasping in alarm as he hoisted her on to the window sill.

'Just drop down and wait a little to the left,' he instructed, helping her shuffle round to slide out of the window. When she was safely on the ground and out of the way, Fox gestured to James to follow.

The young prince shook his head.

'That doesn't look safe,' he complained.

'For storms' sake, your mother just did it!' Cat hissed. 'Fox and I have done it, so stop being such a bloody wuss and take his hand.'

James's ascent was a lot shakier than his mother's, with far more flailing and squirming involved, but Fox kept his grip and with a little help from Cat, managed to get James up and out of the window.

Fox grinned proudly at Cat as she ignored his hand and climbed up by herself, the same way he did. He laid a hand on her back securely as she scrambled up on to the sill, then leaped down on the other side when he saw she was up. She followed, and Fox peered around the corner, looking towards East Gate.

'Looks like Harry and Alice aren't back yet,' he murmured. 'And storms only know where Matt and Ben are. They'll turn up soon, then we can get moving.'

'Should we go where we waited before?' Cat suggested.

Fox nodded; it was as good a place as any, so they herded the two monarchs round the side of the building to the gallery where they could wait with an eye on the gate. It wasn't particularly cold, and yet Cat couldn't stop shaking.

'So what happened?' asked James.

Cat blinked at him in confusion, then realised what he was referring to.

'We followed Nathaniel, and he caught us. We . . . talked.' She wouldn't tell them what had been said in that room. That was for her and Fox to know – at least, until the conversation had to be broadcast.

'No more secrets,' Mary insisted. 'We're out now so there's no chance of guards forcing us to reveal what we know. Tell us what you've been hiding.'

Sharing a glance with Cat, Fox's expression turned serious as he told the monarchs the truth about the children. Tears of sorrow and horror filled Mary's eyes and her lips trembled as Fox spoke, while James went ashen.

'I knew it would be awful, what they were doing, but to go so far as to warp humanity in such a way . . . Nathaniel is more of a monster than I thought,' Mary breathed, disgusted.

'He started bragging about how we could do whatever we liked to this building, because the completed experiments are in a skyship somewhere,' Cat told her, voice hollow. 'He said they were nearly ready for a real war. I told him that we were recording the conversation and all Anglya would hear it. He said . . . he said that we couldn't expose them if we didn't leave the room alive.' She began to shake harder, and Fox held her tighter.

'Nathaniel pulled a gun on me, and Fox stopped him. He threw Fox off, but lost the gun and tried to . . . tried to strangle me instead. Fox shot him,' she said with a lump in her throat. Fox stroked her arm gently.

'Oh, Cat, dear, I'm so sorry,' Mary breathed.

Cat shook her head.

'Why? Wasn't your fault,' she pointed out.

Mary grimaced.

'It might as well be. We wouldn't be in this mess if I had protected my country better.'

Fox looked at her incredulously.

'You were kidnapped and your husband was murdered – what else were you supposed to do?' he retorted, turning back to Cat. 'Are you OK?'

Cat considered the question, then shook her head. She felt like crying, but the tears wouldn't come. Why couldn't she cry?

'Not really,' she admitted. 'But I'll be fine for now.' She had to hold it together, at least until they were safe.

Fox nodded, his arm still around her.

'So how come you two are being so familiar all of a sudden, then?' James asked, jealousy clear in his voice.

'That's what people do when they're together,' Fox replied simply.

James's eyes widened.

'You're . . . together?' he asked.

Cat almost felt sorry for him, but not quite.

'I suppose,' she replied, grinning faintly and squeezing Fox's hand in hers, probably a little tighter than she needed to.

'Oh,' the blond boy murmured softly.

'Well, I saw that coming a mile off,' Mary remarked, though she gave her son a sympathetic look. Evidently she wasn't as attached to the idea of betrothal as James was.

The awkward conversation was halted as East Gate began

to open, and two familiar figures crept through. Cat and Fox immediately got to their feet, startling their companions.

'Harry and Alice are here,' Fox said in explanation. 'Matt and Ben won't be long after, I'll bet. Come on.' Cat led the way, sneaking across the dark walkway towards the gate, and Harry nodded in greeting.

'Good to see you, lass. Where are the boys?'

'No sign of Matt and Benny yet,' she replied. 'But we're ready to go. Nathaniel is dead, and we've got plenty of incriminating footage to add to the broadcast. We just need to get the kids out.'

Harry blinked, then shook his head, astonished.

'Blimey, you have been busy.'

'You can say that again,' Fox piped up, approaching at a far more sedate pace, a half-smile on his face. 'I'd like to introduce you to Mary and James Latham, Queen and Prince of Anglya. Mary, James, this is our fine captain, and his wife Alice.'

Almost in unison, two jaws dropped, and Harry fumbled to make a short bow.

'Your Majesty, Your Highness, it's an honour,' he murmured, and Mary laughed.

'None of that, sir, you're helping us,' she insisted. Alice seemed too stunned to do much else but stare, and Fox cleared his throat.

'We can do proper introductions later,' he cut in, 'but we need to get moving. The alarm could be raised at any minute.'

They were interrupted by a quiet whistle, and all six heads snapped round to see Matt and Ben approaching from the shadows, Matt with his hand on the gun holstered at his hip, ever vigilant.

'Good to see you,' Ben greeted softly, then paused, eyes widening when he spotted the two unfamiliar blonds. 'Storms, you weren't lying. Your Majesties.' He gave a shallow bow, and turned to Harry. 'What's the plan, Captain?'

'Fox, Cat, go back in and get the kids out. I think at this point we can forgo the secrecy. They're bound to sound the alarm soon, anyway. You boys have set all the canisters?' Matt nodded, earning an approving smile. 'Go in with those two, split up and make sure you get every last child out. I'm going to set up the newscast. The four of you meet me when you're done.' He paused, turning hesitantly to Mary.

'Your Majesty, I think it best if you go back with Alice to the ship once we've got the sprogs and wait there while we sort this out. Don't want you and the prince getting hurt, do we?'

Mary smiled gratefully at him.

'Yes, I think that's a very good idea, thank you, sir. After all these years confined, this is a little too much at once. James, dear, come on,' she urged, but the boy shook his head.

'I'm staying. I can help,' he said.

Mary's eyes narrowed. 'James, this isn't a game! If you get in the way, you might get hurt!'

'I can help,' he repeated stubbornly.

Mary sighed, looking at the crew. Fox looked worried, but Cat tried politely to hide her concern. Matt and Ben just shrugged. 'Extra hands might be useful,' conceded Matt.

'Fine,' Mary conceded. 'But you do everything they tell you to do, no matter what, all right?'

James nodded, hugging his mother, and she left with Alice to find somewhere safe to await the children.

After relieving Cat and Fox of their audio and video recorders, Harry clapped Matt on the shoulder, leaving him in charge and heading away to the newscast centre. Cat looked around at her companions, seeing four equally grim faces. It was show time.

22

Ben opened his satchel, digging out two holstered guns and passing one to Fox, who didn't hesitate to strap it around his waist.

'Cat, can you fire a gun?' Ben asked, and she nodded, surprising the others.

'What?' she said defensively. 'My father did teach me a *few* useful things. He didn't have a son, remember?'

Fox stuck a hand in his coat pocket, pulling out his list of room numbers. 'These are the rooms we know contain sprogs. We'll take the lower floors, you stick to this one. We know this place better.' Ripping the list in half, Fox passed one half to Ben, who smiled briefly.

'Will you need any more canisters?'

Fox shook his head, patting his own satchel.

'No, I'm good. We'll drop a few on the inside, the building should go down without any problems. We'll take James with us,' he added, eyeing the blond boy. James didn't look too impressed, but thankfully kept quiet.

'Let's get going,' Cat interrupted before an argument could break out. She grabbed both Fox and James by the arm, turning around and half dragging them towards the alarmed door.

Fox abandoned all finesse and stealth in hacking the door lock, purposefully triggering a loud klaxon. Cat laughed nervously, even as three guards came sprinting around the corner, guns raised. She and Fox got there first, firing and hurrying past the slumped forms towards the staircase, Cat refusing to think about the fact that she had probably just killed a man. All that mattered was getting the children out.

Leaving Matt and Ben to deal with the upper floor, the three teens sprinted for the staircase, rushing down to the floors below. List in hand, Fox called out room numbers, and Cat's eyes scanned the doors ahead of her.

The only guards seemed to be coming from the upper levels, and Fox swore under his breath, having come to the same conclusion as Cat; they would end up facing a huge crush of guards on their way back up if they weren't careful.

The one good thing about the children being kept in labs was that the locks on their cages were feeble at best. Cat slid the bolts aside to let out four terrified-looking girls. 'Just follow me and keep your heads down,' she hissed, already heading back to the corridor. 'We're getting you out of here.'

Fox dropped a canister in the main corridor, James following with a small group of boys behind him. They were all wide-eyed in terror, dressed in grey shirts and trousers. They continued their search for more children, Cat jumping in surprise when a guard came stumbling down the corridor towards her, shooting him quickly in the chest.

'Cat, I'm going to need a hand in here!' Rushing in the

direction of Fox's voice, Cat's jaw dropped at the amount of children kept in the room he'd found. They hadn't seen the room before; it was lucky Fox had checked it.

There was a crash from the opposite end of the corridor, and Fox swore, head turning between the cages and the door.

'James,' he called sharply, pushing his gun into the younger boy's hand. 'Point it at the bad men, and pull the trigger,' he instructed slowly. 'Watch out for the kick, and for storms' sake, whatever you do, don't shoot the canister I left in the hallway or you'll kill us all.'

Cat heard James gulp audibly as she set to work unlocking some of the cages as quickly as she could, flinching at the first gunshot.

'I hit him!' James crowed in surprise.

'Fantastic, now *keep doing it*,' Fox ordered, working at the other side of the room from Cat.

'Just stay calm, kids, we're going to take you to safety,' Cat called out. 'Wait behind James – the blond boy with the gun – and anyone who's still feeling strong, please help those who are having trouble standing.'

Most of the kids didn't look too much worse for wear. Though some seemed slow to react – and were probably drugged – they were all unharmed as far as she could tell. Cat figured they hadn't been in the compound long. But there were a few that would definitely need help.

Cat eventually met Fox in the middle of the room, unlocking the last two cages. They had now gathered quite an impressive group of children – but they were starting to get nervous, several girls and boys having burst into tears.

'Don't worry, we're not here to hurt you,' Fox assured them gently. 'We're going to bring you back to your families, but you have to do exactly what we say, all right?'

The children perked up at the mention of their families.

'I think we've done all the rooms on our half of the list. Fox, you go ahead,' Cat called. 'And, James, you lead the children.' Fox nodded, dropping another canister and running ahead, retrieving his gun from James. He held it out in front of him, poised to shoot. James led the huddle of children out into the corridor, and they followed obediently, filing into rows of two and walking with almost military precision. Clearly they'd had some sort of training while out in the Greaves; maybe they'd even believed that they were going to fight a war, until they'd ended up in the compound.

They reached the staircase without running into any guards, but Cat knew their luck wouldn't last. Sure enough, as they hurried the children up the narrow staircase, Cat heard gunshots from up ahead. Several of the children screamed and flinched. A waif of a girl with a swollen ankle whimpered, lagging behind.

'It'll be all right,' Cat told her with an encouraging smile.

They carried on up the staircase, reaching the ground floor. Here there were many bodies slumped unmoving in the hallway – and Fox stood over them, gun raised. The children all began to run, some of them stumbling as their tired legs refused to cooperate. There was no way to keep track of all of them, and Cat was somewhat glad they hadn't done a count at the beginning; she was terrified the numbers wouldn't match up by the time they reached the ship. Cat picked up the girl with the swollen ankle after she fell for the third time, urging her to climb on to her back. Waiting until the girl's arms were firmly wrapped around her neck, Cat jogged behind the group, beaming when she saw the outer door in sight. At last, they burst out into the open air.

Alice and Mary were waiting at the gate, ready to greet the children. Matt and Ben had yet to return, but Cat doubted they would be much longer.

'James, go with them,' Fox urged, turning serious eyes on the younger boy. James opened his mouth to protest, but Fox cut him off. 'Now isn't the time to play hero. Go with your mother and Alice and get the children to safety.'

James nodded reluctantly. Cat let the little girl down to the ground, where she was immediately transferred on to James's back. She curled both arms around the prince's neck, burying her face in his shoulder. Fox and Cat watched as the group met up with Alice and Mary, who began to group them together, then turned to each other.

'We're not done yet,' Fox said, grabbing Cat's hand.

Together the two of them sprinted around the side of the building towards the newscast centre, remembering the route from Harry's map. When they got there, the building wasn't guarded. Bursting through the unlocked door, Cat let out a choked noise, seeing a group of government workers chained together in a huddle in the corner of the building. Some of them were obviously unconscious, but the few who were awake looked furiously angry, their shouts muffled by the fact that their shirts had been removed and stuffed in their mouths as makeshift gags.

'Well, Matt and Ben *have* been busy,' Fox remarked. Ignoring the struggling workers they headed up the staircase, shoving open the door at the top. The newscast centre wasn't nearly as excitingly technical as Cat had thought it would be; it was a dingy room with a short bench in the centre, and several steadily clicking machines that Cat didn't recognise. There was a large newscast screen in the middle, currently running one of the recruitment casts that Cat was sick of seeing. Especially now; she didn't want to hear about how Collection was a good thing, and families shouldn't fear it.

Harry was hard at work, fiddling with the mechanism of the broadcasting station, barely looking up when they entered. Cat sank down on to the bench, shoulders slumping in exhaustion, and Fox eased down beside her with an arm around her back. Storms, she felt like she hadn't slept in a week.

They were startled by the sound of footsteps on the stairs, and Fox instantly drew his gun, positioning himself protectively in front of Cat.

'Easy, lad, it's just us,' Matt called as he came into view, holding up his hands in a gesture of peace. Ben followed behind him, pulling the door shut. 'Our lot of kids are off with Alice. The only people left alive in that building are government workers,' Matt said, slightly breathless. 'It's ready to blow whenever we're done here.'

'Brilliant. Fox, give me a hand, I can't quite figure out this worldwide broadcasting system.' Harry pointed to an open panel of the machine, where several gears were missing from their plates and half the chains led to nowhere.

Fox nodded, rifling through his bag to find his tool kit and immediately getting to work.

'Right, while he's doing that, lass, you come here.'

Cat obeyed, moving to Harry's side in front of the main machine panels.

The newscast screen had changed to show a fake war report.

Harry tutted under his breath.

'What you're going to do, lass, is shake things up a little. I can separate out all the newscast screens outside of government. With all the commotion, there'll hardly be any government types out of their district. What I want you to do is interrupt the public's evening news report with a little real news.'

Cat stared at the man, eyes wide.

'You want *me* to do it?' she asked in surprise, and he shrugged.

'It was your idea, wasn't it? Besides, people are more likely to believe a sweet-sounding wee lass like you,' he added, winking.

She paused, thinking about it. On the one hand, she would get to speak to the whole of Anglya about what was going on underneath the government's peaceful facade. On the other hand, she would have to speak to the whole of Anglya.

'All right,' she agreed reluctantly. 'What do I have to do?'

She waited for Harry to set up the video footage. Eventually, he turned and gave her a thumbs up, nudging her forward towards a microphone set in the front panel, just beneath the newscast screen. As the screen went black, she took a deep breath, and turned on the microphone.

'Hello, I'm sorry for the interruption. Um, my name is Cat, and there are . . . a lot of things I need to tell you.' She cringed at how awkward she sounded, but carried on regardless. 'That war report you were just watching? It was a fake – old recycled footage edited by someone to make it look like an Erovan battlefield. The truth is that there is no war in Erova. There hasn't been for over seven years. The government's been lying to us, faking newscasts and stopping travel between countries to make sure none of you learn the truth. They're keeping the country on rations to hoard food for themselves and their families, to starve the commoners into extinction so they can make the Anglyan people a *purer* race. And the children . . .' She swallowed hard. 'The children aren't being sent off to war. They're being Collected and held in the government compound. The government doctors have been experimenting on them, "enhancing" them with mechanical limbs and brains and torsos, trying to turn them into the perfect mecha soldiers with no emotions or pain to cloud their judgement, but enough intelligence to make decisions themselves.'

With perfect timing, Harry started the video feed, showing the footage from the room with all the failed experiments, and the footage recorded through windows of the men working on children.

'I'm sorry for the . . . the graphic images. But my friends and I thought it was the best way to get our point across. This is what has been happening to your children for the past seven years. Every time there's a Collection day, every time you promise your son or daughter that they'll be safe, and they'll see you again, this is what our government has been doing to them.'

Fox glanced up from the panel, giving her an encouraging smile, and she continued.

'We're working to bring the government down, this being our first step. But I don't know how long it's going to take us. All I can promise is that we won't stop until your children are safe, and Anglya is returned to its rightful rulers; our monarch, Queen Mary Latham, and her son, Prince James. They are not dead as you have been told. They are still alive, held captive in the government compound, secluded from society, unable to rule their country the way they should. We'll sort that out, but for now ... get your children to safety. Take them to trade ships, merchant ships, anything you can find. I hope it's only temporary, but in case anything happens to us, get them hidden. We'll broadcast and alert the rest of the world right after this, and hope that help will come. We still have work to do – there are still more children to find. Be safe, people of Anglya, and be vigilant.'

As Cat finished speaking, she looked over at Fox, who had finished whatever he was doing with the worldwide broadcasting system, and gave Harry a thumbs up.

'In about twenty minutes you'll hear explosions, and see a lot of smoke coming from the government district. Don't be alarmed, we're responsible. Good luck to all of you. And to the foreign authorities, if this broadcast reaches you – please, we need reinforcements. We're taking our ship, the *Stormdancer*, to find the finished experiments. If you can spare anyone ... we can't do this alone.' She cut the microphone,

allowing Harry to feed in the footage with audio record-
ings at the same time as Fox turned on the worldwide
broadcast system, sending the broadcast they'd just made
out to the rest of Tellus. She crossed her fingers, praying
they hadn't just made things worse.

23

As they watched the footage Harry's friend had pieced together, Cat's stomach churned. She was reliving every moment, astonished that all the evidence had been gathered over two days – it felt like she'd been living in that horror for a lifetime.

Her heart pounded as she watched the new footage Harry had added on; her conversation with Andrew, and the final confrontation with her father. Thankfully, Harry had cut it after Fox had pulled Nathaniel's body off Cat; she didn't think she wanted her first kiss to be shown all over the world. She hoped Andrew's mother was watching, though, to see her son being so very brave. Eventually, the screen went black and Harry shut the machine down, removing the film casings.

'We should get going,' Ben murmured, interrupting the sombre atmosphere in the room. Cat nodded, getting to her feet. The five of them left the room, ignoring the group of workers still chained together in the entrance.

They exited the building and ran towards the open gate. Just as they were leaving, Matt turned and drew his pistol. Cat panicked, thinking there were more guards, until she saw what he was aiming at – a canister, sitting outside the broken door into the government building.

Fox wrapped an arm around her protectively, running with her away from the gate. Cat brought her hands up to cover her ears as she heard the gun go off. Almost instantly there was an earth-shattering explosion, then a series of huge bangs going off inside the building, making her ears ring. When they thought they were at a safe distance, all five of them turned, staring in awe at the enormous pillar of smoke billowing from what was now a pile of rubble; the newscast building was gone, and even parts of the wall had crumbled. There couldn't be any survivors in a blast like that. Matt grimaced, shaking his head and sticking his fingers in his ears.

'I can't hear anything!' he told them loudly, and Ben tugged on his arm.

'You'll get your hearing back in about ten minutes,' he said slowly, making sure Matt was watching his lips as he spoke. He held up ten fingers, just to be clear.

'We need to get back to the ship,' Harry told them, beckoning them all to the nearest side street.

As they neared the city centre, Cat saw people were moving with a sense of urgency, despite the late hour. A woman with two young children was walking, flanked by three burly men, in the direction of the shipyard. Cat hoped that at least one trade ship would risk defying the government and take some children to safety. She saw a blank newscast screen in the centre of a small park and found it hard to believe that mere minutes ago her voice and face had been on it.

Cat kept her head down as they walked, suddenly very aware that her image had just been broadcast all over the country – all over the world. Fox pulled a brown knitted cap over his distinctive red hair, and they quickened their pace, sticking to the shadows, trying to reach the shipyard in safety. They had only dealt with a fraction of the government's forces, and it wouldn't be long before someone came looking for the culprits.

When they reached the shipyard itself, they paused, stunned – everything was chaos.

The shipyard was a riot of activity; people were herding confused-looking children, some still in sleepwear, up a gangplank on to one of the trade ships, helped by the ship's crew in their dark purple uniforms and the dockyard workers. Regaining their urgency, they ducked and weaved through the crowd, and Fox cheered loudly as he saw a guard being tied up and gagged with what appeared to be someone's grubby sock.

They managed to reach the *Stormdancer* without anyone realising who they were, and Cat sprinted nimbly up the gangplank, smiling as she slid through the trap, landing with a soft thud in the familiar shabby hallway.

She was home!

The noise of chatter floated up from the floor below, and they followed the noise to the galley and stopped in the doorway, stunned. The room was full, the children crammed together on the benches and the floor, sharing bowls of hot porridge, eating ravenously as they talked with each other, easily bonding over their shared trauma.

Alice was in her element, a large tureen of porridge in

front of her, Mary assisting her in spooning it into bowls. Cat hadn't known they even *owned* that many bowls. James was helping a boy with a broken wrist eat his meal, and he looked up when he saw them.

'It's about time!' the prince called.

Several of the children cheered when they recognised Cat and Fox, and Alice immediately dropped her ladle, rushing over to hug them both at the same time.

'Oh, I was so *worried*!' she exclaimed, clasping them so tightly Cat wasn't sure she could breathe. Alice released them, only to kiss them both on the foreheads, then moved to accost the rest of the crew, saving her husband for last and kissing him firmly as he stroked her hair.

'We're fine, Alice,' Fox insisted, laughing. 'I promise we'll tell you all about it later. But I think we could do with some rest for now, and something hot to eat. It's been a long day.'

Cat shot him a grateful look as Alice turned on the spot, hurrying back over to the porridge and grabbing another stack of bowls.

'I . . . I want to wash my hands first,' Cat stuttered, staring down at her bloodied palms. That drew Alice's gaze to her hands, and the woman flinched.

'Right, of course. Fox, dear, you'd better go with her, and change your shirt while you're at it.'

Cat glanced up, wincing at the hand-shaped bloodstains on the fabric covering his chest. She'd forgotten about those. She and Fox doubled back out of the galley, crossing to the washroom further down the hall. Fox turned the tap on, and she stuck her hands under the hot spray, not wanting to watch as the pink-tinged water swirled down the drain.

'Here,' he murmured, holding her hands between his and scrubbing gently with a bar of soap. She stood frozen, letting Fox wash away the blood until her hands were finally clean. Even when it was gone, she still felt it on her skin, and wished she could keep scrubbing.

'Thanks,' she said quietly.

He smiled back reassuringly, passing her a towel.

'No problem. Wait here, I'll just go and grab a clean shirt. Won't be a moment,' he promised, ducking out of the room.

Cat looked down at herself; there was blood on her clothes too, but she didn't think she could bring herself to move. All she could see in her mind was blood dripping from her fingers.

When Fox returned, he was only in his undershirt, a clean blue shirt slung over his arm. He led her by the arm out of the washroom, shrugging on the shirt as he did so. He was still buttoning it when they entered the galley. The rest of the crew were sitting with Alice, eating ravenously.

'Sit, both of you,' she urged.

Cat sank down on to the bench between Fox and Matt, leaning her elbows on the table. She stared at the children gathered in the room. The situation felt bitter-sweet; she was glad to have saved them, but her mind dwelled on all the kids they were too late to save. By the look on Ben's face he was having similar thoughts, though she expected that these were focused on one child in particular. Harry began to explain to his wife what had gone on at the compound after she'd left, only to be interrupted when Matt let out a triumphant noise.

'I can hear again!' he exclaimed happily, making Ben snort.

'Damn, I was enjoying your silence.'

Cat smiled at the pair, setting her spoon down in her empty bowl and wearily leaning against Fox's shoulder. He slid an arm around her so she was less likely to fall off the bench.

'And when did that happen, then?' Alice asked, eyeing them pointedly.

Cat blushed, but didn't move. 'Earlier today, actually. After . . . after the talk with my father.'

Alice's smile faltered at that, but she recovered quickly, grinning.

'Well, it's about time! I thought I was going to have to watch you two sniffing around each other for months.'

Cat's blush darkened, and Fox chuckled, sheepish.

'Yeah, well, no worries. You don't have to knock our heads together,' he assured the older woman, his hand comfortably on Cat's waist.

Harry cut in, bringing them back on topic. 'We need to figure out where to start looking for this government skyship. Flying in circles over every inch of Anglyan airspace will take weeks. And that's assuming they're even *in* Anglyan airspace.'

'Any information was probably destroyed in the blast, though,' Matt pointed out with a frown.

Cat's expression grew thoughtful, and Fox raised an eyebrow at her.

'Oh, I know that face – that's your thinking face. What is it?' he asked.

She looked at the rest of the table.

'Well . . .' she began, 'the files in the government compound might have been destroyed, but the files in my father's office at home are perfectly fine. And now he's gone, there's no one stopping me from going back to the house for a visit. I mean, I'm the sole heir so that makes it *my* house, doesn't it?' she pointed out with a smile.

Fox stared at her for several beats.

'You genius!' He leaned forward, kissing her.

James grumbled under his breath about overt displays of affection, which Cat and Fox both ignored, too busy grinning shyly at each other.

'You're still in the same house? The Hunter house?' Mary asked. 'You never moved to the Ingate house?'

'No, Nathaniel refused, even if it was bigger. I think it went to a second cousin or something. Why?' Cat queried, not sure why that mattered.

'If I remember correctly, the Hunter house is big enough to accommodate all of these children. If you're going after this skyship, you can't take them with you – it's far too dangerous. So, you could take them to the house, and keep them there while you finish things,' Mary suggested, looking at the children filling the galley. Cat did a quick headcount.

'Will we be able to get that many kids into the government district without anyone noticing?' Matt asked.

'Have a little faith, Mattie,' remarked Cat with a grin. 'I've been sneaking around government since I was old enough to reach the door handle. I'll manage it.' The tree was the easiest way to get in, but it wasn't the *only* way.

'That sounds like a plan, then. Now, the sprogs look a little sleepy. What say we herd them downstairs for the night? We've got plenty of space in the storage rooms, and I'm sure we can rustle up some blankets for them,' Alice suggested. At her prompting, the group stood up and collected the empty bowls from the children.

'Can I see my mum?' one boy asked, reaching out to Cat as she passed, and she sighed forlornly at his wide-eyed expression.

'Sorry, but you're all going to have to stay with us for a little while. The men who took you from your families are still out there, and we need to keep you safe until they're gone. But I promise you, it won't be for very long.'

Most of the children were listening to her, and there was a groan of dismay from several of them.

'Will we be safe here?' a girl asked, her dirty dark hair escaping from its scruffy ponytail.

'Of course you will,' Fox said with a reassuring smile. 'We'll take you to a safe house in the morning. We won't let the government get to you.' The girl beamed at him, her cheeks dimpling.

'It's bedtime now, dears,' Alice called out. 'You need your rest.'

'Come on, bratlings,' Matt urged from the doorway, drawing several shy giggles. 'Follow us, we'll get you all tucked in for the night.'

The children wearily followed Matt and Ben out of the room. Cat drew closer to Fox, frowning.

'Storms, can you imagine how many are out in the Greaves?' she wondered sadly.

Fox's hand briefly touched her waist, his eyes meeting hers.

'Then we'll go out to the Greaves when this is over and find them,' he promised, pressing his lips to her forehead. 'Come on, you need your sleep.'

Cat sighed, pulling away from him and ushering the last few children out of the room. She could see Ben up ahead, helping children down the manhole. She couldn't hold back her smile when he picked up a nervous young girl, dropping her down the hole to where – she hoped – Matt was waiting to catch her.

They followed the group of children down to the third floor. Matt was directing them through to the storage room opposite the engine room and, peering in, Cat raised an eyebrow. Alice and Mary were busy distributing furs to be used as blankets and allowing children to huddle together in groups of five or six, settling down to sleep in puppy-piles dotted around the room.

'They're so small,' Ben murmured, he and Matt drawing closer to the teens. 'It's hard to imagine anyone would consider them potential soldiers.' His face was tense, the scar on his cheek red where he'd been rubbing it anxiously, and Matt clasped his shoulder firmly. Cat doubted Ben would get much sleep.

Unable to help herself, Cat yawned widely.

'I'm going to head up to bed, if I'm not needed here. It's been a long day.' The three men nodded sympathetically, and Matt ruffled her hair affectionately.

'G'night, girlie. Get yourself some rest, you need it.'

Fox wound an arm around her waist, tilting her head up to press a soft kiss to her lips.

'I'll see you in the morning. Sleep well,' he said quietly, bringing a shy smile to her face. She still wasn't used to being able to kiss him like that.

'Goodnight, all of you.'

Squeezing Fox in a last hug, Cat turned back towards the manhole, climbing lethargically up the ladder. Her eyebrows rose when she saw James waiting in the hallway, leaning against the wall, his arms crossed over his chest. He pushed away from the wall as she drew closer, eyeing her with a look that set her on edge.

'What do you see in him?' he asked, and she resisted the urge to groan.

'James, I'm tired, I've had a terrible day, and I want to go to bed. Argue with me in the morning, if you must,' she said irritably.

'Just answer my question,' he insisted. 'What do you see in him?'

'What isn't there to see in him?' she retorted. 'You've known him for two days, barely. You don't know what he's like, so how can you judge whether he's right for me?'

'He seems like a cocky idiot,' James said sullenly.

She rolled her eyes. 'You don't know him *or* me. It's been years, James. We're not six years old any more. We're not best friends any more.'

'I'm not jealous,' he denied feebly, and Cat snorted.

'Please, you've been looking at me since the moment your mother told you of her betrothal plans. I'm telling you now, I don't care. No contract was signed, and I don't want to marry you. So please, leave me be.'

He raised an eyebrow at her.

'You know it won't last,' he said evenly. 'You gallivanting about with the crew here. When this is all over, you'll be required to take your rightful place in society. You're the heir to the Hunter family, the last survivor of the Ingate family – it's your job to restore the legacy of both families.'

She growled under her breath. 'The Hunter legacy can go to hell for all I care. My father dragged it through the mud and it's best to let it die.'

'The people won't let you do that, though,' James continued. 'Especially not after they find out everything you've done for them. My mother taught me all my life what would be expected of me if we ever got out of that prison, and I can't imagine you getting away with much less, being who you are. They'll expect you to become one of the new leaders – and marrying some low-born skyship boy won't fit in with that.'

Cat was incredibly close to slapping James, but she restrained herself; however irritating he might be, he was still royalty. Moreover, if they succeeded, he'd no doubt be ruling the country in a decade or so when Mary grew too elderly.

'When will you understand that I don't care what the people expect of me? I never have. Who I marry is none of their business, and it certainly isn't yours!' They were interrupted by the sound of footsteps on the manhole ladder, and Ben's head popped up, his smile dropping when he saw them.

'What's going on?' he asked curiously.

'Nothing,' James insisted shortly, turning on his heel. 'Goodnight, Catherine.' He stressed her full name, giving her a pointed look, before disappearing into a spare bedroom. Ben came up beside her, looking at her with a frown.

'What was all that about?'

She sighed, shaking her head.

'Don't worry about it. James is just trying to remind me of my place in society,' she sighed. 'I'm fine. I just wish I didn't have to deal with him on top of everything else.'

Ben's long arms wrapped around her, pulling her close to his chest.

'Ignore him,' he soothed. 'He's just trying to figure out *his* place now he's escaped from the compound. Think how confusing it must be for him right now, Cat. He's never seen more than his mother and a few guards since he was a wee'un, and suddenly he's surrounded by people – and all of them commoners. He's lived on his mother's stories for too long. But once this is all over, he and Mary will go off to Latham Castle and take their rightful positions, and you'll likely not hear much of him after that. And no matter what, you'll always have a home with us.'

'Thanks, Ben. I hope you're right,' she said softly, before stepping out of his embrace. 'I'll see you at breakfast.'

'Goodnight, sprog,' he replied fondly.

She slipped into her room and collapsed on the bed with a bone-deep sigh. She crawled beneath the blankets, curling up in a tight ball. She didn't think she'd quite processed everything that had happened during the day; it felt like a lifetime had passed in only a few hours. She'd gone from being a runaway with two parents to an orphan girl, and suddenly, their rebellion wasn't so secret any more. She wanted to cry, but the tears wouldn't come, and all she could feel was an overwhelming sense of detachment. As if everything had happened to some other girl, and she was just reading about it in a book.

She looked over at the picture of her and her mother tucked behind the mirror, glad she'd taken it from her old room. Something to mourn besides the few hazy memories of her mother when she was well, and the far more solid memories of a frail, bed-bound woman. All the same, that frail woman had been there to listen to her troubles – when she was awake – and hold her hand while she raged about her father and the unfairness of life. She had given her the best advice she'd ever had and while she'd found a new family . . . it wasn't the same.

A choked sob escaped her lips, but her face stayed resolutely dry, and she squeezed her eyes shut, attempting to feel *something*. Still there were no tears, and she bit her lip painfully. Maybe the shock just needed to subside. In the meantime, she could at least get some sleep.

24

For several moments after waking, Cat was confused as to where she was. It was only when she opened her eyes and saw her bedroom that she remembered the events of the day before, and recognised the odd, dull pain in her stomach. She'd experienced more than enough emotions for a lifetime.

Glancing at the clock on the desk, she sighed, reluctantly drawing herself out of bed and into some fresh clothes. She wished she could stay curled up all day and mourn the loss of her mother, but she had work to do.

Their job wasn't done yet.

Entering the galley, she was surprised to see she was the last one up; all the children were spread about the room, and the crew were at their usual table with Mary and James. Seeing a gap on the bench between Fox and Matt, she crossed the room to join them, kissing Fox on the cheek. He smiled at her, shuffling over to allow her to slide into her place between the two men.

'Good morning, sleepyhead,' he greeted her quietly. 'How are you this morning?' His tone was light, but there was concern in his eyes.

'Fine, thanks,' she replied, gratefully accepting her

breakfast from Alice. 'So what's the plan for today, then? Are we heading back to my house?'

Ben nodded from across the table.

'As soon as everyone's done eating. We'll take the kids in groups. You and Fox can go first, show us the way. We have to be very careful, especially just after the explosion. It's being passed off as a furnace malfunction, from what I heard earlier when I went to pick up some food. And the government doesn't seem to have any idea about our little broadcast.'

'I know how we can get in safely,' Cat assured, looking around at the full galley. There were a lot of children, but she was confident she could manage it. 'Once we get closer to Greystone, things should be easier. They won't expect people to be sneaking into government, even if they do suspect rebellion.'

Finishing her breakfast as quickly as possible, Cat slipped a hand into Fox's waistcoat to borrow his pocket watch, ignoring his raised eyebrow. They had to get moving quickly, before too many people were up and about.

'I need to put something warmer on. Meet you back here?' Cat said to Fox.

'Ten minutes,' he replied, getting to his feet to talk to the children. Cat started towards the door, almost groaning aloud when James got up to follow. Was he not going to give it a rest?

'What do you want now?' she asked when they were in the hallway, placing her hands on her hips impatiently. He looked down at the floor nervously, before raising his eyes to look at her.

'I . . . wanted to apologise,' he answered stiffly. 'I was out of line last night. I shouldn't have said what I did. I . . . I was jealous,' he confessed reluctantly. 'I still remember you, you know, from when we were kids. And after my mother mentioned the betrothal plans . . . I suppose I let myself get carried away.'

Cat pursed her lips, but couldn't find it in herself to be too angry. If she'd been locked away for eight years, she'd start developing fantasies too.

'It's fine. If you agree to leave me alone, we shouldn't have a problem.'

His face screwed up in anger, but he composed himself, nodding sharply.

'Of course,' he said smoothly, sounding forced. 'I . . . I wish you the best with . . . him.' The words seemed to cause him physical pain. 'Now, if you'll excuse me . . .' He retreated back into the galley, allowing Cat to go into her bedroom and get her coat.

When she returned to the galley, it was to find the entire crew gathered with the children, looking equal parts anxious and excited. They had been split into four groups, and Cat moved to Fox's side, turning towards her captain.

'Fox and I will take the first lot. Who's following on behind us?' she queried, scanning the faces of each child in her group, memorising them.

'Matt and Benny,' Harry informed her. 'Get your lot in, leave Fox to settle them, then go back and show the boys how to get past the wall.'

Cat nodded, turning to Matt. 'Bring your group to the boarded-up tram tunnel in Kentridge, if you know where that is?' The tunnel was hugely overgrown, and most people didn't realise it still existed. Cat had been using it for years, and never been caught.

'I know it,' Ben assured her. 'We'll meet there. Stay safe.'

'Ready?' said Fox, pulling his knitted cap from his pocket and tugging it over his hair.

She nodded.

'Let's get moving. Right, come on, brats. Stay close together, don't wander off, and be as quiet as you possibly can.' Fox ducked his head, lips brushing over Cat's. 'I'll take the rear and keep an eye out for guards. You just worry about getting us there.'

Leading the kids up to the deck, Cat was buzzing with adrenalin, her grey eyes alert. The children seemed to have slept off the after-effects of whatever they'd been drugged with, and looked around with bright eyes as they stepped into the daylight, as if they'd never expected to see it again. Things were just as chaotic as they had been the night before, but Cat wasn't worried about being caught in the shipyard. With the amount of traders who had been black-mailed into silence now able to rebel against their captains, it was definitely safe territory.

The city itself was less busy, the smoke still rising lazily from the pile of rubble that had once been the government compound. Purple-uniformed guards strode in pairs through the streets, but there were far fewer than Cat had expected; maybe more people had been in the building than she'd thought. Or maybe they'd been very lucky, and the blast had reached as far as the guard barracks. Focusing on her destination, Cat slipped into the familiar network of side streets and back alleys, the sound of small footsteps the sole indication that she hadn't lost her group. She had to hand it to the children; they were quiet as mice.

About halfway there, she paused, turning back for a quick headcount. Her gaze instinctively found Fox's, and his lips curled in a brief smile. All safe and accounted for. Smiling back, Cat set off again. They were drawing closer to Greystone, and she could practically taste safety. The only thing they'd have to worry about past the wall was aristocrats trying to make a sneaky escape before they could be arrested, once the foreign authorities arrived.

She paused at the end of the narrow alley, turning to the children. 'As quick as you can across the square, and duck round the corner same as I do, OK?' she breathed, staring intently at the small faces in front of her. Cat rounded the corner and sprinted across the square, not wanting to take the chance of guards passing through. The children ran as fast as they could, filing in behind her, and when Fox appeared he moved to her side, placing a hand on her back as he counted their group.

'All here,' he confirmed. 'Let's keep moving.'

Cat led the group towards the disused tram tunnel. The weeds grew thicker, ivy clinging to the wall and almost covering the low tunnel. You could only see it if you knew what to look for.

Ignoring the greenery, Cat ploughed ahead, making straight for the gap in the wire that blocked off the tunnel. It had taken her weeks to make that gap, unable to take a knife of any real use out of the house without her father noticing. It was just big enough for someone her size; to get Matt through, it would have to be a lot bigger.

'Knife,' she requested, holding a hand out to Fox. He rolled his eyes, nudging past her with his knife in hand.

'I've got it,' he said, hacking away at the thick wire, slowly widening the gap. Cat wrung her hands as she waited, expecting someone to pop out at them any minute. Surely she couldn't be the only one who knew of the tunnel?

Minutes ticked by as Fox worked, until finally the hole in the wire was large enough. Pocketing his knife, the redhead bent away some of the sharper edges so they couldn't graze people on their way through, then stepped back.

'Lead the way,' he said to Cat. She ducked through the hole with ease, moving aside for the kids to follow.

'We're going to have to be very, very careful now,' she murmured to them. 'I don't need to tell you where we are. But don't worry, it's not far.'

The tram tunnel was merely a street away from her house, and Cat's heart raced as she walked through the familiar neighbourhood. It definitely wasn't home any more.

No lights were on in any of the houses, and Cat mentally hoped that the occupants had been in the government building the night before. Everyone on their street worked directly under her father; if he was involved, so were they. Finally, they came to the front of her house, and she heard Fox let out a low, impressed whistle. Ignoring him, Cat continued, hiding behind a row of bushes along the fence-line as she led the way to the back garden.

'I can't imagine Nathaniel would just leave the back

door open,' Fox pointed out as they reached the door. Cat grinned at him over the heads of the children.

'No, but he *does* leave a spare key under here. Or, rather, I do,' she replied, tilting the flowerpot and retrieving the brass key from underneath. Straightening up, she slid the key into the lock, turning it. It clicked loudly, and she stepped over the threshold, into the familiar hallway.

'Wow,' Fox murmured. 'Your father must have been a right arse if he made you want to give up all this.'

'All the money in the world couldn't make him a good parent, and it didn't make me a happy child. As I think we've established.'

He raised an eyebrow at her, and she could see he was still feeling stunned by the blatant wealth on show.

'To have all this money, all those options, almost nothing stopping you from having what you wanted . . .' His voice trailed off as he met her eyes and saw the frustrated expression on her face.

'You don't get it! You'd have to have seen it from my point of view to understand, but I promise you, it wasn't that simple. I'll probably sell all this when everything is over. Keep a few things for sentimental value, maybe, but . . . most of it is crap.' Fox stared at her incredulously, and she shrugged, looking away in embarrassment. 'Let's just get the kids settled so I can guide Matt and Ben's group through. Come on.'

Mentally running through a list of rooms in her house, she decided that the upstairs living room was probably the best place to house so many people. Not bothering to kick her boots off – what did she care now if she got mud on the carpets? – she led the way upstairs, smiling to herself at the awestruck whispers of the kids as they followed.

'Make yourselves comfortable,' she told them, pushing open the living-room door. 'You're safe here.'

'But it's government,' one of the older boys retorted warily.

'It's safe,' Cat repeated. 'No one who works in government will be coming in here, I promise.' She turned to Fox, running a hand through her hair. 'I need to go back and meet the other group. Are you all right to get this lot settled?'

'Of course. Stay safe, OK?' Cat grinned at his concerned frown, stretching up on her toes to kiss him and lingering longer than she'd intended.

'I'll be fine. You saw how empty it is out there. I won't be long.' Pulling away from him reluctantly, she slipped out of the room and down the stairs, heading out through the back door. She locked it behind her, pocketing the key.

It didn't take her long to get back to the tram tunnel, and she leaned against the wall, listening for footsteps. She wished she'd taken Fox's pocket watch; she had no idea how long it had been since they'd left the ship. How long were Matt and Ben giving her?

A breath of relief escaped her lips as she spotted Ben's curly hair approaching from the alley opposite, and she stepped out of her hiding spot far enough for him to see her. He grinned, ushering his group of children towards her. Matt was bringing up the rear with a little girl on his back. Cat recognised her as the one with the twisted ankle.

'Blimey, I thought they'd filled all these in,' he remarked, eyeing the crumbling brick tunnel.

'No, they just fenced them over. Bricking in was too expensive,' Cat replied, hurrying the children through the gap. 'Come on, it's not far.'

The path back to her house was just as empty as it had been the first time, and Cat kept her fingers crossed it would stay that way.

'Take the kids up to the others,' Ben told her. 'I'll go back and direct the rest. Matt can stay with the kids – you and Fox need to start snooping. The sooner you can find something, the sooner we can get moving.'

'Are you sure?' Cat checked, lips pursed. She knew the route better than Ben; she didn't want him getting caught.

'I'll be fine, trust me.' Matt reached out to clasp his friend's shoulder, ruining his serious expression by ruffling his hair.

'Hurry back, and be safe.' Ben disappeared through the back door, and Cat led Matt and the children up to the living room. Pausing in the doorway, her eyebrows rose.

'I see Sam found you, then,' she remarked drily, unable to hold in a snigger at seeing Fox pinned to the wall by one mechanical hand, a blade protruding from Samuel's other hand which was positioned at Fox's throat. 'Samuel, let him go, he's safe.' Samuel immediately released Fox, blade retreating into his wrist.

'My apologies, Mistress Catherine. He claimed to be a friend of yours, but I do not take chances.' Sam's voice was even grittier than it had been the last time, and it made her wince. Poor thing needed some serious maintenance.

'Don't apologise. You did exactly what you're programmed to.'

'I didn't know mecha servants doubled as security guards,' Fox remarked, rubbing his throat. 'You named it?'

'Of course I did,' Cat retorted. 'I couldn't just call him "mecha". Come on, Ben's bringing the other group through, Matt's going to look after this lot. We need to go to my father's office.' Matt was already getting the children settled with the others, ignoring the mecha in the room completely. He'd probably seen them before when he'd worked at Tinker's.

'Right. Let's see if we can find anything about this skyship.' Still regarding Samuel with distrust, Fox left the room at Cat's side, as she turned to head up another flight of stairs. 'This house is ridiculous. There were just the three of you living here?'

'Yes. We could have fitted in another twenty, I know. But you get used to it, sort of.'

Cat led Fox through the winding corridors, right to the other side, where her father's office was, several doors away from her mother's bedroom. She faltered outside the bedroom door, wishing she could stick her head inside and see her mother resting there, see the smile on her face and sit and talk with her one last time. Pushing the memories away, she carried on, stopping outside the door to her father's office. As she'd expected, it was locked, but she easily hacked the lock, pushing the door wide open.

Fox let out a low whistle, his eyes instantly drawn to the monstrously large desk in the centre of the room. She hated the decor in her father's office; it was disgustingly extravagant, to the point of garish.

Ignoring the bulging filing cabinets along one wall,

knowing they were full of useless business meeting transcriptions and bills and receipts, she went straight for the locked desk drawers, taking the spare key clipped to the underside of the desk beneath a secret panel. Unlocking all six drawers, she beckoned Fox to join her, pointing to the drawers on the other side of the desk from her.

'Help me look,' she instructed, already rifling through the top drawer. Now that she didn't have to worry about her father coming back, she could be as messy as she liked in her search.

Most of what they found was information they knew already; blueprints of every level of the government compound, schematics for the mecha-human soldiers, and transcripts of conversations about Collecting the children and arranging for newscast crews to be sent out to film in the Greaves. However, there were also enough names written in the documents to condemn almost the entire upper level of government.

'Nathaniel was clearly prepared for some pretty serious blackmail, then,' Fox remarked, flicking through a journal full of scrawled writing. 'He could get himself out of just about any accusation they could throw at him with all this evidence.'

'And we can get an awful lot of people *into* some very serious accusations with it,' Cat declared, piling the journals back into their drawers and locking them securely. They would need those later. 'Still, there's nothing in here that has anything about a location for the skyship.' She growled in frustration, about to turn for the door and suggest looking elsewhere, when a memory came to the forefront of her mind. One of the few nights her father had left the door ajar, she'd peeked in to see him standing on a stool, pushing the portrait on the wall behind his desk back into place over something metallic. She'd never been tall enough to find out what it was. Of course!

'Fox! Help me move the chair!'

The redhead gave her a confused look, but obliged, helping her shift the chair back from the desk, right up against the wall.

Cat pointed up at the portrait. 'There's something important behind that painting. I can't reach it, but you can!' she insisted, ushering him to stand on the chair. With his extra inches, he was able to shift the portrait aside. To his surprise, it swung right up, revealing a dark grey square of metal set into the wall, its face inset with enough mechanisms to lock the entire house down.

'Wow. That's one brute of a safe,' Fox remarked, staring at it in awe.

Cat looked at him with raised eyebrows.

'Can you crack it?' she questioned, and he snorted.

'Of course I can! Just give me a little while. This is some pretty sophisticated gear-work. And not the most comfortable position to do it in either,' he grumbled, leaning his knees against the back of the chair to brace himself. He pulled his tool kit from his pocket, eyeing the safe.

Cat hopped up to sit on the desk, her legs swinging absently. It was very odd being in her father's office and not having to worry about him coming in at any moment and punishing her for intruding. Even more bizarre was having *Fox* in her father's office; she didn't think the room had ever seen someone so scruffy in its life.

'Nathaniel didn't skimp on the cash when he had this installed,' Fox muttered, a thin gear wire clamped precariously between his teeth.

'Nathaniel didn't skimp on the cash with *anything*,' Cat pointed out. 'But with this level of security, it's bound to contain something good. Fingers crossed, the information we need.'

She watched Fox work silently for several minutes, until finally she heard several quiet clicks in quick succession. Fox prodded the centre of one of the bottom gears with his wire, turning it gently, and to Cat's delight, the rest of the gears moved with it, slowly shifting the four lock bars to the side. With one last groan of gears, the door popped forward a fraction, and Fox dug his fingers into the groove at the edge to pull it the rest of the way open. Cat was impressed at the sheer thickness of the safe's door. The entire country could sink to the bottom of the ocean, and that safe would probably still survive.

'What have we got, then?' Fox murmured under his breath, sticking his head into the safe. He pulled out several leather-bound journals that bulged with paper, passing them down to Cat. 'Just those five, the rest of the safe is empty,' he told her, dropping down unceremoniously into the chair.

'Really?' She'd thought there would have been something else in there; keys, a weapon, some ridiculously expensive jewel or heirloom.

She passed two of the five journals to Fox, keeping the other three and picking up one from the top of the pile. Scan reading, she ignored most of it; these were her father's personal journals, and mainly consisted of his insane ramblings about what he would do when the country was finally his. Thomas Gale's name turned up several times in passing, which didn't surprise her.

'Here we go!' Fox cried, jumping out of the chair to shove an open journal under her nose. He pointed to a paragraph of cramped writing that took Cat a little while to decipher. 'Read there,' he prompted urgently, and her eyes darted across the page, growing wider as she read her father's writing.

'The skyship is by Hebris! Are they mad? That's right next to the Stormlands! They could be sucked into a hurricane any moment!' she exclaimed incredulously. The Stormlands were known to be impenetrable, running all the way along the world in a continuous storm. No one had ever crossed them, and it was dangerous to even fly near them; the few people who had dared never came back, whether they approached from either the Anglyan side or the Dalivian side.

Fox hummed, his lips tightening.

'Obviously they've got a very skilled pilot to keep them hovering around the edges. And you have to admit, it's a smart idea. No one would be stupid enough to go that far out to the Stormlands, so they'd never be found. Unfortunately for them, no matter how good their pilot is, ours is better,' he said. 'Ben's been out there before. And their ship is bound to be bigger than ours, so they'll have a much harder time trying to get away if they spot us. With luck, the cloud cover should be enough for us to sneak up on them, if we're careful,' he explained.

'We should take these to Harry,' Cat suggested, gesturing at the journals. 'Nathaniel has written about all the weak spots in government, people to bribe, people who would let anything pass by them if it was suggested by the right person. It's practically a guide to bringing the country to its knees.'

Fox nodded in agreement.

'We'll take them back to the ship with us. Are we done here, then?'

'One moment,' she said, rushing back to the desk and pulling open the desk drawers. Taking out all of the material her father had gathered, she passed it up to Fox to transfer to the safe. When everything was securely inside, he shut the door, seeing the mechanisms automatically wind back into place and lock themselves.

'There,' she declared in satisfaction. 'Now we know it's all safe, just in case.' She doubted anyone would come by the house and manage to get past the swarm of children, but should the worst happen, it was good to be prepared.

Fox held out a hand to her. 'Let's go,' he murmured, tugging her towards the door.

25

The living room was full to bursting when Cat and Fox returned, and Cat smiled with relief at seeing everyone had made it across safely. Mary looked more comfortable than Cat had seen her before; of course, she probably knew the house almost as well as Cat herself did.

'What did you find?' Harry asked, standing as soon as he saw them.

'The skyship is over Hebris, just on the edge of the Stormlands. Reckless, but clever,' Fox told him, glancing at Matt and Ben listening in intently.

'Doable,' Ben assured them confidently. 'It's been a while since I've been out that far, but if we have the right weather conditions, it shouldn't be too much of a problem.' He grinned. 'Either way, I like a challenge. Did you find anything else?'

'A lot of blackmail material. Nathaniel was well prepared. If he was going down, he was taking everyone else with him,' Cat said with a frown. 'I've locked most of it in his safe – we can get it after we've found the skyship and hand it over to the foreign authorities. That way they can hold a trial by proxy for most of the government, especially if we've got Mary to oversee things.'

A trial by proxy was only performed when the country itself didn't have enough of an established legal system to perform a trial themselves, and had to call in foreign judges and jurors to conduct the trial for them. She doubted there would be enough people left in government after the arrests to conduct a full trial.

Passing one of the journals to Harry, Fox flipped it open to the page telling the ship's location, watching the older man frown.

'We're supposed to get rain for the next few days, so I can't see the Stormlands being the most welcoming place in the world. Still, if we set course tonight, we can fly through the night and get there as the sun rises. If all goes well.'

'Are we ready to leave tonight? What if the foreign authorities don't arrive in time, or even at all? We'll be awfully vulnerable without military help,' Alice pointed out, concerned.

'It needs to be done as soon as possible,' Cat insisted. 'The longer we leave it, the more likely the government is to discover we know what they're up to. If they find another place to hide before we can bring their skyship down, all our efforts will be for nothing.'

'The lass is right,' Matt piped up. 'We need to get going as soon as we can.'

'We have to feed the sprogs first,' Alice said, looking at the children. 'Is there enough food in the house, Cat?'

'There should be plenty.' Cat bit her lip, a thought coming to her. 'Mary, would you mind showing Alice to the pantry? I assume you remember where everything is?'

Mary nodded, getting gracefully to her feet. 'I'm going to grab a few things from my room, if we have time.'

'We've got time,' said Fox. 'I'll come with you. I have to admit, I'm curious to see what your room is like.'

'It's this way,' she directed, heading for the smaller, metal spiral staircase that led up to her bedroom. A grin was on her face as she opened the door, and she stopped. Fox came to a halt at her shoulder, peering over the top of her head.

'Impressive,' he murmured, and Cat stepped forward, entering the room.

It looked as if she'd just popped downstairs for a glass of milk before bed; her things were still arranged neatly on her shelf, and there was a pile of folded laundry on her chair waiting for her to put in her dresser.

'It's beautiful,' said Fox.

She crossed the room to sit on the padded bench at the bottom of the large window, staring out over the city. Everything looked just the same as it had when she'd last looked through the window, the evening before she'd run away. And yet, everything was so very different . . .

'I thought Nathaniel would have had Samuel pack up my things. Or sold them off, even. I never thought he would keep them.' She didn't know why he'd kept them, and she didn't want to know, but she was glad he had.

Fox moved to stand beside her, and she shifted so she could lean against him. 'So how does it feel to have a common boy all alone in your fancy bedroom?' he drawled playfully, making her giggle, her pulse picking up at his words.

'How do you know this is the first time?' she retorted, trying to match his teasing tone. He winked at her, pushing a lock of hair out of her eyes. Cat's breath caught in her throat.

'I'll be ever so upset if it's not,' he said mock-solemnly, his voice low and eyes bright as they met hers. Cat's lips curved in a smile, his fingers feeling hot where they rested on her neck.

'I'd best spare your feelings, then, and stay quiet.' He growled at her words, though he was smiling, and as he leaned in closer Cat's eyes caught sight of the clock on her wall. They didn't have time for this!

Fox clearly sensed her abrupt change in mood and followed her gaze, his smile faltering as he came to the same conclusion. He coughed awkwardly, stepping away.

'So what did you want to bring with you? You'll need a bag to pack it in,' he reminded her, tugging her gently away from the window ledge.

She opened her wardrobe, dragging a large canvas duffle bag from a drawer in the bottom, leaving it open on the floor and looking at her racks of clothes. Most of them were disgusting: gaudy, hideous outfits that her father had insisted she wear to formal occasions or meetings, but there were a few outfits she actually liked that were too obviously government to pack last time she'd come.

'Is that what the government classes as fashionable?' Fox remarked with a raised eyebrow.

Cat nodded, and he scoffed.

'Well, I suppose all that inbreeding can't be good for dress sense.'

Cat whacked him in the stomach. 'I'm not inbred!' she protested. She rifled through the clothes, occasionally taking something out and tossing it on the bed.

'You wear dresses?' Fox asked, sounding surprised, and Cat glanced over her shoulder to see him holding up a simple, pale blue dress. She shot him a deadpan look.

'Yes, I wear dresses. The only reason I haven't since we met is because we've been a bit busy, and unless there's something you're not telling me, there weren't dresses available among your old clothes,' she said, making him laugh.

'Point taken,' he conceded. 'I just never thought you were the type to actually enjoy wearing pretty dresses. You've always seemed so comfortable in trousers and shirts.'

She shrugged nonchalantly.

'They're far more practical. A dress would blow around something awful on deck. And it would have got in the way all the time back in the compound,' she reasoned. 'But I do like wearing dresses when I can. I'm happy to dress as a boy if it suits what I'm doing, but I'm still a girl.' Her tone was somewhat defensive, and Fox held his hands up.

'I didn't mean anything by it. I think you'll look pretty in a dress. Especially this one,' he told her, holding up a simple purple and silver dress that was one of her favourites.

She blushed, smiling, and added the dress to the pile to be packed.

With her clothes packed, Cat looked around her room for anything she might have forgotten the last time, or not dared to take. After this, she didn't plan on returning to the house, except to collect the children.

'Anything else? Books, maybe?' Fox suggested, studying the overstuffed bookshelf lining the far wall.

Cat snorted, shaking her head.

'If I had to choose only a few of them, we'd be here for days,' she told him with a grin. 'They'll be here for me if I ever want them. Besides, I've read most of them twenty times over. Help yourself, though,' she offered, wandering over to browse the titles on the shelves.

Her finger dragged across the spines along one row, and paused on a dark blue hardback book. 'This is one of my favourites. It's rather well loved,' she added with a rueful smile, pulling it free from its companions. The cover was scuffed and peeling at the corners, and the pages were weathered and creased. It was obvious she'd read it over and over.

Fox reached across to run a gentle finger over the gold lettering on the cover. 'My mother read this book to me when I was younger, and when I learned to read myself, it was the first book I ever read the whole way through on my own. I loved it to pieces. Mum had to sew the cover back on half a dozen times. I used to take it with me almost everywhere, but one of the few times I left it at home, well . . .' He didn't need to finish his sentence; his face said it all. One of the few times he'd left it at home, his entire house had gone up in flames. 'I never managed to get another copy after that. I haven't seen it in . . . years.'

'You can have my copy, if you'd like? I think I can trust you with it,' she offered with a soft smile.

He looked at her, surprised.

'Are you sure? I mean, it's your favourite . . .' he trailed off as she pushed the book securely into his hands.

'It's your favourite too, so I know you'll look after it. Take it,' she insisted.

He paused, pursing his lips, then slipped the book carefully into the inside pocket of his coat. When he looked back at her, his eyes were somewhat shiny.

'Thank you,' he murmured, one hand on her waist as he bent to kiss her. Still amazed that she could do such a thing so freely, Cat's hand slid up to rest on his shoulder.

'We should go back downstairs,' she breathed once they parted, not moving far away from each other. 'We need to get moving. It'll be hell for Benny to navigate the Stormlands in the dark.'

Fox nodded, grabbing her duffle bag off the bed and shouldering it for her. Together they walked back down to the living room, where they found the kids eating under the watchful eyes of the crew.

'All set?' Ben queried when he saw them, and Cat nodded.

'I think so.' She'd definitely be sending someone to get Samuel once things were over; he didn't deserve to be left alone in the house.

'Her Majesty is going to stay and look after the sprogs,' Harry informed her. Cat turned curious eyes on Mary, who smiled wearily.

'I admit I need some time to ... acclimatise to freedom. It's been a long eight years, and I don't think I can stand another adventure so quickly. Besides, we can hardly leave the children to fend for themselves.' Cat didn't argue; Mary looked tired, and it would probably do her good to spend some time in familiar surroundings.

326

'Are you staying too, James?' she queried, not particularly surprised when the blond shook his head stubbornly.

'I want to help,' he insisted. 'I'm coming with you.'

Mary's lips were pursed, and it was clear they had already argued over his decision while Cat had been upstairs.

'We'd better get moving, then,' Harry declared, offering a short bow to Mary. 'Ma'am, we'll see you soon, storms willing.'

'Thank you for all your help, sir,' the queen replied, getting to her feet. 'James.' She pulled her son close, hugging him tightly and pressing a kiss to his hair. 'My darling boy, be safe, and do as you're told. Your country needs you far too much for you to come to any harm.' James swallowed, nodding sharply, and kissed his mother's cheek.

'I will, Mother. I'll be back soon.'

Cat was surprised when Mary crossed the room to her, but obligingly returned the woman's hug. 'Look after my son, Catherine. You may both be grown now, but you were friends once, and I hope you can be again. Keep him safe, and yourself.'

'I'll do my best,' Cat replied, not wanting to promise anything.

Leaving Mary with the children, the crew and James left the house, Cat locking the door behind her. Without a gaggle of children to keep an eye on it was far easier getting back to the ship, though the city was much busier than it had been when they'd left. Despite the cull in numbers, there were now almost twice as many guard patrols as usual, and it made Cat nervous to see so much purple about. The sooner they finished the job and got those in charge arrested, the sooner they could all relax.

'I'll take first shift,' Harry decided, opening the trapdoor on deck. 'Let you get some rest before we hit the Stormlands, Ben.' Ben looked grateful for that, and soon disappeared to his room.

'I'm going to put my bag away, then I'll meet you in the engine room,' Cat told Matt, tugging her duffle bag off Fox's shoulder. Squeezing his hand briefly, she turned away, jogging for the manhole down to the floor below. The familiar mix of dread and anticipation she'd felt in the government compound was returning, and the sooner she got to work the better.

Cat was with Matt and Fox for most of the afternoon, Alice coming down with a plate of sandwiches to tide them over while they got the ship airborne. They worked furiously as Harry pushed the engines to their limits. It wasn't until nearly dinner time that they had things running smoothly, and Cat looked down at her grease-stained arms and clothing. 'I think I'm going to head up,' she mused. 'Have a bath and unpack my things. I'll see you at dinner.'

Matt waved from where he was working on one of the propeller motors, and Fox gave her a lopsided smile, tyrium smudges all over his face.

'See you at dinner.'

Heading back up to her bedroom, Cat perched on the edge of the bed with a sigh, her shoulders slumping. She felt like she hadn't slept in days, and yet it wasn't even close to night time. They still had a long few days ahead.

When she'd finished unpacking, Cat's eyes fell on the contents of her open wardrobe, and a small smile flickered across her face. Fox was surprised that she liked to wear dresses? Well, she'd give him something to be surprised about. Pulling the purple and silver dress that he'd picked out earlier off its hanger, she chose some grey woollen tights to go with it and bundled her fresh clothing in her arms, a towel on top of the pile. Hurrying to the washroom, Cat locked the door behind her and started to run her bath, looking forward to a nice long, relaxing soak.

26

Clean and dressed, Cat towelled her hair until it was only damp, then unlocked the bathroom door and peered into the corridor. It was empty, so she quickly darted back into her room. She didn't want anyone to see her in her dress until dinner. Brushing her hair, she looked in the mirror that hung on her wardrobe door, smiling at her reflection. She looked a lot more like the girl she used to be, but she rather thought she looked years older. Her short haircut made her look more mature, and with all the action and stress over the past couple of weeks, she'd lost the last of her baby fat. She was, dare she say it, quite pretty.

Opening her drawer of jewellery, she found the necklace she was looking for; a simple silver raindrop on a fine chain, with an amethyst gem set in the centre. She carefully fastened the chain around her neck and sat down to pull on her boots. As she did up the last buckle on her boot, there was a knock on the door, and she cursed under her breath.

'It's open!' she called, hoping it wasn't James. She grinned widely when Fox opened the door, her expression growing even brighter at the gobsmacked look on his face.

'Well, do I look enough like a girl now?' she asked with a teasing grin.

When he'd picked his jaw up off the floor, he stepped inside, shutting the door behind him.

'You definitely look enough like a girl, a very beautiful girl, for that matter. Far too beautiful for this scruffy little street rat,' he informed her, half-serious as he moved forward, fingers brushing her cheek to tuck a stray lock of hair behind her ear. Cat felt her face redden, reaching up to rest her hands on his shoulders as he placed his other hand at the curve of her bodice.

'We've been through this,' she told him seriously, voice soft. 'You're not a scruffy little street rat. To me, you're far more of a prince than James is.'

He laughed, pulling her into a lingering kiss, then stepped back and offered his arm with a short bow.

'Well, m'lady, might your prince escort you to dinner?'

She laughed, offering a curtsey before looping her arm through his.

'You may,' she agreed, smiling.

As they walked through the galley door, all eyes turned on them, and Cat blushed fiercely as Matt let out a teasing wolf whistle.

'Oh, Cat, sweetheart, you look wonderful! Did you bring that with you from the house?' Alice asked, and Cat nodded, leaning closer into Fox's side as they approached. James was staring at her with wide eyes.

'Don't you make a pretty little lass, then,' Matt remarked. 'Give us a spin.' She twirled obligingly. 'You'd better keep an eye on your girl, Fox, before someone better-looking makes off with her.'

The redhead raised an eyebrow.

'She'd have to *find* someone better-looking first,' he retorted smoothly.

'Better-looking, I don't know, but I could do with someone with a smaller ego,' Cat sniped, earning a playful nudge from her boyfriend.

'You wound me,' he murmured.

'Cat, would you take Ben and Harry their dinner up for me, please?' Alice asked.

'Sure.' Picking up the tray, she doubled back out of the room, climbing up the ladder one-handed. She nudged the control-room door open with her hip.

'Dinner,' she called.

'Blimey, lass, you clean up nicely! What's the occasion?' asked Harry with a grin, prompting Ben to glance over from where he was engrossed in the view outside the window.

'No occasion. I just brought some clothes back from the house and thought I'd wear one of the dresses. Contrary to popular belief, I do actually like wearing them sometimes.'

'Well, you look very pretty. Has Fox seen you?' Ben asked, turning the steering wheel to central position as he turned to collect his dinner.

'He has. He was quite speechless,' she replied.

'Quite rightly so,' he said with a wink, setting his plate on his lap.

'How long do you think we'll be, Harry?' Cat queried.

'A fair few hours yet, lass. But no worries – if you go to bed, I promise I'll send someone in to wake you up when we get there. Benny and I will be taking shifts all night,' he assured her.

'I'll see you later, then,' she replied, leaving the control room.

Her dinner was waiting for her when she got back to the galley. They were all somewhat tense, despite knowing they were flying as fast as they possibly could, and Cat was uncomfortably aware of James's eyes on her through the entire meal. Afterwards, Alice brought a small sponge cake from the kitchen.

'Should I take some upstairs?' Cat asked, and Alice shook her head.

'No, I'll keep theirs for later,' she assured her, plating up. 'I just thought it might be nice to have a little treat tonight, in celebration of the fact that if all goes well, this entire mess will be over in a couple of days.'

'Shouldn't we celebrate . . . after?' Matt said hesitantly.

'There's cake, Matthew, don't argue,' Fox said sagely.

Matt grinned.

'Duly noted.'

Cat took a bite of her cake, humming quietly in appreciation.

'What do you think will happen when we find the ship? I mean, I know we're going to try and shut them down, but . . . wouldn't it make more sense to just blow them up?' James asked curiously.

'We'll see what we find on the ship,' Matt reasoned. 'And we won't blow the ship up, we'll seize it and fly it back to Anglya – with foreign aid, if they do come – where it'll be searched and stripped until it's back to its bare bones and able to be used as a normal ship again. Then everyone involved will pay for their crimes, and we can make sure there are no experiments left elsewhere, ready to be used.'

Cat frowned as she thought about what would happen when the whole mess was over. Yes, she would love to stay with the crew, but . . . part of her felt responsible for setting the country back to rights. Her father had got them into this state, so wasn't it her duty to get them out? As much as she would love to just fly off into the sunset with the crew . . . she didn't know if she could.

'Everything OK?' Fox asked in a low murmur, his blue eyes concerned, his hand covering hers on the bench.

She shrugged, offering a half-hearted smile.

'Yeah, fine,' she replied unconvincingly. His eyes narrowed, but he let it slide, merely squeezing her hand.

'I might even be able to persuade Harry to settle down and give me some kids after all this!' Alice remarked, making Cat grin. 'He's been making excuses for far too long, and we're not exactly young any more!'

'I think you'd make great parents,' Fox told her sincerely.

Cat knew that Alice and Harry were as good as parents to Fox, and had to agree with him; she rather thought any child would be lucky to have those two as parents.

'What about you, Matt? Gonna settle down when this mess is done with?' Fox asked.

'I don't think settling down is anywhere in my future plans,' Matt said with quiet assurance. 'I'll just carry on here, if Harry and Alice will have me. And if they decide to give up travelling for the family life, I'm sure Benny and I will think of something. I doubt anyone could keep him grounded for long, and he'll need me to keep him out of trouble. How about you?'

The mechanic looked thoughtful.

'Staying on the ship would be nice. Maybe going a bit further afield, seeing parts of the world we've not seen yet. With no one relying on us to bring them food, we could go anywhere.'

Both Matt and Fox looked a little dreamy-eyed at that prospect, and Cat beamed; seeing the world sounded perfect to her.

'I'm going to have to lead a country, aren't I?' James realised, his voice faint and his eyes wide at the prospect. 'Bloody hell.'

'You won't be leading it for a while, yet, dear,' Alice reasoned. 'Your mother has plenty of years left in her. But I'm sure when the time comes, you'll do brilliantly.'

'And the people will already like you, since they'll know you had a hand in helping us bring this mess to light. Any bloke who stopped their children being taken will be all right by them,' Matt pointed out, smiling encouragingly at the young boy.

'I think you'll make a wonderful king,' Cat added.

At her words, he beamed back, looking like a weight had been lifted off his shoulders.

Cat felt that being shaken awake by Fox was becoming far too common an occurrence for her liking, though he was admittedly more gentle about it now. She squinted up at the redhead, who had an apologetic look on his face as he roused her from sleep.

'We're near the Stormlands, so you'll want to be up on deck soon. Matt's rigging the ropes as we speak.'

At the news, her grogginess vanished and she shot up out

335

of bed, making Fox laugh. 'Easy there, sweetheart, there's no rush yet. We're just preparing, so we'll be ready for action as soon as we find their skyship. Get dressed, take your time, wake up a bit.'

She slowed her breathing and calmed herself, smiling sheepishly.

They went straight up on deck as soon as Cat was ready, and despite being bundled up in her warmest clothes, she was still freezing. She could see frost forming on the lenses of her goggles, obscuring her vision, and wiped it off with a gloved hand, squinting up into the rigging to see Matt loosening two swing-ropes with which they could board the other ship. A zip-line would be safer, but that required the cooperation of both ships, which was something they definitely didn't have.

She and Fox hurried over to Harry, who was scouring the cloudy sky for anything that might possibly be another skyship. Cat gripped Fox's arm as the ship lurched abruptly, buffeted by a particularly strong gust of wind. She heard Matt swearing faintly from high above.

'Here, both of you,' Harry said as Cat and Fox approached him, pulling two sets of binocular attachments from his coat pockets, handing them one each. Cat needed Fox to clip hers on to her goggles, having no idea how to do so herself, then flipped them up to rest against her forehead so she could see normally.

'Have you got everything?' Harry asked Fox, who nodded, patting his satchel.

'Recording devices are in here, as are guns, the zip-line brace, and a few ... extras,' he assured them. Cat decided instantly that she had no desire to know what those 'extras' were.

Harry nodded in approval, clapping Fox on both shoulders.

'Get up there with Matt. He'll have the swing-ropes ready for you when we find the ship. Be careful and look after yourselves. Don't do anything stupid.'

Before Cat and Harry could head for the rigging, however, the trap opened, and James's head popped up, clad in a fur-lined cap. When he saw them, he scrambled the rest of the way out of the trap, toppling to his knees almost as soon as he got to his feet. Not letting it faze him, he pulled himself up once more, walking with unsteady steps towards them.

'What in storms do you think you're doing?' Fox snapped. 'The deck isn't the safest place at the best of times, let alone this close to the Stormlands!'

'We got a message,' James panted, ignoring Fox's rant. 'I don't know how, but the Mericans managed to hijack the frequency of the loudspeaker and transmit a message through to the control room.'

Harry let out a low whistle.

'I'd heard they were working on technology that could do that, but I didn't think they'd actually got it running yet. What did they have to say?' he queried.

'They're on their way! They're sending a ship out to meet us, and another two are headed to Anglya as we speak. They'll be with us before nightfall, they said. Ben's speaking to them now to direct them to us. Same with the Erovans — two ships to Anglya, and they've both opened their ship-yards to the trade ships coming in with the children.

337

Apparently all routes to and from Siberene are closed because of storm difficulties, so any ships we had sent that way have been redirected to either Mericus or Erova. They'll talk more about the long-term details when we're all back in Anglya and have the government in custody.'

Cat beamed, whooping with happiness and hugging Fox.

'That's fantastic!' she exclaimed. The Mericans must have already had a ship in the area, to be able to reach them so quickly — it would have taken them days to arrive from Mericus itself. It made her wonder if they'd been monitoring Anglya already.

'Isn't it just?' Harry agreed, patting James on the shoulder. 'Good work, lad. Now, go back below deck before you get blown right overboard.'

James paled, unsure whether to take Harry seriously or not.

'Be careful,' he said to Cat, belatedly shifting his gaze to include Fox as well. 'We're so close, don't cock this up.'

Cat laughed, shoving his shoulder gently.

'Get below deck. We'll see you in a few hours,' she urged.

James saluted them all with a smile, before retreating back to the trap, looking relieved.

'Either way, we need to get moving,' said Fox. 'The Mericans won't be able to do a thing if we haven't found the government ship before they get here. Come on, Cat, we need to get up there with Matt.'

Fox grasped Cat's hand and led her towards the bottom of the rigging. The pair climbed up with lightning speed, meeting Matt at the top, where he had two swing-ropes ready for use.

'Hello, troublemakers,' he said as they joined him, sitting astride the upper mast beam. 'Cat, how do you feel about doing this? I know you've not done a rigging swing before, and, well . . . these are hardly the ideal conditions to make your first.'

She smiled at him, hoping to disguise the fear racing through her at the prospect of swinging from one ship to another, so very close to the Stormlands, hundreds of feet above raging waters, with nothing to support her but a length of rope.

'Can't be too hard, right?' she replied, making Matt snort.

'Always the optimist,' he muttered. 'I'll tie you in nice and safe. There's a reason you've got so many buckles and straps on that flight coat of yours. Not all of them are for decoration.'

'But some of them are?' she asked with a grin, and Fox snickered.

'Well, as you mention it, a good deal of thought went into how dashing I'd look in that coat. I loved that coat,' he informed her.

'Get your binoculars on and start looking,' Matt interrupted them, flipping his own binoculars down and wrapping his arms tightly into the rigging nets to keep himself balanced. Cat copied him, yelping in surprise as the ship began to rock and lurch more violently the closer they got to the Stormlands. How on Tellus were they meant to stay out here for any length of time?

'Should be there any minute now, according to the coordinates!' Harry yelled up to them, and Matt gave him a thumbs up to show they'd heard.

Cat squinted through the haze of cloud that swirled viciously around them, trying to look for any shape or shadow that could possibly be a skyship.

By the gradually increasing tilt of the ship, Cat realised Ben was flying them in slowly decreasing circles; he obviously expected the government ship to be somewhere in the centre.

'There!' Fox cried out suddenly, throwing an arm in an eastwards direction.

Cat turned to see a dark shape half-hidden in the clouds, a rippling scrap of purple fabric at the top of the mast giving it away as an Anglyan government ship. Its base propellers were about four times bigger than its tail propeller, which probably explained how it had managed to stay put, despite the weather.

'Due east!' Matt shouted, and Harry's head whipped around. Nodding when he saw what they were looking at, he shouted down the hatch to Ben.

The ship began to turn, heading in the direction of the shadow in the clouds. Cat could only hope they were approaching the back of the other ship.

Flipping up her binoculars, she wiped the frost off her goggles, feeling herself crunch and crack whenever she moved as a thin layer of ice formed on her coat. Glancing down, her eyebrows shot up when she saw James steadily making his way up the rigging, wearing one of Fox's old flight coats.

'What the hell do you think you're doing?' she exclaimed when he was close enough to hear her.

'Coming with you. I can't stand the thought of sitting around and letting you two do everything. I can help, I swear,' the prince insisted. There was a steely determination in his eyes that told Cat he'd be coming with them whether she liked it or not.

'If you two keep arguing, we'll miss our chance to jump,' Fox interrupted, already securing his swing-rope around his waist and torso. Cat looked past him to see Matt securing a third swing-rope to the rigging, and sighed; obviously the decision had been made for her. James held on to the rigging, letting Matt tie his swing-rope while Fox wound Cat's through the buckle loops in her coat.

'Just jump when Matt tells you to jump, and hold on to your rope. He'll untie them at the top so we can land, and don't lock your knees or you'll break your leg. If you think you're going off course, don't worry – Matt won't cut you loose unless he knows you'll land safely.'

He spoke to both of them, but his eyes were fixed firmly on Cat. Leaning forward, he kissed her hard, their goggles clicking together.

'Trust Matt, and trust the rope. Everything will be fine.'

Cat nodded, poised on the beam, ready to jump. They were nearing the government ship at a higher level than its deck so they would have the height advantage when jump-ing. It didn't look like the deck was manned.

As they drew closer, she gripped Fox's hand, and he turned briefly to shoot her a reassuring smile. James's expression was stony on her other side, the panic obvious in his eyes, and she reached out to him, taking his hand too.

He looked up at her, and she gave him a stern warning look of 'Don't read into this any more than it is', which he returned with a shy smile.

'Get ready,' Matt murmured, eyes fixed on the ship. 'On three. One . . . two . . . three!'

As he shouted the last number, Fox jumped, half dragging both Cat and James with him. Cat heard screaming, and it took her several moments to realise the sound was coming from her own mouth. Shutting it tightly, she swallowed, feeling her stomach clench with nausea as they fell.

Abruptly, the rope pulled taut and she was jerked outwards towards the government ship. Letting go of both boys, she gripped her own rope, practically hugging the thick material as she soared over the bottomless gap between the two ships. Frantically repeating 'Trust the rope, trust Matt' in her mind, she forgot how to breathe as she waited, feeling that any minute now she would reach the apex of her swing and start going backwards, falling into the endless chasm of cloud and sky.

There was another sudden jerk, and then her fall had a distinct downward motion, the deck of the government ship rising to meet her. Letting her knees loosen, she dropped into a crouch and rolled forward when she hit the metal, hearing two thumps that signalled James's and Fox's safe landings.

Standing up and looking to her left, she saw Fox winding his rope into loops on his arm. She copied him, allowing him to untie the end from her body, coiling it with the rest of her rope and moving to untie James, ignoring the way her fingers shook.

She glanced over her shoulder, able to see the clouds raging and the sea swirling beneath them. She imagined herself tumbling into the depths below, and shuddered.

She jumped when fingers touched her hand, glancing up with panicked eyes into Fox's steady gaze. His hand closed briefly over hers, and she smiled, the contact helping to slow her racing heart. Setting aside her fears, she turned her attention to her task.

27

They left the three ropes in a pile on the deck, tying them around one of the shorter mast beams. When the trap began to open several feet away from them, they dived behind a pair of bolted-down crates, Cat peering around the side. The guard who had opened the trap didn't get out fully, merely sticking his head through the gap and looking around, no doubt to see what had caused the noise. Obviously deciding it was just hailstones, he ducked back down into the ship and shut the trap behind him.

'That seemed too easy,' Fox muttered.

'They probably feel pretty secure in the knowledge that no one would find them all the way out here. I know I would be,' Cat pointed out, following Fox to the other end of the ship, where there was a second trapdoor.

James and Cat stood back while Fox unlocked it, pulling it open by the handle and ushering them both inside. The cold metal corridor was deserted and they searched quickly for an empty room.

It happened to be a storage room, filled with crates. Fox dropped his satchel and dug out the recording devices, passing Cat both of hers.

'I've only got two of each so, James, you're just going to have to keep your eyes and ears peeled and be our lookout while we're recording.'

'We should find the main laboratory. The more footage we can get before the Mericans arrive to shut it down the better,' Cat said. They needed to get the faces of government workers on record, or they'd worm their way out of punishment.

'But if the Mericans are coming, do we really need footage? Surely the experiments themselves are evidence enough?' James asked.

Cat shared a look with Fox.

'The government lot are a sneaky bunch. If we don't have footage of them personally involved with the experiments, it's entirely likely that some of them will claim innocence and escape scot-free,' she explained.

'Which we definitely don't want,' said James. 'OK, so how do we find this main lab? I don't think we've got time to search every level of the ship methodically.'

Fox shouldered his satchel.

'We follow the crowd,' he declared, looking quite excited.

'We . . . follow the people who want to kill us,' James said slowly, checking he'd heard correctly. Both Cat and Fox nodded. 'Right. Because in your world, that makes sense,' he muttered under his breath.

'We do it without getting caught obviously,' Cat told him. 'But the main lab is likely to have the most workers. So we need to go where most people seem to be heading.'

James's lips pursed in nervous disapproval, but he nodded regardless.

Fox looked through the window of the door, checking the corridor was clear. He ducked out of sight as two men walked past, then waited several long moments before nudging the heavy door open.

'Quickly,' he breathed.

Cat led the group out of the room and they followed the two men at a distance, ducking around a corner when they entered a room. Before they could decide their next move, the door opened once more and the two men emerged with a metal stretcher on wheels, a sheet-covered body lying limply on it. Cat let out a silent gasp as she saw the unconscious teen; most of the body was covered by the white sheet, but there were large patches of blood soaking through, and the part of the body that was visible looked more machine than human.

'Oh, that's disgusting,' James said under his breath.

They watched as the two men wheeled the stretcher down the corridor until they came to a gated room. One of the men pushed the gate aside, allowing the other to wheel the stretcher into the small room. Shutting the gate behind them, one of the men began to wind a large crank handle set in the wall. Cat's eyes widened as the room itself sank below the floor, until the two men were gone from view.

'They've got a pulley-lift,' Fox breathed, sounding impressed. 'That'll make it harder for us to follow. But presumably, there's a manhole around here somewhere too.'

Walking past the lift, they ignored the few doors along the corridor and turned a corner. Cat grinned when she saw the manhole at the end of a short corridor. Fox insisted on going first, and lay flat on his belly to peer below, checking the corridor was clear before climbing down.

The corridor looked exactly the same as the one above it; plain steel walls and floors, spaced with numbered steel doors, each with a small window. Lamps hung from overhead, swinging with the motion of the ship.

'How far do you think it goes down?' Cat asked in a whisper, and Fox shrugged.

'I'd imagine three levels of labs and workshops, one of sleeping and communal quarters, and one of storage.'

Neither of them needed to voice aloud that in this case 'storage' meant children.

'The main lab is likely to be somewhere on this floor, then. It'll be in the middle of everything,' Cat reasoned.

James tugged on her sleeve, and she turned, eyes widening when she saw three mechanics in overalls and lab coats emerge from a room in front of them. Noticing, Fox held a finger to his lips, gesturing for Cat and James to follow him.

They stayed a good fifteen feet away from the men, and when the mechanics entered a door, it was Fox who rushed forward to peer through the window.

He ducked back down. 'Bingo!' he whispered, beckoning Cat and James closer. He reached into his coat and removed his video recorder, lifting it to record through the window.

Curious, Cat stood on tiptoe to look into the room, and immediately wished she hadn't. The lab was tightly packed with machinery and the two children in the room were barely human any more. One of them – Cat thought it was a boy – had a green and brown camouflage-patterned mask over his face, like a grotesque mecha. His enhancements didn't quite fit his skin, making Cat realise he must have grown a fair amount since having them implanted. She felt sick: how long had he been there?

There were eight mechanics, four for each child, and two aristocrats whom Cat recognised by face, but not name.

'We need audio,' she said quietly.

'We won't be able to get the door open without being noticed,' Fox said flatly.

'I know. I just wish we could.' She kept watching, wincing as sparks flew from the chest plate as one of the mechanics lowered a drill to it. Suddenly, she squeaked in alarm, ducking down and pulling Fox with her.

Without explaining to James, she dragged both boys around the corner, then peeped round it as the door opened. A man walked out and thankfully turned the opposite way, but before she or Fox could hold him back, James flew round the corner, making straight for the slowly closing door. Cat held her breath as the prince reached out and stuck his fingers in the doorway, keeping it open just a fraction.

They crept back towards the lab, Cat removing her audio recorder from her coat, flicking it on and slipping it in the gap above James's fingers.

'Thomas is coming to inspect the stock this afternoon,' said an aristocratic voice. 'Wants to know if we're ready for war after what happened in the city.'

His companion snorted. 'Ready for war? You've got to be joking! We've barely got enough for a single regiment! And we don't even know if they're fully functioning yet!

The man's mad. We would be better off not Collecting in Anglya for a while and kidnapping foreign kids instead. They'll find these saboteurs – there's been no more action since the explosions in the city so I doubt it's an uprising. We should let things calm down for a bit. We've taken too many children and people are getting suspicious, wondering why their kids never come home. It's war, I tell them. People don't come home from war! But I can see that they don't really believe me – they're not as stupid as they look!'

Both men laughed, making Cat feel sick to her stomach. On the upside, it sounded as if they had yet to catch wind of her little newscast appearance, or the danger they were in. She went over her mental list of names, thinking of all the possible men called Thomas who could be running the ship. One sprung to mind immediately.

'Thomas said he wants to bring his younger son out here, soon,' the first speaker said, and the other man chuckled as Cat stood up to peer through the glass in the door.

'To take over the family business?' he asked, but Cat saw his colleague shake his head.

'No, to add to the test subjects, actually. He says he wants both of them involved in his masterpiece.'

This made the other man shudder.

'Told you, the man's a nutcase. Wait, what do you think you're doing! Don't connect that, you'll wake it up!' he exclaimed suddenly, dragging one of the mechanics away from the child he was working on.

'I can't check if it's worked unless I connect it,' the mechanic argued weakly, watching as the fair-haired government man roughly pulled out a chain from the chest plate, tossing it carelessly to the ground.

'I don't care, you can check another time! We've got strict orders not to wake any of them until absolutely necessary, you idiot!'

Duly chastised, the mechanic went back to work. Deciding that was probably all they were going to get out of that conversation, Cat bent down and turned off the audio recorder, attaching it once more to her coat and gesturing to James to close the door. Fox turned off his video recorder and crouched down to speak to them.

'We should find somewhere to wait until this Thomas bloke turns up – it seems like he's running things here. Cat, any ideas who it might be?' he queried, and Cat sighed.

'Definitely one at the top of my list.'

Fox nodded, peering around the narrow corridor.

'How do you two fancy getting a bit cosy?' he asked, his gaze fixed on a storage cupboard opposite the entrance to the pulley-lift.

Cat groaned quietly, glaring at Fox. James looked like he didn't know whether to cheer or scream.

'Come on, it's the best we can do,' Fox insisted. 'We need to stay safe until the Mericans get here.' Opening the storage-cupboard door, Cat grimaced when she saw the dust inside. Still, she settled down in the corner closest to the door. Fox sat next to her, and a disgruntled James squished himself into the opposite corner, sitting on top of some boxes. Closing the door almost completely, Cat leaned her head against the side of the frame so she could see out into the corridor.

'What if he walks in from the other end?' James asked in a whisper.

'He won't, that's a dead end. Both manholes up and down are on the other side of us, and the pulley-lift is right in front,' Cat said quietly. Her mind was still reeling from the information; this Thomas would use his own son as an experiment? Even her father had spared her that fate! Though, she had to admit, he *had* tried to kill her.

Hearing a brief scuffle and a muffled yelp of pain, Cat looked back over her shoulder. She rolled her eyes when she saw Fox and James glaring at each other in the dim light.

'Honestly, both of you, grow up!' she hissed.

'He kicked me,' complained James, sounding far younger than his fifteen years.

'I'm sure it was an accident. What are you – five? Just put up with each other, can't you? For my sake?' she requested in frustration. She didn't get an answer, and assumed that was the end of it – then James spoke again.

'I was just wondering who Fox thinks he's fooling. When all this drama is over, he's likely to move on in search of something more ... interesting. He *is* a commoner, after all, and too old for you. His baser instincts will lead him to stray, eventually.'

Cat wished she could reach over and strangle the young prince.

'I would never find Cat uninteresting, and I have no want or need to stray from her. But even if I did, she wouldn't choose you! You don't realise how much of an arrogant brat you are, do you?' Fox spat in reply.

'I'm right here, you know,' Cat pointed out sharply. 'And

I can hear every word you're saying. James, for the last bloody time, stop trying to get between me and Fox. It will never happen, and I won't stop loving him.'

'You love me?' Fox cut in, sounding surprised.

Cat blushed deeply; had she just admitted that out loud?

'Well, I —' She never finished her sentence, because at that moment, the cupboard door was wrenched open, and Cat was left staring at a horribly familiar face.

28

'Well, well, look who we have here. I was so terribly concerned when I thought my cupboard was talking to itself,' the dark-haired man sneered, his black-brown eyes alight in amusement. He grabbed Cat by her coat, dragging her forcefully from the cupboard.

'Gentlemen,' he snapped curtly, prompting the two guards flanking him to reach for Fox and James.

'Gale,' Cat gasped, glaring at the man she knew all too well.

His smirk widened, and he gripped her shoulder so tightly she thought he would break it. She reached up to her neck, as if trying to pull away from him, and discreetly flicked her audio and video recorders on – relieved when Thomas didn't notice a thing.

'I did wonder where you'd run off to, little Catherine,' Thomas crowed. 'Your father said you had died, but I never believed him. My poor Marcus was *devastated* when he heard the news. His little fiancée, lost to him forever!'

Cat shuddered at the thought of Marcus being *devastated* by her death. He was probably only angry that he couldn't get his grubby little hands on her money.

'I bet he was,' she muttered under her breath, earning a sharp jab in the back. Thomas opened the door to the lab, startling the men inside, who went slack-jawed at the sight of the three struggling teenagers being forced into the room.

'Gentlemen, we have visitors. Why don't you give them a guided tour of our most recent project, hmm?' He dragged Cat over to the table with the teenage boy on it, forcing her to stare at the perverse, twisted mound of flesh and bronze.

'Isn't he beautiful?' Thomas murmured lovingly, stroking the cheek of the camouflage mask. 'I'm bringing Marcus up here soon – he's awfully lonely without his brother. They'll both make wonderful soldiers, though. Both my boys are very strong.'

Cat gasped as she realised just who that boy had once been before the metal and gears.

'Is that . . . Alexander?' she breathed in horror. She'd only met the eldest Gale boy a handful of times – he was three years older than her and deeply unpleasant – but nevertheless, no one deserved . . . that.

'It is my beautiful boy,' Thomas breathed reverently. 'He's ready for the final enhancement, so he can take his rightful place as commander of my army. They're almost ready, you know. My wonderful children are being born again.'

Cat stared at the man in front of her. *He* was the one in charge? She'd always thought that Thomas reported to her father, but obviously she'd been wrong.

'Then, Nathaniel . . .' she murmured, making Thomas laugh harshly.

'Nathaniel was never more than a convenient scapegoat.

354

Tell him the right words and he would believe my ideas were all his own. Insisted on doing all the work, bless him, leaving me free to watch my children grow! My reign will be glorious, Catherine, just you wait! My children and I will unite the six nations and rule like gods, as the Anglyan rulers once did!'

'The other five nations seem to be doing just fine ruling themselves. All you've done is make things worse! Anglya can't prosper if its children are machines!' Cat snarled.

'Its children aren't *all* machines, my dear. Solely the common ones, except for Alexander, who will become their leader. I would have killed the commoners, anyway. Those dirty scum don't deserve to live in our country. No, we shall fill the country with only those of our own pure blood. But what a shame – a child to combine the Hunter, Ingate and Gale lines would have been the perfect heir for our perfect country,' he said with a frown.

'All people in Anglya are descended from the First Men,' Cat recited, as she had learned as a young child in school. It was one of the few things every Anglyan child was taught, regardless of class or status. 'Even the commoners. Our blood is no purer than theirs.'

Thomas glared at her, his dark eyes flashing in anger.

'*How dare you speak such blasphemy!*' he hissed, slapping her sharply across the face.

'Don't you touch her!' Fox roared, earning a slap himself. As both boys began to struggle, their captors clapped hands over their mouths, silencing them.

'It's not blasphemy if it's the truth!' Cat argued. 'Where did the commoners come from, if not the First Men?

Everyone knows the Firsts were the only ones on Tellus and everyone is descended from them. The sole reason the aristocracy are any different is that we're more directly related to them!'

Thomas hit her again, and as her head jerked there was a spark from her coat opening. She froze, panicking, as Thomas eyed her suspiciously.

'I wonder where that little spark came from?'

As he spoke, several more sparks occurred, and Cat cursed as Thomas grabbed the source, yanking harshly on the video recorder. It sputtered and died in his hands, issuing pale violet-grey smoke from its film casing. She almost wanted to cry: it had ruined the footage! She just hoped Fox was recording everything. Her audio recorder was still in place, but without visuals it was useless.

'What's this, then?' Thomas queried, studying the video recorder intently. He let out a chuckle. 'A miniature newscast recorder! Oh, how very sweet! I suppose you've been doing this for a while, you sneaky little brat. Was it you who blew up our Breningarth compound?'

'I saved the children you hadn't touched and got enough evidence to make sure you won't touch any ever again,' she spat fiercely.

The dark-haired man snorted, dropping the video recorder to the ground and crushing it beneath the heel of his boot.

'It *was* you, then. How very . . . heroic. I must admit, it tickles me to know our brave young *prince* was rescued by a street rat and a little girl!' he cried with a laugh. 'But I can't let this continue, I'm sure you understand.'

For the second time that week, Cat found herself facing the barrel of a gun. Her heart pounded; there was no one to save her this time.

'Any last words, little girl?' Thomas taunted, his smirk widening. He flicked the hammer back.

Cat opened her mouth, and closed it again. Should she tell Fox she was sorry, that she loved him? Ask him to apologise to the rest of the crew? Make some comment about how Thomas wouldn't get away with what he was doing?

Before she could decide, she heard a shout of anger and a curse from behind her, and saw Thomas's eyes widen for a fraction of a second. She heard a sharp bang and felt her shoulder jerk back, then she was falling limply to the floor.

Cat didn't dare open her eyes, not wanting to see if she was bleeding. But . . . she didn't feel any pain. Was that what it felt like getting shot? She lay still, eyes clenched shut, waiting for the explosion of pain she assumed would accompany a bullet ripping into her flesh. Nothing came, and she frowned, opening her eyes warily. Immediately, her eyebrows rose, and her jaw dropped.

The only blood in the room was coming from the hole in Thomas Gale's waistcoat, just a little to the right of his heart. The man had fallen to his knees, and was grinning even as foamy blood bubbled from his lips, dripping down his chin.

'My children . . . will succeed . . . where I have . . . failed,' he rasped, more blood dribbling from his mouth with every word, and Cat watched in horror as the dark-haired man began to laugh, falling backwards in a sprawled heap and laughing maniacally until his body grew still.

Looking up, she gasped when she saw what had been going on behind her. Fox and James were both free, their guards slumped unconscious on the floor, and Fox was standing with his gun raised in the direction of Thomas's now lifeless body. The two aristocrats were huddled protectively in the corner with the mechanics, and Fox turned his weapon on them as he crouched at Cat's side.

'Are you all right?' he asked.

She smiled at him, squeezing his free hand.

'Fine. Are you going to make a habit of saving me?'

'Only if you're going to make a habit of needing saving,' he retorted.

'Uh, Fox, Cat? I don't mean to alarm you, but . . . help?' James called, his voice several octaves higher than normal. Both teens looked immediately at where James was standing, beside the table that Alexander lay on. Purple steam was streaming from a small chimney on the boy's neck, and the gears on his chest plate were ticking slowly. 'I'm . . . quite sure this isn't meant to happen.'

'He's been woken. He was never meant to be woken – he's not ready!' one of the mechanics cried out in alarm, rushing forward to look over Alexander's half-metal body. Cat jumped as the door opened forcefully, then laughed in relief when Matt stuck his head in.

'Found you!' he exclaimed happily. 'The Mericans are about five minutes away and we've already set up a zip-line.' He turned, looking back into the corridor behind him. 'Hey, lads, I've found them!'

'Mericans are coming?' one of the mechanics asked fearfully, and Fox, who had stood up, nodded sharply.

'The entire world knows what you've been doing. It's over, you've lost, but if you cooperate with us now, your sentence may be less harsh,' he informed them curtly. The entire group didn't hesitate in raising their hands in surrender.

As Matt entered the room again, Ben and Harry arrived hot on his tail, and grinned when they saw the three teens.

'Was wondering where you three had got to! Everything all right, lass?' Harry asked in concern, seeing Cat on the floor. She nodded, allowing Fox to help her up.

'We need to find the rest of the children,' Matt told them. 'See if . . . see if any can be saved. Cat, Fox, James, you wait here and greet the Merican soldiers when they arrive,' he added with a frown, ushering Ben and Harry from the room.

Cat nodded, walking with shaky steps towards the door.

'How many are here in the skyship, do you think?' she asked, leaning into Fox. He frowned, kissing the crown of her head.

'Far too many, whatever the number. But at least they won't be joined by any more.'

Neither of them saw the movement behind them, and Cat screamed when another loud gunshot went off. Glancing around frantically, her eyes widened when she saw Alexander sitting up on his table, the gun mounted on his bronze shoulder plate smoking. Turning around, hoping desperately the bullet hadn't hit anyone, she screamed again when she saw the red stain seeping rapidly through the back of Fox's shirt. He frowned at her in confusion, then looked down at himself and saw the gaping hole in his stomach. His head lifted, and his gaze met hers, eyes wide.

'. . . Oh,' he breathed, sinking to his knees.

Cat choked back a sob and dropped to the ground, pulling Fox into her lap, stroking his hair.

'Shh, easy, just relax, everything will be fine,' she said in a strangled voice, looking up at James, who was staring at her and Fox in shock. 'Get help! Get a doctor! There has to be one somewhere on this bloody ship!'

Three of the mechanics had instantly rushed to Alexander's table, and one of them reached into the uncovered chest plate and ripped several gears from the mechanism. Alexander froze, the eye-lights behind his mask going blank. Another mechanic bravely broke away from his fellows, reaching out to grab James by the arm.

'I'll take you to our ship's doctor, but . . .' his voice trailed off as he looked at Fox.

'He'll be fine if you get him a doctor! So go!' snapped Cat, and both James and the mechanic left the room. Cat looked back down at Fox, who was deathly pale, his lips tinged blue. She pressed her hands against the wound in his stomach, remembering that pressure helped to slow bleeding.

'Cat, stop,' Fox breathed, and she levelled a glare at him.

'No! You're going to be *fine*, Fox. Just . . . stay awake.'

His blue eyes were knowing, and a little bit sad, and Cat knew then that he wasn't going to recover from his wound. A sob tore from her lips, and she pressed her lips to his copper hair.

'Cat, listen to me,' he murmured, drawing her gaze. 'I love you. I will *always* love you. But . . . I won't be here for you.' He paused, choking out a weak chuckle. 'We could've had years. Decades. Bloody government.'

She shook her head insistently, kissing his forehead.

'No,' she muttered stubbornly. 'Hold on until the Mericans come – they'll help! Just . . . don't leave me, Fox.'

'Not really my choice,' he pointed out drily, slumping further into her lap. 'Be happy, Cat. Our war is over. We won.'

'I *can't* be happy without you, I *won't*!' Her voice was full of anguish as she held him closer. He managed a barely there smile, and Cat tried to ignore the blood spilling between her fingers.

'You have to try,' he told her urgently. 'I'm sorry. I . . . I wish I could stay, but I can't.' His words began to slur, and Cat felt hot tears dripping down her cheeks, landing on Fox.

'Don't leave me,' she begged, kissing his cold lips. 'Please, stay with me.'

'You know . . . James isn't so bad. He'd look after you, at least,' Fox said hoarsely, coughing. When he coughed, blood spattered on his chin, and Cat wiped it away.

'Don't you dare!' she sobbed, holding him tight to her, as if letting him go would mean him disappearing forever. In a way, it did. 'Not now. I don't care about James. He's not you!'

Fox's lips twitched upwards.

'You don't have to. Just . . . be happy.'

He leaned up with what little strength he had left, pressing his lips to hers. She held the kiss for as long as she could, ignoring the taste of blood, even when he went limp and his chest stopped heaving for breath. Feeling the tears dripping from her chin, she broke away, burying her face in Fox's neck, wishing she could feel his pulse, or smell his unique scent of fire and tyrium that she always associated with safety and warmth.

All she could smell was blood.

'Cat?' She didn't turn at the familiar voice, hearing the gasp that told her Matt had realised what was wrong. She hadn't heard him come back. 'Oh, gods, Cat . . . Fox?'

She shook her head, answering the unspoken question as another sob escaped her.

'Storms. I . . . how?'

'Alexander,' she told him quietly, pointing at the now lifeless mecha-soldier on the table. 'Shot him from behind.'

She felt a large hand on her back, and leaned into Matt's arm, still not letting go of Fox's body.

'Gods, I never thought . . . I thought we were safe. I thought we were done with this,' he muttered, his cheek pressed against her hair. 'Cat, I'm so, so sorry, sweetheart.'

A siren began to wail, and Cat winced.

'The Mericans are here,' Matt murmured, making her scowl.

'Too bloody late, aren't they?'

'Cat, we need to find the others, there's nothing we can do for the kids. They're all brain-dead, technically dead. The only reason they're still moving is their machinery. We're getting ready to hand things over to the Merican soldiers.'

Cat shook her head, clinging tighter to Fox's body.

'I'm not leaving him,' she insisted. Matt squeezed her shoulders.

'Just let me pick him up, Cat. I'll be careful, I promise. But we need to go upstairs, and you can't carry him,' he reasoned, his voice low.

Cat bit her lip, but eventually nodded, letting Matt take Fox from her lap. The muscular man cradled the limp body protectively, bracing Fox's head in the crook of his arm.

Slipping the satchel over Fox's head and slinging it over her own shoulder, Cat stayed close by, walking at Matt's side, her hand gripping Fox's.

They took the pulley-lift, Cat wordlessly cranking the lever to raise them to the upper level. When the gate pulled back, she met Ben's eyes, and felt the tears start anew.

'Matt, what are you . . .' Ben trailed off when he saw the blood covering Fox's stomach and Cat's hands. 'No. No, no,' he murmured, shaking his head. 'It can't be true. Tell me that's not what I think it is.'

Matt shook his head, his eyes earnest and tearful as they locked with Ben's.

'I'm sorry, Benny,' he said hoarsely, and Ben's face crumpled. Stepping out of the lift, Cat allowed Ben to run a gentle hand through her hair, pulling her close. But her eyes didn't leave Fox's body.

'Oh, Cat,' Ben breathed, letting her go when Harry approached, flanked by soldiers in the red and white uniform of the Merican army. The man slowed when he saw Fox lying in Matt's arms, all colour draining from his face.

'Harry . . .' Matt shook his head sadly; he didn't need to say anything more. Harry swallowed tightly, his eyes glistening.

'He can't be . . . bloody hell. How am I gonna tell Alice?' he choked. 'Cat, lass, what happened?'

'One of the mecha-soldiers woke up . . . shot him in the back. I tried, I tried to help, I sent James for a doctor, but . . . it happened so quickly. He wouldn't stop bleeding,' she sobbed, gripping the cold hand that didn't grip her back.

'We should take him back to our ship, and get him ready for . . . for burial. We'll bring him home for you,' the soldier on Harry's left said in accented Anglyan.

Matt nodded, stepping closer to the soldier, moving to shift Fox into the man's arms. Cat stopped him, tugging on his sleeve.

'Wait,' she murmured quietly. Stepping up on tiptoe, she brushed the bright red fringe from his smooth forehead, wincing as her fingers touched icy skin. She leaned forward, kissing unresponsive lips.

'Goodbye, William Michael Foxe. I love you, and I always will,' she breathed against his ear, then stepped back, closing her eyes tightly. 'Take him,' she said to the soldier, who nodded, carefully taking Fox's body from Matt. He nodded respectfully to Cat after she'd opened her eyes, a sympathetic look on his face.

'I'm sorry for your loss, miss,' he said softly.

Cat watched as the foreigner walked away with the dead body of the love of her life, and felt like he was taking her heart with him.

29

Swallowing harshly, Cat squared her shoulders, determined to at least finish what she'd started.

The sound of frantic footsteps startled her, and she looked up, seeing James running towards her.

'Cat! I got the doctor, but you weren't in the lab and . . . what happened?' She shook her head, unable to get the words out.

'You were too late, lad. There . . . there was nothing you could have done,' Matt told James, who gasped. He immediately went towards Cat, attempting to put an arm around her. Feeling an irrational bout of anger, she shoved him away, glaring.

'Don't touch me!' she exclaimed. 'He's gone – are you happy? He's dead, you don't have to worry about *competing* with him any more.'

James's eyes widened, and he held out his hands in an attempt to soothe her.

'No, no, gods, Cat, I never wanted this to happen. I might have been jealous of him, but . . . I never wanted him dead. I'm sorry. He was a good man,' he said sincerely, his voice low and calm.

'He was,' Cat agreed, swallowing back another sob.

'Excuse me, sir? Are the experiments contained?' a stocky blond soldier asked Matt, who nodded.

'They're dead – the ones we found, anyway. We were too late to save them. You're welcome to search the ship for survivors, though,' he replied.

Four of the soldiers nodded and walked away, and their commander looked at the assembled crew.

'Why don't you all go back to your ship? Just stay in the area and keep the zip-line connected – we'll send someone over when we're ready to bring the ship back to Anglya,' he suggested.

Cat frowned, but Harry cut across her and nodded.

'I think you might have the right idea,' he agreed.

'But what about the workers?'

'We've got it covered, miss,' the commander insisted, smiling kindly at her. 'We'll arrest the workers and make sure there aren't any dangerous experiments still active. You've done enough. Let us take it from here.'

Biting her lip, Cat nodded reluctantly, allowing Harry to usher her towards the trap leading up to the deck. Harry kept her moving, pushing her gently to the ladder.

She pulled her goggles up when she got on deck, huddling into her coat. There were two soldiers standing guard by the bottom of the mast, and Cat craned her neck to see the zip-line strung taut between the ship's mast and that of the *Stormdancer*.

'You go on up first, Cat,' Matt said, handing her the body-ropes.

She nodded, winding the ropes around her legs and

waist, then scrambled up the rigging to the top of the mast, clamping the free end of the body-ropes into the zip-line mechanism. She landed with only a slight wobble at the top of the mast of her own ship. Wriggling out of her body-ropes, she left them hooked to the mechanism and tugged on the send-rope, prompting Matt to start reeling it back.

Climbing down the rigging, Cat was met on deck by Alice, who screamed when she saw the blood covering Cat.

'Oh, gods, what happened? Where are you hurt?' she asked frantically, moving to fuss over Cat, who ducked away from the older woman, wrapping her arms defensively around her chest.

'It's not mine. I'm fine,' she insisted quietly. She ignored the woman's questions, watching Matt descend the rigging, and squinted across at the other ship, seeing Ben reeling back the mechanism.

'What happened?' Alice asked, her brow furrowing in dread. 'Where's Fox?'

Cat shook her head, unable to speak, and was glad when a long arm rested comfortingly across her shoulders.

'He ... he didn't make it,' Matt told them, and Cat winced at the loud wail of grief that escaped Alice's lips.

Matt hugged Alice tightly, stroking her hair. She was speechless, her sobs muffled by Matt's coat, until she straightened up and composed herself, turning to Cat.

'Oh, Cat, dear ... come on, come with me. We'll get you cleaned up,' she urged, tears running down her face.

Cat allowed herself to be led down the trap, dazed. She didn't struggle, even when Alice took Fox's bag from her and began to strip her of her bloodied clothes, the bath running and a fresh set of clothes folded on the shelf. The water turned pink when she stepped into the bath, even though Alice had scrubbed her hands thoroughly.

She complied silently, allowing Alice to wash her hair and wrap a fluffy towel around her body, only moving when it came to putting on her clothes. When she was dressed, Alice took her along the corridor to the galley. Letting herself be directed into a seat, Cat stared blankly at the table. All she wanted was to hide in her room and cry. She accepted the tea nudged into her hands, but blinked when she heard Alice say the word 'lunch'.

'I'm not hungry,' she said mechanically, making the older woman pause in her fussing.

'Are you sure, dear?' she checked, and Cat nodded.

'I . . . I think I'm just going to lie down for a while,' Cat replied in a quiet voice.

Walking into her own room, the sobs started afresh when she spotted the all too familiar jacket slung over the back of her chair. When had Fox left that there? Unable to help herself, she picked it up and held it to her face, inhaling deeply. Exhaling slowly, she was half sobbing, half laughing; it still smelt of him.

She collapsed on the bed, Fox's jacket hugged tightly to her chest, tears falling freely, hiccuping sobs breaking free. She didn't know how long she lay there, only that she was interrupted by a knock on the door far, far too soon.

'Go away!' she shouted in irritation – flinching when the door swung open and James stepped in. 'Leave me alone,' she spat. 'You're the last person I want to see right now.'

Ignoring her, he walked right into the room and perched

on the edge of the bed. She turned away from him, lying on her side to face the wall.

'I'm not going away,' he told her simply. 'I might not have cared for Fox the same way you do, but I am sad he's gone. He made you happy, I can't argue with that.'

She bit her lip in an attempt to stop the tirade of angry words she wanted to shout at the boy. She knew he was trying to help, but she really didn't want to hear it.

'Then why are you here?' she asked miserably.

He shifted to lean against the headboard, Cat's head next to his thigh. 'Do you want the better-sounding answer, or the truth?' he asked wryly.

'The truth, if you don't mind.' Cat heard a long sigh escape the young prince's lips, and moved on to her back, not quite facing him but not turned away.

'I'm terrified,' he admitted freely. 'There's now nothing stopping Mother and me from regaining our titles, and . . . I'm scared witless. I never thought this day would actually come.'

Cat sighed. 'You'll be a great king, when it's your turn. Besides, you can't do any worse than the last people in charge,' she pointed out.

'Yes, I suppose you're right,' James said quietly. 'But, still . . . I'd be greater if I had a great queen by my side.'

Instantly, Cat shut down. 'Don't. Don't start, not even in jest. It's far too soon . . . he just *died*. Please . . . don't,' she begged in a whisper.

James frowned. 'You're right, I'm sorry. That was insensitive of me. But, you have to know . . . I'm not going to give up. Even if it takes years,' he told her bluntly.

Cat sighed again, bringing up a hand to rub the bridge of her nose, trying to rid herself of the headache that was building.

'James, you'll have a wonderful kingdom and a long reign when the time comes, and I'll be there to help you through it, but . . . not as your wife. And please, allow me to mourn the love of my life before trying to take his place,' she said frankly, desperate for him to leave. He raised an eyebrow at her, an incredulous expression on his face.

'You barely even knew each other,' he pointed out.

'Does it matter?' she said furiously. 'I loved – no, I *love* him, and he's gone. You can't change that, and you can't make me love you!'

'I'm not asking you to. I'm just asking you to remember . . . I . . . we – we were friends once.'

'We were six,' Cat retorted drily. James's lips flickered in a smile.

'Still, we were friends. Closer than friends, even – we grew up together. Maybe one day, we'll be that close again. You're all I remember from before. You and my parents. My father is gone, but . . . I don't want to lose you too,' he admitted. Cat bit her lip; she too had fond memories of those early years. She couldn't blame James for having been kept from human contact for eight years.

'Maybe we can be that close, one day. But don't ever ask for more than that.'

James smiled, looking confident. 'You're only fifteen, Cat. It's too early to say never – you won't need to marry for years yet. I've got plenty of time to prove that you could love me, if you give me a chance,' he replied.

Cat glared at him. 'Get out of my room,' she ordered flatly.

'I've upset you,' he noted.

'Yes, you have. So please leave so I can be upset in peace,' she snarled.

After several seconds, Cat felt the mattress shift as James's weight was removed, and the door creaked quietly as it was opened and then shut again. She buried her face in the soft wool lining of Fox's jacket, feeling it dampen with tears. Why did James have to be so insensitive?

'I won't love him,' she declared softly, not sure who she was vowing to.

Epilogue

'Hold still, sweetheart, you've got a curl coming loose.'

Cat smiled patiently, allowing Alice to fix her hair. She caught a look at her reflection in the floor-length mirror hung on the wall, and despite the circumstances, couldn't help but grin. She looked beautiful. Her hair had grown almost to the length it was before she'd cut it two years ago, and was currently pinned in elaborate curls, accenting the delicate silver and amethyst tiara resting among them. The fine netting of the veil looked like silver mist behind her head, trailing down to her waist, and her dress was . . . perfect.

'Twenty minutes . . . are you excited?' Alice asked, beaming.

Cat managed as close to a sincere smile as she could in reply.

'Could I have some privacy? Just . . . just for a few minutes,' she pleaded quietly.

Alice met her gaze knowingly, patting her cheek.

'Of course, sweetheart. I'll call for you when it's time.'

Cat nodded, turning to the open balcony as Alice made to leave. Leaning her arms against the railing, she stared out over the city, smiling to herself at the angry-looking storm clouds gathering on the horizon. That looked like a hurricane; and that meant good luck. She almost laughed.

The city had changed so much in just two short years; gone were the dirty streets, the multitude of poor and homeless, and the closed-off government district. The city was bright and clean, its people prospering. Once trade had reopened fully between Anglya and the rest of the world, the economic status of the country had shot up; after all, despite everything, Anglya was still the country with the largest tyrium mines. Most of the city had been rebuilt and remodelled, especially the crater that had once been the government compound. There were still plenty of cranes and scaffolding towers around half-finished buildings, but . . . they were getting there.

'Gods, I can't believe I'm doing this,' she murmured with a sigh, glancing up into the clouds. 'And so soon, too. You'd probably hate me for this – after you'd laughed yourself silly and punched him in the face, of course,' she added with a slight smile, remembering hot red hair and an even hotter temper. 'I wish it were you,' she breathed, letting her eyes slide shut. 'I only ever wanted you, but . . . we weren't meant to be.' Laughing sadly, she dropped her gaze to the single large diamond on the platinum band around her finger. It was ostentatious, and not what she would have preferred, but society had its expectations.

'I miss you,' she whispered, as if it were a crime to admit it. 'And I haven't stopped loving you. Not for a moment. I don't love him . . . He's not terrible, but storms, he's not you.' She paused, blinking fiercely as tears threatened to rise. Alice would kill her if she ruined her make-up.

'You'd be proud, you know, Fox.' And gods, if it didn't still hurt to say his name. 'You'd be so *very* proud of what this country has become, of what it's yet to become. And ... I hope you're proud of me too. I'm doing what you asked. I'm doing my duty.' She steeled herself, setting her shoulders back and raising her chin, the action causing her dress to ripple slightly. 'I'm doing my duty, to crown and country.'

'Cat, dear, it's time!' Alice's voice called, and Cat's posture faltered for a fraction of a second before she regained her composure. Leaving the balcony, she left through the doors opposite to find Alice and Harry waiting for her. Despite Alice's playful nagging, the couple hadn't made any move to settle down with kids of their own. Cat had had to call them and the crew in from Dalivia just for the wedding week.

'You look radiant, lass,' Harry said with a fatherly smile, leaning in to kiss her on the cheek. She'd missed the kindly man very much recently. She'd missed all the crew; even when they were in Anglya, it was only for a few days, and she didn't always get the chance to see them. She often found herself toying with the idea of repeating the past, of stowing away to join them once again. 'Are you ready to go?'

'If I say no, does it matter?' she asked wryly, making the man snort with laughter.

'You'll be fine, lass. He's a good lad, he'll take care of you,' Harry assured her, offering her his arm. As she slid her arm through his, she couldn't help but remember heated arguments, glaring matches and her insisting she could take care of herself. But that had been with Fox, and Fox was gone.

She walked with Harry towards a set of tall, ornate double doors. She heard muffled music start up inside, and the doors swung open, revealing a room full of people all dressed in their finery, a deep purple carpet trailing up the aisle to the head of the room. Letting her eyes rest on the young man standing at the end of the carpet, she swallowed, forcing herself to walk in time to the music as they had practised. She had to admit, he looked handsome; his hair, combed neatly to the side, shone like spun gold in the lamplight. Blue eyes bright, and lips pulled into a beaming grin, he was almost the spitting image of his late father at the same age. Standing beside him were Matt and Ben, both looking extremely dapper – if slightly uncomfortable – in their light grey three-piece suits, the vibrant purple bow ties matching the roses pinned to their jackets and the ribbons on their top hats. On the other side of the aisle, Mary was dressed in her royal best, crown atop her head, having easily settled back into her role as queen. She was beaming with joy; Cat wished she could return the sentiment.

Harry walked her steadily past the rows and rows of guests – most of whom she'd only met once or twice, if at all – and came to a halt in front of the blond man. He leaned in to kiss her on the cheek once more, then turned to face the silver-clad holy man.

'Who gives this woman to wed this man?' the wizened minister asked, and Harry smiled.

'I do, sir,' he said clearly, slipping Cat's hand into her bridegroom's.

Cat focused on Ben, who stood opposite her once she turned.

'*You can do this*,' he mouthed supportively, offering a brief smile.

Her lips twitched in reply, and a slight widening of Ben's eyes prompted her to tune back into the proceedings.

'Do you, Catherine Elizabeth Hunter, take James Christopher Richard Latham to be your lawfully wedded husband?'

She met James's eyes. Taking a deep breath, she gave up trying to calm her racing heart, knowing she was about to seal her fate with two little words. The country had been pushing them together since day one; the plucky young heroine and the charming prince she had rescued. And when an entire nation was involved, things like *feelings* had to be pushed aside. She liked James well enough, and she knew their marriage was the best thing for Anglya – storms knew they needed a stable monarchy – but despite his clear wish for more, she just didn't feel that way about him. Cat could only hope he would eventually be content with friendship. It was all she could give him.

I will never love him, she thought fiercely, even as she opened her mouth and resigned herself to a life of politics and social sidestepping, all for the good of her people; for they were hers now, after all. And James was looking to become an excellent ruler, as she had always known he would. Everyone knew they would achieve great things together. Cat just had to focus on that, instead of the ache in her heart at what would never be.

'I do,' she said, her voice ringing through the large room.

Yes, how things changed, over time.